Praise for the
Novels of the Final Prophecy

"Raw passion, dark romance, and seat-of-your-pants suspense all set in an astounding paranormal world—I swear ancient Mayan gods and demons walk the modern earth!"
—*New York Times* bestselling author J. R. Ward

"Andersen's got game when it comes to style and voice. I love [this] kick-ass series . . . a mix of humor, suspense, mythology, and fantasy . . . a series that's sure to be an instant reader favorite, and will put Andersen's books on keeper shelves around the world." —Suzanne Brockmann on WritersareReaders.com

"I deeply enjoyed the story. It really hooked me!"
—*New York Times* bestselling author Angela Knight

"Part romance, mystery, and fairy tale . . . a captivating book with wide appeal." —*Booklist*

"[A] nonstop, action-intensive plot. . . . Ms. Andersen delivers a story that is . . . [a] solid romance and adventure novel. If you enjoy movies like *Lara Croft* . . . or just want something truly new, you will definitely want this."
—Huntress Book Reviews

"Intense action, sensuality, and danger abound."
—*Romantic Times*

"If *Nightkeepers* is any indication of her talent, then [Jessica Andersen] will become one of my favorites. . . . [The book] brought tears to my eyes and an ache [to] my heart. I read each word with bated breath." —Romance Junkies

"[A] terrific romantic fantasy . . . an excellent thriller. Jessica Andersen provides a strong story that . . . fans will cherish."
—*Midwest Book Review*

SKY KEEPERS

A NOVEL OF THE FINAL PROPHECY

JESSICA ANDERSEN

A SIGNET ECLIPSE BOOK

SIGNET ECLIPSE
Published by New American Library, a division of
Penguin Group (USA) Inc., 375 Hudson Street,
New York, New York 10014, USA
Penguin Group (Canada), 90 Eglinton Avenue East, Suite 700, Toronto,
Ontario M4P 2Y3, Canada (a division of Pearson Penguin Canada Inc.)
Penguin Books Ltd., 80 Strand, London WC2R 0RL, England
Penguin Ireland, 25 St. Stephen's Green, Dublin 2,
Ireland (a division of Penguin Books Ltd.)
Penguin Group (Australia), 250 Camberwell Road, Camberwell, Victoria 3124,
Australia (a division of Pearson Australia Group Pty. Ltd.)
Penguin Books India Pvt. Ltd., 11 Community Centre, Panchsheel Park,
New Delhi - 110 017, India
Penguin Group (NZ), 67 Apollo Drive, Rosedale, North Shore 0632,
New Zealand (a division of Pearson New Zealand Ltd.)
Penguin Books (South Africa) (Pty.) Ltd., 24 Sturdee Avenue,
Rosebank, Johannesburg 2196, South Africa

Penguin Books Ltd., Registered Offices:
80 Strand, London WC2R 0RL, England

First published by Signet Eclipse, an imprint of New American Library,
a division of Penguin Group (USA) Inc.

First Printing, August 2009
10 9 8 7 6 5 4 3 2 1

This book is dedicated to those who protect us.
Without you, the world would be a
much more dangerous place.

ACKNOWLEDGMENTS

The Nightkeepers' world is well hidden within our own; bringing it to light isn't always an easy process. My heartfelt thanks go to Deidre Knight, Kara Cesare, Claire Zion, Kara Welsh, and Kerry Donovan for helping me take these books from a dream to a reality; to J. R. Ward for critiques and help each step of the way; to Suz Brockmann for being a mentor and an inspiration; to my many e-friends on the Skywatch message board for always being there for a laugh or cyberhug; to Sally Hinkle Russell for keeping me sane; and to Brian Hogan for too many things to name in this small space.

For a full list of references and recommended reading on the ancient Maya and the 2012 doomsday prophecy, and to explore the Nightkeepers' online community, please visit www.JessicaAndersen.com.

GLOSSARY

Like much of the Nightkeepers' culture, their spell words come from the people they have lived with throughout their history. Or if we want to chicken-and-egg things, it's more likely that the other cultures took the words from the Nightkeepers and incorporated them into their developing languages. As such, some of the words have slightly different meanings and/or spellings in the Nightkeepers' language compared to those of ancient Egypt, the Mayan Empire, and elsewhere.

Entities (people, gods, demons, and other creatures)

Aztec—A complex and warlike Mesoamerican culture that arose as the Mayan Empire lost momentum. The Aztec held sway over much of northern Mesoamerica when the conquistadors arrived in the so-called New World.

Banol Kax—The lords of the underworld, Xibalba. Driven from the earth and locked behind the barrier after the last Great Conjunction in 24,000 B.C. by the many-times-great-ancestors of the modern Nightkeepers, the *Banol Kax* seek to pierce the barrier and wrest control of the earth from mankind. Their greatest opportunity will come when the barrier falls on December 21, 2012.

boluntiku—The underworld minions of the *Banol Kax*, the *boluntiku* are lava creatures that draw their energy from the molten mantle of the earth. The creatures are killing machines that can sense magic and royalty; they travel in an insubstantial vapor form and turn solid in the moment they attack.

ch'ulel—A rare and powerful Nightkeeper mage who can manipulate the life force of all living things.

First Father—The only adult survivor of the Nightkeepers' exodus from Egypt in 1351 B.C. He bound the slaves into *winikin*, led the Nightkeepers and *winikin* to Mesoamerica, and codified their beliefs into the writs and the thirteen prophecies in order to guide his descendants over the millennia until the end-time.

***makol* (*ajaw-makol*)**—The earthly minions of the *Banol Kax*, these are demon souls capable of reaching through the barrier to possess an evil-natured human host. An *ajaw-makol* is an extremely powerful *makol* drawn straight from the lowest level of Xibalba, where the truly damned dwell.

Mictlan—A Nightkeeper capable of wielding the oldest form of magic, with lethal results. (Also see Mictlan under Places.)

nahwal—Humanoid spirit entities that exist in the barrier and hold within them all of the accumulated wisdom of each Nightkeeper bloodline. They can be asked for information, but cannot be trusted.

Nightkeeper—A member of an ancient race sworn to protect mankind from annihilation in the years leading up to December 21, 2012, when the barrier separating the earth and the underworld will fall and the *Banol Kax* will seek to precipitate the apocalypse.

Order of Xibalba—Formed by renegade Nightkeepers, the order courted the powers of the underworld and was wiped out by the conquistadors . . . or so the Nightkeepers believed until the Xibalbans reappeared in modern day with a clear doomsday agenda of their own.

pilli—The nobility of Aztec society. Among the Xibalbans, it refers to the most powerful members of the red-robed, magic-wielding warrior caste.

winikin—The *winikin* function as the servants, protectors, and counselors of the magi, and have been instrumental in keeping the bloodlines alive through the centuries.

Places

Mictlan—The lowest layer of Xibalba, where the most egregious sinners (traitors and murderers) reside, forming the souls of the *ajaw-makol*.

Paxil Mountain—The ancient stories say that the sacred foods of the Maya, maize and cacao (from which chocolate is made), were trapped within this legendary mountain until released by the gods.

Skywatch—The Nightkeepers' training compound is located in the Chaco Canyon region of New Mexico.

Survivor2012 compound—Located in an unpopular offshoot of the Florida Everglades and built on—and into—a massive landfill, this labyrinthine complex was home to the Survivor2012 doomsday cult. Since the death of cult leader Vincente Rincon and the disbanding of Survivor2012, the compound has sat empty. In theory.

Xibalba—The nine-layer underworld of the Mayan and Nightkeeper religious systems, home to the *Banol Kax*, *boluntiku*, and *makol*.

Things (spells, glyphs, prophecies, etc.)

barrier—A force field of psi energy that separates the earth, sky, and underworld, and powers the Nightkeepers' magic. The strength of the barrier fluctuates with the positions of the stars and planets, and weakens as the 12/21/2012 end date approaches.

chorote—A sacred drink that combines both maize and chocolate, two of the most important foodstuffs in Mayan—and Nightkeeper—rituals.

ch'ul—In Mayan mythology, the life force that runs through all living things. Analogous to the Chinese concept of *chi*.

copan—The sacred incense of the Nightkeepers. This is a variation of the Mayan incense, *copal*, and is associated with the great ruined city of Copán, located in modern-day Honduras.

hunab ku—A pseudoglyph associated with the 2012 end date worn by the Nightkeepers' king.

intersection—Located in the sacred tunnels beneath Chichén Itzá, this was the point where the earth, sky, and underworld came very near one another, where the barrier was weakest, and through which the gods could communicate with the Nightkeepers. With the intersection destroyed, the Nightkeepers are in trouble.

jun tan—The "beloved" glyph that signifies a Nightkeeper's mated status. It cannot be formed by a Nightkeeper who also shares a connection with dark magic.

muk—The ancient, ancestral magic that was long ago split into Nightkeeper and Xibalban magic.

tzomplanti—A ceremonial pile formed of stacked human skulls, used as a beacon or a warning sign. Although sometimes associated with the Maya, it is Aztec in origin.

writs—Written by the First Father, these rules delineate the duties and codes of the Nightkeepers. Not all of them translate well into present day.

What has come before . . .

On December 21, 2012, the world will end.

At least, that is what some believe the ancient Maya intended to signal when they set their five-thousand-year calendar to zero out on that day, at the exact moment the sun, moon, and earth will align at the center of the Milky Way in a cosmic dark spot the Maya believed was the mouth of the underworld, Xibalba.

Modern scientific support for the 2012 doomsday theory comes from astronomers and physicists, who predict that this Great Conjunction, which occurs only once every twenty-six thousand years, will trigger magnetic reversals, terrible sunspots, and potentially cataclysmic planetary events. This has caused historians and spiritualists alike to credit the ancient Maya with a level of astronomy not seen again through history until modern times. However, their knowledge of the Great Conjunction—and the havoc it will bring—came from a far older people: the Nightkeepers.

Descended from the only survivors of an incredibly advanced civilization wiped out in 24,000 B.C. during the last Great Conjunction, the Nightkeepers are mortal magic *users sworn to pass their skills from generation to generation until the 2012 conjunction, when they will be the only ones capable of defeating the* Banol Kax, *a group of powerful demons who were bound in Xibalba by the Nightkeepers' ancestors, and will be released on December 21, 2012. On that day, the demons will break through the barrier separating the earth and underworld. They will destroy mankind and rule the earth . . . unless the Nightkeepers stop them.*

Ancient prophecy says that there should be hundreds of Nightkeepers at the end of the age. But in the final four years before the zero date, when the demons begin their assault on the barrier, the Nightkeepers number less than a dozen scattered and untrained magi. Their last king, Striking-Jaguar, reunites the surviving Nightkeepers in time to block the Banol Kax *from attacking the earth. In the process, however, he claims a god-bound human woman as his mate rather than sacrificing her. His love for Detective Leah Ann Daniels defies an ancient prophecy and triggers the next stage in the countdown to the end-time.*

This stage is ruled by the demon prophecies, which are supposed to guide the Nightkeepers in battle as the end-time approaches. The magi race to recover the Mayan antiquities that bear the seven demon prophecies, but they are not the only ones hunting for the missing artifacts. The Order of Xibalba, thought to have perished during the conquistadors' bloodbath, has risen again, led by the redheaded mage Iago. During the spring solstice, Iago invokes all seven of the demon spells at once and uses the power to open a hellmouth connecting the earth and underworld, while sealing the skyroad and separating the Nightkeepers from their gods. Only the power of the love match between Godkeeper Alexis Gray and her destined mate, Nate Blackhawk, allows the Nightkeepers to defeat Iago and prevent the Banol Kax *from coming to earth . . . for the moment.*

In the aftermath of the battle, the Nightkeepers' powers falter without a connection to the gods, while Iago and his followers draw strength from the hellmouth. The Nightkeepers' best hope is finding the lost library of their ancestors, which they believe holds the key to exponentially increasing their fighting magic. The problem? Sasha Ledbetter, the one woman who might be able to lead them to the library her father hid many years ago, is Iago's prisoner. . . .

PART I

LEONID METEOR SHOWER

*This fiery display of shooting stars seems to emanate
from the constellation of Leo, which the modern
Nightkeepers associate with their revered jaguar kings.
It is thought to symbolize a time of great change.*

CHAPTER ONE

One year ago
Somewhere in the Yucatán

Sasha Ledbetter paused, bracing her hands on her knees as she sucked in moist air, trying to catch the breath she'd lost somewhere around the time she'd ditched the dinged-up Jeep to hike the rest of the way to the ruin. "Shit." She wheezed. "I forgot how much I hate rain forests."

They were fine in theory, she supposed as she straightened and readjusted the heavy pack on her shoulders, then used her machete to nudge a thorny vine out of her way. On TV, from the safety of her apartment in Boston, she'd paused occasionally on Travel Channel specials about the low country, though she'd still take the Food Network any day. And she'd babied the half dozen tropical plants she'd grown in brightly colored pots, enjoying them for their sweet scents and lush flowers. But that didn't mean she'd had any desire to return to her childhood haunts. Especially when those haunts came with bloodsucking bugs like the one that kept whining in her left ear no matter how many times she slapped at it. "Get the hint, will you?" She waved at the thing again; it buzzed reproachfully. "God. I forgot about the bugs, too."

She didn't get a response to her complaints, but then again, she was talking to herself.

Traveling alone in the rain forest might not be the smartest strategy for a brunette twentysomething with elfin features and a dented chin—i.e., someone who might be close to six feet tall and fairly muscular, but couldn't look threatening no matter how hard she tried. But she'd spent a chunk of her childhood bushwhacking south of the border and knew how to take care of herself in the hostile, if verdant, environment.

Then again, so had her father, Ambrose Ledbetter, and he'd disappeared into this same rain forest more than five months ago.

Ambrose was missing, presumed dead, according to both the nearest consulate and the university where he'd held court as one of the world's foremost Mayanists. Granted, it wasn't unusual for Ambrose to lose track of a week or two when he was in the field, but five months was too much. He wouldn't have stayed out in the field that long, even if he was hot on the trail of his own personal obsession, a mythical group of warrior-priests called the Nightkeepers, who were supposed to protect mankind from ancient demons in the last few years before the end of the Mayan calendar on December 21, 2012.

Some people—mostly movie producers and nut jobs, as far as Sasha could tell—believed that the zero date signaled the end of time itself. But Ambrose hadn't just believed in the end-time; he'd believed that the legends of the Nightkeepers were real. For the most part, he'd kept the psychosis under wraps in his outside life, playing the part of a sane man, and playing it well. At home, though, he'd let it rip. Which was why Sasha had eventually stopped going home. She hadn't seen or spoken to her father in more than eight years, save for a single brief encounter over the summer. The day after that he'd disappeared into the rain forest.

Missing, presumed dead. The words banged around inside her head as she wormed her way along the narrow trail she'd found partly from childhood memories, partly from a crude map Ambrose's grad student had drawn for her. She paused at the circular clearing that she thought was where they used to make camp, but it seemed smaller than she remembered, and there was no sign of a tent. Granted, the forest claimed everything after a while, even stone pyramids ten stories high, but she still would've expected to find a few pieces of ripstop or scattered equipment. Something, anyway.

Her pulse bumped, but not with hope. After so many months with no word, it was hard to believe that he could still be alive. No, the skim of nerves came from thinking that instead of a relatively peaceful end in the place he loved, maybe he'd been attacked by human predators, bandits who'd taken his equipment to use what they could, sell what they couldn't. The possibility had haunted her ever since she'd learned he was missing—a notification that had been delayed months because he hadn't listed her anywhere as next of kin.

"Don't talk yourself into freaking out," she said, swiping at another incoming bug.

And really, there was no reason to panic. Even though she'd gone to culinary school rather than following Ambrose's charted path for her to become a doctor, she'd taken enough bio classes to know that lack of evidence in favor of one hypothesis didn't prove the opposite. The absence of tent scraps didn't necessarily mean he'd been murdered by bandits. Maybe he'd just camped somewhere else.

Still, she sheathed her machete and popped the snap

on the midback holster she wore beneath her sweat-soaked tee, and withdrew the .22 chick gun she'd bought at a pawnshop a few miles from the airport. Just in case.

Walking as quietly as she could, though she'd lost some of her childhood forestcraft in the years since she'd cut ties with her old life, she eased along the narrow path, which was little more than a groove in the soft rain forest floor. Ignoring the screeches of parrots and monkeys far above in the canopy, she strained to hear other, closer sounds. Nerves fisted in her chest, and the skin at her nape prickled, but again, there was no evidence supporting her fear. There was only the fear itself.

The lush vegetation thinned out as she crested a low rise that might have once been a fortified wall. From that high spot, she caught a glimpse of hewn stone forming a stark grayish white contrast to the surrounding greenery—an entrance leading into the earth. Ambrose's temple. His obsession.

Faint anger twisted at the sight—and the memories it brought—but she ignored it as she headed for the temple entrance, reminding herself she was through chasing love, or even affection. Those were things that had to be given freely, or not at all.

In Ambrose's case, that would be the latter.

A slight downhill slope led to the temple entrance, which was a plain, unadorned rectangle of stone: vertical slabs on either side, twice the height of a tall man, topped with a wide, uncarved lintel. The dark, forbidding doorway led into a high mound of green-covered stone that had once been a huge ceremonial pyramid.

When she reached the entrance, she fished in her pack for the military-grade flashlight that had been another pawnshop find. She'd passed on the night-vision goggles in favor of a decent one-man tent, but thanks to the creepy-crawlies still working their way up and down her spine, she found herself wishing she'd splurged and bought both.

"Man up. You're just imagining things," she muttered, making herself take the first step from soil onto stone. When nothing happened except a ten-degree or so temperature drop, she exhaled a long, slow breath. "See? You can do this." She might be a decade out of practice, and too ready to believe the prickly heebie-jeebies, but it wasn't like she had a choice, really. She'd promised long ago never to reveal the temple's location to anyone else, not even a hint. This had been Ambrose's spot, the center of his life. And in the end, it had most likely been his death.

She needed to search the temple, needed to find his camp . . . and his body. The thought sucked, but she could cope, would have to cope. Besides, she'd had a few days to get used to the idea that he was truly gone this time, and eight years of silence before that to buffer the separation. There was grief, yes, and some stale, leftover pain, but overall, her foremost emotion was weary resignation as she squared her shoulders and started hiking inward, intent on finding her father's remains and bringing them back to the States. Although the ruin and rain forest had been more his home than the apartment he and his non-wife, Pim, had shared near Harvard, he'd always insisted that when he died, he wanted to be cremated and tossed to the wind in New Mexico.

Sasha didn't know why. As a child, she'd suspected that was where her mother had been from, or where she was buried. She'd even visited the spot once, but had found nothing but rocks and wind, making her think that the New Mexico thing was just another of Ambrose's elaborately constructed delusions, one that meant nothing in real terms. Regardless, it had been his request, and Sasha had felt honor-bound to make it happen, even if it meant trekking through the rain forest, slapping at bugs, and fighting the feeling of being watched.

"Besides," she muttered, "it's not like you had anything going on at home. Perfect time for a trip to nonparadise." She'd just been fired for getting too creative with the head chef's recipes—again—and she was annoyingly single some six months after a relationship she'd imagined was leading to marriage had turned out to be going nowhere fast. Figuring she was already depressed, and having been unable to get Ambrose out of her head since their brief meeting over the summer, she had tried tracking him down and wound up discovering instead that he'd fallen off the grid.

Missing, presumed dead.

Tightening her grip on the .22, she forged onward. The bright white flashlight beam made jarringly modern-looking shadows in the ancient stone tunnel, and the creepy-crawly nerves in her stomach started to grow claws. She'd been inside the temple before, of course, but that was years ago, and she'd been with Ambrose. More, that had been back when she'd still seen him as more than he was—a real-life Indiana Jones who'd let her come along on his adventures because he'd wanted her there, more even than he'd wanted Pim, who'd always stayed behind. Eventually, though, Sasha had realized those "adventures" were more uncomfortable than exciting, and he'd wanted her there not for her company, but because he'd needed a fellow role-player in his delusions, which over the years had gone from bedtime stories of magical princesses to twisted, apocalyptic ravings.

An echo of anger brushed against her jangling nerves, but she continued along the stone tunnel, skirting the triggered pit trap near the entrance. Beyond the pit trap, the tunnel continued onward to an intersection, where Ambrose had liked to sit and sip the bitter maize-and-chocolate drink she'd made for him from locally bought cacao.

Sasha was pretty sure that was where her interest in cooking—and chocolate—had started, those hours she'd spent watching the villagers separate the cacao beans from the fleshy pods, then ferment them, roast them, grind them, and finally mix the powder with maize to make the sacred *chorote*, which combined the two plants that formed the basis of the villagers' lives and livelihoods. Ambrose had insisted she'd turned to cooking simply out of rebellion. And maybe that had been a part of it, too.

Still, the smell and taste of *chorote* coated her senses as she approached the tunnel fork. Her brain was so primed to see a campsite, and maybe a body, that it took her a few seconds to process what she was actually seeing. There was no campsite, no body; there was only a wall of rubble. The hewn slabs that had lined the corridor had fallen inward, mixing with crumbled limestone, gritty dirt, and more rocks.

The tunnel had caved in, and the damage looked recent.

She hissed out a breath of dismay as her overactive brain filled with images of her father buried beneath the debris, dying there, crushed and suffering.

"Oh," she said. "Oh, no. *Ambrose*." The name echoed along the corridor and returned to her on a rattle of sound. She ignored both as she rushed to the collapsed spot. Maybe he was close to the edge. Maybe she could get at him somehow. *Maybe*, some foolishly hopeful part of her said, *he's trapped on the other side with all his camping gear and rations, waiting for someone to dig him out*.

She was so focused on the rubble that she initially missed seeing a strange shadow over to one side, partially shielded behind a larger chunk of stone. Then it caught her eye. She froze, disbelieving, then turned slowly and moved around the larger stone to get a better look. Her heart shuddered to a stop at the sight confronting her, then started pounding again, hard and fast. "No," she whispered. Then louder, "No!"

A human skull sat atop a stack of debris that had been carefully formed into the shape of a knee-high pyramid, mimicking the skull piles, the *tzomplanti* that the more warlike Mesoamerican cultures had used to boast of their victories. At first her mind tried to tell her that the skull atop the pile was ancient, an artifact. But it still wore clinging flesh that ended raggedly where the neck had been severed, along with a long, gray-shot ponytail caught at the nape in a ratty leather thong.

She knew that ponytail, knew that scrap of leather. Ambrose had been wearing it the last time she'd seen him.

No, she thought as desperation flared. *Oh, no. Please, no. Not like this.*

Gagging on bile and a huge, awful surge of emotion she hadn't expected to feel, she crossed her arms over her stomach, bent double by the terrible realization that he hadn't died naturally, doing what he loved. *Tzomplanti* were only used for enemies and sacrifices, which suggested he'd been murdered. But who had killed him? Why? And where was the rest of him? She didn't see his body, which somehow made the presentation of his head that much more gruesome. The wrongness of it slammed through her, threatened to take her over. She'd thought she'd been prepared to find him, and maybe she had been, but not like this, never like this. What the hell had happened in the temple?

She shuddered with grief and an awful, racking guilt. But even through those emotions, the old instincts her father had drummed into her long ago flared to life, warning her that she might not be as safe alone in the backcountry as she'd thought.

Her pulse picked up, sending adrenaline skimming through her veins. Someone had killed Ambrose, or at the very least, had cut off his head and arranged him on the *tzomplanti*. That suggested they had been more than bandits. Maybe some of the locals had decided they wanted him out of the temple. But this had been his place for years. What had changed? Had it been politics? Treasure hunters?

Or was it something connected to the massive fantasy that had structured his life? That possibility seemed horribly likely, given that these were the years he'd believed would bring terrible battles between good and evil.

Ambrose had always claimed there were others like him, others who believed the world might end in 2012. More, she'd heard the rumblings, seen the documentaries. Modern culture was catching up with Ambrose's long-held delusions. What if those delusions had somehow spelled his end? What if he'd been killed in an escalating move by people who thought that there was a supernatural war coming, and they were the chosen warriors?

The idea was abhorrent. And, based on all that she'd seen and heard growing up, it was all too possible.

"Oh, Da," she said, using the affectionate nickname she'd dropped years ago, when she'd started to realize that her father might function well enough on a day-to-day basis, but he wasn't all the way sane. "I should've had you declared, should've put you somewhere you could've gotten help." But she hadn't been tough enough to take the step when he hadn't been hurting anyone except her.

"That wouldn't have changed the outcome."

Gasping at the sound of a stranger's voice, Sasha lunged to her feet and spun, holding the .22 cross-handed with the flashlight. The white beam illuminated a man wearing jeans, workboots, and a heavy-metal con-

cert tee that made him look like he should've been in a
rock band road crew, not a Mayan ruin. His hair glinted
with ruddy highlights against the flashlit shadows, and
he was freaking massive, topping her by a good six
inches in height and outweighing her by at least eighty
pounds. Too late she realized that they—whoever *they*
were—must have been monitoring the ruin.

"Don't move," she ordered, voice shaking. "Don't
you frigging—"

Something slammed into her from the side, cutting
her off midthreat. Sasha twisted as she fell, and caught
a quick impression of a woman with long hair and perfect features, incongruously wearing a tiny-waisted suit
jacket and flowing pants. Then the flashlight went flying,
bounced off the wall, and fell to the floor, where it partially illuminated the scene.

Fighting in silence, as Ambrose had taught her, dropping into action-reaction mode even as her thoughts
spun with a city girl's panic, Sasha rammed an elbow
into the woman's stomach, yanked her gun up, and fired
in the man's direction. The .22 went off with the wimpy
pop typical of the caliber, but the big man spun away,
cursing and grabbing at his upper arm. Sasha ducked
and went for a foot sweep, but she was out of practice
and a split second too late. The woman grabbed her by
the hair and slammed her head into the floor, then did
the same with her hand, sending the .22 flinging free.

The world pinwheeled as rough hands grabbed Sasha
from behind, pinned her arms, and lifted her up to her
feet and then off them. The man's booted foot glanced
off the flashlight, which spun and wound up pointed
at the *tzomplanti*, lighting Ambrose's skull with vile
menace.

"Let me go!" Sasha struggled ferociously but her captor didn't even grunt when she got an elbow back into
his injured arm.

"For fuck's sake, stick her already," he snapped at the woman, who had backed off, breathing hard, her eyes glinting with battle rage and glee.

"No!" Sasha strained against his hold, screaming as the woman withdrew a syringe from her pocket and advanced to inject its contents into Sasha's upper arm. The burning sting of the needle was followed by cool effervescence, and Sasha's world went swimmy. Desperation flared as she sagged limply in the big man's hold.

No, she cried inwardly. *Not like this. Please.* She didn't know who she was talking to—she'd abandoned Ambrose's gods when she ran away from him. Strangely, though, she thought she heard a whisper of answer, a familiar voice saying, *Have faith.*

But faith was something she'd never been big on. Hadn't ever had a reason to be.

"Get the light and the gun," the man ordered. "And take her pack. Make sure we're not leaving anything of hers behind."

"What about the skull?"

"Leave it. It'll fuck with the Nightkeepers' heads if they ever find this place." He shifted his grip on Sasha, preparing to sling her over his shoulder. As he did so, the woman snagged the flashlight, and its beam played across the three of them. Sasha moaned when she caught sight of her captor's inner forearm, where he wore a single tattoo. She didn't know the meaning of the bloodred quatrefoil, but she sure as shit recognized the tat's location. It was exactly where the mythical Nightkeepers had been marked with Mayan glyphs representing their bloodlines and magical talents. It was also where Ambrose had worn a huge scar, as though he'd burned away similar marks long ago—or wanted people to think he had.

Despair howled through her as unconsciousness closed in. She fought the drug, fought the reality of her capture, and the growing fear that she was trapped in some giant, live-action role-playing game based on her father's bloodthirsty delusions. And, most of all, she fought the sick heartache that came from knowing there was nobody out in the real world who would think to look for her until it was far too late.

CHAPTER TWO

Present
November 18
Three years and thirty-three days until the end date
The Yucatán

Michael Stone stood atop a midsize Mayan ruin called the watchtower, his dark, shoulder-length hair blowing a little in the sea breeze. Behind him was an expanse of lush, stone-studded greenery; ahead was a white stone cliff that dropped steeply to a gleaming, tourist-dotted strip of coral beach. Beyond that was the vibrant blue-green of the Caribbean.

It was a hell of a view, that was for sure.

The ruined port city was called Tulum, which meant "wall" in Spanish and referred to the sturdy stone balustrade that enclosed the city on three sides, with the cliff and ocean forming the fourth. The fortification was impressive, even in ruins, but it hadn't protected the city from the ravages of the conquistadors and their missionaries. And in the almost five hundred years since Cortés first landed, the place had become a tourist trap, due largely to its small, walkable size and prime beachfront location.

The deets spooled through Michael's brain, courtesy of the report he'd downloaded from his e-mail a couple of hours earlier. It'd been sent by the Nightkeepers' archivist, Jade, his former lover-turned-friend. The thought of her brought a twinge of guilt and regret, but both had become too-familiar companions over the past year-plus, ever since the talent ceremony that had unlocked a shit-ton more than just his warrior's talent. Since he couldn't change the past—his and Jade's or otherwise—he pushed aside the guilt and tried to focus on what he ought to be doing, namely reporting back to home base with a whole lot of negatives.

Still, though, he hesitated, standing alone atop a pyramid where one of his ancestors might have stood centuries earlier. Sunlight glinted on the dark sunglasses that shaded Michael's piercing eyes, which were so dark green they were nearly black in some lights. A sea breeze tugged at his tee, molding the fabric to his big, fighting-lean body as he pictured that hypothetical ancestor, a Nightkeeper mage like himself. The image didn't last long, though, largely because Michael wasn't nearly as deep into the whole ancestor-worship thing as some of the others. Not like the *winikin*, who saw it as their duty—one among many—to remind the Nightkeepers of their history, usually when they least expected or wanted it. Sort of like a Discovery Channel sneak attack. Despite the knee-jerk avoidance the lectures had spawned in him, though, Michael found himself struck by the ruins and their view of the sea. He could almost picture the seagoing outriggers the ancient Maya had used to transport their goods along the coast, the pack trains coming from the inland city-states, and the open-air market that had formed where the two commerce streams met at Tulum's port.

And you're so incredibly stalling, it's not even funny,

he thought wryly, forcing himself to palm his phone out of his pocket and speed-dial Strike's cell.

The Nightkeepers' king picked up on the third ring. "Tell me something good."

"Sorry. I've got bad, bad, and more bad."

Strike's low curse suggested that the others had also come up empty in their ruin-ratting searches for a new intersection, which was a major problem. Ever since the Xibalbans had destroyed the sacred chamber beneath the ruins of Chichén Itzá, the Nightkeepers' powers had been inconsistent at best, weakening at worst. Without a direct connection to the sky plane and the gods who lived there, the Nightkeepers' magic was fading at a time when the few remaining prophecies said they were supposed to be growing stronger, gearing up to fight the demon *Banol Kax* and their earthly agents, the Xibalbans.

Worse, the Xibalbans had direct access to the underworld through a hellmouth located somewhere in the cloud forests of Ecuador, which meant their dark-magic powers were just as strong as ever. The Nightkeepers had tried to find and destroy the mouth, but they'd been unable to find it, suggesting the Xibalbans had tucked the entrance into a fold of the barrier, removing it from the earthly plane.

Given the existence of the hellmouth, logic and the doctrine of balance—which had become a central force in Michael's life since his talent ceremony—said there had to be another access point to the sky, another intersection. The billion-dollar question was: where?

The Nightkeepers had split up to search each of the sites mentioned in their regrettably incomplete archives as being places where the barrier separating the earth, sky, and underworld came very near the plane of mankind, potentially allowing access. Because of the exponentially increased power of mated pairs, Strike and his human mate, Leah; married parents Brandt and Patience White-Eagle; and newly mated Nate Blackhawk and Alexis Gray had taken the likeliest-seeming sites. Bachelors Michael and Sven had each taken a group of lower-priority sites, while the two nonwarriors—Jade and Strike's sister, Anna—provided backup with the help of the *winikin*. On Strike's say-so, the final remaining Nightkeeper warrior, twenty-year-old Rabbit, had skipped the assignment to start his freshman year at UT Austin with his human girlfriend, Myrinne. The kid was on call if anyone needed him.

Six months ago, that would've been a big "no" as far as Michael was concerned—Rabbit was a half-blood, pyrokine, telekine, mind-bender, and juvenile delinquent all wrapped up in one pissed-off package. He might've matured since he'd escaped from his brief captivity with the Xibalbans, bringing Myrinne out with him, but Michael still figured the kid belonged where he was, learning how to be a better human being while the rest of them tried to figure out how to be better magi.

At each of the sites where they hoped to find a new intersection, the Nightkeepers had let blood from their palms and used the sacrifice to call magic, testing the strength of the connection. A new intersection should give them a power boost that was off the charts. Michael's sites had barely registered on his own inner magic-o-meter.

"Are you sure?" Strike asked.

"Positive. There's no sign of an intersection at Tulum, Xel-Ha, Ox Bel Ha, or any of the other sites I tried." Michael might not be able to call the offensive weapons usually brought by the warrior's mark, but there was no way he'd missed an intersection—assuming, of course, that it acted like the one beneath Chichén Itzá. Before he could say anything else, though, he caught sight of an M-16-toting militiaman strolling around the edges of the watchtower's lower level, "I've got company," he reported. "I'll call you back when I get to my hotel, sooner if I need an emergency pickup." Sometimes it came in handy having a king who could teleport.

Michael flipped his phone shut and jogged down the steep, faintly slippery stone stairway that ran down the backside of the watchtower pyramid. When he hit level ground, he headed away from the ruin, angling in the opposite direction from the soldier in the hopes that the guy was just staying visible to the tourists thronging the popular site.

The other man changed vector to intercept, though, which had Michael muttering a curse under his breath. The ruins of Tulum weren't normally under military control; technically they weren't now, but there was a definite armed presence in the region, thanks to an ongoing tug-of-war between the government and a group of resorts that might or might not have been built on protected parkland right next to the ruins. Michael had bribed one of the soldiers to gain access to the watchtower ruin, which was supposed to be closed to the public. But the guy on his tail wasn't the one he'd bribed; he was older and tougher looking, with a serious *don't screw with me; I'm having a shitty week* look in his eyes.

Although Michael had never been one to back down from a fight—fair or otherwise—things were apt to get dicey if the local militia took too much of an interest in him. The fake ID Jox had hooked him up with was good enough to get him across the border, good enough for most airports stateside, but it wouldn't stand up to intense scrutiny. And while the other Nightkeepers could and would spring him out of a Mexican prison if it came to it, they preferred to avoid that sort of thing. The magi didn't exist in absolute secrecy, but they kept a low profile when it came to normal human affairs.

Moving fast, Michael ducked around a man-high pile of rubble that had probably once been a stela. The high pillars had been carved with glyphs spelling out births, deaths, politics, war, and just about anything else human beings of any time period found important. Now, the state of the art in thirteenth-century billboards was reduced to a hiding spot as Michael hunkered down behind the stela. Warning danced across his skin, courtesy of his warrior's powers. But while he might not be able to call fireball magic like the others, he was hell on wheels with its antithesis, shield magic.

As the soldier drew near, Michael pulled a carved obsidian knife from an ankle holster. Drawing the scalpel-sharp blade across his palm, he welcomed the bite of pain and the faint glow of red-gold Nightkeeper power it brought. Before the destruction of the skyroad he wouldn't have needed the blood for a shield spell. Now, though, he needed blood for even lower-level spells.

Concentrating, Michael touched his talent, calling the power of the barrier and using it to cast a thick shield around his body: a faint tremor in the air, a few degrees of refractive index that hadn't been there moments earlier. He couldn't make himself invisible like Patience could, but he'd learned that if he cast the shield at a certain angle from his body, it distorted both light and sound, confusing human perceptions. Once the shield was in place, the soldier shouldn't be able to see or hear him.

Moments later, footsteps approached, boots ringing on stone.

Keep walking, Michael thought as the militiaman appeared, eyes sharp, M-16 still on his shoulder. *Nothing to see here*. Michael wasn't a mind-bender like Rabbit, and thus wasn't actually able to shove the thought into the human's mind, but he figured the power of suggestion couldn't hurt, and he needed the guy to keep going.

Whether thanks to wishful thinking or the chameleon

shield, or a bit of both, the soldier kept going, not even glancing in Michael's direction. Once he was gone, Michael dropped the shield and slipped into a milling herd of tourists headed back toward the hotels. He hadn't gotten far when his phone chirped in his pocket. Seeing the main Skywatch number on the display, he flipped the phone and answered, "Stone here."

"Get yourself someplace private." It was Michael's *winikin*, Tomas, sounding clipped and disapproving. As usual.

Michael stifled a curse at his *winikin*'s tone. The two of them had been close from Michael's youngest years through his teens, when he'd lived and breathed martial arts and aced his schoolwork with minimal effort. Tomas had played the role of Michael's godfather, standing in for parents who had supposedly died in a drunk-driving accident when he'd been a baby. Tomas—short and slight, like most *winikin*—had been there for Michael through college, and had just about pissed himself with pride when Michael had been recruited into the FBI's training program. Things had changed, though, when Michael washed out of the program, then took a high-tech sales job and started partying more than he worked out. Tomas had poked constantly, telling him he was better than his job, that he should do something more, *be* something more. Eventually, they had stopped really talking to each other . . . until almost eighteen months earlier, when the *winikin* had dropped the dime on the infamous, *the Nightkeepers are real, you're one of them, and you've got four years to save the world and six hours to get your ass on a plane to New Mexico* bombshell.

Hello, mind-fuck.

After learning that Tomas was actually his *winikin*, Michael had partway understood where his supposed godfather had been coming from all those years, pushing him to be a fighter, to demand justice, hell, to be the best at whatever he chose to do. But knowing what had caused the pressure didn't really change the fact that his de facto father had stopped loving him—or even liking him—when he'd refused to do as he was told.

The tension between them had remained even after Michael gained his bloodline and talent marks, binding him to the barrier as a full-blood mage. Hell, things hadn't even really improved between them over the past five months, ever since Michael had finally managed to cut ties with his old life and dedicated himself to becoming a better mage. On some level, he'd figured his new level of effort would finally make Tomas happy. That had been a "fail," though. His growing role within the Nightkeepers hadn't made any difference in his relationship with his *winikin*. They still rubbed each other very wrong.

"Get. Your. Ass. Private," Tomas gritted. "Strike needs to make an emergency grab."

Oh, hell. Shelving the interpersonal shit, Michael took a quick look around and headed for a likely looking gap between two buildings on the edge of the hotel district. "What's wrong?"

"Anna just got a phone message from Lucius," Tomas reported.

Michael's warrior talent flared hard, revving his magic and sweeping all the other garbage aside. Strike's sister, Anna, was a Mayan-studies expert at UT Austin; Lucius had been her grad student until he'd gotten himself possessed by an underworld nasty called a *makol*, one of the minion species of the demon *Banol Kax*. In the months since his possession, the Nightkeepers had been unable to find Lucius. Strike hadn't even been able to get a 'port lock, and there were only three things that could foil 'port lock: death, rock shielding, or the efforts of a mage capable of breaking 'port lock . . . like Iago.

"What did he say?" Michael asked as he headed for the alleyway.

"Supposedly, Iago and thirty or so Xibalbans are holed up in the old Survivor2012 compound. They've got Sasha Ledbetter there . . . and they're planning on sacrificing her tonight at the height of the meteor shower. They couldn't torture the library's location out of her, so they're going to see if they can get the answer out of her spirit."

"Oh, hell." Michael hissed out a breath as a complicated mix of emotions mule-kicked him in the chest and an image plastered itself across his mind's eye; a promo shot of a dark-haired woman posing in a restaurant kitchen with a handful of peppers and a ten-inch knife, looking sexy as hell.

Sasha was the only daughter of Ambrose Ledbetter, an old-school Mayanist whose body had been found by Anna and Red-Boar deep in the rain forest near a Nightkeeper temple, headless and buried in a shallow grave. That hadn't been the biggest shock, though. No, the major *oh, holy what-the-fuck* moment had been when they'd found extensive scarring on his right inner forearm, as though Ambrose—or someone else—had burned that skin away.

Did that mean he was a lost Nightkeeper, one who had somehow broken his connection to the barrier, thereby surviving the Solstice Massacre? The magi weren't sure, but that had become an almost moot point when they learned that Ambrose had discovered, moved, and re-hidden the Nightkeepers' ancient library, an extensive repository of spells and codices that should hold all the information the magi were lacking . . . like the location of a new intersection, and what, exactly, was going to happen during the three-year threshold leading to the end date, which was a little over a month away.

Unfortunately, Iago had gotten to Sasha first. The Nightkeepers had been trying to find the Xibalbans' main encampment and mount a rescue attempt since then, with no luck . . . until now.

Michael's gut twisted, partly with relief that she was still alive, partly with sick guilt that she'd been in Iago's power for nearly a year now. Where the Nightkeepers sacrificed their own blood, the Xibalbans drew power from their prisoners and enemies. More, Iago was a borrower, able to divert talents from other magi and use them for his own purposes. There was no telling what foul magic they'd tried on her.

"Godsdamn it," he muttered under his breath. The curse wasn't entirely directed at the Xibalbans, either. If the Nightkeepers couldn't manage to rescue one woman, how the fuck were they supposed to save the world?

The kick of anger brought an answering stir of heat. He'd never met Sasha, but ever since he'd first dug into the file that had been put together by the Nightkeepers' tame private investigator, Carter, he'd been unable to get her out of his head. Part of it was revulsion toward the idea of a woman—hell, anyone—being held hostage by the Xibalbans. But that wasn't what had him looking at her photos far too often, he knew.

There was something engaging about the impish glitter in her dark brown eyes, consistently visible in each of the snaps Carter had culled from a series of restaurant Web sites. The tilt of her dimpled chin carried a hint of go-to-hell defiance he could relate to, and the rest of her stirred his hormones, from her loosely curled dark hair and angular, almost elfin face, to the long, curved fluidity of her body— what could be seen of it beneath chef's whites, anyway.

Carter's factoid-laden report sketched the story of a child who had been raised partly in the field by her father, partly stateside by Ambrose's live-in girlfriend, and had wound up breaking from them both when she left for culinary school. Estrangement, too, was something Michael could relate to, as was her extensive childhood training in martial arts. He'd always been a sucker for a woman with fight training.

Michael had spearheaded several searches of potential Xibalban hideouts over the past few months, but those look-sees hadn't turned up dick, leaving him frustrated and pissed off, and worried about a woman he'd never met, one whose picture was burned into his conscious mind.

She's in the Everglades, he thought, his pulse kicking at the realization that they'd finally gotten a break. But logic tempered the rush of battle readiness, and the stir of bloodlust that wasn't entirely his own.

"It's got to be a trick," he said, thinking aloud. "It can't be a coincidence that Iago suddenly pops up at the old Survivor2012 compound, given how well Leah knows the property."

A former detective with the Miami-Dade PD, Strike's human mate had studied the location as part of tying the site's owner, cult leader Vincente Rincon, to her brother's death and a series of ritualistic murders in the Miami area. With the help of Strike and the others, she'd gotten her revenge on Rincon, and the cult had disbanded. The property, which had been built up out of some seriously swampy land at the edge of the Everglades, had been resold before the Nightkeepers could snap it up. However, Strike and Leah had managed to search the property, discovering several ritual chambers hidden within a labyrinth of tunnels belowground. The compound had sat empty ever since. According to Carter, the place had been bought by a conservationist group looking to preserve the Everglades.

Ten bucks says the conservationists are a front for the Xibalbans, Michael thought. But that didn't necessarily make Lucius's call a trap. Iago could have been drawn there by the compound's history, its isolated location, or the power given off by the numerous Mayan relics Rincon had bought on the black market and reassembled on the property.

"You willing to bet the library on its being a trick?" Tomas asked.

"Doesn't matter either way, does it? We have to check it out." Michael ducked into a deserted alley, where it would be safe for his king to materialize. "Tell Strike he's good to zap."

Tomas hung up without another word. A few seconds later, Michael heard the faint rattle in the air that presaged 'port magic, and then Strike materialized, zapping in maybe six inches off the ground and dropping to a bent-kneed landing.

The king was an imposing figure. Tall, broad-shouldered, and muscular, bigger than even larger-than-average humans, as were all full-blood Nightkeeper males, Strike wore his shoulder-length black hair tied back in a queue, balancing the severity of the look with a narrow beard that traced his jawline. His right forearm was marked with the glyphs denoting him as a member of the jaguar bloodline, as royalty, as a warrior and a teleport. Higher up, on his biceps, where only the gods and kings were marked, he wore the geometric *hunab ku*, the symbol of the 2012 doomsday and the Nightkeepers' king. Even though he was wearing thoroughly modern clothes in his black-on-black combat duds and heavy boots, he looked almost medieval. He could've been a crusader, perhaps, or one of Arthur's knights. Hell, maybe even Arthur himself.

Without preamble, Strike reached out and gripped Michael's upper arm, forming the touch link necessary for him to transport another person. "Tomas has your armor and weapons waiting for you. This could be the break we've been hoping for."

"Or it could be a godsdamned ambush," Michael countered as the 'port magic rose up around them. But ambush or not, he was on board with whatever the king was planning. A fight was a fight. And this rescue was long overdue.

CHAPTER THREE

The Everglades

Sasha awoke, blinking up into the light thrown down by an unshielded fluorescent tube. *Something's different*, she thought. But a quick look around her said it wasn't the scenery.

She was still in hell. It wasn't the Christians' fire-and-brimstone hell or Ambrose's nine-layered Mayan underworld of rivers and roads and monsters, though. No, this hell was one of cool, blank walls and a narrow cot in a ten-by-ten cell with gray walls, floor, and ceiling. This hell was being the prisoner of an enormous, green-eyed, chestnut-haired man who called himself Iago, but whom the others called "Master."

Where is the library? his red-robed, forearm-tattooed interrogators asked her over and over again while drug-spiced smoke oozed from stone braziers carved into the shapes of screaming skulls. Each time, her muscles screamed protest at the crucified position they'd tied her in, roping her to a wooden cross that represented not the son of the Christians' god, but the world tree of the Maya and Aztec, with its roots delving into hell, its branches reaching to the sky. *Where did your father hide it?* Sometimes they lashed her with stone-tipped flails that drew bloody purple-black lines on her body. Other times they didn't hit her at all, but rather somehow put her in agony without touching her, watching with avid eyes as she writhed and screamed.

She would've given anything to make the torture stop, but she couldn't tell them what she didn't know. She'd kept insisting that Ambrose had never told her anything about a library. They didn't believe her, though, which meant that the cycle kept repeating over and over again—days of impotent, drugged fugue interspersed with pain and terror. She thought they might have moved her once or twice, but the details had blurred together, growing ever more distant as her mind insulated her consciousness from the reality her body was suffering. Each time the interrogators had opened the cell door, reality had receded further, her burgeoning fantasies coming clearer.

She knew the waking dreams were nothing more than illusions, constructs that her mind created for her as an escape. But she clung fiercely to the fantasies in her drugged stupor, because if her consciousness was wrapped in the dreams, she wasn't aware of what was happening in the interrogation chamber. And that was a blessed relief.

Sometimes the fantasies brought her to a strange cave, a circular stone room that should have reminded her of the interrogation room and the horrors within it. But she wasn't terrified in this chamber, wasn't hurt. Instead, she was wildly aroused, wrapped around a big, powerful man with long, wavy dark hair and green eyes that reminded her of the pine forests up in Maine. In the dreams, she breathed him in, lost herself in his kiss, and felt, maybe for the first time in her life, like she was exactly where she belonged. Which was how she knew it was a fantasy, because Sasha had done many things in her life, but she'd never truly fit anywhere.

Other times the dreams brought her back to Boston, to the pretty, sun-filled studio apartment where she'd lived across the hall from a firefighter's widow, an elderly ex–concert violinist named Ada, who'd become her friend. Sasha had cooked for her neighbor a few nights a week, gladly trading pumpkinseed dip and spicy barbecued shrimp for snippets of Bach and Mozart, and the knowledge that someone cared whether or not she made it home at night. Only she hadn't made it home, had she? Instead she'd gone looking for Ambrose and wound up in hell, stuck there as her menstrual clock told her months passed, almost a year, while she lay dazed by drugs and hopelessness.

Except she wasn't drugged or hopeless now. She felt sharp and energized for the first time in what seemed like forever.

Hardly daring to trust the sudden change, she sat up on her bunk and braced herself for the pain to hit. It didn't. Instead, nerves and excitement and all sorts of other sharp, hot emotions poked through the numb confusion that had cloaked her for too long.

"What the hell is going on?" she asked, and jerked at the sound of her own voice, the alien clarity of words that weren't drugged mumbles or throat-tearing screams.

Starting to shake now—with hope, with fear—she took stock. She was wearing the sturdy bush pants she'd had on when she'd been captured, along with a too-big navy sweatshirt she'd had for a while now, though she didn't know who she'd gotten it from, or when. Her underwear, T-shirt, and socks were long gone to rags, her boots confiscated. All that was the same as it had been. The cuts on her palms, though, were new.

She stared at the shallow, scabbed-over slices as a

hazy memory broke through. Had she dreamed of a brown-haired man bending over her with a serrated combat knife, his eyes flickering from hazel to luminous green and back again? If so, it was a new, less pleasant fantasy than the others, her imagination run amok. But no, she was positive he had been there; she had the scabs to prove it. Had he done something to neutralize the tranquilizers they'd been mixing in her food for so long? Or had the red-robes withdrawn the drugs for some reason, wanting her fully aware for whatever they had planned next?

But she wasn't just awake; she felt damned good. Energy coursed through her, effervescent bubbles running in her veins, making her want to leap up and run, to scream with the mad exuberance of being alive. More, she was warm. Hot, even, and suddenly needy in a way she hadn't been in a long, long time. Her heart pounded; her skin tingled. She thought of her dark-haired, green-eyed dream man, and ached for him, for the press of his flesh on hers.

Lifting her hands, she cupped her suddenly flushed cheeks, then let her fingertips drift down to skim across her collarbones and along her ribs. Surprise shuddered through her at the feel of smooth, toned flesh. Slowly, almost afraid to look, she lifted the hem of her sweatshirt so her eyes could confirm what her hands had found. Although it seemed impossible, the festering sores on her hips and shoulders had healed overnight, and the cross-hatched welts, scabs, and scars of the repeated whippings had faded from her skin. Her wasted flesh had been restored; her arms and legs were muscled, her butt and breasts rounded, as they had been before her captivity.

Stunned, she let the sweatshirt drop back down to cover her irrationally taut, toned stomach. Her head spun with disbelief, but not with drugs.

If she'd believed in miracles, she would've called it

just that. How else could matching slashes on her palms cause her body to heal itself?

"Doesn't matter," she told herself as the embers of the strong woman she'd once been kindled to a low, guttering flame of determination. "Don't waste whatever time you've got trying to figure out what's going on. Just get your ass out of here."

Rising from the narrow, blanketless cot, she stood for a moment, thrilling to the sense of balance and power that coursed through her, the awareness of her own body. She acutely felt the weight of her sweatshirt and pants, the press of the floor against the soles of her feet. In the back of her head lurked the fear that this was nothing more than another sort of torture, that Iago had given her back herself only to take the feeling away again. But on the heels of fear came determination. "If that's your plan, you bastard, you're going to regret it," she said softly. "That's a promise."

Outside in the hallway, muffled slightly by the heavy metal door of her cell, she heard the measured tread of footsteps in the hallway. One set, heading in her direction. She froze, imagining the possibilities. Was one of Iago's acolytes coming to her room? *Oh, please, yes. I dare you.*

Adrenaline sizzled in her veins and her pulse hammered as she cast around for a weapon. There wasn't time to disassemble the bedframe, if she could even manage the feat, and the toilet was bolted in place. The only other thing in the cell was her meal tray, where a microwaved mac-and-cheese sat half-eaten, a plastic spoon sticking out of the congealed mess.

"It'll have to do," she hissed, grabbing the makeshift weapon and pressing her body tight against the wall, on the hinged side of the door. Letting the handle end of the spoon poke between her fingers, she imagined shoving it into one of Iago's gloating, emerald green eyes. Rage and excitement rose up, nearly choking her. She hated him, hated what he'd done to her, to Ambrose. Hell, for all she knew, the bastard had killed Pim, too. It was Pim's funeral that had precipitated her fleeting reunion with her father in late June of the prior year, and it had been the memory of his grief that had prompted Sasha to call him months later, only to learn that he'd fled to his rain forest. If Iago had been trying to force Ambrose over the edge of his tenuous grip on sanity, killing Pim would have been the perfect trigger. Not because Ambrose had loved her, but because she'd kept him as contained as he ever got, giving his sanity an anchor.

It fit. It played. And it rankled deep inside Sasha as the footsteps paused outside her cell door and the lock clicked. Moments later, the metal panel swung inward and a gray-robe stepped through. Sasha took a split second to make sure it wasn't her brown-haired maybe-ally. Then she attacked.

Now! Propelled by a year's worth of rage and hatred, along with the gut-deep knowledge that this might be her only chance of escape, she attacked. Lunging from behind the door, she slammed the spoon handle into the gray-robe's face. She nailed him in the left eye, the spoon handle sinking in with a moment of resistance followed by a liquid give that made her gag.

Her victim shouted, spun, and staggered, clapping both hands to his ruined eye as blood and fluid spurted. Sickened, Sasha slashed a kick that folded his knee sideways, dropping him howling just inside the door. A second kick, this one to the side of his head, had him going limp. She searched him hurriedly; he was carrying a high-tech com device but no weapon, damn it. Slipping into the hallway, she shut and locked the door, then leaned back against it, gulping air.

Keep it together, she told herself. *You can do this.*

Unable to figure out how to turn off the handheld

com, and afraid it would make noise at exactly the wrong
moment, she ditched it. Then, with her heart hammering
a tempo of fear and victory, her shaking hands stained
with the blood of her enemy, she took off running down
the metal-lined corridor. She had no clue where she was
going, but anywhere had to be better than where she'd
been.

In the blue-black of dusk in the Everglades, eight
Nightkeeper warriors and one human ex-cop materialized in the swamp just beyond the former Survivor2012
compound.

The nine fighters wore black-on-black combat clothes, all
a variation of a tee or turtleneck and Kevlar-impregnated
cargo pants tucked into lightweight, grippy boots. Body
armor went over the top—black again—and their utility belts held MAC-10 autopistols and spare clips of
jade-tipped bullets on one side, ceremonial knives on
the other. Night-vision opticals gave them eyes in the
gathering darkness, and military-grade earpiece–throat
mike combos would allow them to reach out and touch,
as long as there wasn't too much interference.

The ground squelched beneath Michael's combat
boots; the swampy smell was seriously rank, and he was
pretty sure something had slithered out from beneath
him as he landed. He didn't comment, though, merely
registered the peripheral annoyances as he sought the
inner calm he relied on. But balance didn't come easily,
with the possibility of Sasha's rescue so close at hand.
Magic hummed at the base of his brain, responding to
the peak of the Leonid meteor shower; the red-gold
Nightkeeper power was far stronger than it had been
in many months, and carried a jagged, unfamiliar edge
of violence that warned him that his control was close
to slipping.

Anger pulsed beneath his skin, foreign and tempting; it throbbed in time with the blood that ran hot in his veins. Screw stealth and subtlety; he wanted to use a couple of jade-filled grenades to bust open the gates of the narrow causeway leading into the compound, and go in with guns blazing. He wanted not just to rescue Sasha, but to kill the men who had taken her, who had kept her. Who had, he knew, hurt her.

The pounding, overwhelming need for revenge brought sweat prickling beneath his body armor. The heavy iron tang of blood suddenly coated his sinuses and layered his tongue, and for a second he was awash in violence. Horror—and horrible temptation—locked him in place as death flooded his senses. He could feel the flutter of a man's carotid beneath his gripping fingers, smell his fear, taste the moment life cut out and the afterlife took over. *Yes*, something deep within him thought. *Yes!*

"No," he said aloud, gritting the word through locked teeth that he unclenched only long enough to bite the tip of his own tongue, more for the snap of pain than the blood sacrifice—gods knew he was already channeling plenty of magic. That was part of the problem. He didn't know where the dark surge had come from, unless—

His head snapped up and he took a quick look around at the others, but they were focused on Strike as he went over the basic plan one last time. All except Rabbit, who had been 'ported back from UT for the rescue mission. The sharp-featured young man, his former skull trim grown out into a short bristle of brown spikes, glanced over and met Michael's eyes. Rabbit raised an eyebrow. *Got a problem?* the expression said.

Michael looked away.

"I don't sense any wards," Alexis said from the other side of the loosely clustered group of black-clad fighters. Formerly soul-bound to the goddess Ixchel, the tall, blond Valkyrie had retained the ability to sense patterns, both visible and invisible, even after the destruction of the skyroad had severed her connection to the goddess. Michael had to wonder, though, if Alexis was losing the last of her goddess-given skills, because it didn't make any sense for Iago not to have warded the hell out of his hideout.

"Lucius said he'd take care of getting us inside safely." That was from Patience, who tended to be a stubborn optimist, even when things were going to shit. And it was true that Lucius had gotten out a second message to that effect, as relayed by Anna. It was also technically possible that it'd happened the way Lucius claimed: that he'd tried to kill himself back in the spring after escaping from Skywatch, but the *makol*'s powers had healed his injuries, drawing the attention of Iago, who'd taken him into the Xibalbans' fold. There, the mage had used spells and sacrifices to bring the *makol* to the forefront, so it overrode Lucius's human self except during times of increased barrier activity . . . like the one they were experiencing now.

Sure, all of that played. But it was still too damned convenient.

Alexis's mate, Nate Blackhawk, was thinking along the same lines. The dark-haired, slick-looking warrior growled, "Thousand bucks says it's a trap." Nate, a former war game developer, had a decent grip on strategy, and often played devil's advocate to any plan taken up by Strike and the other four members of the royal council, who did most of the Nightkeepers' planning.

"We knew that going in," Michael countered, having been part of the brief confab back at Skywatch. He didn't wear the small, carved eccentric that symbolized an adviser, but these days he often sat in on the meetings and brought his rather unique perspective to the discussions. Not that the others understood exactly how unique that perspective was.

"Trap or not, we're not leaving her in there to be sacrificed," Strike growled. "Even if her father wasn't a Nightkeeper, she's our best connection to the library. Sure, if anyone gets a shot at Iago or a chance to snag Lucius, take it, but remember that the rescue mission is our top priority. Get the hostage and get out. Everything else follows from there. We can come back for the Xibalbans after we get the library and the added firepower it contains."

The tight knot of battle readiness eased slightly inside Michael, making him aware that he hadn't been entirely sure of his king. As their leader, Strike sometimes had to make shitty decisions, like whether to risk almost all of the remaining Nightkeepers in order to rescue one woman who might or might not be a mage's daughter. Michael, on the other hand, was on a personal crusade sparked by a handful of photos and a childhood story he could relate to. He was getting Sasha out, period. And gods help anyone who got in his way.

At the thought, he felt a stir of sharp-edged magic. Blocked it.

Without further discussion, Nate and Alexis melted away from the group and disappeared into the darkness. Moments later there was a surge of sex-charged magic as the mated pair leaned on each other to power Nate's ability to shape-shift to a man-size hawk. A low, alien cry announced the successful shift, followed by the beat of powerful wings. A blur moved past, that of a blond Valkyrie astride a giant hawk. Then the pair took to the air and swept up over the compound, angling precariously through the encroaching mangroves.

"It's pretty tight going," Alexis's voice said quietly in Michael's ear, coming through the earpiece with only a slight burr of distortion. "Not sure how much help we're going to be in terms of recon."

"Just give us a sweep of the area, keeping an eye out

for ambush," Strike said into his mike. He turned to Leah. "You got any last-minute words of wisdom?"

The Nightkeepers' ex-cop queen was blond and classically beautiful, cool-eyed and all business as she answered, "The main building at the top of the hill is just the tip of the swampberg; most of the place is underground, tunnels done in a mix of stonework and prefab steel, sort of the bastard love child of a pyramid and a bunker. The access points are hidden inside temple ruins built into the landscaping; they lead to vertical tunnels running straight down into the labyrinth." She went on to hit the highlights of the location, describing the underground rooms where it seemed most likely Iago would keep a prisoner, as well as the three concealed ritual chambers she and Strike had found during their search. She finished with, "We don't know how long Iago's been here, or how thoroughly he knows the site. Let's assume the worst, hope for the best."

"Story of our lives," Sven muttered from behind Michael. The former underwater treasure hunter had become Michael's closest almost-friend at Skywatch, the two having bonded over video games and nine-ball, and the fact that they were effectively the last two bachelors among the magi.

"Nah," Michael replied, keeping his voice low. "The story of our lives is not knowing enough about any-fucking-thing, thanks to humanity's habit of demonizing and destroying all the shit they don't understand."

"You're clear to move in," Alexis's voice said through the com system. "At least, as far as we can tell. This place isn't ideal for aerial surveillance."

"Understood," Strike responded. "Meet us near the temple of the Diving God." At his signal, the Nightkeepers joined hands, forming the contact that allowed Strike to 'port them inside the compound. The group zapped in right near a low-slung stone edifice carved with Mayan hieroglyphs and the image of the Diving God, an exaggerated figure positioned head-down, as though he were plummeting toward the underworld. Which seemed only fitting.

Michael landed in a crouch, braced for an ambush, but the only sound was that of huge feathers slapping the air as Nate cruised in for a landing and returned to man form. Alexis helped him dress from the knapsack she'd taken to wearing pretty much twenty-four/seven, because of Nate's clothes, only his amulet and armband—both integral to his talent—shifted when he did.

Strike reached to slap the pressure pad that would open the hidden tunnel. Before he could do the honors, though, there was a grating noise, and a stone panel slid sideways into the elaborate carvings of the bastardized temple. A man stood in the opening, broad shouldered, his features obscured beneath the hood of a light-hued robe rendered colorless by the night. Michael tensed, going for his pistols as the figure reached up to push back his hood. Even though he instantly recognized Lucius's pleasantly regular features, Michael didn't stand down until he confirmed that the other man's eyes were normal, not the luminous green of a *makol*.

Lucius looked far more haggard than he had the last time Michael had seen him, his body language gone fighter-tough. On his inner right wrist, in addition to the black slave mark that had failed to blood-bind him under the Nightkeepers' control, he now wore the red quatrefoil hellmark that denoted a connection to the Xibalbans' hellmagic. That shouldn't have been a surprise—how else would Iago have gotten through to the *makol*? Still, though, the sight made Michael wince inwardly. Of the magi, he alone knew that Lucius had been, very briefly, Jade's lover, and that she still mourned him in secret.

Lucius scanned the assembled magi, his eyes locking on Strike. Not bothering with preliminaries, he said, "Follow me." Then he turned and disappeared into the darkness. Moments later came the sound of booted feet on a ladder leading down.

After the briefest hesitation, Strike followed, with Leah at his back. Then, one by one, the others vanished into the earth. Michael took his customary position at the rear of the group, where he could protect them with his shield magic. As a team, the Nightkeepers descended into Iago's realm, braced for almost anything.

Lucius kept iron control of the alien consciousness he'd trapped at the back of his brain as he led the Nightkeepers into the underground labyrinth. The dank air smelled of stale incense and blood, making his stomach churn even more than it already was from the stress of holding the *makol* at bay.

He wanted to stop, drop, and puke, wanted to claw at his own eyeballs in an effort to release the pressure inside his overstuffed skull. Instead, he forced his distant-feeling body to keep moving, putting one foot in front of the other as he led the small group in past the stone-lined rooms Iago used for interrogations. Thanks to the trapped *makol*'s thoughts, Lucius knew that this side of the complex would be deserted, because the Xibalbans were all up in the mansion itself, preparing for the Leonid ceremony and the planned human sacrifice. Which could not be allowed to take place.

Save Sasha, he wanted to tell Strike and the others. *Get her out of here*. He didn't dare speak more than the two words he'd already uttered, though; it was taking all his energy to keep the *makol* in check. But he *had* to lead them in safely, just as he'd fought to get those calls out to Anna—not to save himself, but to save Ambrose Ledbetter's daughter. Sasha.

She was the key to the next stage of the end-time war; he was sure of it, though he couldn't say how he knew. Nor did he understand how, exactly, he'd regained control from the demon within him. The meteor shower had made him stronger, yes, but in theory it would've done the same for the *makol*, which he called Cizin. Despite the mockery of the name, which meant "flatulent one," the creature was strong and fierce. It had been months since Cizin had allowed himself to be shut away at the back of Lucius's brain, months since Lucius had escaped from the dusty, barren road inside his own head to retake control of his own body. Which meant . . .

Took you long enough, the demon's voice said inside their shared skull, sounding very like all of Lucius's über-jock male relatives combining to mock him in dissonant harmony. *You really are an idiot.* With just that split second of warning, Lucius's vision went green around the edges and his hearing sharpened unnaturally.

Shit! he thought with a vicious whip of self-directed anger.

He spun and yelled for the magi to run. At least, that was what he told his body to do, but it didn't listen to him, just kept walking at the head of the line.

And, deep down inside, he heard Cizin's dry, raspy chuckle. *Pitiful*, the creature said in its normal sand-papery mental tone. *Pathetic. You really thought you fought through from the in-between? Please. You're on this plane only because I allowed you to be, so you could bait the trap.* For a second, Lucius saw within the *makol* and gained a flash of its true purpose within the Xibalbans, how its *Banol Kax* masters had used him to gain access to Iago as a toehold on earth. In his mind, Lucius heard a dog's tortured howl, saw a terrible horned creature and the flash of teeth filed to a "T" shape. In that moment, he would've given anything to regain control of his body, to be able to warn the Nightkeepers of what the *Banol Kax* were planning to do, not now, but in the coming year.

But it was already too late. Cizin shoved Lucius back toward the prison of his own mind, a barren expanse of dirt and muddy brown sky, and a road that led nowhere. The in-between.

No! Lucius shouted in a voiceless wail as his *makol*-ruled body turned and beckoned to Strike and the others and whispered, "Her cell is on the next hallway, third down on the right." Which was a lie.

Screaming inside, Lucius fought to break through, to warn the magi, but Cizin quashed him easily as he led the Nightkeepers around the corner. And all hell broke loose.

Sasha's heartbeat thundered in her ears as she turned a corner and found herself at a three-way intersection. She took a quick look around, trying to get her bearings. It was no use, though, because the hallway looked much like all of the others she'd been down so far—bare, with zero in the way of character or distinguishing features. She might be in a repurposed guerrilla compound south of the temple, over the border into Honduras or Guatemala. Or she might be on the thirtieth floor of a highrise somewhere in the States. There was no way to tell.

As long as she kept moving, she could keep the fear at bay. The moment she paused, though, suffocating doubts closed in. How was she supposed to find her way out? Even if she got free, what next? How would she get home? For that matter, where *was* home? Hysteria pressed, making her wonder whether, if she closed her eyes and wished hard enough, she'd wake up back in Boston and find that the last year or so had been a terrible dream.

But she knew deep down inside that this wasn't a nightmare—at least, not a sleeping one. This was a twisted version of reality created by a group of wack-jobs obsessed with acting out ancient prophecies that meant nothing in modern times.

"Their reality is your reality, at least until you get your ass out of here," she muttered, trying to calm her racing thoughts. But which way was out? She hadn't seen any sign of the brown-haired guy she thought might be an ally, didn't have any clue where she was going, knew only that she had to keep moving. Taking a deep breath, she tried to once again become the tough fighter Ambrose had taught her to be, the one she'd rejected in favor of a normal life. Normalcy wouldn't help her now.

Moving quietly on her bare, chilled feet, she passed a row of metal doors and turned another corner, only to be brought up short by the sight of an ancient-looking stone slab blocking the prefab hall. She'd avoided the two other stone doors she'd passed, pretty sure they led to Iago's torture chambers. This door was larger, though, and carved with the image of a winged crocodile, or maybe a dragon.

Her instincts said it was the way out. Then again, her instincts had been known to make some really bad calls.

Whispering a prayer to nobody in particular, she pressed the flat of her palm against a protruding stone that looked like it ought to be a pressure pad. For several agonizing seconds, nothing happened. Then the stone panel grated and slid sideways into the wall. Heart hammering, Sasha stepped through into the corridor beyond.

Excitement kicked when she saw that she'd finally found someplace that looked different from where she'd been. The hallway was more like a tunnel, or a passageway in some ancient ruin. The walls, floor, and ceiling were made of interlocking stone blocks, some carved with worn motifs she didn't recognize, others rubbed smooth, the whole of them pieced together in a pastiche of carved and uncarved sections, as though assembled from several older sources. Light came from bare bulbs hanging off an electric line that was bolted to the low ceiling. There was another doorway at the far end, steel again. What the hell was this place?

Doesn't matter, she told herself. *What matters is getting the hell out of here.* When she did, she was going to find some cops—or mercenaries, depending on where she was—and she was going to come back to kick . . . Iago's . . . ass. Gritting her teeth as cleansing anger surged, Sasha reached for the door. It swung open before she touched it.

Four gray-robes stood in the opening, heavily armed and wearing body armor, as though they were expecting an attack. Or they already were under attack. They gaped at her.

Shock hammered through Sasha, who screamed for the first time since she'd awakened. But then she bit off the cry and turned to run.

"Get her!" the front man bellowed.

She dodged his grab and jammed an elbow into his throat, driving him back into the others. Then she swung the door into him and fled down the stone-lined corridor.

Behind her the door banged back open, and there were shouts of, "Shit, get her!" and "No, for fuck's sake, don't shoot. Iago needs her alive."

Breath rattling in her lungs, she fled up the hallway, heading for the sliding doorway and the prefab tunnels beyond. Booted footfalls rang behind her as she flung herself through the stone doorway and swung back around to scrabble at the pressure pad, trying to get the panel to shut. It started moving, but way too slowly, grating snail-like on its hidden mechanism as the footfalls pounded nearer.

"Faster, damn you!" She hit the button again. Fear sizzled through her, along with the sudden certainty that she wasn't ever going to get out of here, that Iago was going to—

"Leave it, for fuck's sake!" A pair of strong hands yanked her away from the door. "Come on!"

A stranger dragged her down the corridor, hauling her into a stumbling run, but she was barely aware of moving. Her entire attention was focused on the man who had come to her rescue. He was wearing black paramilitary gear over a black muscle shirt, and bristling with weapons. But that wasn't what had her brain vapor locking. What had her in a state of paralyzed shock was the fact that he was freaking huge. He was freaking gorgeous. And he had dark, wavy hair and eyes the same green as the pine forests of Maine.

CHAPTER FOUR

Sasha's brain stuttered in disbelief. No. Impossible. It was just a coincidence that his eyes and hair matched those of the man in her dreams.

Fantasy or not, though, the stranger hustling her down one hallway and across another was seriously impressive. His dark green eyes gleamed from beneath elegant brows, and his lean-bridged nose had a pronounced ridge in the middle. That, along with a square, stubbled jaw and the thick, wavy black hair, made his looks fiercely masculine, while a wide, mobile mouth and the rich gold of his skin saved him from looking too hard. The whole effect was one of raw, potent sexuality.

He was wearing black cargo pants and combat boots, along with a black muscle shirt beneath torso-encasing body armor that revealed the bare skin of his powerful shoulders and arms. He moved with the economical grace of a trained hand-to-hand fighter, and had a small, high-tech-looking earpiece dangling at his collar, and wore a complicated utility belt loaded with a pair of autopistols, spare clips, and a gleaming black glyph-etched knife.

He hooked the earpiece into place, not looking at her

as he said, "I've got her. Where are we meeting up?" His voice was a deep, sexy rasp that had heat chasing across her skin despite the situation.

Stirred by his touch and voice, confused by both his appearance and her response to it, she scrambled to catch up with his long-legged strides as he hustled them along. He was dressed as a soldier and carried himself like a highly trained fighter, and his words suggested that he'd come to rescue her. Yet he didn't wear a logo of any sort—not FBI or SWAT, or whatever the hell other group would be involved in a kidnapping or cult raid. Was he a mercenary?

"Who are you?" she blurted. "What's happening? Where are we?"

"Explanations later," he said as he dodged them down a side corridor, keeping his attention on their surroundings. "We've got to haul ass."

She started to nod, but froze midmotion when she caught sight of his right inner forearm, where he wore two glyph tattoos, both done in black, both images she recognized from childhood lessons: the stone bloodline and the warrior's talent. They were the marks of a mage. A so-called Nightkeeper.

He was one of them, damn it. A role-player. Sasha knew she shouldn't be surprised. More, she shouldn't be disappointed. Because she was both, she stopped dead and yanked away from him, anger giving her strength.

He spun back, brows snapping together over those fierce green eyes as he looked fully at her for the first time. "What the hell?"

"You think you're a goddamn Nightkeeper!"

He leaned in, giving her a close-up of his square, shadowed jaw and the burning intensity of his gaze. "Correction," he grated, the word seeming to vibrate beneath her skin, "I *am* a goddamn Nightkeeper. And right now, I'm your best chance of getting the hell out of here alive.

So are you going to move your ass, or am I going to have to carry you?"

"I don't—" she began, but didn't get any further than that.

He muttered a sharp expletive under his breath and scooped her up against his chest as though she weighed nothing. Outraged and terrified, Sasha drew breath to scream—

And the world went gray-green, then black.

As Michael hustled down the tunnel cradling Sasha's warm, curvy body against him, guilt pinched that he'd used a sleep spell on her. She wasn't all the way under, which argued for her being a mage of some sort. But she'd gone far enough under that he could pick her up and get going.

We've gotta move, not argue, he rationalized. But really, that had been only part of the decision—the other part was that he'd needed a moment to regroup. As in, a moment without her conscious and pushing his buttons, threatening his control.

When Lucius had led the Nightkeepers into the Xibalban ambush, the magi had swung into plan B: Strike, Leah, Nate, and Alexis had dug in to return the enemy fire, while the others had scattered to search the compound, each assigned to a block of high-priority rooms. Michael had started to head for his assigned rooms, but halfway there his warrior's talent had stopped him dead, turned his ass around, and sent him in the entirely opposite direction. He'd radioed his change of plans; to his surprise, Strike hadn't argued. Instead, the king had muttered something about there being no such thing as coincidences, and got Sven and Patience to check his assigned rooms. Ignoring Strike's reference to the writs and the will of the gods, Michael had followed his instincts—or whatever the hell it was—all the way across the labyrinth in the direction of the main mansion. There, he'd practically tripped over Sasha.

He'd imagined rescuing her more times than he wanted to admit, and the scene had usually involved him kicking in a door—or some Xibalban ass—in the process of getting her free. But there hadn't been a door, and she'd gotten at least partway free on her own. With nothing to kick, he'd been off his stride. And that first sight of her in person, where before she'd existed for him solely in the PI's notes and pictures, had done the kicking, with him as the target.

As in the photos, her cheekbones were wide set, her nose slightly tipped up at the end, her mouth lush and bow-shaped, her eyes a deep, rich brown. Her dark hair surrounded her face in a halo of waves and looping curves with no definable style. Her body was long and lean, yet subtly curvy inside faded bush pants and a too-big sweatshirt, and she was tall enough to look him in the eye. He'd gotten all that from the PI's file.

What the file hadn't told him was how the very air around her would snap with energy, or how alive she would be, how vital, when he hadn't dared hope she would come out of her captivity in one piece, either physically or mentally. *Thank you, Lucius*, he'd thought, seeing the slashes on her palms. Their inside man–turned-traitor must have blooded her in an effort to jump-start her connection to the healing magic of a Nightkeeper. And damned if it didn't look like it had worked, providing another point in favor of her having mage blood. He'd guess it was a strong bloodline, too, given how clearly she was thinking, how easily she'd moved . . . and how she felt in his arms as he doubled back along another steel-lined hallway.

His talent-sharpened hearing brought him the sound of quick-stepping bootfalls a couple of hallways over, and he paused to take a listen. *Shit.* They were between

him and the other magi, they were headed his way, and
there were a bunch of them. Outnumbered and cut off
from the other magi, burdened with a mostly unconscious woman, Michael knew he didn't dare fight them,
though part of him thought otherwise.

Heart pumping, senses and reflexes sharpening as
the footsteps drew nearer, he ducked into the shallow
alcove created by a vaulted doorway and cast a chameleon shield that should conceal him and Sasha . . . assuming the Xibalbans couldn't see through his magic.
Then he shifted her to a fireman's carry and pulled one
of his MAC-10s, just in case they could.

Moments later, six heavily armed and armored, tense-
looking gray-robes rounded the corner and headed
along the hallway toward where Michael and Sasha
were concealed. They got to work immediately, splitting
into two groups and checking each room.

Michael stifled a curse, knowing there was no way
they wouldn't notice they were missing a doorway. Pulse
thrumming, he braced himself to make a mess as they drew
abreast of his position . . . and didn't even glance over.

Apparently the chameleon shield didn't just confuse
light and sound; it confused perception and memory.
Nice.

He didn't have time to bask, though, because two of
the men paused just opposite the alcove. "The master
wants us to watch for the mick, and he needs the woman
alive," said the first, a lean-faced man with pale blue eyes
and a hooked nose. "Once we've got her, he'll bring her
straight back to the mountain."

The other guy—a shorter, squatter type with a wres-
tler's face—shrugged, looking annoyed. "That's assuming we find her. It's like she fucking disappeared."

"Don't sweat it," Hook-nose said as they moved off
again. "The *pilli* are on their way. Won't take them long
to sniff out the Nightkeepers' magic."

Michael waited a minute longer, making sure they didn't double back. When he was sure they were gone, he keyed on his throat mike and reported the convo to Strike and the others, finishing with, "Damned if I know what the mick and the *pilli* might be." The only magic sniffers Michael knew of were the *boluntiku*, which were horrifying lava creatures from the underworld itself. "But I've got Sasha. Let's meet up and get the hell out of here."

"Easier said than done," Strike answered. "The ambush team retreated and sealed the exits using some sort of central lockdown, so we're stuck in here. Rabbit felt a pretty good surge of dark magic a few minutes ago, probably teleport, but we're not sure whether Iago's people were coming or going."

"Shit," Michael muttered, hoping to hell Strike was keeping a close eye on the kid.

During his imprisonment, Rabbit had traded Myrinne's life for the red hellmark of the Xibalbans, which had connected him to their hellmagic. That meant the young man could track the Xibalbans' power draws, but also that Iago could sometimes reach him through a mind-link.

"It gets worse," Strike continued. "I can't zap us out of here. Either the resonance from all the stonework has fouled my 'port lock or Iago's got some sort of ward going. Rabbit's trying to burn his way through the ceiling into one of the exit tunnels."

"How's that coming?" Michael asked.

"Not good." The reply came from Rabbit himself.

Michael grimaced, hesitated, then said, "All due respect, but my gut says we don't have time to dick around. Is there a faster option?"

There was a murmur of off-mike convo for a moment; then Strike came back. "The second hidden chamber Leah and I found was clearly Nightkeeper in origin, not Mayan like the rest of them. Maybe the latent power of those stones, plus the group of us linking up, will give me enough to punch through."

Michael hissed out a breath. "I thought solid rock fouled 'port lock, period."

"It screws with my ability to lock onto a destination, but I can still trigger the 'port and get us into the travel flow of the barrier. From there—gods willing—I can lock onto a destination and get us the rest of the way home."

Michael could've done without the "gods willing" part, but it seemed their best option, especially when he heard additional bootsteps in an intersecting hallway. "I'll meet you there."

He keyed off without waiting for Strike's response, as his talent warned that he'd better get his ass moving. Dousing the chameleon shield, in case the approaching group included the Xibalbans' magic sniffers, he moved out, tacking roughly westward through the labyrinth. Soon, the prefab steel–and–drywall construction gave way once again to stones that hummed with old magic. When he reached the place Leah had described as hiding the Nightkeeper-origin secret chamber, he trailed his fingers along the wall, searching for a pressure pad or something that would indicate the location of the hidden doorway. He didn't— *Ah! There.*

He pressed the faint indentation. After a short pause, there was a grating noise and a section of the wall slid aside. Torches flared, lighting a circular stone chamber and providing a familiar ambience. Intricately carved walls arched overhead in a series of concentric rings, forming a circular temple reminiscent of the one that had housed the intersection beneath Chichén Itzá. In this sacred chamber, though, the ritualistic carvings showed a young goddess with vertical lines that looked like tears bisecting her eyes and cheeks. Her hair, worn in a high topknot, cascaded down around her like silk

from an ear of corn, identifying her as the maize goddess, bringer of life and health. Which was just wrong in
a place like this. How had Rincon gotten hold of such a
powerful shrine?

Doesn't matter, he told himself. *Just be glad it's here.*
Because sure as shit the stones held a ton of residual
power; the moment he stepped inside the space, red-
gold Nightkeeper magic hummed resonantly beneath
his skin. And that was just the *one* of the one-two magical punch. *Two* was a hard flare of heat that his body
translated instantly into a burn of lust. *Sex magic*, he
thought, gritting his teeth as the stone doorway slid shut
at his back, closing him in with the buzzing, tempting
power, and the woman who'd become his personal quest
to do something good for a change. *Shit.*

Not that he had anything against sex—far from it—
but this wasn't the time or place for him to put his impulse control to the test.

Swallowing hard, he keyed on his mike and grated,
"I'm here. Where are you guys?"

"On our way," Strike reported tersely, a burst of gunfire sounding in the background. "Might take us some
time, though. We've got company."

"Shit. Do you want me to—"

"Stay put," Strike ordered. "Guard Sasha. We'll get
there as soon as we can."

"Will do," Michael said, but the line had already gone
dead.

Forcing himself not to think about where his hands were
landing, he lowered her gently to the floor, propping her
up against the wall opposite the doorway. The automatic
torches were apparently loaded with incense; the room
was filling with the spicy smell of *copan*, the Nightkeepers' sacred incense. The scent ratcheted his magic higher,
which was going to be a problem. He needed to tamp it
down if he wanted to avoid the Xibalbans' magic sniffers.

He started by squelching the sexual buzz with a couple of breathing exercises and thinking of hockey—colder than baseball, he figured, so better for the job. Unfortunately, once the buzz of sex magic was down to a manageable level, he became all too aware of another power source in the room: the bespelled woman. Power limned Sasha's motionless form, trailing red-gold sparkles across her high cheekbones and accenting the soft curves of her breasts and hips, the long lines of her limbs.

His blood thudded in his veins; his body felt hard and heavy. He told himself to look away, but couldn't. Told himself to swear he wouldn't touch her, but he couldn't do that, either.

What he could do—what he *had* to do—was kill the sleep spell and take his chances.

Sasha woke quickly, with none of the disorientation that had become so familiar over the past year. The first thing she saw was the curving wall of a flame-lit circular chamber, where mad shadows danced on carved stone. That should've brought instant panic. Except it wasn't panic she felt as she stared at the gorgeous stranger who'd grabbed her from the hallway. He stood across the circular room in a fighter's ready stance, with his feet set parallel directly below his wide shoulders, his big, capable hands hooked into his weapons belt, looking very male, very dangerous.

She *should* be afraid. He was armed, and she had a feeling that whatever his hand-to-hand training had been, it went well beyond her own. But fear was far from her first response as their gazes connected. Instead, something shifted inside her, warming her core, tightening her skin, sensitizing her body.

An impossible whisper said that the resemblance was no coincidence, that this was the man she'd imagined in the depths of her despair, the man whose image had carried her through countless interrogations. And now he'd come for her. *What took you so long?* she almost said. Instead, she shook herself inwardly, reminding herself that she'd sworn off making assumptions without proof.

When he didn't say anything, just stood there watching her steadily, his dark green eyes unreadable, she said, "Where are we?"

"Still in Iago's compound. Working on changing that." His short, clipped answers gave away little, yet his voice skimmed along her skin, sounding far more intimate than it should have.

"How'd you put me out like that? Drugs? Vulcan neck pinch?"

"Magic."

Whoa. Wack-job alert, she thought, forcibly reminded that he'd flat-out claimed to be a Nightkeeper mage. She blew out a breath as the greedy churn in her stomach shifted to a twist of disquiet. "No, really. I'm serious."

"Trust me, so am I."

"Shit." She looked away, trying not to let the disappointment feel deeply personal. "You're one of them. A doomsdayer. Part of this . . . sick-assed war game Iago's playing."

"I wish it were a game," he said. "It'd make all our lives a whole hell of a lot easier. Unfortunately, the endtime is very real. Iago and the Xibalbans are real, as are the Nightkeepers, the *Banol Kax*, the prophecies, and the coming war." He watched her as he spoke, as if checking to see how much she already knew. Apparently finding what he'd hoped for, he nodded fractionally, broke from the ready stance, and crossed the room to lean down and offer her his hand. "I'm Michael Stone. It's a pleasure to finally meet you in person."

Sasha took his hand and let him pull her to her feet, his grip warm and reassuring. She was dimly aware that the cut on her palm had almost healed, that he seemed to have a matching slice—or maybe a scar?—on his own. The raised ridges rubbed one against the other, sparking excitement deep within her.

Exhaling a deep breath in an effort to smooth out the jagged edges of an attraction that made no sense, she said, "I'm Sasha Ledbetter. But you already knew that, didn't you?"

"We've been looking for you since late last year. We would've come for you sooner, but we couldn't find Iago's base of ops. I'm sorry."

On one level, the apology made her yearn. On another, it ticked her off. "*We.* You mean the Nightkeepers?" The word conjured bedtime stories of warrior heroes, fearsome monsters, and love affairs that changed the world. And there had been a time in her life that she'd imagined herself a Nightkeeper, dreaming of fantastic magical powers, supernatural enemies, and the darkly handsome mage gods-destined to be her mate. But as Ambrose lost his grip on sanity, he'd increasingly claimed the stories were real, until the day he'd taken it too far. The memory brought a twist of nausea. "Let me guess . . . you want me because of my connection to Ambrose, and the library he supposedly hid."

He didn't bother denying it. "That's part of it."

"What's the other part?"

"We don't just need the library, Sasha. We need *you.* If Ambrose was one of us, then you have power. You're already showing signs of it."

"Bullshit," she said flatly. "If I'm showing signs of anything, it's being held hostage for a year." Except that most of those symptoms were gone, weren't they? What sort of hypothesis fit with that evidence?

Trying to settle the sudden churning of her stomach, she took a deep breath, filling her lungs with the incense-spiced air. When she exhaled, she seemed to lose a layer of tension with the breath. She didn't lose the buzz of heat, though. If anything, it ratcheted a notch higher, making her want to lean into him. Sucking in another lungful of scented air, she looked up into eyes that were nearly black now, with only a thin line of forest green at the edges. Once she stopped thinking of him as SWAT or a local equivalent, and looked beyond the body armor and weapons to the man beneath, there was something grimly piratical about him, a ruthless air that warned he would take what he wanted. The idea shouldn't have kicked up her body heat, but it did. So, too, did the long, dark hair brushing his shoulders, and the muscular ripple of his throat as he swallowed, his eyes locked on hers.

In that breathless, charged moment, she saw his desire, and knew it reflected her own. Which was abso-fucking-lutely nuts. The last thing she should be thinking about was sex. But somehow that was the only thing she could imagine at that moment. Sex. With him.

A shiver worked its way down her neck when she realized what that evidence suggested. More drugs. "What the hell is in this smoke?"

"It's just *copan*," he answered. "Sacred incense." A pause. "Why? What are you feeling?"

Like he didn't know. She gritted her teeth, suddenly grateful for the too-big sweatshirt, which covered the pebble-hard points of her nipples. *You know damn well what I'm feeling*, she thought. *You're feeling it, too*. Unless he wasn't, which was a hell of a sobering thought . . . and wouldn't be the first time she'd mistaken a man's intentions.

Although she hadn't answered, he seemed to take her wince as a response. "This"—he waved at the carved stones surrounding them—"was a Nightkeeper temple. If you're getting a buzz, it's because of the residual power in the stones. That's why we're here—the others'll be joining us soon. When they do, we'll use the power boost from the stones to teleport out." Again, he watched her speculatively.

"You're insane." But even she heard the lack of conviction in her words, the weakening of her resolve in the face of what had to be drugged smoke. "Seriously, what's in the smoke? Some sort of aphrodisiac?"

His eyes glittered. "If you're growing horns, it's magic, not drugs. The man who called us to come get you was the one who cut your palms, hoping to trigger the healing powers of a mage. Seems like it worked."

"No . . ." Her voice had gone whisper thin. "This isn't real." Everything she'd experienced over the past year, and everything that was going on now . . . it was all part of an elaborate, expensive sham constructed around a fantasy world in which Mayan demons menaced the earth and mankind was under the protection of Nightkeeper magi. Which was nuts.

Right?

He continued as if she hadn't spoken. "And given that the healing magic worked, I guess it's no surprise that you're picking up on the sexual aspects of the power too."

"I dreamed you," she blurted. She didn't realize she'd said the words aloud until she saw his eyes go blank with shock for a second, then fill with roaring heat underlain by deep wariness.

"Sasha . . ." His expression softened and he took a step toward her, only to stall abruptly, his eyes losing focus as he touched his ear, where he wore a small receiving device. "Come again?" He paused, grimacing. "Shit. Copy that."

Swallowing hard, she said, "Problem?"

"A delay." He hesitated, as if trying to figure out how much to share. "The others are cut off, and there's a Xibalban search party headed this way."

Dread prickled, cutting through the sensual haze. "If they open the door to this room, we're toast."

His mouth flattened. "I might be able to shield us."

"How?" She gestured around the empty room. "Not much to hide behind."

"It's called a chameleon shield," he explained, watching her carefully. "It confuses perceptions."

"You're insane." *Just like Ambrose.*

He stared at the doorway as though weighing his options. "I'd offer you a demonstration, but I can't risk casting the spell until they're actually here. There's a chance they'll be able to sense the magic."

She shouldn't, absolutely *shouldn't* believe him. The fact that she almost did just supported her suspicion of drugs in the smoke. This whole conversation was part real, part hallucination, and she couldn't tell where one stopped and the other began.

She looked past him to the door. What if it was all lies? What if this was another, more devious method of torture, whether from Iago or another group?

"Don't," he said, following her eyes. "Please. Trust me."

"How can I?" Her voice cracked on the question, though she hadn't meant to let it. "How am I supposed to know what to believe?" She'd been on her own for so long, had had her trust betrayed so many times.

He hesitated a moment, then held out his hand, palm up, baring the elegant black tattoos on his vein-roped forearm.

"I don't—" she began, then broke off with a strangled gasp as a small glitter of bluish white light kindled in his palm, like a tiny piece of Saint Elmo's fire trapped inside it. "Oh," she said aloud. *Hallucination,* she said inwardly. But when she reached out and touched the tiny fireball, she felt its warmth. And his. "I thought you couldn't risk a demo."

"It's my weakest magic," he said, voice husky, eyes guarded. "And worth the risk if it keeps you from kneeing me in the 'nads and taking off." He closed his fingers over his palm, extinguishing the small flame.

"Special effects," she said faintly, trying to hang on to what she knew about how the world was supposed to work.

"What about your dreams?"

She wished she hadn't said anything about the dreams, wished she weren't thinking of them now. But what else could she think of when it seemed that those fantasies were coming true? The circular stone room, the torches, the incense . . . and the man who stood too near her, embodying the heroes she'd grown up hearing about—it was all exactly as she had dreamed. Only she had dreamed so much more.

The rush of desire must have shown in her face, because his eyes darkened. But he held himself still. Waiting.

"What I'm feeling . . . it's not the smoke, is it?" she asked finally.

"The *copan* might be intensifying your latent connection to the barrier, but it can't create something out of nothing. What you're feeling is the magic that's in your blood."

"What if I don't want it to be?" Despite her best efforts, her voice trembled. "What if I just want to go home and forget any of this ever happened?"

"You can't. Iago will come for you."

She shuddered. "Not helping."

"It wasn't meant to be." He paused. "None of us got a vote in this, either, and we've all had days we wanted to bail and let someone else take up the slack, except there wasn't anyone else . . . until we found out about you."

Her head spun—maybe with drugs, maybe with overload—and she tried hard not to let what he was saying matter. "I didn't sign up for your game."

Not bothering to correct her, he said, "I'll do whatever I can to help you adjust. We all will."

"I don't want your help," she said. "I don't want any part of this." But the words sounded weak, even to her. Emotions cascaded; fear, arousal, and confusion spinning together in an overwhelming mélange, pressing inward. Pinching the bridge of her nose in an effort to stave off the insanity she'd apparently inherited from Ambrose, along with his friends and enemies, she said, "I don't know what to believe anymore."

"What do your instincts tell you?"

She smiled with little humor. "My instincts have gotten me fired I don't know how many times because I just *had* to experiment with an in-house recipe. They've hooked me up over and over with guys who say they're ready for a commitment but aren't really. And they sent me off into the rain forest by myself, because I'd promised Ambrose a proper burial. Let's just say I'm not too high on my instincts these days."

"That was then. This is now." He took her hand, turning it palm up so torchlight hit the cut on her palm, which, incredibly, was little more than a thin scar now. "What is your gut telling you to do?"

Sasha couldn't make herself look away from his damned gorgeous green eyes. In that instant, she realized she didn't give a damn what logic dictated, didn't care what it said about her sanity. She wanted him. Call it incense, instability, or magic; she didn't care. For too long she'd been unable to take anything for herself, and this was what she wanted. *He* was what she wanted; he had been since she'd first awakened from the fantasy, warm and wanting, and feeling so damned lonely she'd nearly howled when she opened her eyes and he wasn't there.

"No offense," she said, "but I'm pretty sure these impulses are coming from significantly south of my heart." She was trying to keep it light, trying not to let him know how much the dreams had meant to her. But, in tacit acceptance, she took the last half step that separated them, watching as his eyes blurred, hearing as his breath hitched, and feeling as he shifted to align his body with hers, though they weren't yet touching.

"Then we've already got something in common." He reached for her, cupping one big, capable hand along her jaw and holding her there as he leaned in and touched his lips to hers.

Under any other circumstance, Sasha would've drawn back at his words, which all but spelled out "only sex, no strings." But just then, with her body alight and her brain spinning with incense and desire, the proviso sounded right. And his touch was perfect. The contact brought sparks of light and heat, a sizzle of connection and a sense of *oh, yes* that rippled through her in waves, reverberating and overlapping, heightening as she murmured her pleasure and crowded closer.

Something buzzed at the back of her brain.

At first she thought it was a warning alarm, her unreliable instincts telling her this was a bad idea. Moments later, though, Michael hissed a curse and yanked away from her, putting his big body between her and the door.

A seam appeared in the overlapping stones. Someone was coming in!

Michael crowded her back, sandwiching her between the carved wall and the heavy press of his body armor. His scent surrounded her, sharp and male, resonating with the taste of him. Without thinking, she pressed against him, reaching to touch his hips beneath the armor. His solid strength and the overwhelming *thereness* of him was an anchor, making her feel far safer than she knew she should. But it had been so long since anyone had been anywhere for her, she'd take what she could get.

He tapped his throat mike and whispered, "Is that you guys? Fuck. They're here."

Sasha tightened her grip on him. "That's not your friends, is it?" she whispered as the crack widened, then stilled. From the other side she caught a snatch of low-voiced conversation, some sort of debate. Was the mechanism jammed, or was the hesitation part of a plan, another layer of torture?

Michael glanced back at her, expression resolute as he said very quietly, "I'm going to cast a shield. Cross your fingers that they don't have a magic-sniffer with them." He drew the carved knife from his belt and sliced it sharply across his palm in a move that was all too familiar to her and brought bad memories. Blood welled, looking black in the orange firelight.

Shit, she thought. *The torches*. There was no way Iago's men could fail to notice the flames, or the smoky air. "Should we kill the lights?" she asked, feeling like an idiot for buying into his paradigm even far enough to ask the question. But what if the tiny fireball hadn't been an illusion? What if— She squelched the thought, unable to go there after so many years of denial.

"They'd still smell the incense," he answered in a low whisper. "But if we're lucky and they don't have a *pilli* with them, the shield magic should confuse all five of their senses." He closed his eyes, his face settling into lines of deep concentration as blood dripped from his palm. When the first drop hit the stone floor, Sasha thought she heard a bell chime, and wondered if that meant his magic was working.

Then she wondered whether she'd crossed the border into Crazytown. Because as the door crept open, all she could do was pray that whatever he was doing worked.

Moments later, though, he opened his eyes and bit off a curse. "Nothing, damn it. I can't find the blood magic. I don't know—" He broke off and turned to her abruptly, his eyes hard and hot, and more than a little wild. "I'm sorry," he said inexplicably.

Then, without any other preliminaries, he moved into her, plastered her against the wall with his big, hard, fully aroused body. And kissed her.

Shock held Sasha motionless as his lips touched hers. The first sizzle of contact arced from him to her and back again, and all she could think was *Oh*, and then *Yes*. She might have said the words aloud, because her lips parted and he deepened the kiss, sliding his tongue within to touch hers. His taste was potent and masculine; his strength surrounded her, pressed into her, made her feel that she was safe despite the danger. That she wasn't alone. That finally there was someone on her side.

A red-gold haze rose up inside her, clouding her vision and mind, making the moment all about Michael's kiss. It somehow ceased to matter that he might be just as bug-crazy as Ambrose had been, and that a rumbling noise warned that the door was opening the rest of the way. What mattered was that Michael was holding her, kissing her. And it was vitally, elementally important that she kiss him back.

So she did.

CHAPTER FIVE

With his access to his normal blood magic blocked—maybe because of the nature of the chamber, maybe because the lure of sex magic was so damn strong—Michael had little choice. He kissed Sasha, swallowing her gasp openmouthed and taking it deep with more heat than finesse. And damned if she didn't kiss him right back.

Unprepared for her cooperation—hell, unprepared for *her*—he lost himself in the moment. Her taste was sweet, like the soft, light energy that sang through her, making him feel dark, hard, and hot in comparison.

Danger! his brain warned when his control started to slip.

Ending the kiss and calling on the power it had brought, he summoned the chameleon shield from a seemingly bottomless well of sex magic that was suddenly his to command. He watched out of the corner of his eye as the magic shimmered to life, curling sinuously around the doorway just as the stone panel slid fully open to reveal a small group of heavily armed gray-robes.

There was no shout of discovery, no sudden turmoil. The shield was working, and whatever a *pilli* was, it hadn't shown up yet.

Still, the enemy was very near. The dark warrior in Michael was acutely aware of their positions on the other side of the chameleon spell. At the same time, he was wholly conscious of the woman in his arms.

Sasha twined herself around him, her fingers buried in his hair as she kissed him back, wet and hot, her greed matching his own. Keenly aware that whatever was between them right now was way more about the magic than it was about either or both of them, he broke the kiss, cupping her face to hold her still. "That was enough to trigger the spell."

She looked beyond him to the curving wall of not-light that swirled near the doorway, her lips forming an O of surprise. Then she whispered, "Magic." He couldn't tell whether the word was a question or a curse.

"Sex magic," he said. He meant it as a clarification, but the words hung between them. "Physical intimacy is another way to access Nightkeeper power." Granted, the highest levels of such magic belonged to the gods-destined mated pairs, but he'd been able to lean on Sasha for enough of a boost to jump-start his shield. *More evidence that she's mageborn*, he thought. Not to mention that it'd been a far stronger boost than he'd expected, more than he'd gotten when he and Jade had been lovers. Maybe that was because Sasha's was a stronger bloodline, maybe because he was better trained now, or the end-time was a year closer. "The shield is up," he continued. "We don't have to take this any further. Probably shouldn't." Desire howled, but he held on to his control. Barely.

Eyes intent on the shield, she reached past him and caressed the magic as she had done moments earlier with the small fireball. Now, as then, he felt her touch as if she'd stroked his naked skin. Sensation brought desire, kicking the magic higher, bringing an edge that hadn't been there moments earlier. He nearly arched into the touch, almost purred with the pleasure, even as he told himself to let her go, move away, move on. Once they were back at Skywatch everything would be different. She wouldn't need to be rescued anymore. She wouldn't need *him* anymore, because although she might have dreamed him, the last thing she needed after living in darkness for the past year was a man who lived partway in the shadows.

Lips curving, pupils blurred with sex magic, she moved to stroke the chameleon shield again, but he caught her wrist. "Don't," he said. His voice came out harder than he'd intended, so he softened the order with, "Please."

She met his eyes, and hers widened. "Michael?" Her voice held a faint tremor, but she didn't pull away. He almost wished she would. More, he wondered what she saw in him, and whether it scared her.

It should, he knew, just as he knew damn well he should let her go. But the jagged, primal heat was unassailable, undeniable, compelling him to move in for another kiss. Somewhere in the back of his brain he told himself it would level off the energy that built within him, help him rein it in. But the moment their mouths touched he knew it was a lie. Heat blasted through him, tipping his balance and skewing his world off-kilter. And the magic—of the temple and the night, and the sacred sexual power that was suddenly laced with something more—rose up and swept him away. Magic roared in his veins, lighting his neurons with a howl of, *Yes, yes, this one,* mine*!* as he slanted his mouth across hers, teased her lips apart and plunged his tongue inside, needing more from her, demanding more.

Far from pushing him away, she met him equally and then raced ahead of him, pouring herself into the kiss. He told himself to back off, that she was in the grip of new magic, that she didn't have full control. But he couldn't seem to make that matter as he lost himself in her.

Magic sparked red-gold in the air between them, revving his blood even higher. She felt it too; he could see it in her eyes, hear it in her shuddering inhalation. Then she reached down and cupped him through his combat pants, rubbing the line of his painfully hard erection.

She's not in control, he reminded himself. *And she doesn't know why.* He remembered how it had been for him right after he'd tasted Nightkeeper power—how the need for sex had been sharp and overwhelming, and nothing he could've walked away from. He told himself to back off, back away, that she wasn't entirely rational. But although he'd been raised out in the modern world, with modern mores and ethics, he was a Nightkeeper by blood and magic, and some deeply primitive part of him argued that there was nothing wrong with magic-wrought desire.

Red-gold power crisped the air as she touched him again, shaping him through the tough fabric of his Kevlar-impregnated combat pants. "Gods," he grated, dimly aware that the shield had gone red-gold, shot through with other, unfamiliar colors. Darker hues to match the dark, edgy power that bit at the edges of his mind.

A warning bell sounded at the back of his brain, reminding him of the danger, the *pilli*. The creature that lived within him. But he was lost to reason; his universe had concentrated itself at the place where she was holding him, touching him. He was no stranger to sex—far from it. He loved women, loved the pleasure his body could give them, the moment of their orgasm, and his own. Yet despite all that, he'd been celibate since his talent ceremony more than a year ago, when the shock of gaining the warrior talent had busted through the hypnosis and drug-induced mental blockade, slamming Michael with lost memories and almost releasing the thing lurking within him.

If this bloodline *nahwal* hadn't zapped him into an offshoot of the barrier, he might've slaughtered the other Nightkeepers then and there. The *nahwal's* warning had echoed in Michael's skull: *Your past has put the balance of your soul too close to the darkness. Don't touch the power it offers. And for gods' sake, don't lose control.*

In the aftermath of that vilely nasty surprise, Michael had been a mess. He'd broken things off with Jade and had kept to himself ever since then. Now, though, those three hundred and however many days roared through his bloodstream now, heat and temptation howling for release. But not just any release; his blood and body were clamoring for Sasha—for the woman in the photos, the fighter who'd escaped from her own cell. He wanted her energy, wanted to take it inside himself and use it to light the dark corners of his soul.

He was vaguely aware of a half dozen gray-robes blocking open the damned doorway and taking up positions inside the chamber, looking out into the hallway. As if from a distance he heard radio traffic, reports that the other magi were just around the corner, but meeting heavy resistance from search parties bent on recapturing Sasha. But if Iago wanted her, why had he used her to bait the Nightkeepers into Lucius's ambush? Why not just have Lucius himself call for help?

A half-realized thought gnawed at the edge of his consciousness, warning of something deeper, but it was quickly lost when Sasha kissed him again, then moved against him, restless with desire.

A hard-fought battle raged within his soul. The Nightkeeper warrior in him wanted to attack the gray-robes, helping clear the way for his teammates, and the man in him wanted to rip into them for what they'd done to Sasha. But at the same time he was brutally aware of the *nahwal's* warning. He was already running too close to the edge of his control; killing could put him all the way over.

"We'll be there as soon as we can," he dimly heard Strike report. "Hold tight and keep the woman safe."

I will, Michael thought with the force of a vow.

Magic hummed in his skull—a compulsion for sex, for orgasm, the feeling sharper than before, more protective. Possessive. He wanted to take her, make her his own. He wanted to keep her safe, kill for her, take his revenge on the men who had hurt her. He held the impulses grimly in check, but then she twined her arms around his neck and pressed her lips to his in a blatantly carnal, openmouthed kiss.

And he broke.

Heart hammering, heat roaring through him on a wash of red and gold gone gray at the edges, he returned the kiss and dragged his hands down her curvy body as he pressed her into the wall, his body armor a hard barrier between them. He growled as he reversed the caress, bringing her shirt up so he could reach beneath. Her skin was warm and soft and so very alive under his touch. *She* was alive, arching and quivering, responding beautifully to him as he shaped the dip of her waist, the flare of her ribs, the curves of her breasts. She moaned as, beyond himself, Michael groaned and kissed her, tasted her, touched her.

Somewhere at the back of his brain, beyond the madness of lust and magic, a voice of reason was shouting, *Abort, abort! Bad idea!* She'd been Iago's prisoner for a year, had to be in a fragile mental state. But there was nothing fragile about the feel of her as she pressed against him, demanding as much as she gave, and more. She raked her fingernails along his bare shoulders and arms, making him shiver with the raw power of his response.

The hot, jagged magic grayed his vision and brought

a flash of a high wall with narrow gates inset near the top. Warning buzzers sounded, but he was too far gone within the heat and need to do anything but take the next kiss deeper, take them both higher. He was shaking with desire; they both were.

On the other side of the chameleon shield, he was dimly aware that the gray-robes had taken high and low positions on either side of the doorway, digging in to return the Nightkeepers' fire.

Part of Michael wanted to drop the shield and open fire, taking out the gray-robes from behind. He wasn't sure if that was his warrior's talent talking, or a thought-thread coming from behind the wall, from that hated part of himself. But his priority was keeping Sasha safe. Which he was doing; with each kiss, each caress, the magic ramped higher, the shield grew denser and thicker, seemingly in proportion to his own hard, aching flesh.

He hissed as she loosened the Velcro waist straps of his body armor and reached beneath his tank to run her hands across his heated skin. She drew gentle, inciting trails across his stomach, along his sides, down his spine and then lower to latch onto his ass and pull him into her, anchoring them together at the point where he ached to connect them. He broke their kiss briefly to yank the armor off over his head, then tossed it aside and reached for her, so they were wrapped together, chest to chest, though still clothed.

Her sweetness surrounded him, seeped into him, humbled him. He chased kisses along her jaw and down her neck, heat racing through him as she shuddered and clung. A moment later she pushed him away, but only to create a space between them, room to reach for his pants, and work the fly without undoing his weapons belt. He groaned when her fingers found him, closed around him. Locking his knees so he wouldn't buckle as the blood drained from his buzzing head, he kissed her, pressed his cheek to hers and let himself *feel*.

She stroked his erection, trailing soft fingers along his length. He was so hard he ached, but he held himself still, absorbing the delicious torture until he could take no more. Then, knowing only that he had to be inside her, that nothing else in the world mattered, he shifted to kiss her again as he undid the worn catch of her bush pants, causing them to fall to her feet. He hissed when his hands found her bare skin beneath, then stepped back and looked at the treasure he'd uncovered. The sweat-shirt covered her to the tops of her thighs, but he didn't want to take it off her and leave her bare to the carved stone at her back.

Boosting her up, he cupped her sweetly rounded ass in his scarred palms as she wrapped her legs around his waist, opening to him without hesitation or pretense. He leaned in and kissed her softly, lingering over her silky lips and the taste of her passion.

He turned the shield opaque with a thought, blotting the gray-robes from sight as he eased away from her, cupping her gorgeous, angular face between his scarred palms. He waited until her eyelids fluttered open, dark lashes framing chocolate brown eyes. When their eyes met, he said, "You said you dreamed about me. Where were we? What were we doing?"

"We were here," she said simply. "And we were making love."

Aroused, humbled, caught up in the magic they'd made together, he leaned in and touched his lips to hers in a kiss that started gentle and caught fire from there, until they were pressed together, straining together. Mind hazed red-gold with greedy need, barely aware of the firefight escalating beyond the shield, he caught her hips and boosted her up against the wall, pressing into her, rubbing himself against her slick folds. "Like this?"

Murmuring pleasure, she bit his shoulder, the side of his neck, urging him on with a whisper of, "Don't tease. Not now."

"No, not now." He would have said more, but words left him as he thrust into her.

Her hot wetness gloved him, rubbing with perfect friction. That first moment of joining sent a shock of sensation and pleasure through him, tightening something inside his chest.

The battle hammered on beyond the shield; magic surrounded them; *she* surrounded him, locking her bare feet at the small of his back. And when he pulled back to look down, she smiled up at him and lifted a hand to cup his cheek, rubbing a thumb over the bristle on his jaw. "It's okay," she said softly. "We're good."

He didn't know what she'd seen in his eyes, didn't know why her words loosened something inside him, but they did.

Then, unable to do otherwise, he began to move. Blood roaring through his veins and singing in his soul, he thrust on a surge of heat and power. As he did, Sasha arched against him with an abandon that nearly put him over the edge then and there in a too-quick response he hadn't suffered since he'd been taught control by his first lover—a black belt slightly older than him who had begun his fascination with warrior women.

Sasha might not yet believe she was a warrior, but he'd bet money on it.

Gritting his teeth, he bowed his head and pressed his cheek to hers, straining with the effort of not coming immediately. Their joining was powerful, profound. And it shifted something within him. Magic gathered around them as he balanced on the edge between pleasure and madness. He pistoned his hips, starting slowly, but building fast to set a hard, fast pace that spurred them both through the heat and insanity. They twined together, moved together, and the incense-laden air around them sparked.

It seemed no more than a moment before her nails dug into his shoulders and she cried out, spasming against him. He kept going, driving her beyond the first orgasm to another, driving himself beyond madness. Sensation layered atop sensation, until finally pleasure shock-waved through him in an orgasm that locked his muscles tight on a roar of magic and triumph.

The chameleon shield went red and gold with the purest of Nightkeeper magic as he emptied himself into her and she fisted around him, the two of them locked together in thundering pleasure that drew out from one heartbeat to the next, and the next. It seemed unbelievable that the gray-robes didn't see or sense it as they mounted a concerted rush out the door, leaving the chamber empty, the door still braced open.

Michael was peripherally aware that they were gone, but that wasn't his focus as passion faded to its aftermath and he sagged, bracing himself against the wall with one arm and holding Sasha against him with the other. He should've been wrung out, sated. Satisfied. And on one level he was.

But on another level, fresh and greedy need clawed at him, demanding that he take more, that he take *her*, make her part of him. And that was a level he didn't want to go to. One he wished he could rid himself of forever.

Fuck. His defenses were down. She'd stripped him bare, leaving him wide open. And he'd been so caught up in her that he hadn't noticed, hadn't reacted to the threat.

Closing his eyes, working fast, he tried to find the center of himself, seeking the peace that had kept him sane for the past year-plus, ever since the talent ceremony that had released the creature within him, the murderous alter ego he called the Other. But he couldn't find his center. Instead, he found sex magic still burning hot within him, but its jagged edges growing teeth and claws, digging into him, taking him over. Heat rose again, but this time it wasn't the need to sink himself within her.

It was a far darker, more dangerous need. One she'd brought out in him somehow, even though he'd been able to keep it at bay for so long.

No, he grated inwardly, struggling to keep the Other where it belonged, locked away from the outside world. *Don't you fucking do it.* He envisioned the sky-high dam he'd constructed, piece by piece, at the back of his brain, envisioned locking his other self safely behind it. Instead, the dam bulged obscenely as the Other strained to break through, drawn by Sasha's vital energy, darkness pulled toward the light.

She shifted against him and murmured something into his neck. Strung tight, he pressed his cheek to hers and fought a silent and—hopefully—invisible battle to keep the halves of himself together, fought not to lose control of himself. And in doing so, he missed the moment for soft words and praise.

"I *said*, your earpiece is yelling for you." Sasha turned her face away from him, her body tense. "And let me down."

"Sasha—" he began.

"Let. Me. Down." Her voice was icy.

Shit. He released her, and watched as she retrieved her pants with as much dignity as possible under the circumstances. He didn't know what to say, didn't know how to process what had just happened, either between the two of them or between him and the Other. The sex had touched him deeply. And that was a problem.

But he had to say something. So he went with, "Sorry. Postcoital brain freeze. Let me check in with the others; then we'll talk. I promise." He waited for her nod, which was a beat slow in coming; then he zipped his fly and jammed his receiver back into his ear. He wasn't even sure when it'd fallen out. "Stone here," he grated after keying on his throat mike.

"Godsdamn it!" Strike's voice exploded in his ear. "What have you— Never mind. Are you in the chamber?"

His gut fisted at the king's tone. "What's wrong?"

"We're pinned down, and you've got a red-robe incoming. Deal with it, and for gods' sake, keep the woman alive!" The transmission cut out in a rattle of gunshots, or maybe magic, but Michael could fill in the rest for himself. The red-robe was one of the *pilli*; he'd sensed the magic flaring in the hidden chamber. His and Sasha's luck had just run out.

Michael spun toward her. "Sorry," he said again. And hit her with another sleep spell.

Her eyes flashed with anger for a second, but then she went down, crumpling and lying still, as if too drained to fight the magic this time. It wasn't fair, he knew, but the same mental blocks that wouldn't let him tell the others about his past didn't want her to see what was going to happen next. He wasn't an *itza'at* seer, but he knew that whichever way the next few minutes went, it wasn't going to be pretty.

Tucking her near the wall, he covered her as best he could with his body armor. Then he pulled the shield spell away from the door and put it over her instead. When he'd done the best he could do for her, he stood and turned, cross-drawing his autopistols in a smooth move that had been ingrained long before he joined the Nightkeepers. "Let's do this."

The door slid open as if on cue, and a tall, thin redrobe with hollow cheeks and pale skin stepped through. His eyes went past Michael to the shield behind him, and a look of satisfaction crossed his sallow cheeks. He lifted his wrist and spoke into a comm device. "You were right; she's in here." Then he smirked at Michael. "You might've gotten away with it if you'd kept it in your pants, playboy."

Rage hazed Michael's vision. He answered the taunt by opening fire, putting the autopistols to work with a spurt of dark excitement that echoed his orgasm of only minutes earlier.

The red-robe cast a shield spell, deflecting the bullets as he spoke into his comm, talking fast. Moments later, the *pilli*'s shield rippled. Then, shockingly, the magic flew *at* Michael, wrapping around him and clinging for a second, freezing him in place. It faded quickly, but the delay gave the Xibalban time to pull a stubby black object and lever it at Michael. A Taser. *Shit.*

Michael tried to dodge, but the shield residue left him slow to react as the red-robe fired. The clinging barbs tagged the bare skin of Michael's forearm, just above his marks. He cursed and grabbed for the thing, but he was too damn slow. Electricity arced across the tether, locking him in place.

Pain! It raced through him, freezing him, pissing him off. Mad fury rose within him, bringing with it the hard, vicious power that characterized his other self. Cold logic locked into place, and although his natural healing magic quickly fought the rigor-lock of the electric shock, dulling the pain to a throb and bringing a measure of feeling back to his paralyzed limbs, he didn't let that on to the red-robe. Instead he lay limp and still, hoping the bastard would come over to him to yank the barbs, or to get at Sasha. *I dare you*, he thought coldly, keeping his eyes slitted, his face slack. *I fucking dare you.*

A moment later, dark 'port magic rattled out in the hallway, and there was a thunderclap of displaced air. Michael's earpiece was dead, no doubt shorted to shit by the Taser zap, but he didn't need Strike to guess who had just arrived. The Xibalbans' leader might not have the stones—or the power—to 'port straight into the uprooted Nightkeeper temple, but he obviously had no trouble getting through his own wards to the rock-shielded tunnels below. Which was just more proof the Xibalbans were light-years ahead of the Nightkeepers in terms of magic.

Gods help me protect her, prayed the piece of Michael that still could pray. The Nightkeepers were doomed without the library.

Iago stepped through the doorway a heartbeat later, wearing black leathers, heavy boots, and a slash-metal concert tee. He exchanged a look with the red-robe, then crouched down beside Michael.

"Fug—" Michael began, then broke off with a gargle when the Xibalban grabbed him by the throat and squeezed hard.

Iago leaned in, his pupils going to pinpricks. "Did you just fuck her, or was there more?"

A terrible force pressed behind Michael's eyes, driving a knife into his brain and paralyzing him once again. He would've screamed, but he had no breath, would've writhed, but his muscles were still lax. Then Iago let go of his throat and the pressure snapped out of existence, as though it had never been, leaving Michael to groan with the absence of pain and the sudden flood of feeling returning to the rest of his body.

"His magic's for shit," Iago said dismissively. Lifting an arm, he spoke into a wristwatch comm device. "Set the timer for five minutes, collect the Nightkeepers, and wait for me at the rendezvous. I'll zap the prisoners to the mountain and come back for you before this place turns crater."

He wanted one of the Nightkeepers. But for what? Was he looking to borrow a specific talent? Michael's thoughts churned. Then the redheaded mage moved past him and crouched down beside Sasha, and Michael wasn't thinking about anything but keeping the bastard from touching her.

The shield spell had quit when the red-robe shocked Michael; the sleep spell would wear off more gradually. In sleep, curled on her side, she looked soft and vulnerable as the Xibalban reached out and stroked her pale cheek. Icy rage slammed through Michael. *Get away from her!* he howled inwardly, not giving voice to the words because he didn't want them to hear their clarity and know he was almost back in control of his body, if not his power. And for the first time since the talent ceremony, when his ancestral *nahwal* had helped him recapture the Other and warned him not to touch its power or risk his soul, he didn't give a shit whether he was in control.

Sasha! he raged. *Gods, help me protect her!*

With the skyroad gone, the gods had no access to earth, yet he was suddenly flooded with a heavy, silver, strange magic that wasn't Nightkeeper or Xibalban, but somewhere between the two.

"Shock him again," Iago said to the red-robe. "I'm not taking any chances with this guy."

Letting the strange magic have him, Michael roared and exploded upward, attacking Iago in one continuous, deadly movement. The red-robe hit the Taser trigger and fifty thousand volts lit Michael from within, but this time it didn't shut him down. Instead, the energy smashed through the last of his carefully constructed inner barriers—he felt them give, felt the Other come through fully for the first time since his talent ceremony.

Aided by the element of surprise, he caught Iago in a flying tackle, slamming them both to the stone floor. The red-robe howled and went for his guns, but Michael cast a thick shield spell fueled by blood rage and hatred, sealing him inside with his enemy. Iago shouted and tried to fight back, but he was far better at magic than hand-to-hand. Michael got in under the Xibalban's weak guard and pinned him to the floor, straddling him and getting his hands around the bastard's throat. Iago's eyes bugged and he tried to pull shield magic of his own, but Michael countered it and bore down, leaning in so he could see his victim's fear, the knowledge of his own death.

Only it wasn't fear he saw in Iago's eyes. It was fear . . . and satisfaction.

Michael's grip loosened slightly, just enough for Iago to rasp, "It *is* you . . . or it will be." The Xibalban's eyes narrowed in speculation. "I can wait until you finish your transformation and understand what you really are, why you belong to me."

"Fuck you." Michael leaned in, silver magic spinning up within him. "What am I?"

"She'll show you. And you'll both be mine by the height of the solstice. If you don't come to me, I'll come for you. That's a promise." Then, without warning, dark magic cycled up, 'port lock engaged, and the Xibalban vanished from beneath Michael.

"No!" Slamming palm-first into the stone floor, briefly off balance with his quarry's disappearance, Michael roared with fury and disappointment. Unable to stanch the flow of violence within him, the need to kill, he dropped the shield magic and lunged to his feet—just in time to see the red-robe headed out the door with Sasha's limp body over his shoulder. At the sight, the rage within him redirected itself to killing hatred.

The man's carotid under his thumbs. His pulse stilling in death.

Snarling, Michael moved to cut off the red-robe's escape. The man's face went slack with terror, almost making Michael wonder what the other man saw in him. What he feared. There was no pity within him, though; there was only the hatred, the need for revenge, and the all-consuming call for him to protect what was his.

The red-robe called shield magic, casting it thick and strong in a bubble around him and Sasha, but the thing within Michael wasn't deterred. He felt a jolt of pain, as though a final synapse had soldered itself into place, and a conduit opened up within him, letting the silver magic flow through him. Into him. Shaking with the power of it, the rage of it, Michael leveled his arm toward the red-robe and sent the magic winging toward his enemy, funneling it into the other man while keeping Sasha safe. There was a noiseless detonation, a shock wave of power flinging from man to man.

The Xibalban's face contorted, then went slack and gray. Sasha slid from his shoulder and fell to the floor as he sagged, losing cohesion. His flesh slid on his bones, draping over a skeleton that still fought to stand. Then his inner structure lost its solidity and he collapsed, the bloodred robe tenting around him. When it settled, there was a pile of greasy gray dust with cinderlike chunks beneath. The only recognizable piece that remained was the *pilli*'s hand, looking charcoaled, reaching from the pile as if in supplication. Nearby, Sasha lay curled on her side, still mercifully asleep.

Silence rang in the chamber as Michael stared down at the remains. The killer in him was utterly satisfied. The better man he'd been trying to become wanted to puke.

"Oh, fuck. What did I just do?" *More, what am I? What did Iago know about the silver magic, about him?*

Michael bent double, dry heaving, feeling totally out of control, shaky and sick with it, and afraid of what came next. *Focus*, he told himself. *Get rid of the Other; get rid of the magic. You've done it before. You can do this*.

To his surprise, it wasn't difficult to push the Other back; it seemed sated from the kill, and the magic. Gods, the magic. He could still feel the echo of mad silver power, the thundering might. It fascinated and repelled

him, called to one side of him and scared the shit out
of the other. When it was gone, he was left empty and
all but powerless, with only the faint hum of red-gold
Nightkeeper magic to lean on. And that was a problem.
Where before he'd been able to manage the postmagic
crash that followed big spell casting, now he felt it hammering down on him, threatening to black him out even
though he and Sasha were far from safe.

"Keep it together," he gritted through clenched teeth,
summoning the last of his reserves. With the rattle of
foreign magic gone, he could hear the sounds of battle
from out in the hallway, forcibly reminding him of what
Iago had said about the place cratering, suggesting that
he'd set a self-destruct mechanism.

Save Sasha, he reminded himself, going back to basics
when nothing else made sense. *She's the priority*.

Summoning the last of his reserves, he bent and got
his arms around Sasha. She was warm and lax in his arms,
solid and real. The feel of her centered him as nothing
else had, which was ironic, considering that it was his
rampaging desire for her that had breached his defenses
in the first place. Iago had implied she was the key to
his transformation, whatever that was, and Michael was
afraid the change had already begun. He felt dark and
angry, like he could kill the world even with the Other
locked away.

Holding her close, he breathed in her scent, felt it
seep into him, lighting the darkness and pushing the impulse away. For now.

Then, knowing the fight wasn't over—not by a long
shot—he shifted her to his shoulder. Then, cradling her
with one arm and wielding a single autopistol with a half-
full clip in his other hand, he stepped through the doorway, took in the situation at a glance, and opened fire.

Killing the gray-robes was far too easy.

The closest group went down without a sound, without even knowing they had an enemy behind them until it was too late. They had been ranged across the hallway, firing to keep the Nightkeepers pinned down in an alcove while their reinforcements came up from the other side. The moment Michael neutralized the cover fire, the Nightkeepers burst from their scant shelter and took out the second team with a combination of jade-tips and fireballs. Michael swayed. "Hurry," he rasped. "Iago triggered some sort of self-destruct." There was no sign of the enemy mage; he'd fled the scene, leaving the last of his troops behind.

"She okay?" Strike asked with a dubious look at Sasha.

"Overwhelmed. I thought asleep was better than hysterical." Which was true, though not the way the king would assume.

"Let's get the hell out of here, then." Strike clapped Michael on the shoulder, nearly flattening him. "Good job."

You have no fucking idea, Michael thought with zero humor as he followed the others into the temple of the maize goddess.

There, the magi stared down at what was left of the red-robe's body.

Strike shot Michael a look from beneath lowered brows. "Did Iago do this?"

Now, as before, Michael ran into a mental barrier he hadn't put there, one that tugged at his magic and his instincts and told him that no matter what, he couldn't tell them what he was. It wasn't just fear of their reactions, either. There was something bigger at stake here, something he didn't yet understand. Worse, he didn't know whether it was the light or dark half of himself making the call. He just knew that there was only one possible answer to Strike's question. And it was a lie. "Yeah, it was Iago. His magic misfired."

"Shit." Strike stared at the charred, grasping hand a moment longer, then gestured for the magi to join up for the 'port. "Let's get the hell out of here." When the magi were uplinked, Strike said, "Sorry, gang. I need everything you've got." He leaned hard on the blood links, sucking every last bit of red-gold magic from each of the Nightkeepers, wringing them dry.

Michael's vision grayed. "Son of a—" he began, but got cut off midcurse. The 'port magic triggered and the world slid sideways. As they zapped out, a terrible explosion rocked the compound. Michael felt the scorch of the blast as the last few molecules of him were sucked into the barrier, traveling along the edge of the energy flow.

Then Strike found his 'port lock, yanked the thread, and dumped them all out in the middle of the great room back at Skywatch.

Michael landed flat-footed and nearly pancaked it then and there, but managed to keep himself upright somehow, gutting it out because he couldn't collapse until he knew Sasha was safe.

Easing her off his shoulder, he deposited her more or less gently on a nearby couch, and slurred the words that would rescind the sleep spell. She didn't awaken.

Panic spiked as he said the words again, louder and with actual diction. Still nothing. "Come on, come on!" he hissed under his breath, shaking her a little. Nausea spiked when her head lolled. "She's not coming around. What's wrong?" Had she caught the edge of the silver magic? He touched her throat, reassured himself that her pulse was steady and true, her skin warm. But still, she didn't wake. He said the spell again, didn't feel the slightest hint of red-gold power, even when he dug deep. He was toast.

His vision tunneled to the sight of her face, soft yet strong in repose, her dark lashes forming twin smudges on her cheeks. She wasn't coming around, godsdamn it.

Someone caught his arm, tried to pull him away. He rounded with a feral snarl, grabbing his assailant. "Get the fuck—" He broke off when he recognized Tomas, and realized he'd nearly pitched his *winikin* across the room. He had to get himself under control, damn it. The world hazed muddy red as he looked down into the *winikin*'s narrow, pious face and gray, almost colorless eyes. "Don't give up on her too," he ordered, voice low and dangerous. "Don't you fucking give up on her."

Something flickered in Tomas's face—something that might have been hope. The *winikin* nodded. "I'll see to her. You can trust me."

And the damned thing was, Michael knew that despite everything they'd said to each other—and there had been a shit-ton of it—he *did* trust Tomas, in this, at least. "Don't let anyone question her until I get back," he ordered as the muddy grayness closed in on him.

Tomas frowned. "Where are you going?"

"Away," Michael answered. And, with his soul aching from the burden of his lies, and the knowledge that the last thing Sasha needed was a man with a monster inside him, he finally gave himself permission to pass the hell out. As he slid into the darkness, he heard Sasha's voice in his head, echoing from the moment they were first joined as lovers. *It's okay*, she'd said.

Only it wasn't. Not anymore.

PART II

LUNAR APOGEE

The moment when the moon is farthest from the earth.
A time of reversal.

CHAPTER SIX

Six and a half years ago
Quantico, Virginia

The e-mail had been carefully devoid of information, giving Michael nothing more than a time—midnight—and a meeting place in Hogan's Alley. Which set off all his internal alarms. He might've thought it was from Esmee, the hottie trainee he'd been in heavy flirt mode with since his arrival in Quantico, except that the e-mail address belonged to his superior's superior, who he highly doubted was looking for a quickie behind the post office. So he set out on schedule, and watched his back.

Built by a slew of Hollywood set designers in the late eighties, Hogan's Alley covered ten or so acres of the 385-acre training academy shared by the FBI and the DEA. The Anytown, USA, facade offered plenty of training opportunities, including a bank that was robbed an average of twice a week during heavy training rotations. With no exercises on the schedule for that night, the alley was deserted, but the power was on, the lit storefronts casting eerie shadows on the fake cars parked beside sealed-shut post office boxes. The fall air was unseasonably warm even this late at night, bringing the scents of cut grass, dust, and gunpowder.

As Michael crossed the road, headed toward the theater where the meeting was supposed to take place, he was pretty sure he was under surveillance. Not just by the cameras that monitored everything that went down in the alley, but by watching eyes of the corporeal variety. He could feel them in the prickle at his nape and the stir of tension in his gut. His hands curled into loose fists, and energy flowed through him, warming for a fight.

Down, boy, he warned himself, knowing he was already too close to hair-trigger. Ever since he'd started FBI training, his hotter, harder instincts had risen to the surface. Now, those instincts had him staying in the shadows as he approached the theater entrance, which was seriously dated, like much of the fake town.

A man stepped from the darkness near the entrance. "Stone?"

In his mid-forties, hawk nosed and bald, just shy of six feet but muscled and balanced like a fighter, the stranger wore black, insignialess fatigues beneath a nondescript gray jacket. Michael felt vaguely overdressed in blue dress pants and a patterned oxford. But he'd been expecting to meet with his superior's superior—which this guy definitely wasn't. He wasn't a nobody, though. His eyes were hard and narrow, his bearing military, and he projected a definite air of command, one that had Michael tempted to stand at attention, even though his military service had been limited to a short stint of ROTC in college, which had ended when he'd gotten booted for fighting.

He compromised by standing ready, a balanced position drummed into him by a long line of martial arts instructors who'd attempted to teach him to channel his aggression, with varying degrees of success. "I'm Stone. Who's asking?"

"I'm Maxwell Bryson. I want to talk to you about your psych tests."

Shit, Michael thought, disgusted. *A shrink.* But behind the disgust was fear that he'd blown it before he'd really gotten a chance to prove himself. He'd done his damnedest to skew his test answers toward the norm, responding based on the surface part of himself, not the fighter within, figuring the safer part of him was the one they'd want in the bureau. He'd tried to be so careful. Apparently, he hadn't been careful enough. "What about them?"

"Don't bullshit me. It wastes both our time."

Inwardly, Michael cringed. He hated the idea of washing out of the program, not just because of the embarrassment factor, but because there were parts of it he really liked, aspects of the training and the job he thought would suit him better than anything else he'd tried so far. But beside the dismay rose a twisting curl of anger, and a parade of sensory flashes kaleidoscoped through him: the sensation of gripping the guy by his black fatigues, putting him up against a wall, getting in his face, taking it further. He'd have to deal with the backup he could sense in the shadows on the opposite side of the street, and the camera footage, but . . .

Knowing it was exactly that sort of thought process that'd gotten him into this mess, Michael cut it off midstream, even though it was tempting. Damned tempting. But at the same time his less reactive, more rational self had caught a piece that didn't fit, making him think there was something else going on. He met Bryson's eyes. "You didn't have the boss's boss e-mail me to meet you out here so you could kick me out of the program for fudging psych results. So what's the deal?"

"Then you admit you answered dishonestly?"

"My answers were honest to a point," Michael hedged, figuring the guy already knew that much, if he was asking.

Finally, Bryson's expression changed from cool blankness to a flash of satisfaction. "Now we're getting somewhere. Does this honesty-to-a-point have anything to do with all the fighting you did during your first year or so of college?"

Something stirred in Michael's gut; he wasn't sure if it was warning or interest. Wary, he said, "Shouldn't there be an office and a couch involved in this session?"

The older man made a face. "I'm no shrink. I'm the guy who can give you what you want."

"What do you think I want?"

"Tell me about the fights."

They stared at each other for a long moment. Michael broke first. Telling himself it was no big deal, he shrugged. "They were just fights. Too much alcohol, not enough supervision. You know the drill." Without Tomas around to nag him to hit the dojo daily, the aggression had all but taken over. He'd tried to control it and failed, tried to drown it in cheap beer and found that only lowered his inhibitions.

"I'm not talking about thrashing a couple of frat boys. I'm talking about the fight club you got into after that thrill wore off. You came close to killing a man, didn't you? Scared yourself straight back to martial arts and mind control . . . but that's wearing thin now, isn't it?" Bryson's eyes bore into his. "The further you get into the academy training, the more the monster wants to come out, right? You can tell me. Trust me, I understand. And I can help you."

Michael went very still as his overdeveloped fight-or-flight—emphasis on *fight*—response threatened to kick in, and his dominant self struggled to control the impulse. He counted his heartbeats. When they slowed slightly, and he could hang onto his grip on himself, he glanced at one of the cameras covering that portion of Hogan's Alley. "I don't know what you're talking about."

"Tape's not rolling," Bryson said succinctly. "It's just you and me."

Oddly, Michael believed that. "What about the guy across the street?"

"He's one of mine."

"Who the hell *are* you?" This had to be a total put-on, a trap conceived by the psych types, maybe even a training exercise for the Behavioral Sciences Unit, or some such shit. But even as Michael told himself that, part of him was thinking, *What if it's not a put-on? What if it's real?*

"I'm your best chance at using your natural talents to their fullest," Bryson answered. "I run a small, select unit of men that at present operates under an arm of Homeland Security, although we work outside the scope of the more official paradigms, and have persisted through various administrations, often invisible to even the president. We're . . . let's just say we keep the peace in ways the other branches won't touch."

"You're talking about black ops."

"Among other things." Bryson's expression returned to relentless neutrality. "Ever since the attacks on New York and the Pentagon, we've been looking to expand our ranks, but we require a . . . certain type of individual, so to speak."

And there it is, Michael thought. "A man with the potential to become a killer."

Ever since childhood, he'd been aware of the urges. He'd never acted on the impulses, hadn't done anything on the watch list for serial killers—but there had been times he'd wanted to. Badly.

Bryson shook his head. "Anyone can become a killer, given the right circumstances. What I need is someone who can do the work this country needs him to do, then put it aside and function normally otherwise." He paused, eyes locking with Michael's. "I need a fighter with a borderline dissociative personality, if not full-blown schizophrenia."

Michael swallowed hard, knowing his FBI training was over, one way or the other. "What's in it for . . . for this person? If you found him, I mean."

"I'll teach him to control the impulses, how to use them to be a better man. I'll program him so he can put that part of himself away, and take it out only when and where it will do some good."

"How?" The word escaped before Michael could curb it, or hide some of the desperation he knew had flashed in his eyes.

"The same way I'll blank your memories of this entire meeting if you turn me down." Bryson motioned, and the second man detached himself from the shadows across the road and crossed the street to join them. "Dr. Horn will take care of it."

The doctor wore the same black fatigues but no jacket, and had wisps of white-blond hair crowning his otherwise shiny scalp. His features were pinched and rabbity, and he didn't move at all like a fighter. When he dipped into one of his thigh pockets and came up with a pair of preloaded syringes, though, his movements carried the grace of long familiarity. "Your call, Mr. Stone," he said, his voice surprisingly deep given his unprepossessing exterior. "You in or out?"

Michael locked eyes with Bryson. "If I refuse?"

"You'll wake up in your room tomorrow morning and remember nothing. The e-mail's already been purged from the computer systems, so as far as you'll know, you slept through the night uninterrupted. When you get to your first class, you'll learn that you've been bounced from the program based on your psych profile."

Michael could picture it all too easily; he'd been projecting exactly that scenario ever since he'd been pulled out for a third round of personality tests that most of the others hadn't been subjected to. "And if I agree?"

"Then you receive a very different injection, you come with me, and your training begins tonight."

"How much time do I have to think about it?" Michael hedged.

"About thirty more seconds."

Okay, then, Michael thought, brain racing as he tried to figure his options. But was there really another viable answer besides "yes"? He was being offered exactly the sort of thing he'd been gravitating toward in his training, only on a larger, more immediately relevant scale. A childhood spent listening to stories about magical warriors and saving the world had primed him to want to do the same sort of thing in real life, and the 9/11 terror attacks had only reinforced his need to help. Or at least the need of his better half. His darker side just wanted to kick ass.

What if he'd finally found a way to serve both needs? Better yet, what if it had just found him?

Aware that he'd pretty much made his decision the second Bryson offered to teach him not only to control the violence within him, but to use it for the greater good, Michael nodded. "I'm in."

Bryson's eyes glittered with something sharper than satisfaction. "Good." He waved the other man forward. "Dr. Horn, if you please?"

The doctor pocketed one of the syringes, but kept the other one out as he unbuttoned Michael's right sleeve and pushed the cuff up over his elbow, baring the lighter skin of his forearm. For a second, in the darkness, Michael imagined he saw black marks on the pale skin. But the illusion passed as the doctor moved in and the needle slid home. A pinch was followed by a slow, cool burn that spread up Michael's arm and across his throat, then downward, until it coated his entire body.

For a moment, the world spun around him. Then he was falling.

Falling.

Fallen.

Present
November 19
Three years and thirty-two days until the zero date
Skywatch

Michael woke fuzzy headed and nauseated, which wasn't unusual following one of his unwanted trips down memory's ass. Sitting up in the SUV-size bed he'd had installed in his suite as part of replacing the Southwestern blah decor that characterized much of Skywatch with his own preference of glass, metal, and leather, he groaned and scrubbed his hands across his face, thinking he felt shittier than usual, even given the dream, as though it wasn't just the memories bothering him; it was . . . He froze midmotion as he remembered the rest of the prior day's shitstorm in Technicolor, along with the tastes, scents, and sounds that went with it.

He'd found Sasha. He'd made love to her. And he'd saved her . . . by letting the Other come through and using the forbidden magic to insta-cremate one of Iago's red-robes. And in doing so he'd gotten himself on Iago's radar screen. *Damn it.* Over the past five months, ever since he'd cut the last of his ties with Bryson and Horn, he'd managed to convince himself the Other was safely locked away, that he had the problem under control. Apparently not. The circumstances might've called for extreme measures, but in the end he'd done what his *nahwal* had specifically told him not to—and then he'd lied about it to his king.

Sin upon sin. *How do you think your soul's looking now?*

"Oh, hell," he grated, squeezing his eyes shut behind his hands, even though the weak gesture had never worked before. Still, denial was a natural human response to a situation that had gone well past human-level fuckup status and straight to cosmic proportions. Even worse, part of him didn't feel shitty at all. It felt powerful, self-satisfied, and hungry for more of the killing, more of Sasha. And neither of those things was happening, period. Still, though, urgency burned beneath his skin, and the monster he'd been stirred within his mind.

The Other. That was what Bryson and Horn had called their creation, the piece of him that they had pulled forward and honed into a killing machine.

"Fuck off. Leave me alone." But he knew the memories wouldn't go away on their own. He was going to have to make them leave.

Michael didn't call on the hypnotic conditioning and drug regimen Horn had used to keep the Other at bay—those blocks had given way during his talent ceremony. Instead, he turned to the mental discipline he'd practiced and honed until his inner shields were almost as good as his magical ones. Dragging himself out of bed, he dropped down lotus-style on the cold floor. Straightening his spine vertebra by vertebra, he concentrated on his breathing, voiding his lungs of the old, stale air and replacing it with fresh. He breathed. He counted his heartbeats. And when relative calm descended, he pictured the flow of inner energy, and the dam at the back of his brain.

Concentrating, he cranked the heavy sluice gates shut, feeling the effort as a phantom burn in his arms and back, hearing the clank of mechanisms that didn't really exist outside the construct of his own mind. It didn't matter whether the physical effort or the metallic clangs were real, though. What mattered was his ability to shut off that part of himself.

The good news was that it worked: The sluiceways shut; the dam held. But, as Michael let himself drift within himself for a moment, he was conscious that closing off that part of himself left him incomplete. Although he'd been trying to improve the man who remained outside the dam, he was still a work in progress. Worse, because of Horn's conditioning, when he was fully separated, as he was now, he tended to block his own knowledge of his other half, and what it meant, becoming the surface charmer that had been his cover. *Remember all of it, you self-centered prick*, he thought. *Sasha deserves better than your dissociated ass.* But even as he hung there, suspended between the physical and metaphysical, he was aware of a thrumming current of excitement, one that urged him to get his butt off the floor already and go see her.

He'd been searching for her for a long time now. And he sure as hell owed her his protection from the others after what had happened the night before. Not to mention an explanation.

Feeling the sharp edges of his soul dulling down, he flowed to his feet, hit the bathroom, shocked himself awake with a cold shower, shaved off a layer of stubble, and chewed a couple of Tylenol tabs on the theory that they tasted foul but ought to hit his bloodstream faster that way. Maybe. Movements quickening, he dragged on black nylon track pants and a ribbed white tank, shoved his feet into a pair of rope sandals, and was ready to go.

Six months earlier, he would've been wearing his high-toned salesman duds, even around the mansion, still playing a role he'd been programmed to forget was a cover story. The plan he'd so carefully executed just after the spring solstice meant that he could finally move on, lose the act, and become the guy he'd wanted to be—or at least try to. He'd been doing his damnedest since then to stay in control, to stay out of trouble and do the right thing, hoping to improve the good to bad ratio the *nahwal* had alluded to. But he'd blown that all to hell the night before, hadn't he?

"Probably. But I'd do it again under the same circumstances," he grated to the empty room, knowing that the sentiment did little to ameliorate the heavy debt on his soul. The writs said a Nightkeeper owed his allegiance first to the gods, then to the king, the end-time war, his fellow magi, mankind, and then his own family, wants, and desires. Or something like that. He wasn't much into scripture, but he knew that relationships and personal desire went way down at the bottom of the list. Yet he'd chosen Sasha's safety over his own *nahwal*'s directive.

She's important, he thought. *It was worth it, given how badly we need the library*. More, *he* needed the library. Having exhausted the archive, he was banking on the library having some answers, like whether there was some way to fix what was broken inside him.

And he was so rationalizing. He hadn't been thinking about the library when he'd given over to the Other and its silver magic. He'd been thinking only of Sasha, his thoughts and perceptions telescoping down to *her*. Which was more evidence of how badly off balance she'd gotten him. She was inside him even now, her face right at the edge of his mind, her scent, her taste imprinted on his sensory memory. He'd dreamed of her and had awakened hard and alone.

"Get used to it," he told himself. "Sacrifices aren't easy, and she damn well deserves better." Or rather, she *didn't* deserve a man whose very soul was in question, one Iago seemed to think could become an ally.

Telling himself there was no way in hell he would turn—he'd die first—he headed out of his suite and down the long hallway that led from the residential wing.

The main mansion was a sprawling edifice done in sandstone, wood, and marble, housing a great room connected to a large open kitchen, with a banquet-size dining room that had become a war chamber. Hallways radiated from the great room, leading variously to the residential wings, the archive, a glass-roofed sacred chamber, and forty-car garage. The second and third floors of the main house were empty, as were many of the residential rooms, mute testament to the numbers the Nightkeepers had once boasted. As it had been in his suite, the decor was neutral Southwestern blah, except for the occasional splash of decent art, thanks to Alexis, who wasn't afraid to hit the near-bottomless Nightkeeper Fund for upgrade money, and had a good eye for investments.

Michael paused at the arched doorways that opened onto the sunken great room, glancing over at the big, open-plan kitchen. His system said he needed food. His conscience said he needed to talk to Sasha. He hated how he'd been forced to leave things between them. An orgasm followed immediately by a sleep spell wasn't exactly up to his usual standard. More, there had been nothing "usual" about what had happened between the two of them . . . and she needed to understand that nothing else *could* happen. Especially given what Iago had said.

Ignoring an echo of his own voice rasping, *Mine*, he headed across the great room for the basement stairs, figuring she'd be down there for the time being. He was halfway across the sunken sitting area of the great room when Strike appeared in the hallway leading to the royal quarters, and gestured for him to divert. "Debriefing time."

"Can you give me five minutes?"

The king's expression flattened. "She's still asleep."

"You haven't been able to wake her?" Michael didn't like the sound of that. Even if the counterspell wasn't working, the sleep spell should've worn off on its own by now.

"Not yet." Strike's cobalt blue eyes glinted with frustration and worry. "I've done what I can think of. Even had Rabbit try to bring her around."

Michael's head snapped up. "You had the kid *mind-bend* her? Again?"

Earlier that year, during Rabbit's imprisonment with the Xibalbans, Iago had borrowed the young man's talent—one of them, anyway—and used it to crawl inside Sasha's head and attempt to force her to divulge the library's location. She had fought the invasion hard, and even though the attempted mind-rape had given Rabbit his chance to escape from Iago, the kid's eyes still went haunted when he spoke of the incident and its victim. Michael couldn't believe that anyone had thought another such mind-bend would be a good idea for either party. Strike leveled a long, speculative look in Michael's direction, one that held a measure of satisfaction, as though he'd just gotten an answer to an entirely different question. All he said, though, was, "I made the call I felt I had to make. Remember, we're not just looking at her as a potential new mage; we need the library, and we need it fast. And if that means making some tough calls, that's part of my job description."

Michael saw the logic even though he still didn't like it, on a number of different levels, not the least of which being that he didn't want the kid reliving his and Sasha's encounter in the stone temple, from her point of view. *Oh, holy squick factor.* "Uh . . . what did Rabbit come up with?" His blood hummed in anticipation of the answer; it wasn't that he was ashamed of what had happened with Sasha—far from it. But it was seriously complicated. He didn't need the entire population of Skywatch involved.

Strike shook his head. "Her mind blocked him with some sort of music, just like before." The king's eyes went narrow. "Why? Did something else happen we should know about?"

"Nothing," Michael said with absolute honesty. The others didn't need to know any more than they could guess, at least until he'd had a chance to talk to Sasha about it, and set a few things straight. Which brought him back to the issue of waking her up. "I don't like that she's still out. Should we get her to a doctor?"

"Let's wait on that," Strike said. "Rabbit said he thought she'd come back on her own sometime today, that her brain just needed some downtime to process what happened to her. While he was in there, he set a couple of filters to block off the memories of her imprisonment. She'll be able to remember what Iago did to her, but only if she goes looking for the information. We thought it might help her come back faster."

"That's borderline," Michael growled, but couldn't really say it had been the wrong thing to do. Rabbit had proven adept at installing spell-cast mental filters designed to reroute thought processes. When he and Myrinne were on campus, they both wore filters he'd designed to keep them from talking about the Nightkeepers in public, and to keep him from working magic. That'd been Anna's requirement before she leaned on the UT administration to grant them late admission and dorm singles across the hall from each other, both major concessions at the big school.

"I made a call. You don't have to like it." But Strike's eyes said more than that; they challenged Michael to stake his claim.

He wanted to—gods and the *Banol Kax* knew he wanted to—but he didn't dare. The thing inside him could make him unfit to be a mage, never mind a mate. So instead he growled, "Fine. Whatever. You said you wanted to debrief me?"

"You can have your five minutes with her first."

"I'll take your word that she's still asleep." Even though he would've rather gone straight down to see her, he didn't want to give his king hope of their becoming a mated pair. "Let me grab some food and I'll be right in."

"I've got you covered," Tomas said from the kitchen, surprising Michael, who hadn't realized he was within earshot. The *winikin* skimmed a trough-size bowl along the marble-topped breakfast bar that separated the huge kitchen from the great room; the bowl proved to be filled with scrambled eggs, sausage, and syrup-soaked pancake chunks, all mixed together. "Eat up," the *winikin* ordered. "The king's right. You look like shit."

Michael snagged the bowl before Tomas could do his usual bitch routine over his charge's postmagic food preferences. "Coffee?"

"There's a fresh pot and clean mugs in the suite."

"That'll do." Carrying his breakfast, Michael headed after Strike. The men pushed through a set of heavy wooden doors carved with the royal jaguar motif, and stepped into the main sitting room of the royal suite. Off to their right, a dining table had become a workstation, with laptops, printers, and piles of paper. The kitchen nook to their left was pretty bare, but then again, so were the kitchens in most of the Nightkeepers' suites; the *winikin* did the majority of the cooking in the main kitchen. Hallways sprawled off to the left and right of the living room, leading to bedrooms and ritual areas.

Strike took a spot on the long, brown-upholstered couch, where Leah, Alexis, and Nate sat, forming the core of the royal council. Strike's sister, Anna, sat in a love seat off to one side. She was a lovely woman in her late thirties, with red-highlighted brunette hair and the same piercing cobalt eyes as her brother. Wearing jeans and a soft blue sweater the same color as her eyes, along with an ancient crystal skull that hung from a chain around her neck, she looked tired. Strike must've 'ported her in first thing, maybe on the backside of the trip to return Rabbit to the university.

The final member of the day's council meeting, the royal *winikin* Jox, lounged in a chair on the other side of a glyph-carved wooden chest that was probably more than a thousand years old, and served the jaguar royals as a coffee table. In his late fifties, with his gray-shot hair pulled back in a Deadhead ponytail, wearing jeans and a dark green button-down with its sleeves rolled up to reveal his forearm marks, Jox was the heart of Skywatch. These days, the royal *winikin* was spread thin, looking after not only his true bound charges, but also Leah, as Strike's mate, and Rabbit, who had no *winikin* of his own, but had been partly Jox's responsibility since toddlerhood. The royal *winikin* looked like he could use a serious vacation, but Michael didn't figure it was his place to suggest it. Besides, it wasn't like the rest of them weren't run ragged. There was too much that needed doing, and not enough bodies in residence to do it.

Strike poured him a mug of coffee and handed it over black. "Ready to roll?"

Michael nodded his thanks and took a sip, needing the bite of caffeine. "What do you want to know?" Which was really his way of asking what they thought they already knew.

Leah smiled sweetly. "Nice try. How about you walk us through exactly what happened last night, step by step? And don't skimp on the deets."

So Michael went through the rescue minute by minute. He told them about Sasha's dreams and copped to the power boost he'd gotten from kissing her, though he implied that kissing was as far as they'd gone. He then moved on to describe the red-robe's arrival and Iago's entrance, and was even able to tell them that the Xibalbans' leader was searching for a specific Nightkeeper in addition to Sasha, and needed them both by the winter solstice. Then, for all that he'd vowed to be a better man, he started mixing lies with the truth, hiding the fact that Iago had later said he was the one—and that Sasha would be part of his transformation. He finished with, "Iago tried to grab Sasha and 'port her out, but I slapped the strongest shield I could manage around us both, and Iago's magic misfired and killed the red-robe. I don't know what the deal was with the corpse disintegrating like that—maybe it had something to do with using Xibalban magic in a Nightkeeper temple? Or maybe it was intrinsic to the red-robe? He was definitely a magic sniffer, one of the *pilli*, whatever that means."

Michael made himself stop before he said too much, knowing that the best lies were the simplest. Strike didn't look like he was totally buying the story, but before he could get into it, Anna cut in, saying, "That's why I'm here." With a doctorate in Mayan studies and more than a decade in the field, she was their local expert on the historical stuff. "*Pilli* was a word used to represent a member of the elite nobility. In this case, it probably refers to the more powerful of the Xibalban magi, possibly those wearing the red robes."

Jox frowned at Anna. "I've never heard the word before."

"That's because it's not Mayan," she said. "It's Aztec. Which got me wondering . . . What if, rather than paralleling the Mayan system, like we are, the Xibalbans are patterned after the Aztec?" She paused. "Or, more accurately, what if the Aztec were patterned after the Xibalbans? It makes a twisted sort of sense; the Aztec arose right around the time the Xibalbans split off from the Nightkeepers, and were far more bloodthirsty than their neighboring cultures. Where the Maya largely practiced autosacrifice, the Aztec made huge human sacrifices, taking sometimes hundreds, even reportedly thousands of victims at a time by the mid–fifteen hundreds. Granted, those were terrible times, when the influx of the Spanish invaders brought war, famine, and disease. The Aztec were just doing what they believed would appease the gods . . . but what if it wasn't the gods they were really praying to?"

Nate leaned forward, suddenly intent. "You think the Aztec were being coached by the Xibalbans, that they were actually trying to hook up with the *Banol Kax* to drive the Spaniards away?"

"The timing fits," Anna said, "and it would help explain why the Aztec went so far down a path that most human beings wouldn't consider an option."

Michael's inner tension had settled some as the convo evolved around him, veering away from the red-robe's death. Now he asked, "How does knowing about the Aztec connection help us against the Xibalbans?"

He should've kept his mouth shut. He knew it the moment Strike zeroed back in on him as he answered, "We're not sure yet. Anna is going to work with Jade to put together a rundown of Aztec myths, rituals, and other things that might be pertinent to the issue." The king hit Jade's name harder than he needed to, another challenge.

Normally, Michael let things like that roll off, on the theory that he and Jade had worked things out the best they could, and it wasn't anybody else's business. Now, though, he figured he owed the royal council an answer—on this, at any rate. Choosing his words judiciously, he said, "None of what happened yesterday changes the fact that Jade and I were lovers, but we weren't a destined-mates match. Nor does it mean that Sasha and I are destined, either. Yes, I was drawn to her, and yes, kissing her amplified my shield magic, and yes, she seemed to recognize me. . . ." When he said it like that, it seemed like a no-brainer. And maybe under other circumstances it would have been. But he wasn't the man he was supposed to have been. Just ask Tomas.

"However, Sasha has just been through a terrible ordeal, and, mental filters or not, she's going to need some room. So I'm asking, as a personal favor, if you'll pass the word to lay off the destined-mates rhetoric with her."

Leah, Jox, Nate and Alexis nodded as though that seemed reasonable. Strike, on the other hand, fixed him with a look. "Your *winikin* thinks you've got a commitment problem."

"My *winikin* thinks I've got lots of problems." Michael met the king's eyes squarely, letting him see the determination and control, but not the things that churned beneath. "I swear to you that I'll do my best by Sasha." And that was the man talking. The one who was in control, and was going to *stay* in control, damn it.

After a moment, Strike nodded. "Okay. We'll give you two some room." He turned to Anna. "We need to figure out who Iago was looking for, and why. In addition, we need to know what happened with the red-robe. If that's something new in the Xibalbans' arsenal, we'll have to figure out how to counteract it."

Michael shifted uncomfortably at the list of questions, suspecting that the answers all circled back to him. "I don't think it's a new Xibalban weapon," he said, sticking to his lies. "It seemed more like a misfire of the 'port magic."

"Which is even more reason to figure it out," Strike countered. "I'd hate like hell to do something like that to another human being."

You won't, Michael thought. *It was me. All me*. With the Other locked safely away, he felt the kill weigh sickly on his soul. "What about the word 'mick,' and the mountains the gray-robes mentioned?" he asked, his voice rasping on the question.

Anna sent him a long, slow look before answering. "The prefix 'mic' was used for many things relating to the realm of the damned, which was called Mictlan."

"I thought Xibalba was the Mayan equivalent of hell?" Nate asked.

"Yes and no," Anna replied. "Although Xibalba is the underworld, it's not necessarily a negative place, not hell as the Christians think of it. It's more a realm of challenges that the dead must win through in order to reach their end reward in the barrier or the sky—or reincarnation, depending on which set of beliefs you go with."

Michael frowned. "So there's no punishment for bad behavior?" That didn't fit with what the *nahwal* had told him.

"Wrongdoers get caught up in the challenges, looping endlessly until they learn the lessons they failed to learn on earth," Anna clarified. "Some never learn, just loop eternally. That's the punishment, the hell, if you will. Not Xibalba itself. That's in the formal sense, though. From what's been happening around us over the past eighteen months, I have a feeling the coming of the end-time has shifted the hierarchy in Xibalba, that the *Banol Kax*, who used to be the overseers of the challenges and the dead, have started marshaling them as armies instead."

"Assuming the *Banol Kax* are still a factor," Nate put in, referring to the complete lack of action from that front ever since the destruction of the intersection.

"They are," Strike said flatly. "Just because they've gone quiet doesn't mean they're not a threat. They're doing something, or planning something. We just don't know what."

The current theory was that with the intersection gone and Iago folding the hellmouth into the barrier except as needed, the demons of Xibalba had lost their direct access to the earth, forcing them to work through the Xibalbans and *makol*. But although they might be cut off temporarily, Michael was inclined to agree with Strike's assessment. Given the tenacity of the *Banol*

Kax throughout history, it would be dangerous to assume they would be out of action for long.

"Anyway," Anna said, picking up her thread, "four classes of dead go straight to the sky: suicides, sacrificial victims, women who die in childbirth, and warriors who die in battle. They skip the challenges, having earned their 'get out of jail free' cards by the manner of their death."

"Where does Mictlan fit in?" Nate asked.

Anna hummed a flat note. "Depending on who you ask, it's either a construct of the Spanish missionaries, a sort of culturally relevant hell that they used to threaten the natives—the old 'repent and accept the one true God, or you'll suffer eternally in Mictlan' routine . . . or it's the lowest level of Xibalba, where the true sinners go. Just like there's a group of souls who go straight to the sky, do not pass go, do not collect, there's a group of souls, albeit smaller, who bypass the challenges in the other direction: the traitors and the murderers. Some say these are the souls that become the *makol*."

A chill skimmed down Michael's spine. "What about the mountain?"

"Depends on whether we're talking about the Mayan or Aztec perspective. The Maya believed the entrance of Xibalba was located at the top of a mountain, with tunnels leading to Scorpion River, which formed the boundary of the underworld." She paused. "The Aztec preferred volcanoes."

"Why does that not surprise me?" Strike said dryly. "They sound like a bunch of bloodthirsty psychopaths. Perfect fodder for the Xibalbans."

"Or they were no more warlike than their neighbors before the Xibalbans moved in on them," Anna countered. "Chicken and egg, you know?"

"Were there any volcanoes the Aztec were particularly fond of?" Michael asked. "Maybe one that's extinct now, that the Xibalbans might have taken over as a stronghold?"

"They worshiped Smoking Mountain and White Woman, near Tenochtitlán. East of there is Mount Tlaloc, where the thunder god was supposed to live." She paused, frowning. "There are others, but I'll have to hit the books to be sure."

"It's a start," Strike said. "We'll check it out, but I hate splitting our forces. It's hard enough trying to track the hints handed down to us in the Mayan legends, never mind figuring out the Aztec stuff. Add that to searching for both the library and a new intersection, and we're spread very, very thin."

After a brief hesitation, Anna said, "How about Myrinne?"

"No way." The answer was an immediate knee-jerk from Strike, his expression darkening. Then, catching himself—due at least in part to Leah digging an elbow into his ribs—he toned it down to say, "She and Rabbit just got to school. Let them focus on that for now." It was no secret Strike had sent them to UT partly in the hopes that the two would drift apart in the wider world. So far, though, that didn't seem to be happening.

"She would want to help," Anna pressed. She'd been the one to claim responsibility for Myrinne, based on a debt she owed to Red-Boar, and therefore posthumously to his heir, Rabbit.

But Strike shook his head. "We don't know what she is."

"She's a girl," Anna said stubbornly.

"Who might or might not be the daughter of a witch who might or might not have had actual powers," Strike countered.

"She dreamed of Skywatch before she got here," Anna reminded him. "She described it to Rabbit, right down to the ceiba tree out back." Myrinne's vision suggested that she had seer's powers. It wasn't clear, however, what form those skills might take, whether Nightkeeper, Xibalban, or something else. So far, Strike had forbidden all experimentation. That hadn't stopped Anna from lobbying the point, though. With her own *itza'at* powers dubious at best, the Nightkeepers badly needed a visionary.

"I'll take it under advisement," Strike said grudgingly, and won a nod from Anna. He continued, "For now, Michael is going to focus on this new spell of Iago's, while Anna and Jade do a first pass on the Aztec stuff. Basically, we need anything that'll help us figure out what's coming down the pipeline now that we're bearing down on the three-year threshold."

In the absence of the library, the prophecies actually dealing with the events leading up to the end-time were few and far between. Despite the Nightkeepers' best efforts to uncover additional artifacts with inscriptions that might help, all they had describing the events of upcoming winter solstice was a single carved inscription, badly degraded, that read, *In the triad years, a daughter of the sky . . .*

And that was it. Which wasn't much help at all.

Worse, there was some debate about the actual time period it represented. Anna was convinced that the triad years corresponded to the final three years before the apocalypse. Lucius, on the other hand, had offered another interpretation, back when he'd been in his human guise, living with the Nightkeepers and helping Jade with the archives. According to him, the prophecy referred to the coming of the Triad, a legendary trio of über-powerful magi who were supposed to arise at the end of the age to join forces with the Nightkeepers. Without the rest of the prophecy, there was no way of telling which interpretation was correct. Then again, without the rest of the prophecy, the question was academic. They needed another source for information—which brought them back around, yet again, to the subject of the library.

Draining the dregs of his coffee and figuring he could legitimately make a break for it, Michael shifted in his seat. "If that's it for the debriefing . . . ?"

Strike nodded and waved him off. "Yeah, we're just about finished here anyway. Let us know if she's awake, will you?"

Michael narrowed his eyes. "Don't get your hopes up. I mean it."

Strike turned his scarred palms up in a falsely innocent gesture. "Hey, can't blame me for trying." But then he turned serious. "Look, I know things were awkward for you after you and Jade split, and again when Nate and Alexis got back together."

"That's one way to put it," Michael conceded. With the skyroad gone and no new intersection found, the Nightkeepers needed all the power they could get. Because of that, there was serious pressure on the singles to pair up, whether or not the relationships made sense in real-world terms.

Strike glanced at Leah, a hint of a smile curving his mouth as he said to Michael, "Do me a favor and don't let that turn you off something that could benefit all of us, yourself most of all."

Or it could doom us all, Michael thought. He didn't understand how Sasha, who seemed to embody positive energy, had reached inside him to stir up the Other, and he didn't like things he didn't understand, especially when they had to do with his alter ego. But once again, he was unable to break the silence that came from within him. So instead he said, "I'm just checking to see if she's awake yet."

Because despite the logic that said he should stay far away from her, he owed her an explanation, and an apology. More, he damn well wanted—needed—to see her. It was as simple as that. And as complicated. So he went.

The basement hallway was bland and austere compared to the lived-in feel of the level above. Back when hundreds of Nightkeepers had lived at Skywatch, the basement had been used for storage. These days, though, the storerooms were set up as more or less comfortable cells. Three of them were, anyway, having variously housed Leah, Rabbit, Myrinne, and Lucius when they'd been deemed potential security threats. And although Michael hated the thought of Sasha locked up, a prisoner, there was no arguing the fact that she was still a relatively unknown quantity.

Stopping outside the second of the doors, Michael said a quick spell to drop the ward spell that barred magic users from entering or exiting the cell, and then turned the key stuck in the exterior lock. He was strung tight as he pushed through the door to the sparsely furnished fifteen-by-fifteen-foot cell, exhaling only when he saw that Sasha was there, still sleeping, curled up beneath a blanket.

Wearing a set of Alexis's workout clothes, with her hair bed-wild and the strain of the prior day evident in the circles beneath her eyes, she wasn't the most beautiful woman he'd ever seen. But call it her innate healing magic, call it Rabbit's intervention—hell, call it good genes—whatever it was, even in repose she seemed to glow from within with strength and vitality, and the sort of go-to-hell attitude he'd never been able to resist. And that was a problem, because he was starting to realize he wasn't just attracted to her, wasn't just drawn to her on a magical or even physical level. He was in danger of liking her, of wanting to be with her. He told himself to about-face it and get out of there before he did something they would both regret, but he was already too late. She hadn't been sleeping, after all; she'd been faking it. Now, having no doubt identified him through cracked lids, she sat up and glared at him.

When their eyes met, magic and anger kicked, and every cell of his body lit with desire. Heat rushed through him, tensing his body, hardening his flesh. And he knew he wasn't going anywhere, not just because of the library and the questions that needed answering, but because of her. Problem was, the Other felt the exact same way.

CHAPTER SEVEN

Sasha took a good long look at her latest captor. With the clean, elegant lines of his body visible beneath soft black track pants, and a tight muscle shirt that showed off a whole hell of a lot of muscles, Michael was just as big and gorgeous as she had first remembered, when she'd awoken and found herself far more clearheaded than she would've expected. Or rather, some things were fuzzy while others—like the two of them tearing into each other like crazed nymphos—were crystal.

As their eyes met, heat chased through her. Still, though, she tried to hang on to rationality. What had she been *thinking*? Maybe she'd gotten into a couple of ill-fated relationships far too quickly in the past, but the incident in the smoke-filled chamber had to be one for the *Guinness* book: introductions to orgasm in fifteen minutes or less, with no payment involved. *Hello, sex with a stranger*. She'd nearly talked herself into believing that what had happened between them had come from nothing more than adrenaline and incense, that she'd imagined the connection they'd seemed to forge. But now, as his forest dark eyes looked right at her and saw her, really *saw* her rather than dismissing her or passing by, she knew she was in some big, bad trouble. *He* was trouble. Because even though she knew who and what he was, her blood ran hot for him and her chest tightened with the greedy, grasping need that was her downfall.

She would have cursed him, but she had only herself to blame for the weakness. So many things would've been different in her life if she could've found a way to be happy alone, if she could've been enough for herself. Her ex, Saul, might not have been kind when he'd accused her of clinging too hard, of needing too much, but he'd been right. Even her ill-advised trip into the rain forest had been a quest for her father's posthumous approval. And yesterday? Michael had told her he'd come looking for her, that he and his friends needed *her*, and she'd fallen right in with his plan of hiding until reinforcements arrived. Then, somehow, they'd wound up making love. And for a few moments, she hadn't been alone. The sex had been flat-out, earthshaking, tooth-rattling amazing. More, it had made her feel powerful, as though she'd finally taken something for herself after too many months of having things taken from her. Yet it had to have been a huge mistake. Even though the dreams made him seem more familiar than he ought to, she didn't know him, really. She thought she'd glimpsed something dark and angry in him the day before, something that reminded her too much of Ambrose on a bad day. And although it had been for just a second, and he'd gotten it under control just as quickly as it had flashed, it had been in there. She was sure of it.

Not to mention that she was still a freaking prisoner. She was someplace different from before; that much was evident in the makeshift cell outfitted with a narrow camping cot, a portable toilet, and a small bookshelf that held a couple of paperbacks and a six-pack of bottled water. Still, though, it was a cell.

When he didn't say anything, just stood there staring at her, she tossed aside the light blanket and stood, squaring off opposite him, barefoot, in a fighter's ready position matching his own. Then she lifted her chin in challenge and fixed him with a look. "Well?"

Finally, he let out a long, slow breath and said, "Glad to see you're awake. You had us worried."

"Us?" She didn't let on that she'd been playing possum for the past hour, that she'd seen at least two others checking up on her, a tall, rawboned blonde and a smaller, darker man with gray-streaked hair pulled back in a ponytail much like the one Ambrose had worn. "And where are we?"

"There are a couple dozen of us in residence here, give or take. And you're at Skywatch. Our training compound." He paused. "How much do you remember about what happened last night?"

"I . . . I don't know," she said, buying time while her thoughts churned. *I remember that you're just as bad as Ambrose and Iago*, she thought with a flash of anger that cut through the sensual pull that seemed to anchor her body to his. *I know you believe in the same shit they do, and you think I'm somehow part of it. More, you had me convinced there for a few minutes.*

Granted, her jumbled memories contained splashes of the inexplicable. How had he found her? How had they avoided being seen by the gray-robes? What the hell was the deal with that curtain of glittering light? How had he knocked her out again without even touching her?

But now that she'd slept off whatever had been in the incense, she'd returned to rationality. *They had to be using drugs of some sort*, she thought. *And some special effects to make the magic seem real.* Panic spiraled, bringing a prickle of sweat to her skin, though the room was cool. What the hell kind of rabbit hole had she fallen into? Who were these people? They were Ambrose's kind of people, she knew. And she had to get the hell out of there. It didn't matter that they thought they were the good guys. They were still insane, still dangerous. *I've got to get out of here*, she thought. *But how?* Step one seemed obvious. She needed to get free from her cell and figure out where she was. Iago's labyrinth had proved to be too much for her, but her current accommodations looked to be a converted storeroom. What if the rest of her prison was similarly makeshift?

Scattered thoughts coming together into a plan of sorts, she said, "You want to know where Ambrose hid the library."

Michael stilled. "You know we do."

She lifted her chin, trying not to let the nerves show. "How about we make a deal? I'll tell you everything I know about it, on one condition."

"Which is what—a ticket back to Boston and a vow that we'll forget you exist?" he asked dryly.

She tamped down the kick of excitement brought by the impossible offer. "If you promised me that, I'd know you were lying." She shook her head. "No, no plane ticket. Let's go with straight-up barter instead. You get me out of here and into a kitchen, hook me up with some fresh ingredients, and I'll answer your questions."

His gorgeous eyes went blank for a moment. She'd surprised him. *Good.*

"That's your demand?" he asked after a moment. "You want to cook?"

She shrugged. "You've looked into my background, so you know that's what I do—I cook. I cook when I'm happy or sad, when I'm celebrating with friends or all alone with my thoughts. Cooking is my outlet, one of my greatest pleasures." When the word stirred the physical memory of another, greater pleasure, she hurriedly continued, "I haven't been in a kitchen or touched real food in nearly a year. So, yeah. That's the trade. You give me an hour in a kitchen, I'll you what I know about the library."

A true warrior might not have gone for the pots and pans as her first demand, but she'd never pretended to be a warrior, despite Ambrose's claims otherwise—and his last brutal attempt to prove those claims. She was who she was, nothing more. And in this stupid, screwed-up situation where everybody had the power except her, she needed, for a few moments, anyway, to pretend she was back in her own world. More, she needed to get the hell out of the cell, and a kitchen was a fine place to start.

Michael held her gaze for a moment. Then he nodded slowly. "Let me talk to the others. I'll see what I can do."

"I'll be here," she said blandly.

He looked at her a moment more, then turned with fluid grace and headed for the door, where he paused and said something under his breath. She assumed it was some sort of secret password, one that cued a guard on the other side of the door to unlock it, far preferring the idea of a password over the suspicion that he'd been casting a "spell" to let him through, sort of a Nightkeepers' "open sesame."

Once he was gone, she prowled her cell, trying to remember everything she could about the Nightkeepers. Her childhood had been filled with stories of the powerful magi, their rules and responsibilities. Their talents. Their magic. She knew their legends, knew what drove them. At least, assuming that Michael and his fellow delusionals were buying into the same set of stories Ambrose had taught her. The question was, how could she use that information? How could she—

The lock rattled, interrupting her midthought. The panel swung inward and her pulse accelerated as she braced herself for bad news and the need to come up with a plan B.

Michael stood in the opening, filling the doorway with his body, filling the room with his presence. Instead of coming in, though, he stepped aside. And waved her out into the hallway beyond.

Pulse bumping, she moved toward him, then stalled. "Seriously?" It wasn't until that moment that she realized she hadn't expected her new captors to give in to her demand. It made her suspicious that they had. "What's the catch?"

"No catch." He lifted a shoulder. "Sometimes you've got to offer trust in order to get it in return. I've asked the others to make themselves scarce for the time being, so it'll just be you and me. And a really big kitchen with all the Cuisinart and Copper Clad you could ask for."

She yearned. Tried not to let it show. "Okay. Let's go."

"After you."

She moved past him, but stopped in the doorway, facing him. She was close enough to catch his scent, which she'd caught on her own skin when she'd awakened. *He's a means to an end*, she reminded herself. *And you can't trust him.* The flash she'd seen in his eyes suggested there was far more to him than what showed on the surface. And if that only made her more intrigued, that was her imagination at work again, and she *knew* she couldn't trust that bitch.

At his gesture, she led the way along the short hall, toward a short flight of stairs, acutely conscious of the big, solid man following close behind her, his heat radiating to her skin and prickling each individual neuron to unwanted sensual awareness.

The regularly spaced doors on one side of the hallway all looked the same, and presumably led to more storerooms like the one she'd just been in. On the other side there was a single set of glass double doors. Through them, she caught a glimpse of a huge room filled with high-end gym equipment. The hallway led to a corner behind her and kept going, making her think the building's footprint had to be enormous, far bigger than that of a normal house. Yet the woodwork on the staircase leading up looked more residential than not, and orange sunlight spilled down from above. He'd called the place Skywatch and claimed it was the Nightkeepers' training compound, but that didn't make any sense. None of it did.

Stay on task. Keep focused. Keeping her goals in mind, she headed up the stairs, still too aware of the warm solidity of the man who followed close behind.

Then she reached the main level, took one look at the wide room spread out in front of her, and stopped dead as all thought was swept aside by a powerful surge of emotion, one that welled up and nearly flattened her, scared the shit out of her.

Oh, holy hell. She recognized this place.

Sucking in a breath, she stumbled back, missed a step, and would've crashed down the stairs if it hadn't been for Michael's strong arms catching her easily and holding her against his wide, warm chest for a moment, a few heartbeats when she could feel his pulse hammer in time with hers.

"What's wrong?" he asked, his voice a low rumble in his chest.

"I—I know this room," she said, unable to keep her voice from shaking as she pushed away from him and stood on her own, on a landing that was part of a wide strip running three-quarters of the way around a sunken sitting area. To her left, the space opened to hallways on either side of a huge, open-plan kitchen done in marble and industrial chrome, but not even that lure was enough to snap her out of her *oh, shit* fugue as she kept looking, trying to convince herself that it was just a casual resemblance, that the room wasn't actually the same as the image in her mind. Problem was, she couldn't talk herself into the lie.

"From a dream?" Michael asked, his voice carefully neutral.

"No. A photograph," she said faintly. "I saw it when I was a kid, snooping through Ambrose's things." She'd been twelve, maybe thirteen, and had only just begun to comprehend the depth of her father's insanity, the complexity of the construct he'd built up around a group of people who didn't exist. "It was mixed in with some other papers—tax records and garbage like that, nothing unusual except for this picture of Ambrose in his late teens or so, standing with a couple of other guys, their arms around one another, mugging for the camera." She moved now, walking slowly around the raised platform until the angle was right. Then she looked through the sliding glass doors that led out to a huge blue pool surrounded by a pressed cement patio. "The furniture and paint were different. The curtains. But the room was the same, and the scenery, that was the same. He was here. He lived here."

The photo had been faded, but time hadn't changed the ridgeline in the distance, where the back end of a box canyon rose up in a sheer cliff. Not all of the buildings near the main house looked the same, and there was a tree now where there hadn't been one before. In the distance, though, in the wan, strangely orangeish sunlight of late morning, she could see the regular patterns of light and shadow created by a Puebloan ruin, high on the rear canyon wall.

The scenery matched. The room matched.

"We're in New Mexico, near Chaco Canyon, aren't we?" she asked softly, but didn't wait for his answer. Instead, she continued, "He wanted his ashes spread here. I tried to find the place once, but couldn't."

"It was hidden by a curtain spell for nearly two decades."

"Special effects," she said, her voice going thin. "Desert-style camo netting."

"Magic," Michael corrected, and nudged her in the direction of the kitchen. "Are you taking orders?"

"I don't do real well with orders," she said, seriously grateful for the subject change. "Or didn't your background check mention that was why I'd had nearly a dozen jobs over four years? I have a problem following recipes, and I don't like doing things the same way over and over again." But she let him guide her to the kitchen as she fought to regain her mental footing. So what if Ambrose had lived here when he was a kid? Just because this . . . cult, or whatever it was, went back four decades or so didn't make their paradigm any less bullshit than it'd been when she had finally called her father on the gaps between his beliefs and reality.

She'd been thirteen, just hitting menarche and snotty with it, and had sassed him that the so-called magic he preached didn't work worth a damn. Instead of ignoring her like he usually did when she mouthed off, that time he'd dragged her into his "temple"—a hallway closet he'd done up with stone veneer and a *chac-mool* altar—and locked them both in while he'd chivvied her through the usual ritual of letting blood and burning the sacrificial offerings, as they usually did for each of the solstices and equinoxes. That time, though, his chants had sounded different, more complex. And when, as usual, nothing happened, he'd been furious, accusing her of not believing, of not having prayed hard enough. He'd acted like something should have happened during that particular ceremony, that she had failed him. More, that she'd failed herself.

Later, looking back, she'd realized it was after that ceremony that they'd truly begun growing apart—she in teenage rebellion, he into depression. It had taken several more years and his last final, brutal effort to make the nonexistent magic real before she ran, but that had been the beginning of the end for them.

"Hey," Michael said, breaking into her thoughts with a gentle touch at her elbow. "You okay? Feeling shaky?"

Brought abruptly back to reality—or at least his version thereof—she shook her head. "No. Well, maybe a little. Do you blame me?"

"You want to sit for a while? I'm no trained chef, but I know my way around a kitchen. I could make us something."

His offer reminded her of where they were, and why. And although the memories had knocked her off-kilter, they had also reminded her in lurid detail why she had to get the hell out of there. "I'm fine," she said, forcing herself to focus on the present—and the possibility of escape. Taking a look around, she saw that the large kitchen he'd brought her to flowed out from an upper ledge running around the sunken great room, and was separated from the big space by a breakfast bar that had leather-topped stools pushed into place beneath. The countertops were all marble, the cabinets good wood. The appliances were commercial steel, the pans Copper Clad, as promised, the knives surgical-sharp. Even better, there were fresh herbs everywhere—hung from the rafters in drying bunches, growing in pots, and spilling out of a window greenhouse. A quick check showed that the cabinets, pantry, and commercial fridge and freezer were overstocked with just about anything she could want, especially if her taste leaned toward Mayan cuisine, which it did. Always had.

For a moment, she let herself wallow in the sense of being, finally, someplace that was familiar because of who and what she was, in a way that had nothing to do with her father. But really, her being there had everything to do with Ambrose. And she had to get her ass out of there.

Starting to pull ingredients with more thought to their spiciness than the flavor combinations, she set a trio of hot sauces on a nearby counter and stalled by asking, "Who's the foodie?"

Michael hesitated, and for a second she thought he was going to remind her that the deal had involved her giving him info, not the other way around. But then he answered, "That'd be the royal *winikin*, Jox. He does the lion's share of the cooking, with the rest of us pitching in or being dragooned, depending. Leah's been on a kick to get the Nightkeepers doing more of the house stuff, as part of her whole 'the *winikin* are not your servants' thing. Jox doesn't let too many people in his kitchen voluntarily, though. What you see here is mostly his doing, including the herbs. He and my *winikin*, Tomas, put in a big garden out next to the ball court, with a greenhouse beside it. They've got maize going, along with squash, beans, and about a dozen varieties of peppers. There's even a small orchard. Sour oranges, thin-skinned limes—you name it. If our ancestors cooked with it, Jox and Tomas are probably growing it, or have at least tried to."

Sasha's brain had pretty much shut off after the first part of his answer, though. "You've got *winikin*?" she asked despite herself. She felt like the paleontologist guy in *Jurassic Park*, who'd gotten that *oh, holy shit* look on his face and said, "You've got raptors?" Because that was about how it felt: cloned dinosaurs. *Winikin*. Both unbelievable, but somehow believable within the context.

They're not real winikin, she reminded herself as her head spun and her stomach lurched once again on the sense that she was in way over her head, and sinking fast. *They're just another group of people who've bought into an elaborate and extremely well-funded fantasy.*

Right?

"Or they've got us. Either way." Michael moved to the breakfast bar, dragged out a leather-topped stool, and propped himself up on it, leaning back against the reddish marble bar with his long legs stretched out in front of him as he continued, "Until about eighteen months ago, most of us thought the *winikin* were our godparents and the Nightkeepers were just bedtime stories. Instead, it turned out that *we* were the bedtime stories, that we're the last dozen survivors of the Solstice Massacre of 'eighty four. The *winikin* had hoped—prayed, really—that the war was over before it began, but then the barrier reactivated, the magic came back online, and Strike—he's our king—called us together to become the smallest damn fighting force that ever set out to save the world." Michael's lips twitched, but there was little humor in his expression. "We came here and learned how to connect to the barrier, how to pull the magic. Ever since then we've been playing catch-up, trying to reassemble all the old spells and prophecies, without much luck. Now, we're just over a month away from the three-year threshold, and we're floundering." He focused on her, his gaze direct and silently demanding. "That's why we need your help, both as the daughter of a mage and as the person who knew Ambrose best. He might not have told you where he hid the library, but you know how he thought, where he might've left clues."

The kitchen took a long, slow spin around Sasha. Denial rose up within her, choking her with thick, viscous fear. The story didn't make any sense. Yet at the same time, it did.

The magi had suffered population bottlenecks twice before in their history, once in Egypt around 1300 B.C., when the pharaoh Akhenaton declared Egypt a monotheistic empire and slaughtered the polytheistic priests, and again in the fifteen hundreds, when the conquistadors had converted Mesoamerica to Christianity, starting once again by killing the priests. The Nightkeepers. Each of those slaughters had wiped out all but a handful of the magi. From that angle, Michael's implication of a recent massacre fit with the Nightkeepers' view on the cyclical nature of time and events. It was also consistent with what she saw around her. The mansion was set up for an army, yet Michael had said there were only twenty or so people in residence. That said population bottleneck to her. *Or rather, it does if I buy that the stories are more than an expensive and potentially deadly delusion*, she thought, trying not to lose herself.

Throughout her life, she'd fallen prey to her own imagination time and again, talking herself into realities that didn't exist. Like Ambrose being a good father. Saul being on the verge of proposing. Hell, she'd even believed in the Nightkeepers long ago, had imagined herself fighting demons in the end-time battle, serving beneath the valiant King Scarred-Jaguar, who Ambrose had spoken of as if he were real, like they all were.

Apparently he wasn't the only one who thought along those lines. But that brought up another question: Why had Ambrose left what seemed like the perfect location for him to hang out and indulge his obsessions? Should she take that as a warning in its own right, or a hint that there was far more going on here than she'd even begun to grasp? Her mind spun as she had to ask herself: At what point did delusion become a reality?

It doesn't, she told herself. *So get your ass out of here already*. It was the best chance for escape she'd had in over a year. She couldn't not take advantage of the opportunity, just because her mobile mind had cast Michael into the role of hero and lover, despite all evidence to the contrary.

When she pressed her hands to the counter, she noticed her fingers were trembling. Knowing she was close to losing it, she focused on the scene outside the wide kitchen window, which overlooked a football field–size patch of windblown hardpan, where a darker sand shadow outlined where a building must have stood in years past. To the left of that was a scattering of small cottage-type houses, to the right a huge, spreading tree in front of a big, industrial-looking steel building. In front of the tree sat a high-wheeled vehicle—a Jeep-like chassis riding on fat tires mounted on external shocks. Sasha's pulse picked up at the sight.

"Well," Michael said from right behind her. "You said you wanted a kitchen. What's the next step?"

She hadn't realized he'd moved from the breakfast bar, or that he was so close to her. Sensual awareness skimmed through her, lighting her up. This time, though, it came with the wish that they could have met under different circumstances, as slightly different people. If he'd been a normal guy and she'd been a chef with a little less baggage, she thought they could've made it work. For a while, anyway. But as the people they were, in the situation they were in, there was zero hope. The only sane thing she could do would be to get the hell away from him—from all of it—and build a new life.

"I guess this is the next step," she said, hoping her voice didn't give away her intentions. As nonchalantly as she could manage, she picked up one of the hot sauces, uncapped it . . . and splashed it straight into Michael's face, aiming for his eyes.

"Aah!" He howled and reeled back, grabbing for his eyes with one hand, for her with the other. Sasha went in low, got in an elbow to his solar plexus, hooked his back foot with hers, and yanked. He fell hard, his head banging off the marble counter on the way down. He went limp when he landed, but she couldn't turn back now.

"I'm sorry," she cried, eyes blurring with foolish tears. Then she ran for her life.

She raced across the main room, hit the sliding glass doors at a dead run, and burst out into the open, fleeing captivity and crazy people who believed in impossible things.

The compound was quiet around her, with no shouts of discovery. Not yet anyway. Her breath burned in her lungs as she reached the dune buggy. She hadn't been outside in more than a year; the sunlight blinded her, though it was dim and orange-cast, as though the sun were shining through a layer of smog that was invisible in the clear blue sky.

Throwing herself into the cockpit of the unfamiliar vehicle, she fumbled for the start button, and hissed, "Yes!" when the engine came to life. Yanking the safety harness into place, she hit the gas and sent the buggy churning in a tight one-eighty. Punching it, she powered around the side of the pool, away from the big steel building.

Still no alarm.

Her heart pounded in her ears and her blood ran hot with nerves and building elation as the vehicle slewed out from behind the huge stone-faced mansion and hit a dirt track that led to another, wider track, almost a road. It ran out the front, through a set of open gates.

Sasha hit the gas and flew through the gates. And she was free!

CHAPTER EIGHT

"Oh, for fuck's sake." Tomas's voice came from some-where far above Michael. "You were supposed to let her get the drop on you, not let her split your damn head open. Way to go on the defense."

"Do you mind?" Michael grated. "I'm blinded and dying. The least you could do is pretend to sympathize." But there was some truth in the *winikin*'s dig. Michael had let his guard down too far, as he'd divided his focus between watching her and thinking about the photo-graph she'd described, and what it might mean. And she'd gotten the drop on him way harder than he'd in-tended. Strike's order had been for him to let her escape, not let her kick his ass.

"Jack in," Tomas suggested with zero pity. "You'll heal."

"Son of a bitch." Annoyed with his *winikin* for the lack of concern and with himself for the lapse of vigilance—and more than a little impressed with the one-two Sasha had used to drop him—Michael palmed his father's knife from his ankle sheath, sliced his palm, and muttered the two-word spell that connected him to the barrier: "*Pasaj och.*"

To his relief, the jack-in went without a hitch, and he sensed nothing beyond the pure red-gold of Nightkeeper power. Earlier, when he and Sasha had been face-to-face in the storeroom doorway, he'd thought he caught a thread of silver magic, there and gone so quickly that he might have convinced himself he'd imagined it if it hadn't been for the answering kick of rage that had dimmed his vision for a second, washing her lovely face to grayscale. That part definitely hadn't been his imagination. More, he could swear it'd been triggered by Sasha's nearness, and his primal response to her. Which was consistent with what Iago had said, and so wasn't a good sign. He had to find a way to keep her from lowering his defenses, given that, whether she was ready to accept it or not, she'd come to Skywatch for good.

First, though, he had to make sure she survived her "escape" attempt. Calling the red-gold magic, he leaned on the magic, opened himself up to it, and felt some of the pain ease. A Nightkeeper couldn't heal as fast as a *makol*, but they healed quicker and with far fewer long-term effects than a human. Within a few minutes, his head had stopped spinning and he could see dark and light patches through his watering eyes. "Good enough," he said, aware that Tomas had stayed nearby, though he wasn't sure whether that was because of a sense of duty or a desire to get another couple of digs in. "Did the others go after her?"

"We're on plan," the *winikin* confirmed. "If we're lucky, nothing will go wrong." But they both knew there was no guarantee of that. Sasha was outside the warded protection of Skywatch, and Iago had vowed to get her back before the solstice.

Michael had agreed with Strike and the others that in order to gain Sasha's cooperation they were going to have to prove that their power was real. It had been

Nate's idea to let her escape and then chase her down using magic that was very clearly not special effects. The royal council had voted that the potential reward was worth the risk. He just hoped to hell they weren't proven wrong.

Chaco Canyon

Sasha braced herself against the wrenching jolt as the dune buggy hit another of the huge, hummocky bumps that pockmarked the dirt track that seemed to lead from nowhere to nowhere. She didn't let up on the gas, though.

Heat flickered across her skin—the heat of the desert, the heat of panic. The road she was on had started at the mansion and training compound she'd glimpsed on the way out, and it had to lead somewhere. But she had no clue how long it would be before she hit pavement, or saw a sign or another human being. Worse, she had less than a quarter tank of gas, and knew she was burning through her fuel big-time by keeping the engine pegged as high as it would rev. But it wasn't like she'd had an option on the getaway-vehicle front.

The road curved and she followed it automatically, gripping the steering wheel two-handed to counteract the bumps. On either side of the track, the land fell away to bare dirt dotted with gnarled rocks, windswept into fluidly beautiful shapes. In the near distance, larger rock formations rose seemingly from nowhere, reaching for the sky. Once or twice, she caught glimpses of more regular shapes, doors and windows of ancient Puebloan structures. There was no other traffic, no sign of anyone else in the area. She was free, but far from safe.

Elation battled fear and confusion, and the three emotions called it a draw. Behind them came a twinge of guilt. Or more than a twinge. More like an avalanche, because Michael might be one of *them*, but she'd not only been intimate with him, she had *liked* him, liked the way he'd made her feel she was something special, like she was exactly where she was supposed to be.

"It was just good sex," she said, making herself concentrate on the road. "Don't make it into anything more than that." Squinting against the whip of wind and sunlight, she scanned the horizon, looking for signs of pursuit, of rescue. She saw nothing but sand, rock, and scrub brush, stretching to a clear blue sky. Off to one side of her, paralleling her track, a hawk flew above her, its shadow flattening out on the sand nearby.

It flattened further. Got bigger. Then huge.

Unease gathered in Sasha's gut, spiraling quickly to nerves and then beyond to outright fear. *Impossible*, her rational self argued when the hawk shape continued to grow as it drifted toward the shadow cast by the speeding dune buggy. *That's not real.*

She checked her mirrors, tried to see overhead, but was foiled by the vehicle's hardtop. Then the shadow disappeared.

Terrified, Sasha pressed harder on the gas, only to have the engine cough and choke. "No," she shouted. *"No, damn it!"*

A hawk's cry came from directly above her—a screech of triumph far too loud to come from a normal bird. A *whoosh* sounded overhead, and something slammed into the buggy, sending it shuddering sideways. Terrible thumps and scratches surrounded Sasha as she fought the ignition, nearly sobbing in fear as she tried to get the engine to turn over. She got it going again just as smooth, sharp claws, each at least two inches in diameter at their widest, curved down to take a grip on either side of the hardtop and latched on. Sasha stared at them, breath going dead in her lungs. Moments later, the buggy lurched and went airborne.

Screaming, she twisted the wheel and stomped on the gas and brake in rapid succession, but the vehicle was out of her control. It went airborne, skimming along the surface of the road, then off it, over the softer sand on the verge. Sasha yanked at her safety straps, popping them free as the vehicle dipped and lifted, dipped and lifted, in synchrony with the boom of huge, feathered wings. Then the creature that had captured her slowed, back-winging to hover over a patch of soft sand.

Then the claws let go. The buggy fell a few feet and *whump*ed into the sand.

Not stopping to think or plan, knowing only that she had to get the hell out of there *now*, Sasha flung herself out of the vehicle. She landed in soft sand, stumbled, and went down on her hands and knees, then scrambled up and ran for her life. She didn't look behind her, didn't dare, didn't want to see—

Air rushed and motion hissed overhead, a dark brown blur of feathers and scaly talons with wickedly curved claws. And then the thing landed facing her, beak agape, metal glinting off a gold chain around its neck. It was taller than a man, with a twenty-foot wingspan that it showed her now, flaring its wings wide as it screamed.

Sasha screamed too, and spun to bolt the other way.

A woman stood behind her, MAC-10 aimed with deadly intent.

Sasha froze.

The woman nodded. "Good call." Blond and blue-eyed, tall and stacked, she was wearing jeans, a teal shirt, and slip-on sneakers, and had a small knapsack slung over one shoulder. Black glyphs marked her inner right forearm, but even without them, Sasha recognized her as one of the strangers who'd looked in on her as she'd feigned sleep. Now, the woman lowered the autopistol, shrugged out of the knapsack, and tossed the bag past Sasha, humor glinting in her eyes. "Put your clothes on,

Nate. She looks freaked out enough without adding a naked man to the mix."

A hawk's cry answered, somehow sounding like a chuckle. Then heat rippled across the back of Sasha's neck and arms, and there was a strange noise, almost like a sigh. Then the sound of someone getting dressed.

Impossible, her rational self said, but it didn't sound quite so certain anymore. "Special effects," she whispered, more to herself than to the woman.

The blonde heard her, though, and something like sympathy flashed briefly in her killer blue eyes. "Feel free to keep telling yourself that if it helps. Doesn't make it true, though."

"The Nightkeepers are a myth," Sasha said numbly, repeating the words she'd said over and over to Ambrose, trying to get him to see his delusion for what it was. "It's a bunch of good stories, nothing more."

"Like Alexis said," a man's deep voice intoned, "just because you tell yourself something, that doesn't make it true." There was a thread of amusement in his tone, suggesting an inside joke.

Sasha spun, her hands coming up in automatic defense. But she didn't throw a punch; instead, she froze at the sight of a dark-haired man standing right where the hawk had been. He was tall, dark, and built, and in a way reminded her of Michael. Or maybe a cleaned-up version of Michael, more businessman than pirate. The man's black hair was short and slicked, his jaw clean-shaven, his eyes amber rather than forest green. He was wearing dark cargo pants, sneakers, and a black tee, but on him they somehow came across as dress-down Friday rather than at-home casual. He wore a medallion around his neck, a black cuff of polished stone on his right wrist, and had the knapsack slung over his shoulder. The hawk had disappeared. Or had it merely changed into something else?

Sasha shook her head, so freaking confused she
wanted to scream with it. Or rather, she wanted to be
confused, but was afraid she understood. And that was
what had the screams locking in the back of her throat,
trapping the fear inside her chest with the growing sense
of doom, of guilt. *Oh, Ambrose.*

"Special effects," she said, whispering it to herself as
though the words were a spell.

The blonde looked at the man; Sasha had to believe
they were a couple from the way her eyes warmed as
they touched on his, caught, and held. But then the
blonde's expression cooled as she glanced at Sasha. "I
guess she needs another demonstration," she said, as
though a giant bird that had morphed into a man wasn't
enough proof that either she'd been fully sucked into
the collective delusion . . . or it wasn't a delusion at all.

"No," Sasha said, panic sparking. "Wait—"

But the blonde ignored her and dug in the back
pocket of her jeans, coming up with a cell phone. She
flipped it open, hit a couple of buttons, and said, "Taxi
for three, please."

For a second, Sasha was relieved to think it would
be something as normal as an SUV coming for them.
Then a strange rattle split the air, and a man appeared.
Hovering. In midair, maybe a foot off the ground. He
had shoulder-length hair that was pulled back into a
stubby ponytail at the base of his neck, a close-clipped
jawline beard, and piercing blue eyes. He was wearing
ragged jeans, a concert tee, and leather sandals, and
the whole effect made him look like he should've been
hanging out over a backyard barbecue with a beer in
one hand, grill tongs in the other. Instead, he was hanging in midair.

A moment later, gravity took over and he dropped,
landing easily, as though he'd done it a thousand times
before. Sasha stared, transfixed by the trick, and the

glyph he wore high on his right biceps—the *hunab ku*. The mark of a Nightkeeper king.

"Impossible," she whispered. Except that this time it was the disbelief that rang false, because she could get only so far denying the evidence in front of her.

"Come on," the king said. "Let's go home."

"That place isn't my home," she whispered, pushing the words through a closed-tight throat. The training compound was either an elaborate insane asylum . . . or it was the embodiment of everything she'd spent her adult life trying to escape. The impossibility of it all, the incongruity of it, slapped at her, swamping her and holding her still as the blonde and the man-hawk took her hands and linked their fingers with the king's, connecting the four of them in an alternating male-female circle.

"It should have been," the king said in a voice that brooked no argument. "And if you'll let us, we'll do our best to make it feel like your home now."

Before she could react to that—if she could've even come up with an intelligent response—the air thickened with a hush of anticipation, a skirr of electricity. Then something rattled, the noise feeling as though it came from right behind her ears, her stomach lurched, and the world disappeared, blurring gray-green.

Sasha involuntarily clutched the strong hands on either side of her and drew breath to scream. Before the cry broke free, though, the gray-green disappeared and the world came back into existence around her. They were back at Skywatch, in the middle of the great room. They blinked in slightly above the ground. The others landed easily, flexing their knees to absorb the impact. Sasha, on the other hand, hit and staggered, fighting to lock her knees when they wanted to go rubbery.

The men reached out on either side of her, undoubtedly to keep her from hitting the deck, but she held up both hands, waving them off as panic spiked. "No. Please, just . . ." She trailed off when she realized the room was full, with twenty or so strangers packed into it, making it feel incredibly crowded when she'd spent so much time recently alone.

Her hands were shaking; her whole body was shaking as she reeled away from the small group, fetching up against a soft, high-backed chair. Her heart was lodged in her throat and she couldn't get her breath, couldn't get her balance. "I need—" She broke off, not sure what she needed until she locked eyes on the one familiar thing in the room: Michael.

He moved through the crowd, his reddened, pepper-burned eyes locked on her. "You okay?" he asked when he reached her, his voice pitched low, as though he sought privacy amidst the crowd. He looked more worried than pissed, which surprised her. She'd been expecting rage.

Maybe she was wrong thinking she'd seen something ugly inside him.

"I'm . . . I don't know." The stirred-up, overwrought part of her wanted her to grab onto him, hide her face in his wide, solid chest, and pretend none of this was happening. But her inner fighter, the one who'd given her the guts to escape, had her holding back. The end result was an interrupted physical hiccup in his direction, one that left her awkwardly close to him, with the two of them surrounded by a very interested audience. "Are you okay?" She lifted a hand, focusing on the details, because she thought she'd lose it if she looked at the big picture just then. "Your poor eyes. I'm sorry."

"I'll be fine. We heal fast." Taking her elbow in a firm grip that fell on the border between being supportive and making sure she didn't bolt again, he waved irritably for the crowd to scatter. "Give her room to breathe, will you?"

Everybody moved, but nobody left, which put Sasha

and Michael on one side of the open center of the sunken great room, with the others scattered on an assortment of leather sofas, chairs, and love seats, or standing up on the raised landing, near the kitchen. There was a definite generation gap between the two groups that had separated themselves out by location. The five men and four women on the lower level were younger, bigger, and drew her eyes automatically, all but oozing charisma, while the three men and two women who stood above them, watching over them, were a generation older, as well as being smaller, with a slightly darker cast to their skin, consistent with the Sumerian origins of the legendary servants of the magi. Or what she'd always thought were legends. *Nightkeepers and winikin*, she thought, a bubble of mild hysteria pressing at her throat, threatening to cut off her oxygen. *Gods*.

It took her a couple of seconds to realize she'd used the plural of her childhood rather than the singular God she'd consciously clung to as an adult. When she did, her heart started a long, slow descent to her toes. "Oh, shit. I'm in serious trouble here."

She hadn't realized she'd said that out loud until Michael's fingers tightened on her arm, and he said in an undertone, "Do me a favor and don't make decisions right now. Just suspend disbelief and listen for a bit, okay?"

"I think my disbelief is pretty much shot to shit at this point," she answered, feeling her stomach churn in reaction. "That hawk wasn't a special effect."

"Nope."

"Your king just teleported all of us back here." Her knees threatened to buckle.

"Yep."

"And what happened yesterday was—"

"Turn it off for a little bit, okay?" he interrupted, and she thought his grip tightened in warning before he let

her go and moved away. "Let me do some intros first."
He gestured to the hawk-man and his mate, who stood
hip-to-hip near a long sofa. "You've already met Nate
and Alexis. Next to them is our king, as you correctly
ID'd. Striking-Jaguar."

The tall, black-haired man with the vivid blue eyes
gave her a nod and turned both palms up in a concil-
iatory gesture. "Call me Strike, please. The old-school
names are tough to work with these days. I'm sorry if
the 'port scared you too badly. We wanted to make our
point."

"Consider it made," Sasha said, her voice gone thin
though she stood on her own, keeping herself as strong
as she could in the face of incontrovertible evidence she
didn't want to believe. The man was a teleport. He'd
instantaneously moved the four of them from the desert to the mansion. It should've been impossible, but
she couldn't deny what she'd just experienced. And
she couldn't pass this off as drugs or stress anymore. It
wasn't a dream, wasn't a hallucination. All this was really happening.

Her father might not have been entirely sane, but
he hadn't been nearly as crazy as she'd thought. *Oh,
Ambrose*, she thought on a burst of aching, awful guilt.
Learning the truth didn't make right what he'd done to
her. But it sure as hell explained why he'd done some of
it. In the end he'd been failed by the magic itself. If she
accepted this new reality, then, according to Michael's
story, the barrier had been closed off throughout her
childhood, explaining why his magic—and potentially
her own—had never worked.

"This is Leah," Strike continued, dropping a light
hand on the shoulder of the woman who stood beside
him, and his arresting eyes glinted with satisfied posses-
siveness as he elaborated, "My mate and queen."

The woman—an edgy-looking white-blonde who was

smaller than the others, but still looked fighting tough in the extreme—sent him an affectionate eye roll, then sketched a wave in Sasha's direction. "Leah Daniels, formerly of the Miami PD. I'm fully human, and got dropped into this a bit like you did. If you want to scream, or vent, or shoot something, whatever—I'm available."

That seemed to require a response, so Sasha wet her lips and managed a weak, "Thanks. I'll . . . Thanks."

"Patience and Brandt White-Eagle," Michael said, continuing the intros by indicating a porcelain-skinned woman, also blond, sitting on a love seat beside a square-featured man with dark brown hair. "Patience used to run a dojo. She can make herself invisible, and she and Brandt have a pair of four-year-old twins, Harry and Braden. They're off property, in hiding with their *winikin*, Hannah and Woody." Without giving Sasha time to process that, he moved on to the other sofa, where a tanned guy with bright, interested blue eyes and a stubby blond ponytail was sprawled akimbo. "That's Coyote-Seven, aka Sven. He used to be a marine treasure hunter. Now he moves things from point A to point B with his mind." There was something else in Michael's voice, but before Sasha could think to wonder, he'd turned to the last of the Nightkeepers gathered on the lower level. "And this is our archivist, Jade." The lovely brunette had arresting pale green eyes and seemed wrapped in a layer of serenity Sasha badly envied.

"I was a counselor in the outside world," Jade offered. "I know Rabbit did some work on you, but if you ever want someone to talk to, I'd be honored."

Sasha raised an eyebrow at Michael. "Rabbit?"

"He's one of two other magi who aren't here," he answered without really answering. "Strike's sister, Anna, is a Mayanist at UT Austin. Our resident juvie, Rabbit, is in school there with his human girlfriend, Myrinne, under Anna's supervision, gods help her." When she just stood there, waiting, he finished, "Rabbit's a mind-bender. He put some mental filters into your head to help you deal with what Iago did to you."

The admission didn't surprise her nearly as much as it probably should have. She touched her temple briefly, finding a fragment of memory she hadn't been aware of before. "He interrogated me."

"He tried to. You blocked him." Sending her a look that she interpreted as, *Later*, Michael moved on to the group near the kitchen, introducing the others, who were, as she had deduced earlier, the *winikin*. Jox—a wiry, gray-haired man with kind eyes and several small marks on his inner forearm—was the royal *winikin*, meaning that he looked after Strike and his sister, and had leadership rights over the other *winikin*. Hangdog Tomas was Michael's *winikin*, and didn't look particularly happy about the fact. The two women, Izzy and Shandi, looked after Alexis and Jade, respectively, and the remaining man, a stocky bulldog named Carlos, watched after both Nate and Sven.

The names, bloodlines, and marks piled up in Sasha's head, bringing to life the childhood stories she'd been raised on, making her head spin with wonder, fear, and terrible, dragging guilt. The very air seemed to press in on her, but she tried not to let herself sway, tried not to let the impending panic show. The people gathered in the big room weren't her enemies, she was coming to realize. But she sure as hell wasn't ready to deal with what they might be, what it might all mean.

"Do you want to sit down?" Michael asked.

She shook her head. "What I really want is to get out of here." She didn't think there was a rat's chance of that, though. The last time she'd set foot outside, she'd done her damnedest to escape.

So she was caught off guard when Strike nodded. "Yeah," he said. "I know how that feels."

Michael said, "I'll give her the grand tour." He and Strike traded a look that seemed to mean far more than had been said aloud, but then Michael simply touched her arm, urging her toward the sliders leading out to the pool deck. "Come on. I could use some air too."

She exhaled. "Thanks." Casting a look across the assembled group, she found a thin smile that felt more than a little panicky. "I'll . . . um. It was nice to meet you all."

Gulping air, she turned and headed for the sliders. She had to force herself not to run as she pushed them open, and it took a conscious effort for her not to weep as she stepped through and the world opened up around her, big and beautiful, and full of possibilities that hadn't been hers for so long. "Wait," Michael said. She turned back to find him holding out a pair of pink flip-flops. "Here."

Tears fogging her vision at the small, kind gesture, she nodded mutely, stuck the silly foam sandals on her feet, and headed across the pool deck and through a small gate. Once she was on the hard-packed earth, she struck out at random.

Michael paced her without comment, for which she was pathetically grateful. They walked in silence for a few minutes, past the out-of-place tree and the big metal building it shaded. When they reached the end of the steel span, Michael urged her along a narrow track. "This goes past the firing range and loops back through the ball court and the cottages."

"Fine," she said, though she didn't care where they went as long as she kept moving. Somewhere deep inside, she was afraid that if she stopped, everything would catch up with her, all the fears and confusion, and the terrible, awful guilt that had taken root and was building by the second, telling her that she'd owed Ambrose so much better than she'd given him.

At first she power-walked, trying to burn off the rest-less, edgy energy and outpace her own thoughts. But by the time they were halfway through the loop, the panic had started to drain. As it did, she became acutely aware of the big man who walked beside her, match-ing his strides to hers, giving her the room she'd wanted, yet providing a solid, reassuring presence she was far too tempted to rely on. Their bare arms brushed as they walked, and the contact brought a hum of energy and pleasure. Heat shimmered between them; she almost imagined she could see it . . . then wondered whether she could.

Although Ambrose had been downright nasty to the few boys she'd tried bringing home, he'd been forthright about Nightkeeper sex magic, treating it as a natural ex-tension of power. Now, as Sasha walked beside Michael and felt desire and temptation spin between them, those lessons broke through, perhaps explaining some of what had happened the night before. The words "power boost" and "gods-destined mates" filtered through to her con-scious mind, though she did her best to ignore them, knowing it would be far too easy to talk herself into something that would not only excuse the fact that she'd had sex with a complete stranger about ten min-utes after they met, but also suggested there might be the possibility—hell, a mandate—for a future between them.

Don't go there, she told herself. *Just . . . don't.*

Still, she was jarringly, achingly conscious of his body, of the way he walked, the way his muscles played one against the next. "I didn't believe you," she said, feeling like it needed to be said. "I thought you were part of some elaborate, overfunded role-playing game that had somehow turned real for the people inside it."

He was silent for a moment before he said, "In a way, it'd probably be better if that were the case. At least then we wouldn't be looking down the barrel of a three-year countdown with no fucking clue what we're supposed to be doing."

She didn't know what to say to that, didn't know how much of it she wanted to know, how much of it she could handle just then. So she walked. And in walking, she stared up at the sun. As she'd noticed before, it was a strange, orange-yellow color.

Michael followed her gaze. "It's like that all over the world. Nobody knows what's wrong with it," he said without her having to ask. "There are theories, of course— pollution, lack of solar flares, changes in magnetism—you name it, there's someone out there arguing in favor of it as a theory. But nobody knows for sure."

"Is it . . ." She trailed off, not yet ready to shift her paradigm so far as to ask about the pending end of the world. "Did Iago do something, or the *Banol Kax*?"

"We don't know. We need more information, and we're out of options." It was an indirect nudge, a subtle interrogation.

"I don't know where the library is," she said. But for the first time, the tightness in her chest and stomach came not from the hated question, but from a new understanding of the situation, and its urgency.

At the end of the age, the 2012 prophecy held that the magi would number in the hundreds, that they would form an army powered by the might of the gods. Instead, there were, what, ten or so of them? And if she was reading their forearm marks correctly, only Leah— a human—and Alexis wore the marks of the Godkeepers who were supposed to be the keys to the end-time war. In the absence of manpower, they must have gone looking for spell power, only to find their repository gone.

Ambrose, what did you do? Why? The why might not be a simple or logical answer, she knew. Even stipulating

that he hadn't been as crazy as she'd thought, he hadn't
been sane, either.

"How about you tell me what you do know," Michael
said, "and we'll go from there." Once again, she had to
wonder if she'd really seen that flash of darkness within
him. There was no sign of it now; that was certain.

"I hadn't been close to my father in more than eight
years before his death," she answered, "so when Iago
first asked me about a hidden library, it wasn't an effort
to play dumb, because honest to God—gods, whatever—
I'd never heard of it. When Ambrose was in one of his
manic phases, I couldn't get him to shut up about the
Nightkeeper crap." She paused, wincing. "No offense.
Anyway, if he'd known about a library back when I was
still living with him, he would've told me. I'm sure of
that much." More, he would've insisted that she become
involved. "At first I thought the library itself was just another part of the mythos."

"I take it something convinced you it was real?"

She nodded, exhaling a long, slow breath. "A few weeks
after Iago grabbed me from the temple, he brought me
one of my father's journals. It wasn't dated or signed—
they never were—but I recognized the writing style." Or
lack thereof. When Ambrose was on one of his Nightkeeper rants, his scholarly acumen devolved to repetitive
babbles and fragments of things that she now realized
might have been actual spells. "In it, he mentioned swimming through some sort of cave system toward where
he thought the library should be, and instead finding a
scroll. On it was a spell he couldn't use. He took it and
hid it. He didn't say where, not even a hint."

"You're sure?"

"I'm positive. The rest of the entries were a combination of lecture notes, complaints about his students,
and . . . well, ravings, really." She met his gaze squarely.
"Ambrose had mental problems. I don't know if it was

a true split personality. More likely, he was manic-depressive. He existed day to day on a decently functional balance, especially when he was at the university. But at home or in the rain forest, when something set him off, he was . . ." She trailed off, uncomfortable with the words that came immediately to mind, such as "impossible," "off his rocker," or Pim's favorite, "fucking nuts." Ambrose had been a demanding, sometimes cruel man. But apparently not all of what she'd dismissed as ravings actually had been. So in the end she went with: "Difficult."

Michael's expression had gone shuttered as she'd spoken of Ambrose's problems. Or maybe he was simply disappointed that she'd gotten so little from the journal. "Are you absolutely sure none of what he wrote, even the rantings, contained clues to where he hid this scroll?" he asked.

She shook her head. "I went over and over the journal, and told the red-robes all the places I could think for them to look." She shrugged, though the movement didn't even begin to encapsulate the months of pain and terror, which still existed within her, even though they'd been blunted by a mind-bender. "I'm sorry. That's all I've got." She wasn't just talking about information, either. As she'd been talking, the adrenaline that had sustained her to that point had drained suddenly, leaving her feeling wrung out, strung out. "Honestly? If I knew where to find the scroll or the library, or anything that would've helped lead the Xibalbans to either, I would've told them months ago,"

Michael's eyes flashed, his voice going rough. "Then he would've killed you months ago."

"There were days that would've been a relief."

She wasn't aware of him moving, had no warning before he was suddenly in her space, gripping her arms and leaning in, eyes blazing. "*Don't* say that. If you had

died, one of our best hopes for a connection to the sky
would've died with you."

Her first thought was relief that although he was furious, there was no sign of any darkness from him. Her
second was even simpler: It was desire, hot and hard,
revving her body from zero to want in an instant.

His eyes locked on hers and his breathing went ragged.
Heat crackled in the air around them, along with a faint
thread of music, as though someone had cranked up a
stereo out on the pool deck. But too much had changed
for her, too quickly. That morning she had wished she
could have gotten to know Michael in the "real" world.
Now that her real world had been replaced by his, in a
paradigm where their being lovers didn't seem so out of
the question, where did that leave them? Where did she
want it to leave them?

She didn't know, and she couldn't figure it out while
he was touching her. Suddenly stepping closer didn't
seem like such a smart idea. She eased away, tugging to
free her hands from his. When they didn't tug, she said
softly, "Michael, let go."

For a second something flashed in his eyes—a hard,
angry expression so at odds with the man that she froze
in shock. Then it disappeared and he jolted in place,
looking down and seeming surprised to see that he was
gripping her hands.

"Gods, I'm sorry," he said quickly. He released her and
stepped back with deliberate care, holding his hands out
in an *I'm unarmed* gesture. "I won't touch you again."

The air around them stilled; the music faded. Something seemed to shimmer on the air for a moment, as
though he'd just made a silent promise. "Not ever?" she
asked, trying to tell herself the sinking in her gut wasn't
disappointment.

He shifted and looked away. "We need to talk about
that."

"And by 'that' I take it you mean the sex."

He stopped in the dirt track and turned to face her squarely. He met her eyes, but his expression was closed now, giving away little of the man within. "What happened last night was amazing, but it went way farther than I'd intended. Too far. We need to back away from . . . from that aspect of things going forward. Skywatch is a pretty big place, but there's not much privacy. I think it'd be better if we agreed to keep what happened last night just between the two of us."

She stood a moment, staring at him until he broke eye contact and looked away. When he did, she let out her breath on a hiss, unable to believe that somehow, under the most abnormal circumstances she could've conceived of, she'd managed to find herself on the losing end of the *Let's not make this into a bigger deal than it really is* speech. "You're kidding me," she said hollowly. "You've got to be abso-fucking-lutely kidding me."

A muscle worked at the corner of his jaw, but all he said was, "I'm sorry."

She told herself it was better this way, that the hints of anger she'd caught from him were a warning sign suggesting maybe he wasn't the solid, likable guy he seemed. More, she told herself not to cling, not to let him think it had meant anything more to her than it apparently had to him. *He's just another hunter*, she told herself, for the first time realizing that she'd inadvertently fallen into another of her old patterns by opening herself to a man who valued the chase and capture more than the long term. In this case, granted, the chase had been finding her, the capture her rescue, but still, once he'd gotten her, he'd realized he didn't really want her all that much.

What was it about her that attracted the hunters? she wondered on a spurt of self-directed disgust. More, why did she continue to be attracted to *them*? Sure, those men tended to be smooth and dangerous, tended to know their lines and moves, which she supposed explained the attraction. But once they'd caught their prey, they moved on, leaving the tattered remains behind. She *knew* that, damn it. She shouldn't have been surprised—been there, done that more times than she wished to count, even with Saul, whom she'd picked precisely because he hadn't looked like a hunter on the surface.

But, logical or not, she *was* surprised to hear it from Michael, not the least because, even as they stood there faced off opposite each other, electricity hummed in the air between them. She knew damn well the attraction wasn't one-sided. That couldn't be her imagination.

Could it?

Summoning anger, more at herself than him, she said stiffly, "That's fine. Let's just forget it happened."

Michael was watching her steadily, and she had a feeling he saw more in her face than she meant him to. But he said only, "That might not be so easy."

She narrowed her eyes. "I've got a long-term contraceptive implant, if that's what you're worried about."

"No." His flinch suggested he hadn't thought that far. "I was more thinking about the others. They're probably going to try to throw us together. Not just because of what happened last night—which I edited for public consumption, by the way—but because I've been hung up on finding you for a while. Ever since I saw your picture, in fact."

"I'll try to take that as a compliment," she said, though it wasn't easy.

"And then there are your dreams," he continued. "You imagined me before you met me."

"I dreamed of a dark-haired, green-eyed man. That's a coincidence."

"There's no such thing as coincidence," he said, and it sounded like he was quoting something. "There's only the will of the gods." The words echoed in Ambrose's voice, as well. He'd been fond of saying things like that. Okay, technically he hadn't said things like that. He'd said those exact words, time and again.

Sasha exhaled, feeling stretched very thin. "So which is it? Are we cooling things off, or did the gods themselves intend for us to be a couple?" Because that had to be where he was going with this.

"We're cooling it," he grated between clenched teeth, the obvious tension in his body belying his apparent conviction.

"Fine. Whatever." She looked along the track, then back toward the compound. "You want to head back in? I don't think I'm in the mood to walk anymore." What she really meant was that she wasn't in the mood to walk with him.

"Sasha . . ." He trailed off. Lifted a shoulder. "I'm sorry. We shouldn't be putting all this on you at once."

She had a feeling that wasn't what he'd been about to say. When he didn't continue, she shrugged irritably, hating that she'd let him matter too quickly. "I'm figuring out that you guys don't have much of a choice, given the present circumstances. You know, 'When in the triad years' and all that."

Michael stopped dead, his face draining. "You know the prophecy?"

"From Ambrose. He said my mother taught it to him." She paused, unnerved by his expression. "Why?"

"Because we've been busting our asses trying to find the whole thing, hoping to hell it'll tell us what to expect next month, during the winter solstice." Michael paused. Swallowed. "Do you know the rest of it?"

Instinct told her to lie, but the terrible hope etched in his face forced the words. "'In the triad years, the daughter of the sky will defy love, conquer death, and find the lost son.' " She hesitated, then forced herself to go all the way. Taking a deep breath, she said, "My mother said I was the daughter of the sky. According to her, the triad prophecy is about me."

CHAPTER NINE

After that announcement, Sasha quickly found herself the center of an all-hands-on-deck meeting in the main room. Michael sat her on one end of the big sofa and stood behind her as though guarding her—or perhaps making sure she didn't bolt. Then he had her repeat what she'd told him about the library and, more important, the prophecy.

"'In the triad years, the daughter of the sky will defy love, conquer death, and find the lost son,'" Strike repeated thoughtfully. "And you say your mother taught it to Ambrose?"

Sasha nodded. "That's what he told me, anyway. She made him repeat it over and over again until he had it memorized, and then asked for his blood vow that he would teach it to me." The memory pinched with the sense that, in turning away from Ambrose, she'd failed the mother she'd never known. She'd thought she was doing the right thing by protecting herself from him. How was she supposed to know he'd been telling the truth?

"What else did he say about your mother?" Strike pressed.

"Nothing, really. He always called her 'Lady.' " A shiver collected within Sasha as she wondered whether the endearment had actually been something more. Like a title. "You guys don't have a . . . a nobility, I guess you'd call it?" The question felt like a huge leap. It was her first overt acknowledgment that her mother, too, might have come from Skywatch. Even that she herself might've been here as a baby. She'd been born two years before the massacre. It was possible.

"Only the queen, really," Jox said, "and her kids are accounted for." The royal *winikin* frowned. "We've been over and over the records, trying to figure out who Ambrose might have been. But back then, the Nightkeepers were pretty scattered. The royals, advisers, instructors, and other key magi lived here year-round, along with the students, but most of the others had homes off-site. Everybody gathered here on the cardinal days, but there might've been a thousand or more people total. So none of us necessarily knew everyone by sight. And what records we kept were badly damaged during the massacre."

She let out a long breath, disappointment quashing the quick stir of a hope she'd barely even acknowledged. "So we might never know who I am. Assuming I'm someone."

"You're someone," Michael said in a tone that brooked no argument. "That's not in question. What we need to figure out is what the prophecy means." He paused, then said reflectively, "We have a few key phrases to work with. First, we've got 'daughter of the sky,' but the sky means the gods, and all humans are the children of the gods, right? So that probably means there's a closer connection." He eyed Sasha, then glanced at Jox. "Were any of the gods supposed to have children on earth?"

"Not as such," he said.

Wanting to derail that hypothesis as quickly as possible, and preferring to avoid any discussion of how she might "defy love," especially in the aftermath of the oddest dumping she'd ever experienced, Sasha said quickly, "Ambrose thought the part about conquering death meant I was to be a healer. He tried to steer me toward med school." Understatement of the year. "He didn't know who the lost son might be."

Patience made a low sound of distress. "What if it's one of the twins?"

"I'll get a message to Woody and Hannah, telling them to watch their backs," Strike said, referring to the *winikin* who had taken Patience and Brandt's twin boys into hiding, for their own protection during such unsettled times. "But if I had to guess, I'd say the prophecy probably relates to someone old enough to make a difference when the zero date comes. Snake Mendez is a possibility—he's the last of the magi, and he'd qualify in the 'lost' category, at least in terms of his soul."

Michael leaned in and said in a low voice, "Mendez is the last of the known Nightkeepers. He's doing an extra six months for aggravated assault, which is a bonus. That way we know where he is, without actually having to figure out what the hell to do with him."

Jox said slowly, "We *thought* Mendez was the last of the magi, until we found out about Sasha. If she survived outside the formal system, maybe there's a chance others did, as well."

There was a moment of wistful silence before Strike said, "I don't think we can put too much hope in that. There's nobody else out there like Ambrose, at least that we're aware of."

Leah nodded. "I think we should focus on the things we can control." She looked at Sasha and said, "I know you've been over this a thousand times, but I'm sorry, I have to ask: Do you have any idea where to look for the scroll your father mentioned in his journal?"

Which was essentially a backhanded way of asking,

Where is the library? Sasha made a face. "I don't. I'm sorry." She paused. "I'm assuming you've searched Ambrose's temple?"

Now it was Strike's turn to grimace. "To the best of our ability. It's guarded by an entity of some sort that's able to both take corporeal form and mind-bend full magi. The thing nearly killed Anna, and it's gone after us a couple of other times when we were in there, searching. We didn't find anything." He paused. "We did recover your father's skull while we were in there. It seemed wrong to just leave it. The next time we're out there, we'll exhume the rest of him, and bring him back for a proper funeral."

Sasha's throat closed on a surge of emotion. "Thank you. He'd . . . Thank you."

The king nodded. Then his expression softened, making him suddenly seem far less imposing, far more human. "You look exhausted—you're probably ready to turn it off for a little while, huh?"

"Beyond ready," she said.

Strike nodded. "Jox will show you a couple of suites; choose one and crash. When you're ready to start moving in for real, tap him for decorating and clothing money out of the Nightkeeper Fund. Get what you want, no limits, though be advised that he starts wincing after a while."

"I . . ." Sasha trailed off, sort of guppy-gaping at how things had done yet another quick one-eighty on her. "What?"

"You're one of us," he said implacably. "If you're going to be hit with the responsibilities and dangers, you should get the perks, too."

Her mouth went dry. "You don't know for certain that I'm a Nightkeeper." And for the first time, she felt a tug of longing, a desire to belong to these people, to live the adventures she'd dreamed of as a child.

The king tapped the geometric *hunab ku* on his upper arm. "I have faith. The gods may not be able to reach us directly anymore, but the plans they helped put in place long ago are still coming to fruition. You're a child of prophecy, Sasha, just like I was." His expression reflected an odd mix of regret and satisfaction. "I would wish for you to have an easier time of it than I did, but I have a feeling it's one of those doctrine-of-balance things, that the greater the challenge, the greater the reward." He looked over at Leah, and his face lit with love.

"Thanks, I think," Sasha said, carefully not looking over her shoulder, where Michael still stood guard.

He growled, "Don't thank him yet. He hasn't gotten to the catch."

But Sasha shook her head. "I already know. I'm my father's daughter, after all." She paused. "You want me to undergo the bloodline ceremony," she said, and saw the confirmation in their faces. Oddly, she wasn't as upset as she would've thought. "When?"

"The full moon," Strike answered immediately. "On December second, thirteen days from now."

She nodded, because what else was there to say, really? She'd woken up a prisoner, and would go to sleep that night a potential mage. So much had changed, yet plenty was still the same. She was still at odds with her father, even though he was more than a year in the grave. And once again, she'd set her sights on a hunter, and imagined he felt more than he really did. At the thought, she glanced over at Michael and saw him deep in convo with the pretty brunette archivist, Jade, their heads bent together with intimate familiarity. When Strike cleared his throat, her gut-check was confirmed. *Well, hell*, she thought, *just what I don't need*. Best-case scenario, she was an ex. Worst-case, she was a current. And Sasha so couldn't deal with that level of drama right now, so she focused on Strike. Her king. And how weird was that?

"You said something about assigning me a real room?" she asked.

Strike watched as Michael and Jade disappeared down a hallway beside the kitchen. "What the—" He caught himself with a glance at Sasha. "Sorry. Right. Check with Jox. He's . . ." A quick check showed that the *winikin* was gone. "Try the greenhouse," Strike suggested. "He goes there when things get hectic."

"Then I think he and I will get along just fine," Sasha said, and dredged up a smile that felt only a little thin around the edges. She headed for the sliders leading out. And she damn well didn't let herself look back, down the hallway where Michael and Jade had gone.

Twenty minutes after the meeting broke up, almost exactly twenty hours after he'd lost himself in Sasha's body and let the Other escape, Michael stared at the reference Jade had dug up for him, and cursed hollowly.

He'd asked her to search for references to silver magic and rage. Because he'd claimed to have seen it coming from Iago, she hadn't thought twice about the request—aside from a grimace of disgust at his description of the corpse. Using the computerized database she and Lucius had put together, she'd searched all the scanned, translated pages they had on file, and had come up with a likely reference.

Michael stared at the computer screen, which was split between the scanned page and Lucius's translation. The reference had come from the journal of a missionary who'd worked in the Mayan highlands in the mid–sixteenth century. Lucius had done a very rough, vernacular translation from old-style Spanish: *The village elders speak of great white-gold magicians who used to live with their ancestors in the sky pyramids. These great magi fought against the devil himself, wielding a silver-gray magic called* muk. *But the* muk *held too much evil, it was too easily corrupted, and the magicians split it in half, taking the red-gold half for themselves and banishing the darkness to Xibalba.*

From there, the passage devolved to proselytizing, but in the margin was a red-lined note tagged with Lucius's user name. *Don't know what the hell this* muk *is—I've never heard of it before, and I can't cross-ref it anywhere, but I think we can assume Nightkeeper magic was the "good" side of it, hellmagic the bad. Not sure if the ancestral joined magic is even still around, though it's probably worth looking into, as it'd make a hell of a weapon . . . if we could find a way to control the stuff and keep it from turning to the dark side.*

"Weapon, yes," Michael muttered under his breath. "Control, maybe." Was that what was going on with him? Were the lies and rationalizations evidence that the silver magic was corrupting him? Or had he come precorrupted, thanks to the Other? And how the hell did a government-created alternate personality relate to the ancestral magic that preceded Nightkeeper power? More, how was Sasha involved with the Other and the magic? Iago had implied that she was important to his transformation, and that his transformed self would be of use to the Xibalbans, and that fit with the way she broke through his defenses without trying. But at the same time, there had been moments when touching her, being with her, had helped level him off, as though she strengthened not only the monster inside him, but the man. And it wasn't like he could tell her any of what was going on—he'd tried earlier, and had vapor locked on the words. As far as she knew, he was . . . hell, he didn't know what she thought he was at this point. All he knew was that he couldn't risk it, couldn't risk *her.* Not until he knew what he was, and why Iago wanted him.

"Shit," he muttered. "We need more info, as usual."

"Was that what you were looking for?" asked Jade from her desk in the corner.

"Yeah, thanks," he answered, but he doubted she heard him. She hadn't looked up from what she was doing, and her tone had suggested she was mostly asking to be polite, and to indicate that she could make herself available if he needed help. All of which was quintessential Jade—always supportive, always *there*. Even after the talent ceremony, when he'd been too screwed up to continue as her lover, she'd tried to help him.

I'm sorry we couldn't bring Lucius back with us, he wanted to say. He didn't, though, because she'd already made it clear she didn't want to talk about it. She preferred to deal with her problems alone, in silence. He could relate, though in his case it wasn't necessarily a preference. *Fuck it*, he thought. He was so damn tired of being alone in a house full of people.

Then, knowing that swearing about it wasn't going to get the job done, he printed the page and closed the file. After a quick glance to make sure that she'd gone back to her work, he tapped a few keys, got into the code, and, with a twinge of guilt that was weaker than it should have been, he deleted the file, scrubbed it from the directory, and replaced the citation with a dupe of another page he pulled at random.

As he headed out of the archive, sketching a wave, he sought the back of his brain, expecting to find one of the sluiceways cracked, letting through the dishonesty he associated with the Other.

It was shut. That move had come entirely from him.

Shit. Michael stalled in the hallway, not liking that realization one bit. He didn't want to be the liar, didn't want to be corrupted. But at the same time he couldn't stop thinking of what Lucius had written. *It'd be a hell of a weapon.* And it would. It had killed the red-robe but spared Sasha, who'd been slung over the man's shoulder. More, the power had felt bottomless. What if, rather than transforming to the monster within, which was what he suspected Iago had meant, he became a man capable of wielding the monster's power on behalf of the Nightkeepers?

Or was that nothing more than rationalization?

Frustration kicked in his veins, bringing a wash of anger that warned he wasn't quite as in control as he'd thought. He'd been planning to head for his suite, but detoured for the sliders instead, knowing it was time to burn off some steam. Over the months, he'd learned that it wasn't enough to be mentally strong. Sometimes he just had to go kick the shit out of something.

A too-tempting target presented itself when Tomas appeared in the doorway leading to the main mansion, his expression thunderous.

Michael held up a hand. "I'm really not—"

"I don't really give a shit if you're in the mood or not, Romeo." The *winikin* closed on him, five foot six of pissed-off moral compass intent on beating some sense into his charge's head. "You need to stop fucking around here."

Right, Michael thought, *because your telling me what to do has worked so well in the past.* "I'm doing the best I know how to do," he said finally. "And that's all I'm going to say about it." Except he knew that wouldn't be enough for the *winikin*. How many times had they gone around in some form or another of this argument?

The *winikin* just shook his head in disgust. "Your mother and father would be ashamed."

Fuck. Anger slapped through Michael, rage and shame mingled into a nasty, vicious brew as Tomas went right for the jugular. His fingers twitched for the knife he wore strapped to his ankle, but he left it sheathed. The blade had been his father's, one of the few pieces he had that connected him to his bloodline. Michael wasn't as into the whole "what has happened before will hap-

pen again" as some of the others were, and didn't base
his life on the history and predilections of his bloodline
as much as he might, but he'd done his homework, and
knew something of his parents. Jeraden and Silva Stone
had been loyal soldiers, strong magi. And in a bloodline
that had a reputation for producing more than its share
of unmated bachelors, depressives, and suicides, they
had found the strong, binding love that had earned them
the matching *jun tan* forearm marks of a love match, a
mated pair. They had lived together, loved together,
borne a son together. And they had died together in service to their king. Theirs was an honorable legacy. His
fuckups were his own.

"Leave them out of this," he said tightly.

"Get your head out of your ass, boy," Tomas bitched.
"You and Jade weren't a match. Fine. But are you going
to look me in the eye and tell me that the gods themselves didn't put Sasha in your path?"

"The intersection's gone. The gods can't reach us
anymore."

"That's not an answer."

"It's the only one you're getting." The only one he
could give.

The *winikin* glared up at him. "When did you get to
be such a prick?"

Takes one to know one, Michael would've said on another day, during another fight, and they would've been
off down another familiar loop. But the anger was too
close to the surface now, the violence too tempting, the
Other too near. "Do us both a favor and leave it. I don't
want to hurt you."

The *winikin*'s eyes went wide and he fell back a step.
"Michael? Are you okay?"

Michael didn't have an answer for him, so he did the
only thing he knew how to do these days to keep himself
from doing something terrible: He walked away.

Pushing past the *winikin*, he headed down the hallway toward the main mansion, ridden hard by jagged teeth of anger, and the tight rein he held on it. When Tomas called his name, he almost didn't turn back. But although the affection had long ago bled from their relationship, their history remained. Michael stopped and looked at his *winikin*. "Yeah?"

Bleakness edged the other man's eyes. "I'm asking you, as a personal favor, to go talk to Sasha. You didn't see the look on her face when you took off with Jade."

Michael stifled a curse; he hadn't even thought that one through. "It wasn't like that."

"Don't tell me. Tell her."

For a change, he couldn't argue with his *winikin*. "Where is she?"

"I think she was headed outside to find Jox. So probably the garden or the greenhouse."

Michael nodded. "Okay. That much I can do."

But as he cut through the deserted great room and headed outside, frustrated excitement kindled at the thought of seeing her again. His skin heated as his mind filled with the memory of losing himself inside her. He wanted to taste her vitality again, wanted her chocolate brown eyes laughing up at him, challenging him. He wanted to know she was okay after everything that had happened, wanted to tell her it would get better, even if that was a lie.

But he couldn't go to her, didn't dare. The blood ward surrounding Skywatch might protect them from enemy magic coming from outside the shield, but it didn't quell magic coming from within, dark or otherwise. And right now, with his desire gone silver around the edges and the killing rage held back by only a thin grip on sanity, he didn't know if he could, either.

Feeling the darkness rise up within, he turned away from the path leading to the greenhouse and headed off in the other direction instead, toward the ball court, out of sight of the others. He knew only one sure way to regain his center, his control.

He would fight himself. And, gods willing, he would win.

Jox's garden was a wide, rectangular swath of rich dark earth that contrasted sharply with the arid surroundings, making Sasha suspect that the humus had been trucked in. Several different varieties of maize grew in graceful rows along one side, nearly ready for harvest, while squash, pumpkins, and other late-season vegetables grew on the other side. Above and around the crops, PVC pipes showed where an irrigation system made up for what the skies didn't provide in the way of moisture, and reflective screens and frost-retarding drapes were stacked against a nearby shed. The setup was expensive and extravagant, but she was pitifully grateful for the splurge as she crouched down, pressing her palms to the moist, yielding surface. She closed her eyes for a moment, feeling a layer of tension ebb.

Even if she hadn't needed to speak with Jox, she would've visited the greenhouse sooner rather than later, because her love of green plants was second only to her love of cooking; truly, the two were intertwined. Although she'd never had the space to grow more than a window-box garden, the feel of soil against her palms had always soothed her, centered her. And she was sorely in need of peace just then.

Beside the garden loomed a geodesic greenhouse formed of a central dome and several radiating spokes. The complicated setup—again, top-of-the-line, like everything she'd seen within Skywatch so far—was geared to use solar energy for heating, cooling, and regulating humidity. She was impressed even before she slipped through the door. Then she got her first look at the plants being grown inside, and was blown away.

She stopped just inside the door. "Wow."

Instead of a traditional central aisle and square planting beds or tables leading off it, a pathway of textured cement wound through the space, twisting among potting tables and beds full of knee-high flowering plants, then disappearing into a grove of sour oranges and thin-skinned key limes. The air inside was moist and redolent with the fragrances of fruits and flowers, the earthy smell of compost, the sharp tang of granular fertilizer. Music emerged from speakers set high around the space, something with a country twang, turned to a low murmur.

She inhaled deeply, drawing in the fragrances of a hundred different flowers and the perfect smell of moist earth. Out of the corner of her eye, she caught a flutter of movement as a butterfly wafted on an unseen air current, lifting to alight on the fine sprinkler mesh overhead.

Jox was just inside, perched on a metal stool pulled up to one of the potting benches, where he was transplanting small, delicate shoots from peat pots to five-inch rounds. He glanced over at her, his eyes kind. "I had a feeling you'd find your way here."

"Strike said you could hook me up with a room that has an actual bed."

"And you have questions, and need a moment of peace, away from the others."

A layer of tension fell away, and she exhaled. "Oh, holy shit. Do I ever."

Jox nudged another of the metal stools with a foot. "Have a seat." He pushed one of the flats of peat pots toward her, along with some larger pots. "Transplant."

She climbed onto the stool, took a peat pot and turned it in her fingers. It was very real, very mundane. "I don't know where to start," she said, meaning the questions, not the potting.

"It'll come to you. But work while you talk."

She started transferring the seedlings to their new homes, and was soothed almost immediately by the rhythm, the *winikin*'s undemanding silence, and the flicker of butterfly wings here and there. "Tell me about Michael," she said finally. It probably shouldn't have been the topic foremost on her mind, but there it was. She'd dreamed of him, had sex with him, been dumped by him, all in the space of twenty-four hours. An entire relationship done on fast-forward.

The *winikin* hesitated, as though weighing his response. "If you had asked me about him a year ago, I would've said he was a classic example of a male of the stone bloodline. They generally come in two flavors: Most of them are handsome and charming, but not stayers—the type who wind up bachelor uncles rather than mated fathers. They're good in a fight, but don't go beyond what's asked of them. In the second category are the heavyweights, like his parents. They fight fiercely, love fiercely, protect fiercely—and often burn out early, like shooting stars."

"I take it Michael's a type A Stone?"

"Up until this past spring, I would've put him firmly in the first category. Slick and charming but . . . a little insubstantial. He was here, but he wasn't always present, if you know what I mean. Particularly after his talent ceremony, it seemed like he was always locked away in his room, on his phone, doing some sort of business. He was edgy, jittery, always looking over his shoulder. If anything, I'd say that back then he was waiting for something."

"What?"

"Not sure. Whatever it was, I think he found it, or dealt with it, or whatever, right after the spring solstice.

It wasn't an overnight change, but looking back, it was pretty abrupt. Over the space of maybe a month, he went from business casual and vodka tonics to muscle shirts and beer. Not that there's anything wrong with nice clothes and expensive drinks, but they never quite seemed to suit him, like they were an act. Anyway, after that, the personal phone disappeared, and he started sitting in on council meetings and working like hell on his magic."

"What happened in the spring?"

Jox lifted a shoulder. "A whole bunch of things: Nate and Alexis became mates, Lucius went *makol* and disappeared, Rabbit escaped from Iago and came back with Myrinne, the magi fought the *Banol Kax* at the hellmouth, Iago destroyed the intersection. . . . I'm not sure which of those things, if any, triggered the changes." The *winikin* paused. "Please understand that I wouldn't be telling you this if I didn't consider you an interested party."

She smiled with little humor. "Let's say I'm trying very hard not to be interested, because he's made it clear he's not."

"Bullshit. He nearly tore the place apart last night when he couldn't wake you up, and he got into it with the king this morning over making sure everybody gives you some room to find your balance here. And the way he stood over you in the great room, glaring at the world? That's not the behavior of an uninterested man."

She tried not to let it matter, but warmth curled around her weak, needy heart. "Fine. He doesn't *want* to be interested, which in my experience is worse than disinterest, and drags on a lot longer." She fell silent, concentrated on the feel of potting soil between her fingers. She told herself not to ask, but asked anyway. "What's the deal with him and Jade?" Might as well get it out there.

This time there was no hesitation, as though the *winikin* had known it was coming. "They were lovers for a couple of months right after the barrier reactivated. It was during the gap between their bloodline and talent ceremonies, when their hormones were raging. It ended after the talent ceremony, and they've been friendly since."

The *winikin* didn't say how friendly, and Sasha didn't ask. And although she could've guessed they had been lovers, the sex-magic parallel brought a wince. He'd become Jade's lover to defuse the pretalent hornies. He'd become Sasha's lover to fuel the chameleon shield. Although she wanted to think it had been more than that, his actions since said otherwise.

Jox glanced at her workstation. "You potting or plotzing?"

"A little of both." She got back to work, but stayed pensive. The more she learned about the situation, the more she realized how little she actually knew. "If I could go back to when Ambrose was alive, and talk to him about what's going on now . . ." She stopped, shook her head. "You know what? That's a lie. I don't want him back." It felt good to say that, she realized. She didn't have to forgive everything just because he'd been telling the truth about the Nightkeepers.

Jox shoved another flat across the table to her, a different kind of seedling. "Keep transplanting. It helps."

Their eyes met over the furry, optimistic greens. She saw sadness in his eyes, but didn't think he'd thank her for bringing it up. So instead, she said, "You said you thought I'd come here. Why?"

"Because growing and cooking are inextricably intertwined," he said. "Along with healing."

"I'm no healer." But she passed a hand over the soft leaves, drawn to them. "What are they?"

"Cacao."

Her lips curved. "Chocolate. My favorite."

"I had a feeling."

Letting that one pass, she commented, "You're ambitious. I didn't think cacao grew well in greenhouses, or at all in areas like this."

"Neither do ceiba trees like the one out in the courtyard." Jox returned his attention to the other seedlings, which had the round, waxy leaves of a member of the squash family. "The cacao can be your project, if you like."

Suddenly, she couldn't think of anything better. "I'd like that. Thanks." And as she started with the seedlings, working side by side with Jox in a comfortable silence, she realized that she'd found her little bit of peace, after all.

CHAPTER TEN

November 22
Lunar apogee; ten days until the full moon
Three years and twenty-nine days until the zero date
University of Texas, Austin campus

Blood sparking with magic despite the mental filters that prevented him from using his powers outside of Skywatch, Rabbit stalked across campus, pissed that Anna wanted him and Myrinne to stay at her place in Austin, with her dull-assed human husband, for the whole Thanksgiving break. Worse, when he'd challenged her on it, Strike had made it a royal order. A royal pain in the ass was what it was.

Rabbit wanted to be back at Skywatch, where he could use the magic that was as much a part of him as his own blood and bones. He was trying to make good on his screwups . . . but how the fuck was he supposed to figure out how to call up a new three-question *nahwal* from his godsdamned dorm room?

The three-question *nahwal* was—or had been—an oracle bound to answer three questions per Nightkeeper lifetime. He hadn't meant to kill it; he'd wanted only to ask his questions, but the thing had attacked him and it'd come down to kill or be killed, leaving the Nightkeepers in dire need of an oracle of some sort. The answer was obvious—to him, anyway. He had to get his ass back into the barrier and see about summoning a new *nahwal*. Except Strike wouldn't let him until he had the right spell. To find the spell, they needed the library. To find the library, they needed the three-question *nahwal*.

Was he the only one who saw the disconnect here?

His mood must've shown in his face, because he saw a guy from his calc class start to lift a hand in greeting, then abort the motion and get real interested in the contents of his knapsack. Rabbit didn't give a crap, though. Calculus was small stuff. Hell, *college* was small stuff.

Granted, it wasn't nearly as bad as high school had been—at least he wasn't still a ninety-pound weakling who regularly got his shit knocked loose. But he was frustrated by the day-to-day grind of classes when he could be—should be—doing much more important things. The Nightkeepers needed all the power they could get. So why in the hell was he stuck in Austin? Okay, so it'd been blatantly obvious that part of the whole "let's send Rabbit and Myrinne off to college" thing had been intended to split them up by getting them out of Skywatch, where they'd been flat-out living together in his old man's cottage out behind the main mansion. But that hadn't worked, had it? They were still a couple. And if there was a small frisson of doubt deep within him on that last point, he was sure as hell going to ignore it, because when Myrinne had come to live with him, he'd made three promises: He'd promised her he'd protect her from the other Nightkeepers, some of whom were dubious about having her around. He'd promised her that he'd be the only one who ever worked magic on her. And he'd promised himself, on his own blood, to do whatever it took to keep her with him. No matter what.

He headed straight for her door and knocked softly. When Myrinne's voice called, "Go away, I gave at the office," he grinned and let himself in.

Unlike his room across the hall, which was haphazardly organized at best, Myrinne's space was neat and fresh. Although Rabbit had urged her to spend what she wanted out of the Nightkeeper Fund—gods knew there was plenty in there—she was acutely conscious of her status as, in her words, a charity case of the magi. So she'd bought only a simple, neutral rug and bedclothes a few shades deeper, then accented the space with the things she and Rabbit had recovered from the New Orleans tea shop where she'd spent most of her life. The end result was an eclectic mix of voodoo kitsch and halfway decent crystals that somehow suited her perfectly.

Myrinne herself stood at her desk, bent over her laptop, banging off a quick note or IM or something, which gave him an excellent perspective on her ass. She glanced back and grinned at him, her straight dark hair hanging off to one side, her dark brown eyes gleaming with mischief. "Hey. Where've you been?"

Something loosened in his chest at the warmth in her tone and the sparkle in her eyes. Those hints, coupled with the rear view he suspected wasn't an accident, told him she was in one of her good moods, and gave him an idea of how they could spend the next couple of hours. She was wearing low-riding jeans and a formfitting cropped sweatshirt that had ridden up to show off the curve of her waist. He couldn't see the tattoo that traced around her navel, but knowing it was there, knowing that—gods willing—he'd be getting up close and personal with it soon, was a huge turn-on.

Given that her mood had been seriously up-and-down over the past few days, he was grateful as hell to find her on an upswing, especially with the buzz of frustration humming in his veins, looking for an outlet.

"I was talking to Anna," he said in answer to her question. "It's a no-go on getting back to Skywatch over Thanksgiving break." He glossed over his own frustration because it morphed into another kind of heat as he moved up behind her, cupped her strong, slim waist, and slid his hands along her smooth skin.

There were still times he halfway expected her to haul off and smack him for touching the goods. Chicks like Myrinne had never been interested in him before, and despite his growth spurts and the added confidence the magic had given him, he still sometimes had trouble believing she was actually with him. Actually wanted him.

She turned, smiling, slid her arms around his neck, and rose up on her tiptoes to press her lips to his. Rabbit leaned into the kiss. Despite the filters, power flowed through him, hot and hard, and he was instantly ready for battle, for sex, for anything and everything.

"Did you tell her why you wanted to go back?" Myrinne whispered against his mouth, as her hands slid up beneath his sweatshirt and his body temp headed for nuclear-meltdown territory.

"Huh?" It took him a moment to process the question, struggling to put the words together when he would've much rather been concentrating on the feel of her fingers on his belt, the taste of her mouth and throat, the softness of her breasts in his hands. "Um. No, I didn't. She'd just tell me not to worry about it, that they're working on it."

"What are you going to do next?" she asked in between kisses.

"Dunno," he said, trying to get her bra undone with some semblance of grace.

"I've been doing some research, and I think there might be something we could do from here."

The last thing he wanted to discuss was research.

"Sure, I'm game. As long as it's not Nightkeeper magic."
The filters allowed him to talk about it when he was
alone with her, though when he was alone with her, he
wasn't usually thinking about magic. At least not of the
blood-sacrifice variety.

"It's not Nightkeeper magic," she assured him.

"Okay. Fine." *Whatever. Busy here*.

"Good." Her eyes went wicked and she started walking him in the direction of her bed, which was made up
in mounds of fluffy pillows and other soft, girlie things,
and scented with patchouli and vanilla. "Pencil me in for
the night of the full moon."

"You can have all the nights you want," he said, not
really giving a crap what he was saying at that point,
as long as they were headed for the bed. When they
got there, he fell back and pulled her with him so they
dropped to the mattress together, laughing and wres-
tling with clothing.

It was the last coherent thing either of them said for
a long, long time.

Skywatch

The days flew and Sasha's life accelerated to a blur,
enough so that she could almost avoid thinking about
the approaching bloodline ceremony. In fact, whether
by virtue of the mental filters or simple denial, she found
herself living almost entirely in the moment, taking in
the information pertinent to her new life without really
putting it into the structure of her old existence.

Little by little, she settled in. She tapped the Nightkeeper Fund and ordered some clothes, going with comfortable, functional pieces that were more feminine than
the type she'd typically worn before. She didn't know if it
was backlash from her captivity or being around the in-
nately sexual Nightkeepers, but she was far more aware

of her body than she'd been in the outside world, more conscious of the way she looked, the feel of her clothing on her skin. She stopped short of staring at herself in the bathroom mirror, but was conscious that there were changes there, as well. Her hair had grown out from its short kitchen cut, and the curls tended toward the unruly side, but aside from blunting the ends, she left it alone, deciding she liked its unpredictability. Although her weight was the same as before, her face was thinner now, her arms and legs more muscular, her hips and breasts rounder. She suspected the changes were magicwrought, but didn't look too closely at the underlying reasons; she could only deal with so much Nightkeeper reality at any given time.

Still, she nested, adding some personal touches to the suite she'd chosen because of the big bow window that stretched nearly the length of the kitchen nook, offering a shallow shelf where she could grow herbs. She outfitted the nook with what she considered the essentials in both cookware and ingredients. And there, when she had a free moment or two, she filled herself once again with the love of her art.

She made *recados*, the flavor pastes that formed the basis of most Mayan dishes, reminding her that no matter how hard she'd tried to reject Ambrose's teachings, she'd constantly gravitated back toward the villagewrought flavors of her childhood. She char-grilled maize, not realizing until later that she'd automatically pricked her finger with a paring knife and let a few drops of her own blood drip onto the food, an old habit she'd picked up after a knife slip and a drop of blood had felt oddly right, yielding a meal that had far outstripped her usual efforts. She'd fought to break the habit, and managed to keep it in check when working commercially, but it occasionally crept back into her personal cooking. Now she let herself follow the dictates of her soul, recogniz-

ing the autosacrifice as a nod to the gods she was trying
to let herself believe in, an acknowledgment of the inex-
tricable link between maize and life itself.

It had been her favorite of her father's stories, in
fact: how the gods had made mankind from maize. According to the legend, when the creator gods Tepeu and
Kulkulkan first raised the earth and sacred mountains
from the water, they populated the lands with animals,
but quickly became dissatisfied with the animals because
they were unable to speak or worship. Determined to
create beings that could raise their voices in praise of
the gods, Tepeu and Kulkulkan then tried to build men
and women out of mud, but the mud people were soft
and weak, and quickly fell apart. The creators next made
men from wood and women from rushes, but although
these people held together okay, they didn't understand
the world around them. Frustrated, the gods sent them to
live in the rain forest canopy as monkeys. Finally, Tepeu
and Kulkulkan summoned maize, ground it into powder,
mixed it with their own blood to form dough, and used
the dough to shape the first humans. That was why the
gods thereafter required sacrifices of blood and maize.

As the days passed, Sasha relearned that story, along
with so many others, during daily lessons with the
winikin. These were followed by afternoon weaponry
and hand-to-hand drills, along with basic magic classes.
She wouldn't get her true access to the power until after
her bloodline and talent ceremonies, but she practiced
the spells so she'd be ready for whatever came next.
After dinner she often sat down with Jade, looking for
holes in her knowledge, and finding a couple of places
where Ambrose's stories filled in gaps. The more they
compared notes, the more it seemed likely that Ambrose had left Skywatch prior to the Solstice Massacre.
Which begged the question of why he'd left, who Sasha's

mother had been . . . and whether she'd been magebred. Lots of questions. No real answers.

During those long talks, Sasha and Jade formed a budding friendship despite—or perhaps because of—having Michael in common.

Sasha saw very little of him in the days leading up to her bloodline ceremony . . . at least in the flesh. To her dismay, she still dreamed of him most nights, reliving their lovemaking in the sacred chamber. Her mind replayed each touch and sigh, and the way they'd come together without pretense, honest in their desire for each other. Magic or no magic, they had connected, or so she believed in the deep of night. In the mornings, when she awakened alone and aching, she found that she couldn't even curse him for how it had ended. She could only wonder *why* it had ended. Granted, he was a free man; he had the right to say "no thanks." But on the rare occasions when she did see him, he looked haggard, and he stared at her with a dark, hungry expression that he tried to conceal when he caught her staring.

More, he *did* things for her.

The first incident was her second day at Skywatch, when the king himself had broken the news that Iago had torched her apartment soon after he'd captured her, presumably to confuse the Nightkeepers' search for her. Sasha's initial shock had turned to worry when she realized that Ada wasn't among the listed survivors. But Strike told her that Michael was already on it. Carter's report on Sasha had mentioned her friendship with the widow, and Michael had taken it from there.

He wouldn't talk to her, apparently, but he'd take the time to find out what had happened to a firefighter's widow in her seventies, simply because she'd been Sasha's friend. Which didn't make any sense.

The next day, Nate—Skywatch's resident techno

geek—had shown up at her suite and handed her his latest castoff laptop, which, although a hand-me-down, still had way more bells and whistles than anything she would've bought for herself. Then he'd taken a few hours, taught her how to use the toys, and brought her up to speed on the latest Web sites and current events. He'd accepted her thanks but made sure she knew it'd been Michael's idea, Michael's request.

That had left her fuming. He'd dumped her. So why couldn't he leave her alone?

But despite her annoyance, she kept the computer. The Net access helped her feel reconnected to the larger world without leaving the compound. The first few days, she had no desire to leave. Then, just as she was starting to get itchy to explore, Sven returned from a short assignment—bloody, battered, and drawn—to report that a couple of red-robes had jumped him just outside the gates of Skywatch. Although a thorough search of the area had turned up nothing, the magi had to assume the Xibalbans were watching the compound, which meant that Sasha wound up under house arrest, at least until her bloodline ceremony.

It wasn't the hardship it might have been. She studied. She cooked. And when she needed some peace, she went to the greenhouse, where Jox and Tomas made her welcome, giving her time and company when she wanted it, space when she needed it. And let her know that they would have wanted her there, even if Michael hadn't asked them to make sure she felt at home.

In fact, she heard so many variations on the theme of "He told me, 'Make her feel welcome, damn it!'" that she could almost hear the words in his too-familiar rasp. She was tempted to track him down and demand an explanation, but didn't because he was so obviously avoiding her. And because she was determined not to chase affection. Never again. So instead she studied the magic that might soon be hers and tried to ignore the fact that it felt like Michael was courting her thirdhand while at the same time pushing her away.

That is, until one morning a few days before the full moon when she opened the door to her suite and found three file-size cardboard boxes sitting in the hallway just outside her door. Her name was written above the address for the postal drop-ship location the Nightkeepers used to maintain a layer of anonymity, and the boxes were plastered with stickers that read, FRAGILE, RUSH DELIVERY, and THIS END UP. Assuming the packages contained the new mixer and bowls she'd ordered online, she lugged them into her suite and attacked the first one, punching through the layers of tape with a kitchen knife.

Instead of commercial packing, she found wadded newspaper within. A white envelope lay on top, her name written across the front in spidery handwriting.

Familiar spidery handwriting.

"Ada?" Sasha whispered, nearly dropping to her knees when her legs went wobbly.

She reached for the envelope with trembling fingers, then hesitated, half afraid the note and boxes would disappear, proving to be a figment, a wish. Instead, the envelope crinkled beneath her touch. If this were a posthumous delivery, she had to assume Michael would have been there to break the news. Or, more likely, sent an emissary. But this . . . this had to mean her friend was alive, that she'd survived the fire.

"Thank you, gods," she whispered.

She opened the envelope and pulled out the single sheet of paper, then blinked back tears at the sight of the familiar stationary, which was watermarked at the top with Ada's name intertwined with that of her husband, Charlie, who'd been gone nearly a decade but lived in her heart. Or so she'd always claimed. *Dear Sasha*, the letter read in Ada's nearly illegible writing.

*I can't begin to tell you how happy I am to know
that you're okay. I'd be terribly mad at you, but
your Michael explained about the robbery and wit-
ness protection, so I know you couldn't have clued
me in before the trial, and you can't contact me
yourself now.*

Sasha's mind stuttered a little, not just on the fabricated WitSec protection, which she supposed was as
good a story as any to cover her disappearance, but on
the words "your Michael." She reread them a few times,
then made herself move on.

The letter continued:

*When I told him that I'd moved out after you disap-
peared, but before the fire, your friend—and dare I
hope he's more to you?—asked me if I'd brought
anything of yours with me, and of course I had. You
asked me to look after things, and I did, even when
they said you weren't coming back.*

*So here are the survivors, dearest heart, packaged
with my fondest wish that your new life is a won-
derful one, and you find someone special to share
it with—someone who'll challenge you, make you
crazy, make you bigger than you'd be on your own.
Someone like my Charlie was to me. That is what I
wish for you, dear friend. But having seen your Michael, I wonder if you haven't already found him?*

It was signed, *All my love, Ada*, though Sasha almost
couldn't read the signature through the blur of tears.

In a flash, she was back in Ada's pretty kitchen, fuss-
ing with a batch of spicy shrimp while her friend "fiddled
around," as she called it, padded violin tucked beneath
her chin, rosined bow sliding smoothly as she segued
from Beethoven to Bach, from Mozart to others Sasha

couldn't name, some that she suspected were Ada's own creations. "Find yourself a good man," the widow had often said, her eyes crinkling at the corners. "Someone who'll love you like my Charlie loved me." After Saul, when Sasha had suffered through a series of bad first dates, and a few worse second ones, she'd decided Ada had gotten one of the good ones, that there might not be a Charlie for her.

Now, her eyes locked on the name in the last paragraph. *Michael*. He'd found Ada for her. He'd asked her to send . . . what?

She didn't even care that her hands shook as she broke the seal on the top box, hardly daring to hope that Ada had— Yes, she had! The clay pots were packed one against the next, the greens protected with inverted Tupperware containers duct-taped into place, with airholes perforated into the top. "Hello," she breathed, knowing she should probably feel like an idiot for talking to her plants, and not giving a crap. "Do you remember me?"

Laughing a little, crying a little, she unpacked all three boxes, which yielded eighteen pots, all but two of which were her personal cooking herbs. Those last two were the fat, furry African violets that always made her smile. And smile she did, as she watered her green friends and arranged the pots in her kitchen window, setting the few shade lovers off to the side. She stood back and felt a tear fall as she saw that she'd arranged them almost the same as they had been back in Boston. Then she swiped at her face, and told herself to pull it together as determination firmed within her.

She was going to track down Michael and thank him, whether he liked it or not.

Michael's blood was running hot and hard as he blasted away with both autopistols, one in each hand, running through his clips without pause, then slapping a fresh pair home and getting back into it before the targets could even reset. He was jonesing to run and roll and kick some major ass, but Skywatch's firing range was static. No Hogan's Alley here—it was all paper targets and a half dozen pop-ups he'd already Swiss-cheesed into submission. He could've gone hunting for a partner for the techware laser tag he'd instituted a few months earlier; the high-grade military equipment was pretty close to the real thing—good enough for training runs, anyway. But he wasn't in the mood for company; he was in the mood to blow some shit away.

The dam was intact, the sluiceways shut, but that didn't seem to matter these days. His inner caveman was alive and well, and loose within his skull. He wanted to throw his head back, beat on his chest, and howl into the strange orange sun with frustration, anger, and the shitty unfairness of Sasha's being there, yet beyond his reach. He couldn't touch her, didn't dare. Not when she was the one who'd stirred up the darkness within him, calling it so close to the surface. Too close.

He was holding the Other at bay, but just barely. And he was spending a hell of a lot of time and energy burning off the edges.

"Whatever it takes," he grated, slapping home another pair of clips and hitting the reset button at his right elbow. "Whatever it fucking takes."

"Words to live by," a voice said from behind him, filtering through his ear protectors. *Her* voice.

His whole body went tight in an instant. He would've given anything to scoop her up, carry her into the gun shed, lock the door, and lose himself with her, inside her. Because that wasn't an option, he slammed down every inner shield he possessed, set the autopistols aside, stripped off his protective glasses and earplugs, and turned toward her, moving slowly, trying not to let her see how the sight of her got his body jamming.

She stood a few feet away, at the edge of the rubber-padded cement that formed the main firing platform, with its waist-high reload counter and protective baffles. She was wearing crisp new jeans that hugged her long legs and a clingy green shirt that cinched beneath her breasts. Her hair was a mass of dark curls surrounding her face, and she was wearing a touch of mascara to accent her vivid brown eyes, a slick of lip gloss that caught his eye and made him think of her long, slow kisses and the murmur of pleasure she'd made at the back of her throat when he'd touched her, when they'd touched each other.

He'd crossed half the distance between them before he was aware of moving, was reaching for her before he could make himself stop. The spark of silver that flashed through him, though, stopped him dead in his tracks, and had his voice going low and harsh. "You shouldn't be here."

But she shook her head, holding up her hands as though to ward him off. "I came to thank you."

It took him a moment; he was too caught up in the edges of battle rage at first to remember. Then he did, and he fell back a step. "Oh. That." He didn't pretend to misunderstand. "I had Jox get her a fake ID, and we moved her to another apartment within the retirement complex, just in case Iago goes looking deeper in an effort to find you." They couldn't forget that the Xibalban wanted Sasha. And once Michael had met Ada Moscowitz and seen the older woman's relief when she learned Sasha was okay, he'd known he wouldn't be able to walk away without making things as right as he could. He'd wanted the widow to have some closure, wanted Sasha to have a piece of her old life within Skywatch.

And he should've had Strike give her the boxes and pretend it'd been his idea, damn it. But he'd wanted . . .

hell, he didn't know what he wanted. Or rather, he knew exactly what he wanted, and didn't dare take it.

Her lips parted on a soft sigh. "Then I owe you even more than I thought."

"You don't owe me a godsdamned thing," he said flatly. When that didn't seem to be enough for the edgy heat that was kicking through his system, he added, "Don't make me into some sort of hero, sweetheart. That was payback."

He wanted her to be pissed at him. Instead, she rolled her eyes. "Try again, cowboy. One good deed I might've bought as guilt. Four or five good deeds—and those are the ones I know about—make me wonder what the hell game you're playing."

"Shit. I should've known they'd blab. Frigging Yentas." Trying really hard to be an asshole, he shrugged. "Fine. You're welcome. Go away." He lifted his protective glasses. "I've got to get back to work."

Her eyes went past him to the pop-up targets—this week it was a group of tough-looking men in urban gang gear, packing Uzis. Most of them were headless. "Looks like you're doing just fine."

"What part of 'go away, I don't want your gratitude' are you not getting?"

If he'd figured that was rude enough to make her leave, he'd been way off. She looked back at him, the glitter in her gorgeous brown eyes going from irritation to speculation as she moved to the apron of the firing platform, closing the distance between them until he could've reached out and touched her, tracing the curve of her cheek, shaping the swell of her hips and breasts.

"Don't," he gritted from between clenched teeth. *Don't push me. Don't tempt me.*

The air between them steamed with the memories of the two of them straining together, his big body pinning her to the wall, helpless against the burn of pleasure. Her scent filled his lungs, bringing him the taste of her, the feel of her. They weren't touching, weren't kissing, but his whole body lit as though they were. He held still, told himself to take a big step back. Couldn't make himself move.

"What's wrong, Michael?" she asked, lifting her chin in the defiant challenge that got inside him, turned him on. "You don't want me, remember?"

"I never," he grated, voice rough and low, "said I didn't want you." The words were out before he could call them back. "I *ache* for you." *Whoa.* He really hadn't meant to say that.

Her expression went sharp. "Then . . . what, you're playing games? The thrill of the chase isn't enough; you need to manipulate the people around you, too?"

Sweat prickled along his spine as the heat demanded that he touch her, take her. Yet he couldn't, damn it. "You don't understand."

"No shit, Sherlock. How about you try explaining it to me?" She lifted a hand and splayed it on his chest. "Your heart's pounding."

"I'm pissed."

"You're turned on," she countered, "and so am I." A flush rose high on her cheeks at the admission. "So . . . you want to tell me why, rather than giving us a chance, you're up here beating the shit out of a bunch of targets—and from the looks of you, yourself too—trying to get yourself too damn tired to feel the burn?"

"I . . ." He wanted to. By the gods, he did. If she understood that much about what he was doing, maybe she could understand the rest, at least as much as he did. Hell, maybe she'd even have some ideas. But he couldn't find the words for what was happening inside him, the shame and the anger, and the daily battle to hold on to himself. He'd tried to tell her, but hadn't been able to. He'd tried to drive her away, but hadn't been able to do that, either, because he'd betrayed his own good intentions through his friends. Had that been his subconscious sabotaging his conscious intent? Maybe. Probably. Gods, he wanted her.

He wanted her beneath him, surrounding him. Arching up against him as she came. But more than the physical, he wanted to sit with her, laugh with her, be with her. But above all, he wanted to keep her safe. And to do that, he had to keep his hands off her.

Or did he? He was nearly dead on his feet, and the target practice had burned off the leading edge of the anger. If there was ever a time he'd be able to keep himself level around her, it was now. And if the logic was self-serving, maybe even coming from the corruption brought by the silver magic, in that moment, with Sasha close enough to touch, he was having trouble caring. He'd run himself ragged each day until he dropped into bed too exhausted to do anything but sleep. And in sleeping, he'd dreamed of murder and magic.

He needed something different to take with him tonight. He needed *her*.

Control, he reminded himself. Drawing a deep breath, he counted his heartbeats, feeling them slow beneath her palm. Then he leaned into her touch and dropped his head, zeroing in on her glossy lips. Her darkened eyelashes fluttered to her cheeks as she tipped her head back in tacit agreement. He wanted to crush her to him, wanted to take her deep in an instant, but held himself in check. *Hold it together*.

Slowly, he leaned in. Softly, he touched his lips to hers. Then he paused, assessing. The magic stirred; the Other pressed at the edges of his consciousness but remained in check as he increased the pressure fractionally. Her mouth opened beneath his; their tongues touched. Retreated. Touched again. And then, daring to test the limits of his knife-edge control, he took the kiss deeper, trying to tell her the things he didn't have the words for. *I want to be with you*, he said in his kiss. *I'm sorry for the things I've done, the things I can't tell you about.* And then as he pulled her to him and took her lips in a branding, blatantly carnal kiss, something shifted within him.

She stiffened and started to pull away, then hesitated as he gentled the kiss, trying to tell her the things he didn't have the words for. After a moment, she brought her hands up to grip his wrists, and her mouth opened to him.

Yes! exulted the creature that was him. His blood raced, burning in his veins, seeming to stretch his skin from within as he crowded closer to her, taking the kiss deeper and deeper still as his hands slid from her shoulders to the crooks of her elbows, then down to the soft skin of her wrists. He moved to link their fingers as the heat gained an edge of wonder, a sense that—

She shifted, spun, and drove a knee into his side, below his ribs. Completely unprepared for attack, entirely off balance on every level imaginable, Michael let go of her and fell back. His body dropped automatically into a fighting crouch, while his head fought for control, fought not to go after her as she moved past him. Then he wished he *had* gone after her, because she grabbed one of the autopistols and leveled its business end in his direction.

He froze. "Those rounds are live, sweetheart."

"Do you really think now is the time to 'sweetheart' me?"

"Possibly not."

She regarded him levelly, holding the weapon waist-high with the ease of a childhood familiarity that had come back to her with, according to Jox, amazing speed. The *winikin*, who was their resident gun nut, had waxed enthusiastic over her dead aim at close and middle distances, though he'd allowed how some of the others, including Michael, were far better sharpshooters. They were sure as shit at close range now, though.

"Do I have your attention?" she inquired, pinning him with a glare that held a bright-eyed edge of the same passion that hammered in his veins. It was a short leap from sex to combat for him. Apparently for her too.

He spread his hands away from his body, indicating helplessness on many levels. "You've had my attention from the first second I saw your picture."

"Damn it, that's what I'm talking about!" Her eyes narrowed in fury, but she let the muzzle of the autopistol dip an inch. "You don't get to *say* stuff like that; you don't get to kiss me like you just did, or do what you did for Ada, and then tell me you're not interested in me."

"I never said I wasn't interested." Even that much was an effort to get out; it bumped up against the fused-shut part of him, the part that made him work around the things he couldn't say.

"Then what are you? Because I've got to tell you, I don't have a frigging clue."

I'm crazier than your father ever was. I'm a split personality that some powerful men made worse. I'm a time bomb. A killer. And you, who are an angel, bring out the devil in me. His mouth worked, but none of that came out.

Her expression flattened; her eyes went hot with disgust and fury, aimed not at him, but at herself. "Yeah. That's what I thought. *Shit*, I did it again." Spinning, she squeezed off three rapid bursts of gunfire in quick succession, rocking the three nearest Uzi-toting pop-ups. Then she slapped the pistol back on the counter and stormed past him, jaw set.

"Sasha . . ." He held out a hand to stop her, but then let it fall, because what could he say? It would be better for both of them—for all of them—if she were pissed at him.

She turned back at the edge of the cement pad. "Don't do me any more favors, okay? Just leave me the hell alone. My whole life, I watched Pim wait around for Ambrose to get tired of chasing his dreams and settle down. I swore I wouldn't be that woman, swore I'd hold out for a man who wanted to be in a relationship with a woman rather than an idea. Then, when I thought I'd found him, it turned out that he'd wanted the relationship, yes, but then he wanted to move on to the next, and the next after that. Saul didn't want me; he wanted the idea of me, which was just as bad." Eyes dark, she opened her hands, as though letting her own dreams fall free. "And you . . . I don't know what you want. It's like you're two different people—the guy who rescued me, who made love to me, who kissed me just now . . . and then the guy who warns me off at the same time he's tracking down an old lady and having her ship my herbs so I'll have a piece of myself back." She paused expectantly.

He ached for the girl whose father hadn't known how to love anyone but the life he'd left behind, for the woman who'd sought answers for herself and found only pain and confusion. He hated knowing he was adding to that pain.

If I could find a way to make it work for us, I'd do it, he wanted to say. But he didn't see any answers on the horizon, and he was losing hope that he ever would. So in the end, he said only, "I'm sorry, Sasha. I'm so damned sorry for all of it."

She closed her eyes for a moment. When she opened them again, her mascaraed lashes were damp with tears. "Is that all you're going to say?"

"It's all I *can* say." And that was the truth.

"Okay." She swallowed hard, and nodded. "Okay. I guess that's it, then." She turned away without another word and headed back down the path with her spine straight and her shoulders unbowed.

He was the one who slumped and hung his head, wishing to hell he could go back in time and change the decisions he'd made, the things he'd done. She made him want to be a different, better man. But he'd wished for that a thousand times since his talent ceremony and it hadn't happened yet. He was who and what he was, and had had to find a way to make that work for the Nightkeepers, not the Xibalbans.

So, moving very deliberately, he replaced his earplugs and protective glasses and turned back to the counter, picking up the weapon that was still warm from her hand.

He sighted on the pop-ups she'd hit, expecting to see them blasted through the 'nads. But they weren't. Each of the men was shot center mass, clean through the heart. The sight made him want to howl her name.

Instead, he very calmly, very methodically shot the rest of the targets to shit.

PART III

FULL MOON

The moon is in opposition to the sun, meaning that it is large and bright in the sky. This night is associated with insomnia, insanity, and magic.

CHAPTER ELEVEN

December 2
Full moon
Three years and nineteen days until the zero date

Sasha had never before been aware of a full moon as anything more than a passing thought, as a pretty white circle in the night sky, brightening the darkness. But as the sun set on the night of her bloodline ceremony, she thought there was something different about this particular full moon, something different about her body. As she sat alone in her suite, waiting out the last hour before the ceremony, her skin felt too tight on her bones and her body temp flashed from hot to cold and back again. She didn't know if the stirred-up feeling was nerves or the sensation of the Nightkeepers' magic strengthening as the barrier thinned with the approach of the three-year solstice. Probably both. And honesty compelled her to admit, inwardly at least, that she was jittery about being one-on-one with Michael to the degree they would need for the ritual.

The king had declared that since the two of them had already proven that their magics were compatible,

Michael would be the one to act as her main point of contact during the bloodline ceremony. Michael had argued—rather unflatteringly—against the plan, but had been overruled. The others would all be involved in the spell; she'd need all the power she could get, given that she was attempting a cardinal-day ritual on a noncardinal day, one that wasn't a solstice or equinox.

Michael would be her main point of contact, his power the conduit through which she would enter the barrier and gain her bloodline mark. More, they were hoping the additions they'd made to the traditional ritual would enable her to summon her bloodline *nahwal*. Assuming that Ambrose's knowledge had been integrated into the *nahwal*, it might be able to tell her how to find the library.

That was the theory, anyway. And it all hinged on her ability to lean on Michael, his ability to boost her magic. But what if they'd lost that capacity?

She'd barely seen him since that afternoon out at the firing range, but she'd been acutely, achingly aware of him. That was her problem, she knew, her stupidity. But she wouldn't let herself dwell on it. Of all the things she'd taken away with her from the year of captivity with Iago, she'd gained a hard-edged practicality, and the ability to slap a lid on her emotions when she needed to. She didn't fall into fantasies of her old life anymore, didn't let herself dream of a man who'd made it clear he didn't want to be right for her, despite the apparent signs suggesting that the gods intended otherwise, or had at one point. For all they knew, Iago's destruction of the sky-road had disrupted the gods' plans on earth, and her and Michael's destined pairing had been collateral damage.

A brisk knock sounded on the door of her suite, peremptory and forceful. *Michael.* Despite her best efforts to shield her heart, heat gathered in her core, alongside the nerves. "It's open."

He pushed the door inward, but didn't step over the threshold. Instead, he stayed in the hall, framed in the doorway. He was wearing the same battle armor and fighting clothes he'd had on the first time she'd seen him, along with a floor-length black robe that had long, pointed sleeves and a line of black beadwork around its edges. He looked dark, sexy, and mysterious, and every inch the warrior-priest. *Damn him.*

"It's time," he said. "You ready?"

She took a deep breath and nodded. "Yeah." She stood, instinctively smoothing down the set of black-on-black combat clothes she wore along with a robe that was similar to Michael's in style, but in fabric that was the deep blue of a novitiate rather than the black of a mage. Jox had pulled the clothes from storage, where they had been locked since the massacre. She hadn't asked who they'd belonged to, hadn't wanted to know then. But now she found herself wondering who had worn the gear before her. Which made her think of the mother she'd never known. Who had she been? What had she been like? Why hadn't she left Skywatch with Ambrose? Had losing her broken him, or had he been broken before that?

There were too many questions with too few answers, on too many levels, leaving Sasha feeling lost and cut adrift. Then again, she was quickly realizing she wasn't that far behind the other magi in that regard. They had all come late to the magic, and were struggling in the absence of a solid knowledge base. And they were counting on her to fix that.

She hoped to hell she didn't let them down.

She crossed the room to face Michael. His eyes were dark with emotion, with secrets, but he didn't share either with her. Instead, he took her hand, lifted it to his lips, and pressed a kiss to her palm. "I'll be right there with you. We all will."

Shit, she thought. Leave it to him to be sweet when she needed it most. *Bastard*.

Fear of failure crowded close around her: fear of failing herself, failing her new friends, failing Michael . . . hell, even failing Ambrose more than she already had. Her feelings toward him remained complex, but they were softening some as she became more and more a part of Skywatch and began to understand that the writs guiding the Nightkeepers weren't the same as the mores of modern humanity. The magi lived primarily for their responsibilities to the magic and the war, meaning that sometimes personal desire had to take a backseat to necessity.

But still, that didn't excuse what Ambrose had done during that last solstice ceremony she'd been with him. The memories of that terrifying night had crowded far too close as she'd prepared for the bloodline ritual.

"What's wrong?" Michael asked, watching her carefully. When she didn't answer right away, he let go of her hand, but didn't move away. "You can talk to me."

Then why can't you *talk to* me? she nearly asked, but knew there was no point. She should wave him off, say she was fine. But instead she found herself answering. "I left Ambrose because he almost killed me."

Michael went very still, his eyes intent on hers. "Tell me."

It was easier than she would have thought to get started, even though she'd never told the story to another living soul. Only she and Ambrose had known what happened that night. "It was the winter solstice when I was almost eighteen. He . . ." She faltered, remembering the fear and pain, and the crushing sense of betrayal. "It was one of his bad times. Knowing what I know now, he must not have realized the barrier was sealed, the magic nonfunctional. Every cardinal day during my childhood, we blooded our palms and enacted the proper rituals. When

I was thirteen, right after I hit puberty in earnest, he put me through the talent ceremony, then got pissed when it didn't work. After that, I balked, and started trying to talk him into getting help." She paused, her lips twitching without humor. "I thought maybe he'd get better if I proved to him that the Nightkeepers didn't exist. It didn't work."

"Your bloodline must be a stubborn one."

She snorted, and her chest loosened with the realization that Ambrose really was in her past. The knowledge made it easier to go on. "That last time, he didn't give me a choice. He locked us both in the ritual chamber, which wasn't unusual. But this time . . ." She faltered. Okay, maybe it wasn't easy after all. "He held me down and tied my wrists and ankles." She flashed on a circular room with torches and incense, and a wooden cross in the center of the floor. *No*, she thought, *wrong ceremony. That was Iago, not Ambrose.* "He must've figured if a little blood was good, lots would be better, because he opened my wrists and let me bleed out into a bowl filled with oil. The last thing I remember was the smell of my own blood burning."

"Son of a *bitch*," Michael grated. His body had gone hard and tight, his face to stone.

She didn't meet his eyes. Couldn't. "I don't know if he meant to sacrifice me and lost his nerve, or if it was a bloodletting that got out of hand. I woke up in the hospital, where everyone acted like I had tried to kill myself. Because, of course, that was what he'd told them."

At the time, she'd felt pathetic. Now, she just felt . . . tired. Drained.

She'd known how much that past ceremony had been overshadowing her preparation for today's ritual. What she hadn't realized was that telling Michael about it would ease the tension. Or not ease, she realized as he muttered a vile curse. Instead it seemed that he'd taken her tension into himself. His body was rigid, his expression locked. And the anger she'd glimpsed before was full-force in his eyes.

Her transient sense of peace quickly became a hard fist of nerves. "Michael?"

He closed his eyes, as though he didn't want her to see what was inside him as he said, "I wish the bastard weren't dead. Because then I could kill him for you."

Sasha took a step back before she was aware of moving.

She should be horrified, she knew, and part of her was. More, she was scared by the intensity of his words, the dead-flat delivery that suggested he meant every word, and was fully capable of carrying out the threat without hesitation. The rational part of her said she should close the door between them and call one of the other magi for help. Maybe all of them.

Another part of her, though, saw that he'd gone very pale, that he didn't look like himself anymore. His high cheekbones stood out in stark relief, and the dark shadows of his sunken eyes looked like sockets. She could have been staring at a skull for all the life she saw in him at that moment. The memory of what Ambrose had done to her, so close to the surface of her mind, told her to get the hell away from Michael, that he wasn't the man she'd thought him. But the stronger woman, the one who was increasingly coming out in her at Skywatch, had her standing her ground and reaching out to him.

He flinched. "*Don't* touch me." But his voice sounded desperate, as though he longed for her touch.

So she ignored the mad anger in his eyes, in his face, and closed the gap between them, and framed his haggard face between her palms. "He's gone," she said simply. "He can't hurt me anymore."

"But I can," he rasped. It sounded more like a plea than a warning, and he dropped his forehead to hers.

"You won't," she said, not sure where the certainty came from, not sure she could trust it. "Not today. Today you're going to watch over me. You're going to protect me."

A long shudder racked his body and something shifted in the air around them, a sense of some watching presence leaving, though not going far. She didn't track the sensation, focusing instead on Michael, who raised his hands and gripped her wrists where she still cupped his stubbled jaw in her palms. Instead of pushing her away, as she half expected him to do, he held her in place. They stood a moment, their foreheads pressed together, leaning on each other. And she felt, for those brief few seconds, the same connection she'd found with him in the sacred chamber—a sense of being whole. Being home.

Unfortunately, she knew it wouldn't last long. Whatever was within him, whatever was between them, it was far from resolved.

With a final squeeze of her wrists, he broke the almost-embrace and stepped away. His eyes, when they met hers, were back to those of the man she knew, clear and very serious. "The next time you see me like that, promise me you'll run away."

She lifted her chin. "No." *Tell me what's going on*, she wanted to scream, but didn't bother, because she knew he wouldn't. "Promise me you'll talk to someone. If not me, then Jade. Or Tomas."

His eyes flickered with an emotion she couldn't define. "I can't," he said softly, but his words were laced with regret.

"Then we're at an impasse." Making herself be strong and stand apart when she wanted to cling, or maybe shake him until his teeth rattled and she knocked loose some damned sense from his stubborn skull, she shrugged her blue robe tighter around her, smoothing the heavy fabric. "Come on. Let's do this."

Without waiting for his answer, she swept out of her suite and headed for the sacred room where the ritual would take place.

The bigger spells and important ceremonies had previously been held in the altar room beneath Chichén Itzá, but with the secret tunnels beneath the ancient city now gone, and no luck so far in identifying another intersection, the magi were left with the smaller ritual room at Skywatch, a temple typically used for weddings, funerals, and naming ceremonies. Now, out of necessity, it was being pressed into service for heavier-duty magic.

Sasha hesitated at the entrance to the circular room, where torches lit the carved walls and the *chac-mool* altar, and soft curls of *copan*-scented smoke curled from stone braziers. The scene was like a pastiche of memories, combining the filter-blurred sensory images of the torture she'd endured at Iago's hands with the hotter, more immediate memories of being with Michael. Or with the other version of Michael—the edgier, sharper one she'd dreamed of the night before.

He touched her arm. "You okay?"

Shifting away so his hand fell to his side, she nodded. "I will be."

The large, man-shaped *chac-mool* sat at one point of the compass, and torches were affixed at the others. The altar itself was set atop a large slab of cement that was tinted the red-gold of the Nightkeepers and the gods. Jox had told her that the cement had been mixed with the ashes of hundreds of magi, carried with the Nightkeepers while they searched for the place that would become their home. The ashes gave the site an artificial power boost that was weaker than that found at the true sites in the Mayan territories, but was better than nothing. The chamber was full of robed figures, and Sasha had to push back a shimmer of fear at the sight of two in bloodred.

One of the red-robed figures turned toward her, and she nearly fell back, losing the face to the memory of Iago's red-robes. But when he pushed back his hood, she recognized Strike, who she'd come to like, if from a distance, over the past two weeks. He'd proven to be an odd combination of mage king and normal beer-drinking, football-watching guy next door. In a way, all of the Nightkeepers were combinations of their former and present selves. As for her . . . well, they'd see, wouldn't they?

Wearing a thin strand of jade beads around his forehead instead of the elaborate headdress and dangling celts of the traditional regalia, the Nightkeepers' king looked every inch the leader, but his eyes were kind and concerned. "Are you ready for this?"

Sasha lifted her chin, drawing strength from the knowledge that Michael was right behind her. "Apparently I was born for this."

"Then let's get started." Strike gestured for the others to take their positions.

The magi formed a circle in the center of the room, sitting cross-legged, knee-to-knee. Strike and Leah, in the red robes of the royals, sat with their backs to the *chac-mool* altar. Patience and Brandt took their places on one side of the royal couple, Nate and Alexis on the other. The setup emphasized the linked power of the three mated pairs, united in love and magic. The four unmated singles completed the circle: Jade next to Michael, then Sasha, with Sven on her other side. It was a small circle. Anna and Rabbit, who Sasha hadn't officially met yet, had stayed in Texas. Even if they'd been there, though, Sasha thought the ghosts in the room still would've outnumbered the living by a large margin. The *copan*-scented air all but reverberated with the memory of the hundreds of ceremonies that had taken place there, the new lives celebrated, new pair-bonds sealed, and the funeral rites that had passed the fallen on to their death challenges.

A cool breeze stirred the hair at Sasha's nape, though there was no open window, no source for the chill that walked down her spine.

When the magi were seated, the door opened and the *winikin* filed in ceremonially, and handed each of the magi a stone bowl holding a folded bit of parchment, an ear of maize, and a small cup of *chorote*. Normally, the ceremony would've involved a simple bloodletting and burning of the blood-soaked parchment. The other items were part of the effort to help Sasha invoke her bloodline *nahwal*. The actual details had been largely Jox's idea, based on Sasha's obvious affinity for maize and cacao. Once the *winikin* had dispensed the ritual items, they filed out, remaining silent. At the door, though, Jox turned back and sent Sasha a wink that warmed her. The kind, clever *winikin* had become her bedrock, proving to be the sort of man—and the father—she'd often wished Ambrose had been.

When the *winikin* were gone, Strike pulled a carved stone knife from his belt and used it to cut his palms. The others did the same, except for Leah, who used a modern combat knife, as befitted her human status, and Sasha, who didn't have a knife because they were bloodline specific. Until they knew what bloodline she belonged to—assuming the ritual went as they hoped— she was weaponless.

"Here." Michael palmed his knife from his ankle sheath, and passed it to her unblooded.

"Thanks." Sasha took the blade, which was warm from his body, making the transfer both intimate and faintly erotic. Or was that the effect of the *copan* smoke, and the memories it invoked? Either way, she felt some-how both steadier and more unsettled with him beside her, with his knife in her hand. *Focus*, she told herself, and cut her palms with two long, shallow slashes, managing not to think of the past as she did so.

She hissed out a long breath that started as pain and ended as something else when the magic trickled into her, kindling a red-gold hum at the base of her brain, one she remembered from the night of her rescue, though it felt different now, less edgy and more welcoming. The hum—which was how the others consistently spoke of the magic—had seemed a rattle before. Now it was more of a river's babble, or the basis of a song.

It was odd how many things made her think of music these days, when she'd never before been musically inclined, and couldn't carry a tune if her life depended on it. But recently as she'd tended her struggling cacao seedlings out in Jox's greenhouse, she'd caught herself humming softly, a faintly martial beat that echoed in her skull. Even as she thought about it, the hum twined itself around that marching beat, matching the tempo of her pulse.

Unsure whether that was part of the magic or not, she passed the knife back to Michael, bracing herself against the kick of heat brought by the touch of his fingers on hers as he took the blade. He didn't acknowledge the unintentional caress, though; he seemed almost ferociously intent on his actions as he cut his own palms. Around the circle, the magi held their bleeding hands over the ceremonial bowls, letting their blood soak into the parchment held within, turning it dark in the dim light. Using a small torch that was passed hand-to-hand, they each lit the parchment, which sputtered and then caught fire, releasing magic in the burning of blood. Then, deviating from tradition, they each reached for and drank the *chorote*, which tasted like very thin, very cheap instant hot chocolate, only with a chewiness that was more unexpected than actually unpleasant. The taste made Sasha think of the village near Ambrose's temple, and the kind strangers who'd let her hang around while her father lost himself in his dreams and work. And eventually, in his madness.

Sven made a face and said, "Urk." The rest got their drinks down without complaint.

After the *chorote*, they each picked up their ear of maize and passed it through the smudgy smoke that came from the slow-burning parchment. That part of things had been adapted from an old birthing ritual, when a new baby's umbilical blood had been collected on parchment and burned, and maize seeds were passed through the smoke and then planted. According to the ritual, children who ate maize plants grown from their own blood-spelled seeds were stronger, healthier, and smarter. The magi were hoping the act itself would strengthen them for the ceremony. Afterward, Jox and Sasha would plant the seeds and integrate the grown maize into the Nightkeepers' diets, on the theory that they needed every bit of power they could get these days.

Sasha leaned in and inhaled the pungent smoke. She felt as if she were floating out of her body, though at the same time she could feel the press of the stone floor beneath her. Which made sense, because for this ritual, her spirit would enter the barrier while her body remained behind. The idea of being disconnected like that brought a thrum of fear, but she pushed it aside, telling herself that she'd trained for this. Whether she liked it or not, she'd been born for it.

"Link up," Strike ordered, and the magi joined hands, one to the next, sharing blood magic. The hum notched higher, becoming music inside Sasha's head: not just the martial theme now, but a twinkling, twining blend of sound. Strike said a short, guttural spell, and the torches went out, leaving the magi in darkness broken only by the cool moonlight coming from above through the glass ceiling.

Tipping her head back, she looked up at the full moon. She held Michael's hand on one side, Sven's on the other, and felt their power flow into her, and hers into them. She could feel the differences in the two men through the blood-link. Sven's touch seemed to bring a whisper of strings and rippling harp tones. Michael's touch didn't seem associated with any particular piece of the music flowing through her. Maybe the martial theme she kept hearing was her brain's way of interpreting his power?

Unable to answer that question, even for herself, Sasha braced herself for her first jack-in.

"In we go," Strike said. Taking Leah's hand, he sealed the circle. Then, leaning on the power brought by the love between the three couples and the teamwork that bound the others, the Nightkeepers said in unison, "*Pasaj och.*" And jacked in.

Sasha thought of a *nahwal*, holding an image culled from a dozen descriptions fixed at the forefront of her mind, hoping against hope that it would cause the barrier transition to bring her to her bloodline *nahwal*, in a manner analogous to Strike's 'port targeting. That was the theory, anyway.

There was a moment of dizzying nausea, of extreme disorientation. The world went gray-green and she had the sense of speeding without moving, of flying while staying still. Then she blinked into a universe of gray-green mist and sky, dropped a couple of inches, and landed on her feet, stumbling only slightly.

Fog rose to her knees, camouflaging a soft, yielding surface underfoot. Overhead hung clouds the same color as the mist that surrounded the small group of magi, who clustered together, still linked hand-to-hand. There was nothing in the mist as far as she could see, except—

Oh, holy hell, she thought, adrenaline spearing through

her at the sight of a humanoid shadow approaching through the mist. She'd done it. She'd found her blood-line *nahwal*.

The shadow drew nearer, resolving itself into a human-shaped figure without nipples or genitalia, no hair or distinguishing features, only skin across bones, with black, pupilless eyes. The hum of red-gold magic at the back of Sasha's skull trilled upward as though the magic were welcoming its own. "Ambrose?" she whispered.

Michael nudged her forward, whispering, "I'm right behind you."

Setting her balance through force of will, Sasha lifted her chin and stepped forward to meet the *nahwal*. Then things got weird, because as it drew closer, she saw that it wore a single earring, a bloodred ruby that glowed dully in the strange gray-green light. The *nahwal* weren't supposed to have any distinguishing marks aside from their bloodline glyphs. Except for one ... and that wasn't possible. She couldn't be linked to the royal jaguar—

"Father," Strike breathed, bringing her brain to a stuttering halt.

The *nahwal* didn't acknowledge him; it kept advancing on Sasha, its black eyes fixed on her. Disbelief and panic collided inside her. She wanted to back away, wanted to run, but her feet wouldn't move; they seemed stuck in place, glued by the clinging gray-green fog. She held out her hands in a *stop* gesture, as though that would deter the creature, even though she was the one who'd called it, who needed to speak with it.

It halted when her hands were nearly touching its leathery, desiccated chest. And incredibly, horribly, it smiled—a too-human expression on an inhuman face. "Welcome home, child," it said in a voice that was made up of several voices speaking in harmonious descant. "We've been waiting for you."

Tears burned her eyes and an unexpected sob welled

up in her throat. "Where's Ambrose?" she asked, knowing instinctively he wasn't inside the creature she faced.

"His path led another way." Reaching out a desiccated hand to her, the *nahwal* folded its fingers around her wrist; it said, "You are the second daughter of the jaguar king. Find yourself. Learn the magic that is in your blood. All else will follow from there."

The world tilted beneath Sasha, though the barrier firmament itself didn't move. Confusion battered her. Her eyes locked on the dual marks on the creature's inner forearm, the jaguar and the royal *ju*, and her voice shook when she said, "Who *are* you?" Deep down inside, though, she knew. Maybe she'd always known, had struggled hardest against her destiny because she'd known it would take so much from her.

"I am yours. You are mine." A strange burning sensation took root where the *nahwal* held her wrist. Moments later the burn faded, and the *nahwal* released her and started backing away, fading into the fog.

"Father!" Strike said.

This time the *nahwal* looked at him. "Take care of her as I did not."

"Wait!" Remembering the plan, and what they'd hoped to learn from her *nahwal*, royal or not, Sasha surged forward, grabbing for the *nahwal*'s arm as it continued retreating. "Where is the library? Do you know where Ambrose hid the scroll?"

Michael shouted, "Don't! Let go of it!" But his voice quavered strangely on the last few words.

Sasha turned back, only then realizing that the *nahwal* had continued retreating as she'd spoken, that it had pulled her away from the others, though she'd had no sensation of moving. She saw Michael's mouth move, shaping words, but she couldn't hear his voice, couldn't hear anything over the sound of wind that suddenly arose from nowhere and everywhere at once. She tried to let go of the *nahwal*, but couldn't, tried to yank away, but couldn't do that either. Panic slashed through her as the scene wavered and started to fade. She screamed, scrabbling for purchase as she felt herself sliding sideways. She heard the music but didn't know what to do with it, about it.

Michael shouted something and lunged for her, but he was too late. Just as his fingers brushed her arm, a giant force picked her up and yanked her through the gray-green nothingness.

"Help," she cried. *"Help me!"*

The sense of movement accelerated and the wind whipped past her with howls louder than her own. Her forearm burned. Panic jammed her chest and her pulse thundered in her ears. Then, abruptly, the wind and movement cut out. The air went wet and warm, and she was surrounded by leaves. She hung in midair for a heartbeat before gravity reasserted itself and she slammed down, landing sprawled in a wet, leafy layer of rain forest debris.

She lay still for a second, gasping for breath. There was no magic in the air, no sign of the others. And even though she knew her body should still be back in the sacred chamber at Skywatch, she had to wonder, because what she was experiencing felt very, very real. The soil beneath her felt real; the moist air smelled real, with the scent of green things and rot. She was in Mayan territory, she knew instinctively, recognizing the feel and smell from her childhood.

With the realization came a burst of excitement and understanding. She was in a vision showing her where the library scroll was hidden. She hoped.

Scrambling up, she stood, shaking. The heavy robe was far too hot, but she didn't dare take it off, wasn't exactly sure what it symbolized within the barrier—if she was even in the barrier now. She scanned the scene, saw trees and undergrowth, more trees and more undergrowth—a profusion of greenery and the occasional color-burst of flowers. Parrots called in the canopy, the melody soaring up over a background of monkey chatter. Familiarity settled around her as she caught the white flash of carved stone and recognized the entrance to Ambrose's temple. She'd been right all along, she realized. The scroll had to be in there, somewhere. But where? How was she supposed to find it?

"By looking around, idiot," she told herself. Trying to banish the memory of what had happened to her the last time she'd searched the temple, she inhaled a deep breath and headed for the faint trail.

She'd gone barely three steps when something stirred in the middle growth to her right, bending leaves and branches.

Sasha froze, her heart pounding into her throat as she thought of jaguars and other jungle predators. Her hand slapped for her weapons belt, but it was empty. The magi traditionally wore only their knives into the bloodline ceremony, with the potential mage going unarmed.

Sticking to that particular tradition might have been a mistake.

The branches rustled again, the disturbance man-high, making her think of bandits, Iago, and the entity the others had seen in the so-called haunted temple. They'd described it as looking like a *nahwal*, but one that spoke with only a single voice, and walked the earth rather than the barrier. It had attacked Anna, nearly killed her. Was that what was coming for her? Sasha wondered. And if so, should she stay put, or run? The latter option wasn't likely to gain her the answers she needed, but she was also all too aware of the danger she was in. And that she was alone.

For all that the lack of privacy had chafed at times over the past couple of weeks, she'd grown used to the sense of safety in numbers. Now, even that was gone.

Use the magic, she thought, knowing she should be able to do something with the red-gold hum that sounded within her. She managed to kindle a tiny fireball, and the success brought a buzz of magic and rightness, a click of connection within her own soul. *This is me*, she thought. *This is who I am.*

But the fireball was of little use there in the rain forest. Why was she there? What was she supposed to be doing? As a last-ditch effort, she tried to short-circuit the jack-in. "*Way*," she whispered, which was the spell word that was supposed to take her back to her body. It didn't work; she stayed where she was. But the flare of magic called something else.

A low, feral growl sounded from the undergrowth, sending her pulse into overdrive. A second growl answered the first. For a moment she couldn't tell where the sounds had come from; they seemed to surround her. Then two dark shadows emerged from the undergrowth—big black canines that were rottweilerish in size and shape, but had long tails, and pure black coats that lacked the distinctive tan markings of the breed. They wore no collars, no means of restraint. And they stalked toward her, stiff legged and growling, with their heads low and the fur between their shoulder blades standing in menace.

Magic prickled across her skin, warning her that they weren't just dogs. But what the hell were they?

Whatever they were, they were closing in on her, one from each side. *Don't turn your back on them*, she told herself. *Don't panic; don't run.* But her heart hammered in her chest and adrenaline surged through her veins, making her want to flee and hide, to fight, to do anything other than stand her ground.

Then the branches and shadows moved again and a humanoid figure stepped out into the orange-dappled sunlight. As Sasha focused on the newcomer, her heart shuddered in her chest and a low moan escaped from her throat as she saw the creature Red-Boar had called the mad *nahwal* . . . and recognized it. The desiccated skin was that of a *nahwal*, but the creature wore bush clothing and a long gray ponytail tied back with a worn leather thong. And on its forearm was a wide, gnarled scar.

"Ambrose?" she said, her voice cracking to a whisper.

His path led him elsewhere, the jaguar king had said, and now she understood. He'd stayed in the place of his death, waiting. But for what?

She didn't know if he was a ghost or a man, or something in between, stuck in the process of merging with the *nahwal* of his own bloodline. His eyes weren't the flat matte black of a true *nahwal* . . . but as he advanced on her, she saw that they weren't normal, either—they were glazed over with the look she'd seen only once or twice, when Ambrose had been in the throes of the worst and most violent of his psychotic episodes, when he'd grown violent and mean, and Pim and Sasha had gone to a hotel for a couple of days until he returned to himself.

Only Sasha didn't see any hope of return in his eyes now. She saw only the madness, as though his death, and whatever had happened to freeze him in this halfway state, had stripped him of his better parts, leaving the insanity in control.

"Oh, Ambrose," she breathed, fear and sorrow flaring to life within her even as she took a step back, away from the advancing demi-*nahwal* and his snarling black familiars.

There was no recognition in his face. He just kept coming in slow, measured treads as Sasha retreated, eventually backing into a tree. She pressed against it, pulse hammering with guilt as she thought that she'd brought him to this. Because she hadn't believed. *Gods*.

"Ambrose," she said, forcing the word from between dry lips. "It's me, Sasha. Your princess." That was what he had called her in his good moments. His princess. She'd never before thought it'd been anything but a nickname. "I need to talk to you about the library. I need you to tell me where you hid the scroll."

He hesitated, and for a second she thought she saw the man she'd known in the eyes of the creature that faced her. Then that blink was gone and the demi-*nahwal* lunged at her, reached for her with fingers gone to claws, its mouth splitting in a multitonal scream of mad rage, baring pointed fangs.

"No!" Panic slashed through her and she broke. Spinning, she bolted, breath locking in her lungs as she ran for her life. Moments later, the snarling familiars lunged in pursuit.

Michael cursed and flailed against the wind and the darkness that gripped him, holding him suspended in the middle of nothingness. He twisted against the invisible force, howling with rage, with the need to get to Sasha, to protect her. As she'd been sucked into the mist he'd followed her and grabbed on tight, refusing to let go, but it hadn't mattered. She'd been yanked away from his grip, and he'd wound up someplace black and empty, a space without light, without time.

"Sasha!" he shouted into the nothingness, and got no echoes in return.

Magic swirled around him, harder and hotter than it should have been. He grabbed onto it, threw himself into it, only then realizing that the power glinted silver in the blackness; the sluice gates had cracked and the Other was nearly loose within him, brought to the fore by the combined magic of the Nightkeepers and the lure of the blood-link with Sasha.

"No," he grated. "Get back, damn it. She's not yours!"

She's not yours either, the Other said in the deadly inner tones he hadn't heard in a long time. *She's ours*.

In an instant, Michael was plunged into a vision, into a memory that wasn't his own.

Three years in Bryson's employ, two dozen confirmed kills, and twice that in completed missions, and the Other's existence had come down to a single syringe. The creature within Michael had seen its own destruction in Dr. Horn's eyes.

"It won't hurt," Bryson had said as they'd stripped the Other of its weapons, its passports. Its reason for existing. "You won't remember a thing." But by "you" he'd meant Michael, not the Other. Because the Other would soon cease to exist, blanked forever by the same cocktail of drugs and hypnosis that had so cleanly separated it from the Michael personality, creating two halves: one a murderer, one a man.

"No," the Other howled, straining against the binding restraints as Horn approached. "No!"

The syringe descended and the world went black.

"No!" Michael shouted, fighting the darkness, fighting the end of himself. Instinctively, not sure who he was, which part of himself, he tipped back his head and shouted, "*Pasaj och!*"

He was already jacked in, but now another layer of magic slammed into him, around him. The world exploded around him, detonating with Nightkeeper magic, forcing the Other out of his consciousness, out of his head. He leaned on the red-gold magic, opened himself to it, choosing life over death. This time, at least.

"Gods help us," he yelled into the darkness. "She needs me!"

The world exploded around him again, and he blinked out of the darkness and into the light. Back on earth, or a vision version of it. He materialized within the glare of the reddish orange sun, surrounded by thin white clouds. The earth was green below him. Very far below him. The canopy of a rain forest was broken here and there by the tops of pyramid ruins.

Oh, shit, he thought as panic spiked. He'd blinked in way too fucking high.

For a split second, he hovered. Then, howling, he fell. Air whipped past him as he tumbled, spinning, cursing up a storm, like that was going to help a godsdamned thing. Air screamed in his ears and the ground lunged up to meet him at an impossible speed. He was going to die, he realized with fatalistic certainty. That was what the Other's vision had been trying to tell him. It hadn't been a threat. It'd been a warning.

He couldn't fly, couldn't 'port, couldn't do gods-damned anything but shield, and—

Shit, he realized. *That's it! A shield*. Almost too late, fighting the wall of air that pushed against him at terminal velocity, he contorted and yanked his knife from his ankle sheath. Slashing both palms, he called up the red-gold Nightkeeper magic and threw the strongest, most yielding shield he could manage, casting it in a sphere around his body.

Leaves and branches slashed as he plummeted through the canopy. Monkeys screamed and dove for cover; parrots burst from their perches in a fury of red and blue feathers. As Michael caught sight of the shade-dappled ground, he cast a second shield, one that pressed into the ground, giving as he approached, slow-ing his velocity. He hit hard, caroming around the inner sphere as it slammed into the earth and dug a hell of a crater, meteorlike.

Pain thundered through him, and his head spun from

the impact, but he didn't have time to be hurt. The moment he was down, he heard a woman's scream. *Sasha!*

He dropped the shield magic and tumbled out of its embrace. The warm, moist rain forest air smelled of blood and rattled with dark magic. He could feel it in his skull, in his chest, and suddenly found himself fighting the mad lure of hellmagic, and the strength it threatened to offer the Other.

"Sasha!" He lunged into the forest, chasing the sounds of a struggle.

He broke into a clearing, saw her on the ground, pinned beneath two black, furry beasts that looked like dogs but had too-smart eyes and bared their teeth when they saw him.

Michael didn't hesitate for a moment. "Me!" he yelled. "Fight me, damn it!"

He heard a roar from behind him, spun to meet the new attack, and gaped for a second at the sight of a *nahwal* on earth, nearly seven feet tall, with claws and fangs and bright, mad eyes. It went for him. Roaring, he ducked under the attack, then straightened up, inside the *nahwal*'s guard. He reversed his knife and jabbed the hilt into the creature's throat in a vicious blow that sent it reeling back, gagging, as a human would have done under the same attack.

Sasha screamed, "Michael!"

Michael spun as one of the black dogs leaped upon him, jaws snapping too close to his face. Jamming a knee into the beast's groin, he held it off long enough to get his knife up and into it. Blood gushed over his hand, hot and iron-scented. An unearthly howl split the air, and the dog disappeared. *Poof*, gone. *Magic*.

Lunging to his feet, Michael grabbed the second creature away from Sasha, cutting its throat in an automatic swipe. It went down in a spurt of blood. Seconds later it vanished.

Breathing hard, with battle rage running hot under protective instincts more intense than any he'd ever felt, he rounded on the *nahwal*, which had recovered from its throat jab and now bared its teeth, hissing. "Are you going to die as easily as your mutts?" Michael demanded

"No!" Sasha grabbed Michael's arm and tugged him back. "Don't kill it."

Thinking he recognized the scene, the creature, he tried to shake her off. "If I can kill it here, in spirit form, it'll be gone from the outside world, and we'll be able to get into the temple without it bothering us."

"You can't kill him," she said. "It's Ambrose."

Ambrose? He stared at the creature. The flinch nearly cost him.

As if in response to its name, the *nahwal* screeched and charged Sasha with murder and madness in its eyes. Reacting instinctively, Michael yanked Sasha against him in a hard, possessive hug and threw up a thick protective shield around them both.

The *nahwal* bounced off. Screaming in frustration, it clawed at the shield, trying to gouge its way through.

Inside the protective bubble, Sasha threw her arms around Michael, shaking hard. He hugged her back with equal intensity as relief crashed through him. He'd gotten to her in time.

They clung together for a few seconds, while the *nahwal* howled and fought the shield. Then Sasha pulled away. "I tried the '*way*' spell. It didn't work for me."

"Shit." That was not good news. Michael could feel the silver magic poised at the edges of his mind, but he shied away from its power. What if in using it to get Sasha and him home, she wound up tainted by the darkness too? He couldn't risk it.

"We need more of a power draw to get out of here,

right?" She met his eyes, her lips turning up at the corners, but her expression remained wary.

He got it. More, it was so obvious that he wondered why his thoughts had gone straight to the silver magic. Or rather, he knew why and didn't want to accept it. "Power, it is," he said, shifting her in his arms, blocking the Other as hard as he possibly could these days, as he leaned down. And kissed her.

Sex magic sparked around them, reassuringly red-gold, though not nearly as powerful as the silver *muk*. It would be enough, though. They would make it be enough.

Her arms came up and around his neck as she leaned up on her toes up to press her body into his. He slid his hands down her sides, catching her around the waist, holding her close as he'd imagined doing so many nights since they'd been together. Her mouth opened beneath his; their tongues touched. Desire flared, hot and hard, but with an edge of tenderness that was theirs alone as they kissed and kissed again. But even as he kissed her and called the red-gold Nightkeeper magic, he was aware that the Other was there as well, called by Sasha, empowered by her.

She's ours, his alter ego had said, and that had definitely been a threat.

I won't let you have her, Michael thought fiercely. *I won't*. He reached for the red-gold magic, hoped to hell it would be enough. Ending the kiss, he pressed his cheek to hers and whispered, "*Way*." Home.

And the world disappeared, leaving the howl of the mad *nahwal* to trail off into a silence broken, deep down inside Michael, by the Other's raspy whisper. *Don't make promises you aren't man enough to keep*.

Sasha clung to Michael as the world went gray-green and swept them up into the barrier on a mad whirl. They were torn apart, but she barely had time to shout his name before her soul slammed back into her body and the world took shape around her, becoming the sacred chamber back at Skywatch.

Thank the gods. They'd made it back.

Moaning, she cracked her eyes open and tried to regain feeling in her stiff body, which was all but frozen cross-legged. Expecting to see everything the same as it had been when the ritual began, it took her a moment to realize that wasn't the case. She was holding Michael's hand on one side, but they were the only two magi still sitting in the ceremonial circle. Most of the others had left the chamber. Strike remained, though; he stood just inside the door with Jox at his side.

They were staring at her.

Sasha didn't know what to think about that, what to think about any of it. Her head was spinning and she was ravenous. She was also stirred up, heated by Michael's kiss, and her head was full of the things that had happened inside the barrier. Ambrose was haunting the temple; it made sense, it fit. But at the same time it didn't. She now remembered hearing him whisper, "Have faith" to her as Iago had taken her away. But if he'd been there, why hadn't he saved her? Had he *wanted* the Xibalbans to have her? Why—

"Sasha." Michael tugged his hand from her too-tight grip and nudged her arm. "Earth to Sasha."

Torn from her whirling thoughts, she stared blankly at him. "What? Oh." She flushed at the heat in his eyes, and felt an answering kick of desire within her. But then he looked past her, his expression going strange and rueful as he nodded to the others. "I think those two want to talk to you."

"What? Why?"

"Check your wrist."

Adrenaline shot through her system when she real-

ized she'd all but forgotten about the point of the bloodline ceremony in the chaos of what had followed. The
nahwal, she remembered. That had been Scarred-Jaguar;
hadn't it? The royal *nahwal* was the only one to retain
personal characteristics. But why had the royal *nahwal*
come for her?

She became acutely aware of the slight tingle that
spread across her inner forearm, seeming too large for a
single mark. *Oh, shit*, she thought, afraid to look, afraid
not to. Before she could make the move, Jox crossed to
her, leaned down, and offered his hand. His sleeve slid
back to reveal the marks on his forearm.

Where before there had been two jaguar glyphs
above the *aj-winikin*, now there were three.

Something inside Sasha went still. Shaking, caught in
her oldest and strongest fantasy, the one where she had
an actual family, she pushed back the sleeve of her soiled,
dragging robe. Shock slammed through her at the sight
of not just one mark . . . but four. The jaguar. The royal
ju. The warrior. And something she didn't recognize—a
talent she hadn't yet tapped.

She hadn't just gotten her bloodline mark; she'd also
gotten her talent marks, along with an unexpected, terrifying glyph that couldn't be true. The *ju*. The mark of
the jaguar kings. "I'm not . . ." she began, then trailed
off. She looked up at Strike. "Ambrose was my father."
She paused. Swallowed. Said in a smaller voice, "Wasn't
he?"

Strike's face was crowded with emotion, but his voice
was matter-of-fact when he said, "The *winikin* stepped
in as our guardians. Apparently, Ambrose stepped in as
yours."

Jox had tears in his eyes. "I'm sorry, child. I didn't
know. I would've looked for you if I did. I would've done
whatever it took to find you."

A hot, messy ball of emotion gathered in Sasha's

throat and clogged her chest as she realized that if this was true, if she was really a child of the jaguar bloodline, then Jox should have been her *winikin*. She should have been raised as Strike and Anna had been, with love and a fair-minded understanding of who and what they were. Not blood and madness.

"Who am I?" she asked Strike.

The king looked simultaneously shell-shocked and hopeful. "The *nahwal* said you're his second daughter. That would make you Anna's and my baby sister . . . the one who was supposedly stillborn two years before the Solstice Massacre."

Sasha opened her mouth, but nothing came out.

It was Michael, solid beside her, his eyes dark with an indefinable emotion, who said, "Looks like it was more than a nickname . . . Princess."

CHAPTER TWELVE

University of Texas, Austin

As it got on toward midnight on the night of the full moon, Rabbit killed the music, set his book aside, and started pulling himself together for his late date. Myrinne had told him to come to her room at ten of twelve, not before, and she'd been serious about the timing. So he was following orders, despite the buzz of anticipation that'd played hell with his concentration in the hours leading up to the rendezvous.

He didn't know what sort of surprise she had planned, but he was hoping it involved getting naked. He also hoped it wouldn't include any of the witchy stuff she'd been increasingly into lately. If Anna or any of the others knew Myrinne had been dabbling with Mistress Truth's spell books and paraphernalia, they'd shit a brick. Rabbit was skirting deep trouble by not saying anything to them, but what was he supposed to do, rat out his girlfriend? That was so not happening. Besides, it was all harmless stuff, not even real magic, as far as he could tell. It seemed to be mostly about centering personal energy flows and crap like that, which made it little more than a glorified yoga class with some extra candles and crystals. If she got in any deeper, he figured he'd say something. For now, he was just glad the rituals seemed to have smoothed out the edges she'd developed in the first few weeks they'd been on campus, when she hadn't wanted to spend much time with him, preferring to be on her own, or hanging with friends he never seemed to meet.

Lately, she'd been spending more and more time with him, and seemed happier overall. He figured he could overlook the yoga stuff if this was the end result. Gods knew she'd had some major life upheavals over the past year. If this was how she needed to deal, then so be it. It wasn't like he could judge—he'd spent most of the months following his old man's death hanging out in the pueblo ruins behind Skywatch, smashed on the drug-laced, highly alcoholic *pulque* he'd snagged from Jox's not-so-hidden stash. In fact, when he thought about it that way, she was probably dealing with things better than he had.

At exactly ten to midnight, his blood buzzing pleasantly with anticipation, Rabbit crossed the hallway and knocked on her door.

Her husky voice called, "Come on in."

He opened the door and his pulse kicked to find the lights off and fat red candles flickering, and Myrinne wearing the long black silk bathrobe he'd bought her a few weeks ago after she'd bookmarked it on his Web browser as a hint. Her hair was loose and lustrous, and she wore the jade bracelet he'd given her over the summer.

Rabbit grinned. *Hello. Guess I'm getting lucky tonight!*

It wasn't until he stepped into the room and locked the door at his back that he saw that the candles weren't ambience, after all. At least not entirely. They sat at the points of a six-pointed star that was drawn on the linoleum floor in red electrician's tape, with a double line through the middle of the star.

Myrinne's expression went wary at his double take. "Problem?" she said, her voice faintly challenging.

Rabbit squelched his first few responses, which were all variations of, *Oh, fucking shit, baby, are you* trying *to get me in trouble?* She deserved better than that. Of anyone at Skywatch—or anyone in his life, ever—she'd been the first to be entirely on his side, no matter what. The others kept trying to make him fit into their prophecies, their rules, not seeming to understand that a half-blood, by definition, didn't conform to the Nightkeepers' rules. Hell, in the past, no half-blood would've even been put through the bloodline ceremony and allowed to perform magic. It was a case of luck, lack of manpower, his own strong magic, and eventually Strike's royal *this is how it's gonna be* that had gained him acceptance as a Nightkeeper, over his old man's strenuous objections and dire predictions.

And whether because of those predictions or because he was truly a screwup at heart, he'd blown up one opportunity after another, most of the time literally . . . until he met Myrinne. She'd been the first one to appreciate him—and maybe even love him?—for who and what he was, for what he could do. She wasn't afraid of him, hadn't been from the first. In fact, she was always encouraging him to practice more, work harder, develop the multipronged talent that set him apart from the others.

Could he do any less for her?

So he took a deep breath and forced himself not to freak out at the sign of the star on the floor and the suspicion that this wasn't exactly the kind of date he'd had in mind. Unable to think of a better response off the cuff, he said, "Nice candles."

Some of the fight drained out of her, and she smiled at him, candlelight catching her eyes. "The star represents the two of us. You're the fire sign—no-brainer—which is the upward triangle, and I'm earth, which is the downward triangle with the line through the middle. Put the two together, and you get the transected star."

He liked the symbolism just fine, with it joining the two of them together and all. But he wasn't sure he liked where he thought she was going with the rest of it. "Myr . . . you know we can't do magic, right? We swore blood oaths to Strike and Anna."

She crossed to him, moving through the star with a smooth sweep of her robe, somehow avoiding all the candles in the process. On one level, Rabbit thought sourly that if he ever tried that while wearing, say, his ceremonial robes back at Skywatch, he would've lit his shit right up. On another, more primal level, his skin tightened at her approach, and his jeans, baggy though they were, grew uncomfortably tight in the crotch.

Stopping very close to him, close enough to kiss, to touch, she did neither, instead raising an eyebrow in challenge. "We swore a blood oath not to do Nightkeeper magic. This isn't."

Rabbit's breath left him in a whoosh, and his brain clicked back into *oh, shit* mode. Technically, she was right, but he knew damn well that the technicality wouldn't save him from getting his ass handed to him if Strike or Anna found out. Or Jox. Or, hell, any of the gang back at Skywatch.

But you're not at Skywatch, are you? said a small, sly voice inside him. *They sent you away to grow up. Who's to say this isn't part of the process? It's called making your own decisions, asshole. You might want to give it a try sometime.*

"Besides," Myrinne continued, lifting his right hand to press a small kiss at his wrist, over the bloodred Xibalban mark he'd accepted from Iago in order to save her life, "don't you have questions?"

He went still. "You've got an answer spell?"

"It's called scrying," she corrected, "and yeah. Especially since tonight is the esbat—the full moon—I think we should be able to figure out where you can find the spell to call a new three-question *nahwal*. Or heck, maybe we'll even call up the spell itself." She paused tellingly. "That's assuming that you get behind this a hundred percent. It won't work if you're not into it, or if you don't trust me."

"I trust you," he said immediately, realizing that he'd begun to sweat lightly, which sucked, because he was wearing the last of his clean shirts. "It's just . . . if it's not Nightkeeper magic—"

"It's not," she broke in. "No blood sacrifice, no barrier. It's all about flames and mirrors."

"Then are you sure it'll answer questions about Nightkeeper magic? Does it . . . I don't know . . . acknowledge other magic systems?"

It was the right thing to say, he saw immediately from the gleam in her eyes. "It's more along the lines of self-hypnosis, allowing you to access your own natural visions and your connection to other levels of sight and knowledge," she said. "It's all very low-impact, very natural. Honest."

He shouldn't do it, he knew. He should back out as gracefully as possible, hoping she didn't take it the wrong way. But even as he told himself that, he couldn't help thinking about everything that'd gotten fucked up because he'd killed the three-question *nahwal*. If the Nightkeepers still had access to its answers, they might've rescued Sasha sooner, found the library, found a new intersection . . . hell, they might've even dealt with Iago by now. Who knew?

"What . . ." Rabbit faltered. "If these visions come from my magic, or my ancestors, or, shit, the barrier or something, then it's Nightkeeper magic." But the protest didn't sound convincing even to his own ears. He kept picturing what Strike's face would look like if he showed up at Skywatch and announced that he knew how to summon a new three-question *nahwal*. Or better yet, that he'd already summoned it. That'd have to make up for some of his more spectacular disasters, right? And, tangentially, it'd prove to them that Myrinne belonged with the magi, and with him, because she would've been his catalyst for recovering the *nahwal*.

Right?

She slid her hand down his forearm, across his bloodline mark—the peccary—and his main talent mark, that of pyrokinesis. When their fingers linked, she squeezed, conveying her sympathy and support. Her affection. "Trust me," she said again.

How could he not? He might've saved her from Iago, but she'd saved him right back. He was alive because of her. He didn't just trust her; he loved her.

"Okay, let's do it," he said finally, and was rewarded by her brilliant smile.

She leaned in and kissed him hard, slightly off center, but was gone before he could correct the angle and follow up with more. She skipped back across the star, making the candlelight dance. "Sit here," she ordered, pointing to one spire of the star. "That's the top of your triangle. I'll sit at the top of mine."

They linked hands over the flickering candles, making a small, intimate circle of two. Myrinne said some sort of incantation about the mother and the earth, and being young and seeing all that was to be seen. Rabbit didn't totally follow all of the words, not for lack of trying, but because she was so damned beautiful in the candlelight that he couldn't stop looking at her, couldn't take his eyes off the play of light and shadow across her face.

The bloodred candles were faintly scented—how had

he not noticed that before?—and whatever was in them made his head spin, made his body feel light.

"Look into the mirror," she said now. A faint smile touched her lips. "You can look at me later. Promise."

"I'll hold you to that," he said, feeling an added layer of heat kick into his bloodstream. He looked into the mirror, where she had placed a slender candle made of clear wax, or maybe some sort of crystal. Whatever the components, it made the candlelight refract at all sorts of crazy angles. The flickers merged and separated, always moving, never the same. The patterns fixed his attention, drew him in. "Cool," he breathed, and heard his own voice as if from far away.

"Now, ask your question aloud; then hold it in your head as you keep looking into the flame and the mirror."

He stared into the patterns, imagining that he saw men and women in the flames. "How can I summon a new three-question *nahwal*?" The flames skipped and danced, showing nothing but light and shadow. For a second he saw an animal—maybe a coyote?—and something that might've been a boat. But then it was just flames and shadows again, and nothing more.

After a few minutes, when their clasped hands were starting to get damp with sweat, she said, "Anything?"

Rabbit shook his head. "Nothing I'd call an answer."

"Maybe the way you said it was too specific. Maybe you'd be calling the same old *nahwal*, so the word 'new' in the question short-circuited the answer. Or maybe the answer isn't replacing the *nahwal*; maybe there's some other sort of oracle you can summon instead."

"Good point," Rabbit agreed, adding, "Damn, you're smart." He felt a little drunk and a lot horny, sitting there holding her hands, achingly aware that she was naked beneath the robe. But he made himself focus, and asked, "What can I do to help the Nightkeepers?"

Again, he thought he saw patterns in the reflected light—a burning tree, a big house in flames—but nothing that gave him a clue how to fix what he'd broken.

He glanced sidelong at his and Myrinne's intertwined fingers, and at the stark marks on his forearm: three black, one red. In contrast, her forearm was creamy white and unmarked, which made him ache. He wanted her to wear his *jun tan*, wanted the world to know they were bound to each other. But no matter how much he wished for it, no matter how much he loved her, the gods hadn't marked them as a mated pair. Not yet, anyway.

"Try another question," she suggested. "Maybe one that's more personal. Something about you rather than the Nightkeepers."

"Are—" He broke off, ashamed to realize he didn't have the chops to ask if he and Myrinne were destined mates, partly because he didn't want a "no" from the candle flame and partly because he didn't want one from her. So he fudged it, saying aloud, "What is my destiny?" Inwardly, though, he asked the question he really wanted the answer to: *How can I make Myrinne mine?*

Nothing happened. He sighed, frustrated and more disappointed than he would've thought, given that he hadn't really believed her so-called scrying spell was going to work in the first place. "I guess I'm not—" He broke off as the reflected flames suddenly turned liquid and blurred together before his eyes. "Holy shit. I think it's working."

Myrinne said something, but he couldn't hear her, couldn't hear anything but the pounding of blood in his veins, in his head. His heartbeat sounded like ritual drums, his bloodstream like a waterfall. *What is my destiny?* he asked inwardly. *How can I make Myrinne mine?*

The world went silent, as though his heart had stopped entirely. The liquid flames merged and separated, merged and separated . . . and then they roared up, reaching for him. And when they touched him, they burned like fury.

Rabbit felt his mouth stretch wide in a scream, but couldn't hear his own voice, could hear only the horrible roar of flames. He was dimly aware of Myrinne shaking him, then leaving him to beat at something nearby. He saw her mouth move in panicked shouts he couldn't hear, couldn't respond to. He could only curl in agony, screaming silent howls of pain that quickly turned to denial as he blinked back into the vision and saw himself standing over Myrinne, who lay at his feet in a spreading pool of blood, her lovely eyes wide and fixed in death. As he watched, a drop of blood fell from the ceremonial knife he held in his fist, to land on her upturned, waxen face.

"No!" He writhed, pushing the image away, rejecting it, rejecting himself. "No, I won't do it; *I won't*!" He heard the words now, heard them echo inside his skull.

And in those echoes was embedded another voice, deeper yet familiar, growling, "Then fucking get rid of the hellmark, shit for brains! As long as Iago can find you, he can control you, and the gods can't touch you. Get rid of the godsdamned hellmark, or you're godsdamned screwed."

"Red-Boar?" His voice cracked on the name as his lungs filled with the acrid smell of char. He doubled over, coughing and retching, dimly aware that Myrinne's dorm room was full of smoke, the fire alarms shrilling. "Dad!"

"Come on!" Myrinne hauled him up. "We've got to get out of here!"

The room was aflame around them. For real.

Rabbit's head swam, he was nauseated as shit, and he felt like he had one foot on the earthly plane, one foot somewhere else. He couldn't wipe the hellish visions out of his head, couldn't do anything but moan and lean on Myrinne as they staggered out into the hallway and joined the stream of bodies headed out of the dorm.

There were a few screams and a surge of the traffic flow when they staggered out of the burning dorm room and the other students realized that there actually was a fire, that it wasn't a drill.

As they shuffled down the stairs, packed cattle car–tight with the other evacuees, Myrinne yanked Rabbit's cell out of his pocket and speed-dialed. Shouting over the din, she said, "Anna? We need you. Meet us outside your office building. And bring me some clothes." She was still wearing her black silk robe, and didn't have any shoes on. Rabbit noticed those details as if from a great distance away.

When they hit the great outdoors, his breathing eased but his head didn't clear. If anything, the spins were getting worse and he was feeling less and less connected to his body by the second. "I d-d-don't think we should leave when the fire's in your room . . ." he got out, then lost the thread of his thought.

Waxy face. Blood dripping from a knife.

"Anna will fix it," Myrinne said, hustling him away from the crowd. "She'll call admin and tell them where we are, and some version of what happened."

That had him glancing back over his shoulder to the dorm, where flames licked out an upstairs window. He moaned, a low, broken sound, and turned away, hanging his head and gulping oxygen as he and Myrinne staggered to Anna's office.

Strike was going to fucking kill him this time, he thought. But behind that thought came another, a whisper in a dead man's voice: *Get rid of the godsdamned hellmark, or you're godsdamned screwed.* Which made sense, because the hellmark not only connected him to the first level of Xibalba, it bound him to Iago, giving the Xibalban bastard access to Rabbit's head under certain circumstances. So getting rid of the hellmark made sense . . . but it wasn't exactly an original concept. Strike and the others had tried everything they could think of to break the hellbond, but none of the spells had worked.

"What about it, old man?" Rabbit croaked, earning a wide-eyed look from Myrinne. "Want to tell me how the fuck I'm supposed to get rid of the damned thing?"

The darkness rose up, grabbed Rabbit, and dragged him down. He pitched forward, nearly taking Myrinne down with him as he collapsed against the side of the art history building. An he passed out, an image flashed through his brain, that of a carving, rough-hewn and powerful, showing a glyph that wasn't Mayan, but far older: a scorpion with a double zigzag line beneath it.

Skywatch

Michael stood on the upper level of the great room with his back to the wall, watching over Sasha from afar because he didn't dare get within touching distance. She sat on one of the big sofas, describing the barrier vision the *nahwal* had sent her into. When she was done, Michael filled in with a few of his own observations.

Finally, Strike summed it up: "So it seems like a good bet that the library scroll is somewhere in the temple, and Sasha is probably the key to gaining access, given that the thing we've been calling the mad *nahwal* is Ambrose's ghost . . . or I guess demi-*nahwal* is as good a term as any." He paused, his lips curving. "Meanwhile, on the 'oh, holy shit' front, Sasha got her bloodline mark, the warrior talent, another talent we're going to have to look into, and—hello, bonus—the royal *ju*." He was playing it pretty cool, but blinking a little too much, evidence of what it'd meant to him to gain a sister.

Sasha's answering smile was strained around the edges. "That's going to take a little while to sink in, I think."

"For all of us," Leah said from her position beside Strike. She dropped a hand to his shoulder and squeezed. "So can I be blatantly practical and suggest we call it a night and reconvene tomorrow? We all pulled a fair bit of magic tonight, and probably shouldn't make any major decisions until we've recharged. Let's eat and crash."

"I second that," Sven said from his position flat-out on the floor in the middle of the great room. "I'm whupped."

As if that'd been the signal they were waiting for, the *winikin* moved in and started shepherding their charges toward food and then bed. Jox beelined for Sasha, his face alight, as if to say, *This one's mine!* On one level, Michael was overjoyed for her. If any of them had needed to step into a ready-made family, it was her. More, Sasha, Strike, and Anna should be able to uplink and increase one another's power significantly—the sibling bond wasn't as powerful as the twin bond or that of a mated pair, but it was meaningful nonetheless. With Strike and Leah's Godkeeper bond negated by the destruction of the sky-road, Sasha's ability to amplify the king's power would be invaluable in battle, since she also wore the warrior's mark.

Which meant that while there was no denying the power of the sex magic boost she and Michael made together, she didn't technically need him for the magic anymore. She could lean on Strike or Anna. Michael told himself that should be a relief, that the less she needed him, the better off they all were. He'd gotten away with kissing her to bring them both back out of the barrier, but he had a feeling the Other had been almost ... toying with him. Like it was waiting for something. But what?

Big surprise, he thought, irritated. *More questions, no*

answers. He shifted against the wall, strung tight with a restless, edgy energy entirely at odds with the postmagic burn he should've been feeling. He wanted to run into the night, wanted to pick a fight, wanted to throw his head back and howl at the moon.

Fuck all that; he wanted sex. He wanted Sasha, hard and fast, tight and wet around him, bowing back, her name tumbling from his lips as he pounded himself against her, poured himself into her, marking her as his own. Lover, killer—he didn't even totally care which aspect of him got the score, as long as he was buried deep within her, and they were—

Oh, shit, he thought, squeezing his eyes shut as he figured it out. The hormones.

Sasha might have gotten her bloodline and talent marks at the same time, but that didn't mean she was totally clear of the hormone surges they'd all experienced between their bloodline and talent ceremonies. In fact, from the look of her flushed face and the way she'd suddenly become the center of attention in the kitchen, where Jox was plying her with tamales and some sort of seafood concoction, Michael would've bet his left nut she was on the brink of a really compressed version of the pretalent hormone surges. And it was going to be a Very. Long. Night.

Peeling himself away from his wall perch, he took a step in her direction, then made himself stop. She didn't need him near her right now. In fact, he should stay the hell away from her for the duration.

You'd rather someone else do the honors? a sly voice said from deep within him. He wasn't sure if it was the Other or his own black mood talking. Either way, it was a valid point, Michael thought, glaring down at Sven, who'd pried himself off the floor to join the testosterone party in the kitchen. The other magi were happily mated—they'd soak up some of the sex-magic buzz she was giving off, then take to their own beds. The *winikin* weren't sensitive to the magic, so they were safe. But Sven was neither mated nor a *winikin*. And as Michael watched, he moved in, dipped his head toward Sasha with intimate familiarity, and said something that made her laugh.

Rage flashed through Michael, blinding him. For a second all he could see was Sven's eyes bugging, his mouth drawing wide in horror; all he could feel was the hammer of the other man's carotid under his thumbs as he choked the living shit out of the bastard who'd pretended to be his friend, then taken his woman. He—

Oh, shit. I've got to get the fuck out of here. Blinking hard in an effort to banish the horrible sensory image and the way it both repulsed and tempted him, Michael spun and headed for the sliders. He nearly plowed over Tomas, who stood in his path.

"Out of my way. I need air."

The *winikin* stood fast. "You need food. How about we head over to the kitchen and I can—"

"Not the kitchen," Michael said, his voice going ragged. "You want me to eat, snag me something and bring it out. You know where I'll be." He was pretty sure the *winikin* had followed him out to the ball court at least once over the past few weeks.

"Do you really care so little for the will of the gods?" the *winikin* said, eyes narrowing. "I know you too damn well to believe you haven't picked up on it. She's for you. Don't you get that?"

Desire flared so hot that it felt like desperation. "I can't—" Michael almost got it out that time before the inner shields slammed down, stopping the words in his throat.

Tomas made a disgusted noise, and Michael figured the next thing out of his mouth was going to be a variation on the old, *Get your head out of your ass and take some damned responsibility, for gods' sake!* Instead, the *winikin* fixed him with a look and said, "I want you to promise me something."

The seriousness of his tone had Michael focusing on the other man. "Maybe," Michael answered, momentarily distracted by the sound of Sasha's laugh when Sven—the bastard—said something else to her. He growled. "On one condition. You promise me that once we're done here, you'll grab Carlos, and the two of you will get Sven good and drunk. I want him legless until midday tomorrow. Understand?"

"It's a deal," Tomas said immediately.

Reluctantly, Michael refocused on him. "What do you want from me?" The question might've started as a reference to the promise at hand, but once it was out there, it somehow expanded to cover so much more than that. Even if he'd been able to talk to Tomas about his work with Bryson, he suspected the *winikin* still would've found fault somehow. There had always been something, going back as far as he could remember. There was perfection. Then, beyond that, there was Tomas. "Let me guess," he said when the *winikin* didn't answer immediately. "You want me to shape up and be a better man. You want me to work harder, try harder. You want me to give what's between me and Sasha a chance. Better yet, you want me to pair up with her, regardless of what my gut is telling me, just because the signs say we're meant to be. News flash, *winikin*: The gods aren't here anymore. We're on our own."

He expected Tomas to bark at him, and was disconcerted when the other man just shook his head, looking sad and strung out. "You're so much like him. It scares the hell out of me sometimes."

"Like who? My father? I don't know why that would scare you. You've always made him sound like the model mage, the ideal."

"He was. I was talking about his brother. Your uncle Jayce."

Michael zeroed in on him. "I didn't know I had an uncle Jayce. Let me guess—he was an underachieving disappointment, a general blot on the stone bloodline until he semiredeemed himself by dying for his king during the Solstice Massacre."

"No, actually. He was a brilliant man, a wicked fighter, and a highly respected mage . . . until the day he killed himself."

A beat of silence hung between the two men before Michael could bring himself to say, "You think I'm suicidal?"

Maybe not now. But there had been days.

"No. But then again, nobody thought Jayce would kill himself," Tomas answered. "Least of all his *winikin*. My father."

Michael winced. "Oh, shit. Sorry."

The *winikin* culture was one of protection and support. It was a *winikin*'s job to keep his charge alive and functional. Although suicide wasn't necessarily a sin in the Nightkeeper world—far from it—he had to figure that an unexpected autosacrifice would be seen as the ultimate failure for the suicide's *winikin*, whose job it was to keep the magi alive and kicking.

Uncle Jayce, Michael thought as a few more pieces fell into place. He supposed that explained even more of Tomas's control-freak ways, though it didn't make him any easier to live with. "I'm not going to off myself now," he said, letting the last word acknowledge Tomas's instincts.

When he'd come to Skywatch, Michael hadn't had a clue he was anything but a salesman with an eye for women and a good, if slightly shallow, heart. When Bryson had terminated him as an operative, Horn had used him as a guinea pig, splitting his halves so thoroughly, he'd thought his cover was really him. That is, until he'd jacked in for his talent ceremony, his bloodline *nahwal* had laid the warrior talent on him, and he got a hell of a "This is your life, Michael Stone!"

In the aftermath, hell, yes, he'd thought about killing himself. All he'd been able to think about was murder, reliving the Other's kills over and over again. He'd eventually regained control, and had decided he could do the Nightkeepers more good than harm by staying alive. But still, it had definitely been an option.

Unlike the Christian viewpoint of suicide as a sin, in the Nightkeeper culture it was the act of greatest sacrifice to the gods, thereby earning a trip straight to the sky. Michael figured that, in his case, it might at least balance out the bad shit. But at the same time he couldn't help wanting to think the gods really did have a plan for him, that they wouldn't have let him get so far toward damnation without some reason.

Unless, of course, his destiny wasn't in their hands anymore. The barrier had been sealed when he took Bryson's job offer. It was possible he'd damned himself beyond the gods' redemption long before the Nightkeepers were reunited, that he was laboring under majorly false delusions now. If that was the case, then Sasha had been meant for a different version of him—the one that had told Bryson to stick his job offer, that he was no killer.

Except he *was* a killer. And he hadn't turned Bryson down.

He glanced over to the kitchen once again, only to see that Sven was no longer hanging all over Sasha. Instead, he was sitting at the breakfast bar opposite Carlos, downing shots in rapid-fire succession, amidst catcalls from the others. Jade sat nearby, working on a bottle of wine, apparently having also decided in favor of self-medication.

Michael glanced at Tomas. "You and Carlos already

had that cooked up, didn't you? You're taking out the competition on both sides."

The *winikin* lifted a shoulder. "You're not perfect by a long shot, but Sven has some major growing up to do before he'll know what to do with a mate. You, at least, know how to keep a woman happy."

"Not necessarily," Michael said, thinking of the parade of women who'd passed through his life, starting with Esmee, the FBI trainee he'd dated soon after leaving the academy. He'd hung onto her too long, not realizing that she was the first in a long line of women who would be hot on him at the beginning, then fade when they realized he couldn't give them the deep emotion they sought. "Is that what you want me to promise? That I'll give it a go with Sasha?"

But the *winikin* shook his head. "That's between you two and the gods. I want you to promise that if you ever do think seriously about sacrificing yourself for the good of the Nightkeepers, or to quiet whatever it is that's going on inside your skull, you'll come talk to me first. Or if you can't talk to me, you'll talk to someone."

Michael's throat went dry. "That . . . Yeah. That I can promise." He didn't like that the *winikin* saw as much as he did. But at the same time, it shifted something inside him, something that said, *If only.* If only he'd turned down Bryson. If only he'd taken his FBI training more seriously, made less of an ass of himself. If only he'd grown up sooner, like Tomas had wanted him to do. *Damn it all.*

The *winikin* nodded. "Thanks. Go on, then. I'll pull together some food for you and leave it by the path." He paused and nodded toward the kitchen. "Unless you've changed your mind?"

Sasha, Strike, and Leah were chatting animatedly while wolfing down whatever Jox had put in front of them. Carlos and Sven were going strong on the shots.

Nate and Alexis, Brandt and Patience had already decamped to their suites, no doubt to take advantage of the contact high from Sasha's sex-magic buzz. For a moment, Michael yearned. Because he did, and because the Other's darkness stirred beneath the want, he turned away. "I'll be outside."

Tomas nodded. "Your call." But his tone said, *You're an idiot.*

When Sasha finally wound down enough that she thought she could sleep, she headed for her suite, feeling as if she were floating on feet that barely touched the floor.

Part of her euphoria came from the barely realized amazement of finding her family, finding that she was royalty—she thought that would become a reality over the next few days, not all at once. Another part of the bubbling dizziness came from sheer exhaustion; she wasn't just physically tired—she was mentally drained, and felt like she'd been sucked dry of both thought and energy. She was dragged down by having seen what Ambrose had become, but energized by the promise that the scroll was somewhere inside the temple. And the magic that had come from Michael's kiss hadn't yet faded, though it had been hours.

Body tingling with the sensual awareness brought by sex magic, she jittered around her small apartment as the night deepened and the mansion quieted around her. She checked her herb family for their water status—all good—and straightened things in the kitchen and main room that didn't need straightening. Her laptop failed to hold her attention, as did the paperbacks stacked beside the couch. She thought about taking a shower, but it wasn't until she vetoed the idea because it meant going through the bedroom that she admitted to herself what the problem really was.

She was horny. And not just a little. A lot.

It wasn't like she hadn't known what was going on out in the kitchen; she'd caught the looks, and the not-too-subtle jockeying for the mated pairs to get very near her, then slip away, bright-eyed and holding hands. She'd snorted inwardly when Carlos had waylaid Sven with a bottle, and suffered a pang when she saw Jade anesthetizing herself similarly. The pretty brunette had silently toasted Sasha with her glass, and mouthed, *Go get him,* across the room, giving her blessing again, though Sasha had long known the coast was clear on that account.

No, the *winikin* and magi had conspired to make it easy for her and Michael to be together in the hormone burn of the aftermath. What they didn't get, because they didn't know, was that it wasn't going to happen. Their exchange prior to the bloodline ceremony suggested that he wasn't just pushing her away to be an ass. There was something going on with him, something dark and angry inside him that he didn't want her to see. She didn't know whether to give him the space he seemed so desperate for or talk to one of the other magi about it or what. But she knew one thing: She wasn't signing on for anything long-term with a man who had both commitment *and* anger issues. She wasn't Pim, damn it.

But what if it's not long-term? she asked herself, moving restlessly around the space that was quickly becoming her home. *What if it's just for tonight?*

He'd first kissed her to fuel his shield spell, and though he'd later apologized for how far it had gone, she knew the sex had given him a hell of a power boost. What if she went to him now, and asked him to return the favor?

On another day, under other circumstances, she never would've considered a booty call. But the Nightkeeper ways were different from those of the outside world, often for logical reasons. Like this one. And once the idea took root, she couldn't shake it. Didn't want to. She was hot and bothered, wet and wanting; strange tingles skimmed over her skin, heating her, making her ache with the need for sex. For *him*.

She'd changed out of the combat clothes into flowing drawstring pants and a tight tank, with a sweatshirt over the top. Figuring that—gods willing—she'd be out of the clothes pretty damn quick, she didn't bother switching to something else, instead jamming her feet into a pair of slip-on sneakers and heading out of her suite, her pulse already bumping, her body ready for hard, fast sex.

As she skimmed down the hall, she knew her eyes were too bright, her cheeks flushed, and she hoped to hell she didn't meet anyone coming or going, because they would know exactly what she was up to. Tacit permission was one thing; the walk of shame was another.

Breath backing up in her lungs, she stopped outside Michael's suite, which was a corner unit with hallways on two sides, one leading to the mansion, the other connecting to the *winikin*'s residential wing. She knocked quietly. When there was no answer, she knocked a little louder, then risked it and stuck her head through the door, took an interested glance around the slick glass-and-chrome tables and black leather furniture, and called his name. There was no answer. Michael's suite was empty.

"Damn it," she muttered under her breath. "Where the hell are you?"

"If I might make a suggestion?" a familiar voice said from around the corner leading to the *winikin*'s wing.

Sasha blushed and shuffled around the corner, following the voice to its source. She found Michael's *winikin* sitting just down from his door, reading a well-thumbed hardcover. "Were you waiting for me?" she asked, feeling awkward in the extreme.

"Hoping," he said, with a small, tired smile. "I was hoping."

"And your suggestion?"

"Try the ball court. These days he goes there almost every night and fights himself into exhaustion."

"Oh." She winced at the image that engendered. "Do you . . . Never mind." She didn't want Michael to think she'd been sneaking around behind his back, quizzing his *winikin*.

But Tomas answered. "He has problems managing his temper sometimes. He was an angry kid, got worse in his teens. That was why all the fight training, not just because it's expected of a mage child, but because it was the only way I could think to keep him in check. I thought the military would be a good choice for him. That didn't stick, but he found his way into FBI training on his own. I thought it'd be a match. It wasn't. And since then . . ." The *winikin* spread his hands. "He's trying."

"He's been much worse since I came, hasn't he?"

"Yes, but that's not necessarily a bad thing. You might be just the motivation he needs to make him buckle down and fix himself. The process is not uncommon in the bloodline."

"So that makes it okay?"

"Of course not. But it makes it . . ." Tomas paused, trying to find the right word. "Manageable. The Stones that have the problem eventually figure out how to control it. You met him at an awkward time, that's all."

She stared at the *winikin*, not sure whether he totally believed that himself. "And that's all it is, right? Nothing, um, magical?" She still wasn't totally comfortable discussing magic as a reality. "There's not a really nasty talent in the bloodline, right?"

He glanced away, shaking his head. "Mostly warriors." He paused, then met her eyes once more and said softly, "That first night, when he brought you out of Iago's compound, he handed you off to me and made me promise not to give up on you, no matter what. So

I'm asking for the same thing from you. Don't give up on him. Please."

"I—" She broke off, unable to make the promise. "I don't want to." But at the same time, she had to protect herself.

"I understand." Tomas closed the book, let it rest on his thin knees for a moment. "The gods brought you to him. I just hope he'll listen to them better than he ever listened to me." He stood and inclined his head in a half bow. "Good night, Princess."

Then he turned away and headed for the *winikin*'s wing of the mansion, leaving Sasha to stare after him.

When he was gone, she told herself to abort the mission. Maybe she should follow Jade's example and drink herself to sleep. But the idea didn't appeal nearly as much as the image of Michael somewhere outside under the full moon, fighting himself into oblivion. She considered the options for all of five seconds. Then she pushed through the sliders and headed out into the moonlit night, intent on a hunt of her own.

CHAPTER THIRTEEN

Outside, the moon was lower than it had been before, during the ceremony, and gone yellow with its declination. Some small part of Sasha noted that it wasn't orange or otherwise off-color, confirming the latest reports that whatever was wrong with the sun, it wasn't the atmosphere's fault.

The larger part of her, though, focused on her footing, and the growing sense of nervy panic at what she was about to do—not only the booty-call aspect of things, but the prospect of disturbing Michael at his most private.

Still, though, she didn't turn back. She padded across the ash shadow where the great hall had stood in Ambrose's day. The ceiba tree that had grown from its ashes was black in the wan moonlight, its leaves limned in gray. Then she forged onward and passed into the wide space between the tall, parallel walls that formed the I-shaped ball court, where small stone rings were set high overhead as the goals of the ancient game, with its life-and-death stakes.

She was dimly aware of passing a tray of covered food,

but she focused entirely on the man at the center of the open space.

Barefoot and naked to the waist, wearing only the loose black track pants he favored around the compound, Michael wielded a pair of curved swords as though they were extensions of his arms. He moved as one beautiful, balanced whole when he spun, leaping into the air to avoid the swipe of an invisible attacker. He landed and lashed out, then flowed away again, his movements liquid and lovely in their perfect violence.

Sasha was hardly aware of moving, but she drew closer to him, crossing the packed earth that her ancestors had used for a game that had celebrated the daily rise and fall of the sun, the cycle of life itself. This night, though, the lone player wasn't celebrating anything. He was trying to burn himself out.

The moonlight gleamed off his skin; shadows edged the sharply defined muscles that slid beneath. His wide shoulders bunched and flexed, and the strong column of his spine curved elegantly as he reversed, redirected, then swept low and pinwheeled out of his phantom opponent's reach. There was no sound but the brush of his feet on the trampled dust, and the flare of his nylon pants. The silence made the whole scene feel otherworldly, as if she were standing outside herself, looking down on the scene.

Then he paused, holding a final triumphant form for several heartbeats before he broke the kata, set the swords aside, and turned to face her. Eyes dark in the night, he said, "You shouldn't have come."

She held her ground, tipped her head in acknowledgment. "Probably not. But I collect what I'm owed. You've used me twice to ramp up your magic. Now I need you to help me burn mine off."

He didn't pretend to misunderstand. "I owe you distance, not another go-round."

"I'm not sure that's your call." Blood hummed beneath her skin, pulsing in time with her heart, with the tension that sprang to life between them, hot and wanting.

"Then whose call is it?"

On impulse, riding the burn of her blood, she said, "I'll fight you for it. Winner chooses. Sex or distance."

"I don't want to hurt you."

Too late, she thought, but didn't say, because what would be the point? She was coming to realize that he hadn't intentionally hurt her; he was stuck in a loop of desire feeding into anger and back again, and not sure how to deal with either. So she jerked a thumb over her shoulder. "You haven't eaten yet, and you've been out here, what, an hour already? I'm guessing the edge is off."

"Not even close," he growled, eyes fixed on her with an intensity that sent shimmers of heat along her neurons to gather at her center, where they coiled, thrumming with desire.

This was the man she wanted, the one she'd come looking for. She tipped up her chin. "I'm willing to take my chances."

He stared at her a moment longer as the night closed in on them, the silence broken only by a whisper of wind running along the top of the ball court walls, and a coyote's eerie howl in the distance. Finally, moving so slowly that she was acutely aware of the change in each muscle, the exquisite control he commanded over his own body, he came to a ready position and inclined slightly in a bow. Acknowledging her challenge. Challenging her in return.

Adrenaline and burgeoning hormones hummed in her bloodstream, along with a sparkle of nerves that warned her she was already in over her head. But she didn't back down, didn't wimp out. She'd come outside for him. If this was what he was willing to give her, she'd take it. Then, gods willing, she'd take more.

Hyperconscious of her own body and the brush of cloth on skin, she skimmed out of her long-sleeved shirt, leaving her in the tight sports tank and flowing pants. She kept her sneakers on for the benefit of grip, bouncing on the balls of her feet a couple of times to test her balance and loosen muscles that threatened to go tight with excitement and need.

He watched her in utter stillness, the only movement the dark gleam of his eyes as they tracked her with an intensity that made the touch of his gaze into a caress. But when she squared off opposite him and mimicked his earlier bow before dropping into a balanced, fight-ready stance, he didn't make a move in her direction. Instead, he moved away, circling her slowly. She turned, keeping their eyes locked as he reversed the rotation, moving back widdershins.

They moved in synchrony, staying a constant distance apart, on a rotation that made it seem like they were dancing without touching. Then, without warning, he moved in with a foot sweep that nearly caught her, would've flattened her if her reactions had been any slower. She jumped over the top of the attack, touched down, and hopped again immediately, expecting a return sweep. But there was only his dry chuckle as he disengaged and resumed his circling. "The follow-through is too banal. I try not to do what's expected of me."

"So I've noticed." Knowing he was toying with her, she dampened the flare of irritation, reversed the circle, and closed on him from the side with a hip check–sweep combo that used a bigger opponent's leverage against him.

He twisted away from the meat of the throw, dropped himself, and rolled away, flowing to his feet with an elegance that tightened the knot of desire riding low in her belly. She didn't want to fight him; she wanted to feast on him, wanted her hands on him. But as she closed with him again, dodged a sweep-kick, and went in low, aiming an elbow into his kidneys that landed with a satisfying jolt, she was jarringly aware that he was doing everything he could to avoid touching her. He wasn't throwing punches or going for holds or throws; he was using his legs and feet, his balance and body mass.

"Put your damn hands on me," she snarled, closing and going for a hold. She gained purchase for a moment, putting the two of them face-to-face. She saw the fire in his eyes, felt the heat pouring off his skin.

He gripped her for a second, convulsively, and leaned in, his eyes hard and hot, and a little frightening. She saw the kiss coming, welcomed it with a flare of raw lust that wouldn't let her fear him. Then he flipped her, and the world spun a full revolution around her before she slammed to the ground, only to find him there, cradling her neck and hips in his arms to break her fall.

Enraged, she bounced to her feet and faced him, hands balled into fists at her sides, breaking the practiced positions for one of pissed-offedness. "Don't baby me, godsdamn it. *Fight me.*"

"I can't." His eyes were a little wild in his face, his chest heaving with far more exertion than he'd evidenced while practicing alone, though they'd done little but circle each other.

"You can," she insisted. "Just stop holding back. I can take a punch."

"You *want* me to kick your ass?"

"I want to live, damn it. I want to celebrate being free of Iago. I've got a bloodline now, a place in the world. He can't take that away from me. Nobody can." Startled by the freeing truth of it, she tipped her head back to the sky and laughed aloud. As if called by her joy, a sense of power flowed through her, a heady elixir that made her feel wholly feminine, yet strong with it rather than soft. She caught a thread of that foreign, marchlike music, and embraced it, sent the heat of her blood toward it, and welcomed it inside her when it washed back to her on a staccato rattle of drums.

Red-gold sparked at the edges of her vision—or was that in the air itself? She wasn't sure, but it gathered, stormlike, as she locked eyes once again with Michael, the man who'd rescued her, then turned away from her. He wasn't turning away now, though. He was staring at her hungrily, as though something she'd said had finally gotten through whatever was keeping him from making the move they both wanted.

She stepped into him, getting inside his space and looking up at him in direct challenge. The heat from his body echoed into hers and back again, binding them together. "And no, I don't want you to kick my ass," she said in answer to his earlier question. "I'd much rather do this."

Reaching up, she twined her arms around his neck, where the long hair at his nape was damp from his exertions. And then she kissed him, pouring all of the red-gold hope and magic that was within her into him, coaxing a response, demanding it. *Want me*, the kiss said. *Want me enough to get past whatever is hanging you up here. Want me enough to risk a relationship, risk a commitment, risk whatever it is that you're really afraid of.* And though she'd gone out there looking for a single night, the adrenaline high of sparring with him, of pushing him to the limits of his self-control, brought her all the way back to naked honesty, and the admission that she didn't just want this one night. She wanted more. She wanted everything. And so she poured everything into the kiss, and hoped to hell it would be enough.

Michael knew he should've sent her away the moment he'd sensed her there, watching him. He cursed himself for the weakness that prompted him to let her stay, the hubris that had convinced him he could handle it, that he could handle *her*. Instead, she'd leveled him almost immediately with her challenge and then taken him out at the knees with her kiss, and with the magic that spiraled through him, tempting him. Making him yearn.

He leaned into her, letting go of his control enough to cup her slim, strong waist and return the kiss half-measure, holding back, holding tight to the self-discipline he'd found through the katas he practiced in the darkness, using their rhythm and routine to keep the energy flow contained, the sluice gates shut. But even as he let go that much, and let her heady, intoxicating flavor seep through the sturdy barriers he'd erected around his soul, he could feel the Other's excitement, almost hear its voice. *No*, he said inwardly. *You're not welcome here.* And he turned his back on the creature within and let himself slide into Sasha's kiss, though he knew he was running a major risk. The feel of her in his arms once again made that risk seem worthwhile.

Her lips parted beneath his. He tasted her desire, felt it in her fingernails digging into his back. More, he felt the new magic in her, the sparkle of red-gold power. It was strong and sure, seeming so much purer than his own. He embraced it, leaned into it, and felt it push back the darkness inside him.

Take me, her kiss said. *I need this. I need you.* And gods knew he remembered the hormone burn of new magic, and the craziness it brought. But this was more than hormones, he knew. There was a connection that bolstered his magic and touched his soul, making him believe, for the moment, at least, that anything was possible. He'd managed to block the rage while they had sparred, had managed to keep the Other behind closed doors. That made him think he could keep blocking his nemesis, keep himself in control even when his body begged to be set free, out of control. Letting that control slip another degree, he deepened the kiss and let his hands follow the tug of gravity down from her waist to her curved buttocks, which filled his hands perfectly when he cupped her, drew her up and around him, then turned and pressed her against the carved ball court wall.

Her eyes glinted in the moonlight. "This feels familiar."

"One of these days we'll make it to a bed," he said, and wished he could believe there would be another time for them.

"It's a date." She wrapped herself around him and fastened her teeth on his lower lip, nipping gently at first, then increasing the pressure. Lust speared through him, hard and hot, and it was all he could do not to take her then and there.

His thoughts didn't extend past that prospect. There was no thought of tomorrow, only of that night, and the payback she'd demanded, that she'd challenged him for. She might not have won the fight by points or throws, but he'd ceded it to her rather than risk the edge of violence that rode the periphery of his mind, begging to be set free. *Not happening*, he told the Other. *She's mine. Not yours, not ours. Mine.*

He touched her through the thin fabric of her pants, kissed her throat, her cheeks, the point of her chin, as heat rose within him, threatened to take him over. He wasn't sure anymore whether it was her magic or his, the Other's grasping will, or a combination of all three, but his control wavered as temptation leaked through, borne on her sparkling, newly minted red-gold magic, which seemed somehow determined to reach inside him and find the places he wanted kept hidden.

"Let me love you," he whispered against her lips, barely aware of what he was saying anymore, knowing only that he needed to lose himself in her, while keeping a piece of himself separate. "Let me have you."

"Yes." That was all she said, all she needed to say as she twined around him, flowed into a kiss that started hot and went hotter, heading straight to flash point. Their tongues and teeth clashed, bringing a nip of pain, a taste of blood.

It was the blood that put him over the edge.

Pain detonated at the back of his brain, and silver magic spewed out through a broken sluiceway, called by the blood sacrifice and, he thought, Sasha's gloriously positive energy. The power reached for her, called to her, and he heard the jarring dissonance of music gone wrong.

He jerked away from her with an inarticulate cry, suddenly suffused with the Other's memories, which were drenched in the blood of his victims. Michael saw staring eyes, torn throats, and tangled limbs, and knew that his alter ego was throwing them at him, using the dead as weapons in an effort to disorient him, to make him give way fully. Forcing his way through them, wading through their blood, Michael slogged to the dam and reached for the sluiceway, using the mental image to shape his efforts to force the Other back where he belonged, away from his conscious mind.

He doubled over, gagging at the sights and smells, and the knowledge that none of the horrors were fabricated. The Other had made those kills and washed himself in that blood. And, dissociated or not, the Other was a part of him. Which meant *he* had done those things. Those were *his* hands in the memories, his blood singing with death and violence. Michael might have killed as a Nightkeeper—both Rincon's *makol* and Iago's disciples—but he hadn't enjoyed the brutal task. His other half not only gloried in killing; it existed solely to kill.

"What's wrong?" Sasha's voice seemed to come from very far away, from the other side of a river of blood.

She was still too near him, though. When she stepped toward him, he held up his hands to ward her off.

"Don't," he grated. "I . . . I can't do this. I'm sorry." He didn't want her to see him like this, couldn't tell her, even now, what was going on with him. More, the gray, clinging *muk* was attracted to her, wanted to wrap around her, seduce her. And he couldn't—wouldn't—let that happen. When she hesitated, he waved her off, almost violent in the action. "For fuck's sake, would you just leave me alone?"

She stood her ground for a moment, during which her features came clear through the blur of silver and the effort he was expending to push the Other back beyond the inner barrier that segregated the soul they shared. He expected to see hurt, maybe fear of whatever she could see inside him. Instead, she looked flat-out pissed.

Brown eyes flashing, she fisted her hands at her sides like she wanted to take a swing at him, street-style this time, with none of the trained finesse she'd shown earlier. He didn't blame her for the impulse, wouldn't blame her if she went ahead and punched him. Instead, she lifted her chin in her trademark *go to hell* gesture and said, "Oh, I'm going, all right. And you needn't worry about fighting me off again, because I'm done with this. You want space? Fine, you've got it, playboy. I might want you, but I sure as hell don't need your shit." She spun and stalked off, stiff legged, body screamingly tight with fury. Pausing at the edge of the ball court, she kicked at the tray Tomas had left for him. "And for fuck's sake, eat something and go to bed. Whether either of us likes it or not, I have a feeling I'm going to need your help getting into the temple and finding the library scroll. The gods apparently got it wrong as far as us being compatible, but that doesn't stop our magic from resonating. So get your shit together, will you?"

Magnificent in her fury, she turned and disappeared

into the darkness, leaving her words to ring into silence on the night air.

Michael watched her go, aching with the loss, and the knowledge that she'd been meant for the man he should have been. She was his warrior, his equal—at least, she should have been. Given the choices he'd made, the things he'd done, they were badly unequal now, with her so much better than him, her soul so much purer.

For the first time in nearly eighteen months, he wondered whether his first instinct had been the right one, back after his talent ceremony: that it might be better for him to sacrifice himself than risk taking her down with him. Taking all of them down. But in the end, he was a selfish man, too proud to really believe the world would be better off without him, too greedy to let go of his life until he was absolutely positive there was no other way.

He should get the fuck back to work, he knew, should keep fighting to burn off the restless, edgy energy she'd renewed within him, the kind that made him want to go after her, to give her everything he could, and damn the consequences. Instead, he sat cross-legged in the dust and ate the food Tomas had brought him, tasting nothing, knowing only that it fueled the burn within him, but didn't come close to filling the emptiness.

When the plates and bowls were empty and he registered only that he was full, finding no satisfaction in the feeling, he stood and returned to the center of the court, where the waning moon lit a diminishing patch of earth. His muscles ached a protest when he took the first ready position, having stiffened during the break, but those small pains didn't even start to get at the burning within him. He had hours to go yet before he collapsed, exhausted.

"The longer you wait, the longer it's going to take, asshole." He forced his fists up, pushed himself through the first set of positions, feeling them catch initially and then begin to flow, as his body loosened from the tension of sex magic, and his center allowed itself to be redirected away from Sasha, turning inward, where he needed to be. He launched into the phantom fight viciously, almost inhumanly so, sparring with his inner demons, and the ghosts of the dead. He fought his desire for a woman who deserved so much more than he had made himself, so much more than he could offer her. And he fought himself, hating what he had become, but not seeing any hope of ever being otherwise.

Sasha's anger carried her all the way back to the mansion and across the pool patio, where she faltered, not entirely ready to go inside and admit defeat. "Damn him," she muttered, breathing past the tightness in her throat that came from rage and frustration and a barely acknowledged kernel of unease. She focused on the rage and frustration, though, because those were easy. She could hate Michael for being the worst sort of hunter— the one who seemed sincere in his intentions, who acted like he was trying to do the right by her, only to shut things down when they started getting too serious. Saul had been that kind of hunter. And she hadn't realized it until far too late.

She didn't even think it was all about the rage with him. She'd seen him fight the anger to a standstill enough times to believe he could control it. But that was the key, she knew—control. He couldn't control something that involved another person, couldn't be sure of his victory if the two of them got involved. So he'd bailed. Again.

This time at least she'd been forewarned, had buffered herself—somewhat—against the sting of rejection. It had still hurt, yes, but it had pissed her off more. Being mad she could deal with, she told herself. It was far better than being needy and heartbroken.

But as she paused on the pool deck and stared out

across the nearby rock formations toward the dying moon, she couldn't avoid the small brain worm that said he truly had seemed sincere, that something within him had changed—with more than just the angry darkness she'd seen before. His face had been different at the end, and his eyes had flashed almost silver. More, she'd felt a kick of power from him; one that had felt strange to her. Not that she was an expert on what magic should feel like, but still . . . Which was worse, she wondered: for him to be mentally unbalanced or magically tainted? And what should she do in either case? What *could* she do? Even Tomas, who was supposed to be his advocate, thought it was just a too-quick temper and some impulse control problems. If she cried wolf to her new teammates . . .

"There you are!" Jox's voice said from behind her, sounding breathless and harried.

She turned, something kicking at her, putting her into full battle readiness in an instant. *The warrior's talent*, she thought, recognizing the signs of the magic activating, and wondering why it hadn't done so before, with Michael. Then Jox stepped into the light that came through the sliders, and she got a good look at his face, and she stopped thinking about her own problems. "What's wrong?" she asked quickly.

"There was an incident at the university," the *winikin* reported, crossing to her and urging her the way he'd come. "Strike just got back. Rabbit's unconscious, and we need your help reviving him."

She went along with him, but was baffled. "Why me?"

"Just hurry. Strike will explain everything."

Figuring she would have to live with that nonanswer, Sasha followed him into the darkness, hoping to hell she could do whatever it was they needed her to do, not just because she owed a personal debt, but because she was a Nightkeeper now, damn it. She would do whatever it took to get the job done.

CHAPTER FOURTEEN

Jox led Sasha to Rabbit's cottage, and pushed through the front door without knocking. They stepped into a plain kitchen that had the clean, orderly look of disuse. The next room was a sitting area, with doors off it leading to a pair of bedrooms and a bath. The decor was an odd mix of outdated early eighties furniture and accessories that were heavy on silly pig motifs, overlaid with a layer of modern things—tossed clothes, a pair of sleek laptops, and various high-tech entertainment gadgets.

Sasha glanced at Jox. "You guys didn't clean out the place after his father died?" She'd bet money nobody born in the past two decades had chosen the china pigs. That would've been the work of his father's first wife, before the massacre.

"Trust me, we tried," Jox said. "But Rabbit is, among other things, incredibly stubborn. He wanted his father's stuff left the way it was, despite—or maybe because of—how messed up their relationship was." The *winikin* gestured toward the bedroom on the left. "He's in there."

Sasha braced herself, then stepped through.

The decor was similar to that in the other room, with a big, plain bed, outdated furniture, and college-kid detritus. Two chairs were pulled up next to the bed; Strike sat in one, and a brunette in her late thirties sat in the other. In the corner, a pretty, dark-haired girl in her late teens, maybe early twenties, was curled up in a third chair, pretending to be asleep. On the bed a sharp-faced twentysomething lay twitching, his face working as though he were trying to talk, trying to scream.

Sasha instinctively drew back and bumped into Jox. Voice hushed, she asked, "What happened to him?"

"He got lost in a spell of sorts," said the woman. "After that, we're not sure." She stood and reached out to Sasha, though most of the room separated them. Letting her hands fall, she said, "This isn't the best time for introductions, I know, but Strike told me about you. I'm . . . I'm Anna. Your sister."

Sasha's brain vapor-locked on two simple words: "holy" and "shit."

She stood frozen in place, staring at the woman who should've been a stranger, but wasn't. Not because they'd ever met before, but because it was like looking in a fractured mirror, with pieces the same, pieces different. Anna was probably ten years older than Sasha. Where Anna's eyes were the same brilliant blue as her brother's, Sasha's were dark brown. Anna's face was round, her features soft and regular, whereas Sasha's face was all about points and angles. But through those differences, there were jarring similarities in the shapes of their eyes and mouths, their hairlines, and the burnished red highlights she didn't think came from a salon.

My sister, Sasha thought, her hands going clammy.

"We didn't know you were alive," Anna said, tears crowding her eyes. "If we had known we would've brought you home. I swear it."

The scene froze as Sasha realized that with the exception of Myrinne, the people in the room were the ones she should've grown up with. Jox would've been her guardian, Anna and Strike her older sibs, Rabbit their younger tagalong. She knew she should be full of emotions, but instead found herself strangely empty. In the aftermath of the scene with Michael, which was still sharp and painful in her memory, she was numb to more drama.

"Let's talk about it later, okay? Tell me what happened, and why you think I can help." She paused. "You do know I'm a chef, right?"

Strike said, "Rabbit tried to call a new three-question *nahwal* and wound up nearly burning his dorm down instead. He walked out of the building under his own power, but collapsed soon after." He turned a baleful look on the young girl in the corner; she played dead. "Myrinne convinced Rabbit to try a non-Nightkeeper scrying spell, some sort of pseudo-Wiccan shit she must've learned from Mistress Truth back at the voodoo tea shop. We're not sure what sort of magic they tapped into, which is why we're hoping you can help."

A chill came out of nowhere to chase down Sasha's spine. "Why me?"

"Because of this." Anna reached out and tapped Sasha's forearm, not the jaguar or the symbol of royalty, or even the warrior's mark, but her talent mark, which consisted of six small circles that followed a curving, ninety-degree corner, looking somewhat like part of a string of pearls draped over a man's thumb. "Jox described it to me earlier this evening. I'm pretty sure I know what it means."

Sasha's chill turned into a full-on shiver. "Is it something about the sky prophecy?"

"Maybe, maybe not," Anna answered. "Either way, it's the *ch'ul* glyph."

"And that means what, exactly?" Sasha had the sudden sensation of balancing at the edge of a very tall cliff, headed for a very long fall.

"*Ch'ul* is essentially the essence of all living things. It's the energy flow that makes up the barrier and gives life and sentience." She paused. "The creator gods used *ch'ul* to animate the maize people, creating mankind. Next to the gods, only a special sort of mage called a *ch'ulel* can directly manipulate *ch'ul*."

Sasha pulled her sleeve down over the glyph. "I thought all of the magi could wield the barrier energy."

"Every mage can use the power of the *ch'ul* contained within the barrier. But only a *ch'ulel* can alter the flow of *ch'ul* within living things, including plants and people." Anna paused. "There are only a couple of references to the *ch'ulel*, all Mayan, not Nightkeeper. In one of them, she's called the daughter of the gods."

"Oh." Sasha hugged herself, trying not to shiver.

Anna stepped closer and reached out to rub Sasha's shoulder gently.

The supportive, almost maternal gesture unaccountably made Sasha want to weep. *No time for this*, she reminded herself. *Rabbit needs help.* "That's what you want me to do? Alter his energy flow?"

"The *ch'ulel* is a positive force, which means you can give energy, maybe in certain cases siphon it from one place to another, but only when it is freely given. You can't take life away . . . but you might be able to give it. On the most basic level, you should be able to promote growth and healing . . . which would also be consistent with the whole 'defying death' part of the triad prophecy."

Sasha closed her eyes on a messy wash of guilt and pain. "Ambrose was right about that, too. I was supposed to be a doctor, not a chef. I even screwed that part up."

"Or else," Anna said reasonably, "your love of food is integral to your ability with plants, which is part of being a *ch'ulel*. For all we know, you access your gifts through food sacrifice rather than blood."

Sasha swallowed hard. "I'm going to need time to practice, time to figure out how to use . . ." She faltered, the concepts of *ch'ul* and *ch'ulel* too big for her to even conceive. How, exactly, was she supposed to deal with the idea of controlling the flipping Force? She wasn't Yoda, for chrissake.

"The other magi found their talents naturally," Jox assured her. "Strike performed his first 'port blind, the day the barrier reactivated. It eventually brought him to Leah. Patience first blinked invisible to protect the twins. Nate became the Volatile to save Alexis. You'll do fine."

"They were all trying to reach or protect the people they love," Sasha pointed out. "I've barely met Rabbit."

"True, but you and he have shared a mental link twice now," Jox pointed out. "We're hoping that'll help." The *winikin* leveled a look at her. "You have to at least try."

Aware that Myrinne had slitted her eyes and was glaring at her, Sasha glanced down at Rabbit. He had quieted, and now lay still. But not in a good way. Instead of looking peaceful, he looked . . . absent. As if there were nobody home inside his head or body. "Of course."

"Do you want me to get Michael?" Jox asked quietly. "Strike and Anna should be able to boost you through your shared bloodline, but we already know for certain that you and Michael are compatible."

Magically, anyway, Sasha thought. But she nodded. "He's either down by the ball court or on his way back to his suite. I'd bet he's still out at the court." She wasn't going to jeopardize whatever chance she might have to help Rabbit just because she'd rather not be around Michael.

"Anna and I will link with you, too," Strike said. It was more a statement than an offer, but if Sasha had been inclined to demur, one look at his and Anna's faces would've changed her mind. They were worried as hell

about the young man, whether or not his girlfriend saw
or believed it.

She nodded. "When Jox gets back with Michael,
we'll uplink." The words seemed strange coming off
her tongue. It took her a moment to realize the odd-
ity came from the utter lack of disconnect within her.
She'd bought into the magic, bought into her new life.
She wasn't worried about escaping, denying, or even really understanding what was going on. Her greatest fear
at that moment was failing the young man lying too still
on the bed, stretched out flat with his arms at his sides,
like he'd already gone to corpse.

"What exactly happened?" she asked.

There was a pause while Strike and Anna looked at
Myrinne, who played dead. Or maybe she really was doz-
ing; Sasha wasn't sure. Shaking his head, Strike turned
back and said, "He was trying to help us out and things
backfired. Literally." He went on to describe what had
happened, presumably as relayed by Myrinne.

"The spell is basic occult," Sasha said.

Anna nodded. "It shouldn't have done anything, really. My guess is that he got into his own powers, which
he isn't supposed to be able to touch with the mental filters in place, and now he's trapped behind the blocks."

Strike frowned. "But he installed the damn things.
And he was up and walking for a while after the spell, so
I'm not sure that makes sense."

Anna faced her palms to the sky in a "who knows?"
gesture, then turned expectantly to Sasha. Strike did the
same, so they were both looking at her, waiting for a
miracle.

Sasha's heart lumped in her throat. "I can't promise
anything."

"Just do your best," Strike said softly. "That's all any
of us can do."

Nodding and taking a deep breath that did jack shit

to settle her nerves, Sasha moved to the side of the bed. Rabbit looked like he could've been any of the young guys, more balls than brains, that she'd worked with in a dozen kitchens. Yet according to the stories, he was the most powerful of the magi, an unpredictable half-blood with a good heart and bad luck.

Gods, she thought, for the first time sending her thoughts outward, winging toward the sky, hoping that somehow, somewhere, someone—or some*thing*—was listening. *Help me help this kid.* When that didn't seem like nearly enough, she went a layer deeper. *Help me help the Nightkeepers.* And at that, she thought she felt a shimmer within, a faint hint of heat, a stir of echoes. Or maybe that was just wishful thinking.

Steeling herself, she touched Rabbit's wrist, where the hellmark stood out in violent bloodred while the marks of the peccary, the warrior, and the fire starter were done in reassuring Nightkeeper black. When she opened herself up to the world around her, she felt . . . nothing special. His arm was just an arm, a little cooler than it maybe should've been, and faintly clammy. But beyond that? Not a damn thing. Remembering something she'd seen one of the village elders do as part of asking the gods to heal a dying woman, she said, "Is there any *chorote* left?"

"I'll go get it," Strike volunteered, and bolted. He returned a couple of minutes later with not just the sacred drink, but Michael and Jox, as well, making the room suddenly feel far more crowded than it had before, filled with Michael's presence, and her deep desire not to have to deal with him just then.

But that was the coward's way, she knew, and whatever her father had raised her to be, it wasn't a wimp. So she watched him come through the door, forcibly banking the chemical reaction that had heat spiraling inside her at the sight of his broad shoulders and wide chest, which were draped now with a silky white button-down that he wore unbuttoned, showing a strip of ripped torso beneath. Bracing herself, she looked up and met his eyes. To her surprise—and faint disquiet—there was no sign of the wild violence that had blazed in him down at the ball court. There was only the man she'd come to know there at Skywatch, the one who'd found Ada for her, the one who'd followed her into the *nahwal*'s vision and saved her life a second time. This was the man she wanted, she realized, not that other, angrier part of him, the part he kept so well hidden most of the time. But what good did it do her to want only half of the man? It was impossible to take the good and ignore the bad. She'd learned that the hard way. Never mind the question of what, exactly, that anger meant.

He moved up beside her and looked down at her, eyes intent and shadowed with regret. "I'm sorry about before," he said quietly, while the others pretended not to hear. "I should've—"

"We've been over this," she interrupted. "I don't want to hear it again. What I want is for you to shut up and bleed."

His eyes flickered with surprise, and maybe a gleam of appreciation, but he said nothing, simply palmed his knife from his ankle sheath and held out the blade to her. She cut her palms and handed it back, and waited while he, Strike, and Anna all followed suit. Then Strike passed around the small thermos of *chorote* he'd snagged from the mansion, and they each took a sip. Sasha wasn't sure when the magic started; one moment it was just there, humming at the back of her brain, sounding almost like a song, like the voice of the lover she wished Michael could have been for her.

Mimicking the ritual she'd watched the village healer perform, she let her blood fall into the half-full flask to mix with the remaining *chorote*. Then she uncovered

Rabbit, who was clothed in only a pair of blue bike shorts. Even though he was a young man, his body showed the development of a Nightkeeper male, big and muscular. Sasha let drops of the blood-and-*chorote* mixture fall on his neck, and then on each of his shoulders, elbows, wrists, hips, knees, and ankles, the spots that made up the thirteen points of health in Mayan spiritual medicine.

Aware that Strike and Anna had already joined hands and uplinked, she held out her free hand, bleeding palm up. Strike took her hand, blood-to-blood.

The contact rocketed through her, a potent combination of heat and power, and a warm sense of something that she didn't recognize. Something that might've been family. She heard their songs playing through the contact: Strike was a trumpet fanfare; Anna was strings and a woman singing softly in an unfamiliar language. Theme songs, she realized. Somehow, her brain was translating their *ch'ul* into song.

"Easy," Strike said, his voice soothing. "We've got you."

And they did, Sasha realized, feeling how Strike—*my brother*, she corrected inwardly, trying to get used to the idea—was regulating the power flow, buffering her from overloading with too much, too soon. She nodded her thanks.

Within the small, crowded room, Jox had faded into the shadows, standing apart from the magic, but ready to help if needed. Myrinne had given up all pretense of sleep; she was still curled in a protective ball, but her eyes were wide open, and fixed on Sasha. When their gazes connected, Sasha saw a mute plea beneath the sullen mistrust. *Help him*, the girl's eyes said. *Don't let him leave me here alone.* And damned if that didn't resonate.

Sasha nodded again, though she wasn't entirely sure what she was agreeing to. Without looking at Michael, she said, "Okay. Let's do this."

He moved up behind her, bracketing her body with his much larger one as he reached around her and placed his hands atop hers, one where she touched Rabbit, the other where she was linked with her brother and sister. Despite what had happened between them earlier, she had to force herself not to lean back into Michael's reassuring warmth and solidity. For a moment, she felt nothing from him. Then a small shudder ran through his big frame, and the red-gold power flowed into her from him, sparking the kernel of magic at the back of her skull to a flame. Feeling self-conscious, she murmured, "*Pasaj och*," gaining another layer of power from the barrier itself. For a moment the magic filled her up, threatened to spill over. She felt larger than herself, as though the skin stretched over her flesh and bones; it wasn't an unpleasant sensation—it was just *full*.

She heard Strike's and Anna's music, heard the martial theme she'd begun to suspect was her own, though it didn't seem to suit her, wasn't what she would've picked for herself. She heard nothing from Michael, which was strange because she'd caught something off him earlier, back at the ball court. A creepy-crawly tracked down her spine when she remembered that had been when his eye were strange, the anger at its worst. Not wanting to analyze that any further, she focused on Rabbit, seeking to forge with him the same sort of link she shared with Strike and Anna, that of energy and music, and the reciprocal flow of what she thought might be *ch'ul*.

She got nothing. Rabbit was a blank. She got no music from him, no power. No energy flow. Nothing. It was like she was touching a piece of furniture. Or a corpse, she thought, shivering a little. "I can't find his music," she said softly. "Where is it?"

"What music?" Strike asked.

"I think that's how my brain translates *ch'ul*—as music, though gods know why, given that I can't carry a tune in a freaking bucket. Anyway, everyone I've touched since coming out of the ceremony—and a few people beforehand, as well—has given me a sense of . . . a theme song, I guess you'd call it." She paused. "Jox's is low and twangy; Strike's has trumpets blowing a fanfare." She didn't mention the inconsistency of Michael's theme. "I think I need to find Rabbit's song in order to channel him our energy and call him back."

She wasn't sure that would make any sense, the way she'd said it, but Strike nodded. "I visualize a yellow thread connecting me to my 'port destination, and give it a mental 'yank' to initiate the magic. I think our minds come up with ways to interpret the magic within a paradigm that makes sense to our brains, using our experiences. For me it's string; for you it's music."

"So what am I supposed to do, sing to him?" she asked, looking down at Rabbit, who was too pale, his skin verging almost on gray.

"Just keep trying," Anna said softly, her eyes brimming with worry.

So she tried. And tried.

Still, nothing happened. Rabbit lay there, unchanged.

"We're forgetting something," Michael said suddenly. "Rabbit wasn't able to mind-bend Sasha because he couldn't get through the music inside her head, which is consistent with what she's experiencing now. What if I don't know, their talents just aren't compatible? He wears the hellmark, and *ch'ul* is a power for life and good, right? Maybe his connection to Xibalba is blocking the *ch'ul* magic, and vice versa."

It made a hideous sort of sense, Sasha realized. Hideous, because there didn't seem to be any way around it. She glanced at Strike. "Please tell me you have a plan B."

His mouth was tight. "This was it." As if conceding defeat, he gave her hand a last squeeze and released it.

Anna, too, stepped away from their uplink, leaving Michael the only one still touching her. After a moment, he too broke the connection and moved back.

"I'm sorry," Sasha said hollowly, failure echoing alongside grief. She hated that she hadn't come through when her new friends and family had needed her. Did that mean she wasn't a *ch'ulel*? Or was Michael right, and she and Rabbit were simply incompatible? But if that was the case, did the fact that she couldn't hear Michael's song mean that the two of them weren't compatible, either?

It seemed depressingly possible.

"What now?" Strike asked. It seemed like a rhetorical question.

"Let me try," Myrinne said unexpectedly.

"Not an option," Strike said flatly. "You're the one who got him into this."

"Then I should be the one to get him out, don't you think?" The young woman uncoiled from the chair. With her average height and dark, Gypsy-lush looks, wearing jeans and a hooded sweatshirt that was cropped off at her hips, she would've come across as just another college kid if it weren't for her eyes, which looked far older than her chronological age, and her mouth, which tipped up sensually at the corners, somehow seeming to suggest that she'd been there, done that, and no sort of depravity on earth could surprise her.

The look in her eyes nudged Sasha's mind back to her time with Iago, pushing at the filters and making her chest ache. What in gods' name had the girl lived through? What had happened to her?

"Maybe we *should* let her try," Anna said slowly. "Her ritual put him under. Maybe she can bring him back."

"No fucking way," Strike said. "For all we know, the next woo-woo shit she tries on him will kill him. Besides, whatever's going on, it's nothing more than self-hypnosis bringing out Rabbit's latent talents—and gods know what else he's got hiding in there that we don't know about yet. He's caught in Nightkeeper magic, maybe Xibalban. The woo-woo shit doesn't work." Sasha didn't think he'd thank her for pointing out that, given the existence of magic, it wasn't logical for the Nightkeepers to claim its sole possession. But something of her thoughts must've shown on her face, because he fixed her with a look. "You think I should let her, don't you?"

She started to give him a *whatever you think is best* answer, but then stopped herself. Maybe it was her warrior's mark, maybe the feel of Michael's eyes fixed on her, silently challenging her to step up into the life she'd chosen, the one that had chosen her. "I think," she said carefully, "that unless you've got a viable plan C, you should give her the chance."

"If she could've woken him up, she would've done it back on campus," Strike countered.

"Not after he lit the dorm." Myrinne faced the king with a scowl, looking very young and slight in comparison, but defiant as hell. "You don't think it's magic? That's fine with me—let me do my self-hypnosis shtick. Can't hurt if that's all it is, right?"

Caught in his own logic, Strike cursed under his breath. He glanced around the room, tallying a silent vote. Sasha and Anna had already cast their votes. Jox opened a hand, as if saying, *Beats the hell out of me*.

Michael held the king's eyes for a moment, then nodded. "I say let her try. He's fading fast." The gray cast to his skin predominated now. "Alternatively, you could 'port him to that hospital in Albuquerque. But you've got to do something."

Strike shook his head. "There's no point giving him over to human doctors. He's lost in his own magic."

"Then give him a reason to come back," Michael said bluntly. His eyes were fixed on Sasha as he said it.

Irritation flared—with him for making it seem like she mattered, and with herself for the quick buzz brought by the words. Damn hormones.

"Fuck." Strike turned back to Myrinne. "What do you need?"

"Nothing from you," she said sharply. She slipped from the room, returning quickly with a small metal dagger inset with crystals at its hilt. Taking the seat beside the head of the bed, she pulled the nightstand slightly away from the wall. On it was a fat red candle, halfway burned down in a saucer decorated with flying pigs. She opened the nightstand drawer wide and fished for a box of matches, smirking slightly when Strike looked away from the big box of condoms, torn open and most of the way empty.

He's got a life that doesn't include you, the action—and the expression—said.

"Make a circle," she ordered. "No bloodletting, and don't lean on your magic. Clear your heads. I don't care if you believe in this, but keep the negative thoughts out." Her eyes flicked to Jox, who was edging for the door. "You too." Something in her voice said, *Especially you*, as if the *winikin* had more power here than the others combined. Which didn't make any sense, really, because a *winikin*'s marks might be magic, but the *winikin* weren't magic users, hadn't ever been. At Strike's nod, though, Jox joined hands with the others in a circle that surrounded the bed and included Rabbit, with Myrinne on one side of him, Strike on the other. Sasha ended up between Michael and Anna; she caught a buzz of sexual heat and frustrated anger from one, a trill of harps and song from the other, but suppressed both to focus on Myrinne's ritual. As she did so, she sent a second prayer: *Gods help us all*.

Instead of using the knife to cut herself or Rabbit, Myrinne placed it on his blanket-covered chest. She lit the candle and put it, pig saucer and all, on Rabbit's stomach, which dipped flat beneath the covers. The assemblage wobbled for a moment, then stabilized as Myrinne took Anna's hand on one side, Rabbit's on the other, and said, "We welcome the element of fire, symbol of willpower and courage. We call to the south for inspiration and passion. We call on the goddess Nephthys, ruler of magic and secrecy. And we call on Rabbit to return to us. He is fire, willpower, and courage. He is my inspiration and my passion." Releasing Anna's hand, Myrinne leaned in and kissed Rabbit on the cheek. "It's time to come back now. Follow the sound of my voice and the energy of the people who love you."

There was no hum of red-gold Nightkeeper magic, no song, no change in the air or the flickering candle flame. For maybe half a minute, absolutely nothing happened. Then, as if someone had thrown a switch, Rabbit's chest rose in a long, drawn-out inhale, and the knife and candle set on his chest moved with the ripple of a long shudder racking his body. Then his eyelids flickered.

Relief curled through Sasha like a song, and she instinctively tightened her fingers on Michael's. Whatever Myrinne was doing, it was working.

Rabbit's consciousness swam up through the sticky layers of gray, fighting inertia, fighting the tide that threatened to suck him back down. He didn't know where he'd been, didn't know what he'd been doing, didn't even know where he was going, only that the familiar contralto voice drew him onward, to a glittering silver interface where the grayness met something else. There was light beyond the interface, and the sense of motion and life. And the voice. *Her* voice. As he struggled up to the surface, the clinging layers started to fall away and he started reconnecting with himself, with memory.

He affixed the voice to a name—Myrinne—and an emotion: desperate love. At the same time, he saw flames and heard himself scream her name. *A waxy face. Blood dripping from a knife.*

No! Instinctively, reflexively, he threw a mental block over the nightmare. It wasn't a true vision, he knew. It'd been a projection of his own terror that no matter how hard he tried to do the right thing, he always fucked everything up, usually destroying shit in the process. But not her. Never her. She was a metaphor for the good stuff he screwed up. That was all. He wouldn't ever hurt her.

"That's it, kid. Open your eyes," another familiar voice said, accompanied by the brush of cool fingers over his forehead. *Anna*, his mind supplied.

"Rabbit, you've got to come all the way back." That was Myrinne's voice, and those were Myrinne's fingers holding his, squeezing encouragement. He latched onto the promise of her, the reality, using that to pull himself the last little bit through the grayness to the interface, then shove himself through.

He jolted back into his own body and spun, disoriented, as his consciousness fought to reconnect with the shell it was supposed to inhabit. When he finally got his eyes open, he found himself blinking up at a whole damn crowd gathered around the bed in his old man's cottage back at Skywatch. Which reminded him that he'd set Myrinne's dorm room on fire. *Shit*.

"You're back," Strike said.

Rabbit's knee-jerk response was something along the lines of, *Duh*, but he managed to squelch it, saying instead, "Sorry it took so long." He braced to get his ass chewed up and spit out. Gods knew he deserved it—he'd broken his "no Nightkeeper magic" vow, if not to the letter, then certainly by intent. Worse, he didn't have a damn thing to show for it except more property damage. He hadn't gotten the answers he'd been looking for, and didn't know what to make of the answers he *had* gotten.

There was an awkward pause, as though Strike couldn't decide whether to hug him or strangle him. In the end, the king didn't do either; he just turned away, muttering, "Glad you're okay," under his breath.

"You scared us," Anna said, but instead of censure, there was mostly relief on her face, and in Jox's eyes. Which made Rabbit realize that they were pissed, yeah, but they were also damn glad to have him back. The knowledge warmed him. It humbled him, to the extent that he could be humbled. Why did he keep forgetting that they weren't his old man? Why did he keep assuming the worst about their reactions, and then being surprised when they went the other way?

"He should rest," Myrinne said pointedly. In case the others didn't get the nonhint, she followed it up with, "Go away. I'll let you know when he's up for an interrogation."

Strike ignored her to lean over the bed. "I'll kick your ass later for pulling this stunt . . . but given that it's a done deal, I've gotta ask: Did you get any answers?"

Yeah, Rabbit thought. *I'm just not sure which question they belong to.*

What is my destiny? he'd asked. *How can I make Myrinne mine?* And he'd gotten a response of sorts. He just wasn't sure what the hell it meant. Choosing his words carefully, he said, "The images I got were all jumbled up. I have a feeling they weren't anything, really, just pieces from inside my head . . . except for one of them. Just before I passed out for good, I blinked into a ceremonial chamber and felt a hell of a power surge. Like maybe it was an intersection."

There was a collective indrawn breath. Strike said, "Can you describe it? Could you get back there?"

Rabbit grimaced. "I didn't really see the room; it was mostly a blur. But there was a stone tomb in the middle of it, a big one with a scorpion carved in its side, along with some wavy lines." He paused. "The thing was . . . the symbols weren't Mayan, I don't think."

"What were they?" Strike asked, his voice deadly intent.

"Egyptian." He looked from Strike to the others, and raised an eyebrow. "Anybody up for a field trip?"

CHAPTER FIFTEEN

The next morning, after catching up on sleep and calories, the residents of Skywatch assembled for an all-hands-on-deck meeting, at the picnic tables set beneath the big ceiba tree. Rabbit was there, with heavy circles beneath his eyes and a faintly mulish look on his face. But at least he was vertical. Myrinne sat beside him, with Anna on his other side. Sasha had originally taken a seat between Jox and Sven, in a cowardly effort to avoid dealing with Michael. Her best efforts were foiled, though, when he arrived, big and grumpy-looking, and thumped Sven on the shoulder. "Move."

Clearly hungover, Sven merely winced and slid down. Sasha divided her glare between the two men, annoyed with Sven for being oblivious, with herself for the kick of physical reaction that coursed through her when Michael's shoulder touched hers, and with Michael for being . . . hell, for just *being*.

Before she could decide whether or not to change seats, Strike brought the meeting to order, standing up at the head of the table and saying, "Okay, gang. Suffice it to say that a whole lot of things have changed over the last forty-eight, some for the better, some not." He paused and looked at Sasha. "First and foremost, I want to officially welcome Sasha to the family, quite literally. I'd like to start by having Jox go over what we've pieced together so far."

The *winikin*, clearly prepped, stood up from his seat. Once he had everyone's attention, he began, dropping into what Sasha had learned to recognize as his storyteller mode, eyes half-closed, as though he were describing vivid pictures seen in his mind's eye. "Nearly two years before the massacre, the queen gave birth to a baby girl. As far as anyone alive today knew, it was a stillbirth. The funerary bundle was made and burned, the child's ashes added to those beneath the altar here at Skywatch."

Sasha was aware that everyone might be looking at Jox, but their attention was on her. She hadn't heard the story, but suddenly couldn't sit still for it. She'd waited so long to learn about her mother; now that the time had come, all she wanted to do was get up and pace off a sudden case of restless nerves. Just when the jitters were nearing the breaking point, though, Michael touched his booted foot to her sneakered one beneath the table, a brief, supportive pressure that said, *You can handle this.* And she could, she realized, exhaling a long breath and drawing in the next. But she didn't like that he'd been the one to remind her.

She shifted her foot away from his as the *winikin* continued, "Based on what the *nahwal* said about Sasha being his second daughter, and the way the timing fits, it seems that the baby was either stolen from the queen and replaced somehow with an appropriate substitute ... or that the queen herself was involved in the deception. We don't know which of those was the case; we may never know. Sasha's mother made Ambrose memorize the triad prophecy, and insisted that it related to Sasha. In a way, this suggests the queen's involvement. She was the most powerful *itza'at* of her generation, so it's certainly possible that she foresaw Sasha's importance to the end-time war, and knew she had to keep her alive at all costs . . . perhaps even by lying to her husband and her people."

Sasha's head buzzed as thoughts collided and separated within her, threatening to tip her brain toward overload. "But why send me away?"

It was Anna who answered: "An *itza'at* can foresee the future but not change it. If she envisioned the massacre, or a dark future at the very least, she might have thought to spare you."

"Why not send all three of us away, then?" Sasha asked, then wished she hadn't. Because if their mother had sent her to safety, it meant she'd knowingly left her two older children in harm's way.

Strike didn't look offended by the question, though, saying only, "Either she'd seen Jox raising us—but not you—in relative safety . . . or she had no foreknowledge of our fate, but couldn't risk sending us away, because it would look like she didn't believe in the king's plan to attack the intersection."

"Treason is one of the few things considered a true and absolute sin," Michael said out of the corner of his mouth. "It's good for a one-way trip to Mictlan."

"That's—" Sasha broke off, not sure what she wanted to say, what she *could* say. She was only beginning to understand what it meant to be a Nightkeeper, how her decisions had suddenly become plural, impacting so much more than just herself.

"The king's writ spells out the responsibilities of the leaders," Strike said. "Personal desires are pretty far down the list." He glanced at Leah. "Lucky for us, the jaguars are known for being not only stubborn as hell, but willing to rewrite the rules to suit themselves." He returned his attention to Sasha. "Our mother made the choice she made—I have to believe it was her choice, in retrospect. She grieved deeply when the baby died, and again around the time of the funeral, which was a few months later. She and the king drifted apart for a bit too. In retrospect, what Anna and I remember of that period is pretty consistent with her having made some hellish personal choices."

"If that's true . . ." Sasha trailed off, trying to find the right question amidst the clamor of them in her brain. "If this was her plan to keep me safe and make sure I made it to the end-time, then why did she send me with someone like Ambrose? Why not a *winikin*?" But what she was really asking was, *Why not someone stable, who had half a clue how to raise a child and introduce the Nightkeeper ways gently, rather than like magical boot camp for the criminally insane?*

It was Jox who answered: "Even narrowing it down to the inner circle of the royal jaguars and their close friends, we're still not sure who Ambrose was, for the same reasons as before—lack of records, too many people to choose from. But I think it's safe to say he would've been someone the queen trusted implicitly, someone she thought would keep you safe and raise you well." The *winikin* had clearly guessed her unspoken question, because he continued, "We have to assume that his orders from the queen included his severing his connection to the barrier. Every mention of the spells capable of breaking the barrier connection suggest that they are, quite literally, hell. If we take the trauma of the spell, and add that to his being abruptly cut off from the culture he'd spent his entire life training for, he must have . . . broken inside somehow. The queen would have picked him thinking he could handle it. Unfortunately, that wasn't the case."

You can say that again, Sasha thought. But for the first time in a long time—maybe ever—the anger and regret that tainted her memories of Ambrose were overlaid with a new degree of empathy. She'd been a part of Sky-watch for only a few weeks, but already her life was in-tertwined, to different degrees, with her teammates, and the *winikin*. What would it be like to have that feeling of belonging, multiplied several hundredfold, and then have it yanked away? More, he would have been a func-tioning mage, capapble of tapping the barrier for power, for answers. Maybe he'd even had a cool talent. A lover. Gods, a family. Then, on his queen's order, he'd left all that behind to undergo the worst sort of trauma, sever-ing his connection to his entire life. And after that he'd been alone, adrift with a newborn baby, acting on stand-ing orders to protect her and raise her as befitted a prin-cess. Was it any wonder he'd lost it, that his priorities had gotten badly skewed, the delivery harsh in the extreme? Could she really blame him for breaking?

Sasha became aware that the tables had gone silent, that everyone was looking at her.

"You hanging in?" Michael asked.

She nodded. "Just rearranging a few very deep-seated preconceptions." Like the one that said Ambrose had never wanted her, never loved her. He'd given up his *life* for her. How could that not be a form of love?

And at the thought, she had the glimmer of an idea, a strategy that might just get them into the haunted temple.

"I have something for you," Strike said, gesturing for her to rise. "Come around here."

Keeping the nascent plan to herself for the moment, she stood and joined him at the front of the group, in an open spot beneath the edge of the ceiba tree's reach, where the shadows gave way to sunlight. Nerves hummed through her as she realized, from the seri-ous expression on his face, that they'd moved into the formal-acceptance part of the morning's meeting. She'd halfway expected something along those lines. What she hadn't expected was for her stomach to go tight, for it to matter to her as much as it suddenly did.

She, who'd never wanted to believe in the Nightkeepers, now wanted to belong to them. She wanted to be one of them, wanted to fight with them, for them. She wanted her birthright, damn it.

Standing straight and tall in the strange orange sunlight, looking every inch the king even without his regalia, Strike pulled a gleaming black knife from his belt and held it out to her, haft-first. "Sasha Ledbetter, as a member of the jaguar bloodline and the royal house, this knife is yours by right of descent and the warrior's mark," he said formally. "Will you accept it?"

Her breath went thin in her lungs at the sight of the etched knife, which was sand-polished obsidian, worked with the jaguar and the *ju*. "Whose was it?" she asked softly, curling her fingers into her palms to keep from reaching for the blade, even though she was dying to snatch it from him. She didn't know whether the impulse came from her newly minted warrior's instincts or a chef's appreciation of a good edge, but she wanted the knife, wanted it badly.

"The queen's."

The queen. Her mother. The woman who'd saved her by giving her to a madman. Sasha wasn't sure how she felt about that, wasn't sure what to think about the things she'd just learned. But she could no more refuse the knife than she could undo the past. She wanted the blade, wanted the symbol. She reached for it, then hesitated and looked at Anna. "You don't mind?"

"Warrior's prerogative," Anna said. "Go ahead, please." She touched the heavy chain she wore at her throat. "I've got our mother's pendant."

Our mother, thought Sasha, her heart kicking in her chest at the realization of a childhood wish fulfilled, though not how she ever would've expected it to be. *Not now*, she told herself. *Later*. She could process everything later. Her time wasn't entirely her own anymore, and the Nightkeepers had priorities other than welcoming their newest member.

Throat closing, she took the knife, which was warm and heavy in her hand. As she tested its weight, Strike stepped forward and kissed her on the cheek. "Welcome home," he said simply. Then, moving to her side, he waved the others forward to formally welcome her into the group. Anna was first, and gave her a big hug. The others greeted her one by one, both *winikin* and magi, with a handshake or brief kiss, acceptance as one of them. More, acceptance as royalty.

Michael held back until last. When he finally moved up to face her, the intensity in his eyes brought a jitter to her stomach and a skirr of warning from her warrior's mark. Instinct said for her to back away, but pride had her holding still and offering him her hand rather than a kiss. He ignored the hand, leaned in, and touched his lips to hers. For a moment, she thought she heard his voice inside her head, a soft whisper: *I'm sorry for last night*.

Then he withdrew, leaving her to stare after him, trying to figure out if that had been wishful thinking or not. More shaken than she wanted to admit by the suspicion that she'd just touched on Michael's thoughts, another sign that they were destined—or had been at one point—to be mates, she gripped her new knife convulsively. Forcing herself to ease up, she returned to her seat as the others took theirs. She didn't move away from Michael, didn't want to deal with the questions the move would raise. And, damn it, she would've been physically aware of him regardless of where either of them sat.

Strike brought the meeting back to order. "Jade?

Anna? One of you want to bring us up to speed on where we stand with the Aztec research?"

In the weeks since Sasha's rescue, although she'd been immersed in her studies, she'd been aware of the Nightkeepers' ongoing efforts to find Iago's stronghold, or at the very least project the Xibalbans' next set of moves in the countdown to the end-time. Strike had sent teams to check out several of the mountains the Aztec had considered sacred, but they'd come back with a whole lot of negatives. The Florida compound was a crater, and there was no sign of Iago or his people anywhere else. It was like they'd disappeared, though not even Iago had power enough to tuck a few hundred Xibalbans into the barrier. Apparently it was far easier to fold away inanimate objects than people—it required serious magic to get a sentient being across.

Their inability to find Iago or catch a hint of any Xibalban activity on earth had left the magi trying to guess what they would try to do on the night of the winter solstice, when the three-year countdown began. Also, there was no sign of the *Banol Kax*. Instead of reassuring the magi, it had put them on edge.

Anna stood and walked past the tables to take Strike's place. "I'm going to assume you've all read—or at least skimmed—the report Jade sent around last week. Suffice it to say that the deeper we go into the research, the more it looks like the Xibalbans all but created the Aztec empire, and that, if it hadn't been for Cortés's arrival and the subsequent Spanish conquest, the Xibalbans and Aztec might have wound up ruling all of Mesoamerica." She paused. "Based on what we've seen from the Xibalbans so far, I think it's a pretty good bet that Iago is planning to complete that rulership. I don't think he's trying to ally himself with the *Banol Kax*, as we had originally believed. I think he destroyed the intersection and hid the hellroad with the prime purpose of barring them from the earth for the time being."

"But why?" Strike asked, frowning.

"I think he's trying to preempt the end-time itself."

That brought a murmur of surprise from the assembled group. When it died down, Anna continued. "The Aztec calendar was akin to, but not identical to, the Mayan Long Count. It delineated a five-thousand-year cycle broken into five periods, called suns. Each sun began with peace and prosperity, then deteriorated toward chaos, whereupon the gods rose up and destroyed their creations in order to bring them back to life, purified. The first period—the Sun of Precious Stones—ended when the jaguars and other animals rose up and slaughtered mankind. The Sun of Darkness ended with the destruction brought by a huge hurricane. The Sun of Fire was destroyed when fire rained down from the heavens. The Sun of Water ended in a terrible flood. The final and current period, called the Sun of Movement, is destined to end on December 24, 2011, almost exactly a year *before* the actual zero date. On that day, a terrible earthquake is, at least according to Aztec prophecy, supposed to tear the earth apart." Anna spread her hands. "Game over."

Michael frowned. "What good does it do Iago to precipitate a full apocalypse? Unless he's an idiot—which I don't for a moment think he is—he's got to have a plan to keep the earth intact and install himself as ruler, presuming that's his goal."

"There's an even more specific Aztec prophecy dealing with their end date," Anna revealed. "It predicts that the Life Tree will bear a new sort of fruit, namely a new world order. At that point, the god of death will remove his jade mask, revealing himself as Quetzalcoatl, god of peace, and returning the great emperor Moctezuma back to his rightful place as the ruler of all creation."

She paused. "I suspect that Iago is taking this to mean that the earthquake will destroy civilization but not the earth itself, making room for the Xibalbans to move into power. He may even see himself as the reincarnation of Moctezuma, the god-king who ruled the Aztecs at the time of the Spanish conquest."

"But if the Xibalbans are an offshoot of the Night-keepers," Sasha said, thinking aloud, "then how did they come up with a different zero date? Is there a conjunction on the earlier date, too?"

Anna shook her head. "If you ask me, it's an artificial date, one designed to preempt the Nightkeepers' end-time."

"It might work, too," Michael said grimly. "If Iago's magic is stronger than we think, and he's truly managed to trap the *Banol Kax* in Xibalba, we could be in serious trouble here."

"I think it's more likely that it suits the lords of darkness to remain below for now," Anna said. "But you're right that we could be in trouble, either way. Which is why I think we need to plan a raid on the haunted temple as soon as possible. Hopefully, we can get past the demi-*nahwal* now that we have Sasha with us." She paused, then looked at Sasha. "We need the library now more than ever. Please tell me you've got an idea of what we should do."

Sasha nodded. "Maybe." *Hopefully.* "The *ch'ulel* talent didn't work on Rabbit, but as Strike pointed out, those of you who've found your talents outside of a formal talent ceremony have done so in the process of saving someone you love. I think we can make that work for us here."

Strike raised an eyebrow and looked from her to Michael and back. "How?"

She smiled, well aware that the expression carried an edge. "This doesn't involve Michael. I'm talking about

Ambrose. We had a . . . difficult relationship, but I did love him." She paused. "If I can use that love, or what's left of it, to trigger the *ch'ulel* talent and heal his spirit, I might be able to bring him back to his version of sanity. At a minimum, I may be able to prevent him from attacking us. Who knows? I might even get him to lead us to the scroll, or answer some questions." Gods knew she had plenty of those.

There was a moment of speculative silence before Strike nodded, a smile curving his lips. "Yeah. That could work. Let's do it."

"The hell," Michael growled. "No way she's going in there. Or have you all forgotten what the demi-*nahwal* did to Anna?" He rounded on Sasha. "He made her slash her wrists and she damn near bled out. Sound familiar?"

Her stomach knotted, but she forced a sharp-edged smile. "I'm an old pro, thanks. And I don't remember asking your permission for any of this."

His eyes snapped to her. It wasn't until that moment that she realized he'd been deliberately not looking at her through most of the meeting. He'd touched her just twice, once playing footsie, and again during her formal acceptance into the group. He'd been banking his magic those two times, she realized, because now, when he reached out and cupped her chin in his hand, his touch all but seared her with red-gold power tainted with that strange, compelling power she'd sensed in him the previous night.

In a flash, the hormones were there inside her, wanting him. *Damn them.*

She nearly jerked back, but forced herself not to. Narrowing her eyes, she said, "I'd appreciate it if you wouldn't touch me. Or if you're going to touch me, then *touch me*, for chrissake. Make up your mind—do you want me or not?" In that moment she didn't care that they had an audience of nearly two dozen, and that she'd be living with all of them for the foreseeable future. All she cared about was getting through Michael's thick-assed skull that he couldn't push her away with one hand while touching her with the other. It was making her crazy, and she didn't do crazy.

For a moment she thought he was actually going to answer her, that he might finally let rip with what was really going on inside his head. Instead he shoved to his feet. "Shit." To Strike, he said, "I'll catch up with you later on the planning. Just keep one thing in mind: If she goes into the haunted temple, I'm going in with her. That's not negotiable." He followed up that declaration by stalking off along the path that bifurcated out of sight, one branch leading to the firing range, the other to the ball court. He didn't look back.

"And there he goes," Sasha murmured, too annoyed to be embarrassed, too tired of his inconsistency to be truly surprised, or even all that hurt, though she suspected that would hit her later, in private. "Pain in my ass."

A muffled snort from Jade made her feel better, though it probably shouldn't have. For a second, she was tempted to ask the others about the strange silver magic. But she didn't.

Muttering something uncomplimentary under his breath, Strike turned away from watching Michael's strategic retreat, and returned to the matter at hand. "We'll start at the campsite and exhume Ambrose's body. Maybe that will attract his spirit outside of its normal boundaries, allowing you to talk to it where it's not necessarily at its strongest. We need to recover the corpse regardless."

Sasha nodded gratefully. "I promised him a proper burial." She flashed back on that last time she'd seen him, when he'd asked for the old promise once again. Working the time line, she'd realized that had been right after the summer solstice, when the barrier had reawakened. He must've sensed it somehow, despite having been severed from the barrier. He'd known, and he'd gone south to the temple. Maybe he'd intended to reconnect himself somehow, and bring her proof of the magic. Who knew?

"He'll get his funerary rites," Strike promised.

"Red-Boar . . ." Anna's voice caught a little on the name, then steadied as she continued, "Red-Boar and I buried the remains near the cenote clearing. I didn't have any trouble with the mad—um, with the demi-*nahwal* until we got closer." She paused, then asked Sasha, "Do you have any thoughts on the dogs you saw in your vision?"

She'd thought about them numerous times, thank you very much. Big, gaping jaws tended to make an impression. But in all honesty she had to say, "Michael didn't have much trouble neutralizing them, so I don't think they're an actual threat to us in this context. More bark than bite, and all that. Besides, it was a vision. I'm not sure why, but my instincts say they weren't really part of the scene, that they were in the vision to tell me something else. Question is, what?"

Anna pursed her lips. "Dogs play any number of parts in Mayan, Aztec, and Nightkeeper mythology, but if we stick with the big one that seems the most relevant at the moment, we're looking at the sky. More specifically, the sun."

A chill ran across Sasha's skin. She wasn't the only one who looked upward at the pale, orange-tinted ball hanging midsky.

On the other side of the table, Jox frowned. "You think the dogs Sasha saw were the companions?"

"Companions?" Sasha queried.

"According to legend, the Mayan sun god, Kinich Ahau, starts at one horizon and travels across the sky each day, shedding light so mankind and his crops can flourish, et cetera, et cetera. When he reaches the other horizon, he enters the underworld and Night Jaguar takes over the sky. During the night, Kinich Ahau has to sneak through Xibalba without getting caught; he has two companions to help him get through the challenges of the underworld—a couple of black dogs. They help guide the sun god beneath the plane of mankind, until he comes out on the opposite horizon each morning as the sunrise."

Sasha looked up into the strange orange sky. "So why would I see these companions in my vision?"

Anna turned her palms up. "If we're lucky, the answer to that one too will be in the haunted temple."

Sasha nodded. Forcing herself not to look in the direction of the ball court, she said to Strike and the others, "Okay. Let's pick a day."

Strike glanced at the sky. "The next conjunction of any real power is going to be the Geminid meteor shower."

"Which is when?" Sasha asked.

"It peaks on the fourteenth."

Sasha grimaced. That was eleven days away, and just seven days prior to the winter solstice. "There's nothing sooner?"

"Sorry, that's the best we've got. Besides, there's the connection between Gemini and twins. Could give us a bit more of a boost than otherwise."

"Then that'll be the day." Suddenly realizing she'd taken over a meeting—and a decision—that wasn't hers to take or make, she spread her hands in the king's direction. "Sorry. Habit. I always got in trouble with the head chefs for overstepping."

"It's your plan, your temple, your foster father, and your talent," he said reasonably. "I'd say you've got the right."

For a few heartbeats, the statement of support made her feel very alone, as though he'd just stuck her out in front of their tiny army. Which made her wonder whether this was how their father had felt, leading the Nightkeepers into battle when so many of his advisers had argued against the move. And that brought a nasty parallel to mind. The jaguars didn't just have the reputation for being stubborn and rule benders, she knew. They also had a habit of being led into trouble by their dreams and visions, believing in portents that others didn't see. Strike had defied the thirteenth prophecy to take Leah as his queen, based on his visions, and had nearly paid the ultimate price. Their father had led the Nightkeepers to slaughter on the weight of his dreams.

"What if . . ." She trailed off, then forced herself to say it. "Do you think I could be misinterpreting the vision? What if the scroll isn't in the temple, after all?"

Strike turned his scarred palms to the sky. "We do our best. It's all the gods can ask of us these days."

Late that night, exhausted enough that he thought he might finally be able to sleep, Michael dragged his ass into the mansion through the garage, doing his damnedest to avoid anyone seeing him. He didn't want the looks, or the questions.

When he'd first arrived at Skywatch, he'd been a hundred percent into his salesman persona—a little too slick and pretty, a lot insubstantial. That had been the Nightkeepers' first impression of him, and he'd only reinforced it in the weeks and months after the talent ceremony, when he'd been so fucked-up inside his own head, he'd clung to the familiar, easy role, one that had seemed so much safer than the thing he'd rediscovered within himself. And now, even though he'd been evolving over the past six months, he could tell that he was backsliding in their eyes. *That's just the way he is*, he could see them thinking, and wished to hell it could be different, wished he could make them understand. But he couldn't. It was as simple as that.

He was doing what he had to in order to keep Sasha safe, to keep her whole. And if he was the only one who could ever know it, then he'd have to be satisfied with that. He *would* be satisfied with that, he told himself, as long as it meant she was safe. He hated the idea of her going into the temple after Ambrose, but if she was determined to do it, then he'd be right behind her. And if the demi-*nahwal* went after her, it would have to get through him first.

On that thought, he turned the back corner leading to the residential wing. And stopped dead, then ducked back behind a concealing corner pillar at the sight of Sasha lingering in the doorway to her suite with Sven standing too near her, an arm braced above her on the door frame. Sven leaned in and said something, then smiled when she laughed.

Sick, dark anger sluiced through Michael in an instant, curdling his blood and making him want to kill. And for a split second, even the rational side of him actually considered it, wanting in that instant nothing more than to remove Sven from Sasha's presence. Permanently. Michael tasted blood, and for a heartbeat thought it was the Other sending him more death images, almost welcomed them. Except he knew damn well that the sluice gates were closed, the dam secure. He'd meditated long and hard on his defenses, sharpening the skills until he shook with the effort. No, the blood didn't come from the Other; it came from him. He'd bitten his own tongue until it bled, bringing power and madness, bringing danger—not to himself, but to the man who stood no more than thirty feet away, being his usual careless, charming self.

Michael wanted to charge down the hall and yank

Sven away from her, wanted to sweep Sasha up in his arms and take her, brand her as his own. But she'd been right to call him on his bullshit earlier in the day. It wasn't fair to her—to either of them—for him to play around the edges of the attraction, going as far as he could without summoning the darkness, without it seeing her and drawing her in. Then, when he went too far, pulling back and shutting her down. If there was a male version of a cock tease, the split inside him had him in danger of being that guy, at least when it came to her. He wanted her, but couldn't have her. Which meant he should stay the fuck away from her already.

The hallway noncuddle broke up, with Sven sketching a wave and heading back to the main mansion, undoubtedly to hit the rec room for some *Grand Theft Auto* or some such shit, not having a clue how close he'd come to nonexistence. Sasha angled to disappear into her suite, but then paused, turned, and fixed Michael with a look. "Well?" she said, her voice sharp with challenge.

He froze for a second, then straightened and stepped out from behind the column to stand, unspeaking. Not because he didn't want to talk to her, but because he'd already said everything he was physically able to say to her, and it wasn't enough. They both knew it wasn't enough.

She stared at him for nearly a minute, as though waiting to see if he would finally explain what the hell was going on. When he didn't move, didn't say a word, she turned away, stepped past the door, and shut it firmly at her back. After a moment, he let himself into his own suite three doors down and slept a few hours, alone, exhausted, and plagued by dreams of love and death, and the blurred line between the two.

PART IV

THE GEMINID
METEOR SHOWER

*The peak of this meteor shower is associated with
moderate barrier activity, but it can fluctuate wildly,
much as the Hero Twins could be tricky and unpredictable.*

CHAPTER SIXTEEN

December 14
Peak of the Geminid meteor shower
Three years and seven days to the zero date
Skywatch

As the battle-clad Nightkeepers gathered in the main room in preparation for the temple raid, Sasha perched on one of the big couches and tossed her mother's knife from hand to hand, sending the blade spinning in a glitter of polished obsidian. It was a habit that seemed to have come with her warrior's mark, along with the ability to nail a moving target with the queen's blade at fifty feet, sometimes more. Not that she intended to throw the heirloom if she could help it—she wore machine pistols on her hips, and had developed fireball magic of better than average strength and accuracy.

In the eleven days since her bloodline ceremony, she'd proven deft in all of her magic lessons, as though Strike and Nate were reminding her of the spells instead of teaching her anew. The *winikin*—especially Jox—had nodded as if to say, *Of course, she's a* ch'ulel, but she'd ignored that pressure. Or tried to, at least. Some days it got hard.

She might be projecting a calm exterior—she was doing her best, anyway—but inwardly she was scrambling to keep up with herself, with the new skills she was learning, and the new confidence—and insecurities— they brought. She'd come to Skywatch a victim, and in less than a month had become a princess and a top-notch mage; she'd found her family, and had found some forgiveness for Ambrose, and the hope that he could forgive her, as well. And she'd found and lost a lover. That piece weighed on her, despite her best efforts to just walk away from it.

She glanced up, looking for Michael, knowing she would find him nearby, not too close, but never far away, either. True to his word, he'd insisted on partnering with her during what they'd come to call the temple raid. He might not want to be with her—or not enough to get past his inner shit—but he seemed bound and determined to protect her. Part of her thought she should've turned him down, maybe replacing him with Sven, who along with Jade had become her friend, filling some of the empty hours when the mated pairs were off doing mated things. But Michael had had refused to let another mage take his place. Period. And to be honest, she hadn't argued too hard. She liked Sven, but he was a bit of a lightweight still. If she had to have any of the magi at her back, she'd take Michael despite their problems, because she knew that once he'd committed to a course of action, there was no swaying him, for better or worse.

So they would go in together, but not together. Story of her life.

Focus your ass, she thought as the warriors came together in the center of the great room, with their *winikin* up above, clustered in the kitchen area. With the winter solstice and the three-year threshold exactly a week away, it was time for her to step up and fulfill her destiny. At least, that was what she kept telling herself in the darkest hours of the night, when she lay awake and alone. And again now, when the idea of puking was sounding really good.

"Okay, people," Strike said as he appeared in the arched doorway leading from the royal wing. "It's time."

The Nightkeepers would all 'port to Ambrose's old campsite, save for Jade, who offered nothing in the way of fighting skills, and Anna, who had gone back to Austin. Thanks to a sizable donation from the Nightkeeper Fund, which had repaired the dorm and bought them amnesty, Rabbit and Myrinne had also returned to school, wearing even stronger mental filters than before. However, because Red-Boar had once used his mind-bending talent to wrest Anna's consciousness away from the demi-*nahwal*'s grip, Strike had 'ported Rabbit back to Skywatch that morning to participate in the raid. In the event that the demi-*nahwal* attacked the magi, it'd be up to him to pull their minds back.

The young man had arrived sullen and dark visaged, muttered something about having a fight with Myrinne, and promptly disappeared in the direction of his cottage. Sasha had gone to see if he was okay, but he'd ignored her knock and she hadn't pushed it. Now he lifted his hand in a gesture she thought was part acknowledgment, part apology.

She nodded and felt a little less alone, while thinking inwardly that if her least complicated ally was a loose cannon with a penchant for torching real estate, she was in trouble.

At the thought of allies, she tried very hard not to look at Michael. She was all too aware of him, though. He wore the same outfit he'd had on when he'd rescued her, when he'd made love to her that one time. She tried to tell herself it meant nothing, that those were his combat clothes. Still, her own slick black fight wear chafed in the face of sensory memories that came all too easily.

"Link up," Strike ordered. The magi formed a circle, cut their palms, joined hands, and jacked in. Standing between Strike and Michael, Sasha was all but over-whelmed by maleness and magic, and by the sharp dif-ference between the two men. Trumpets and silence. Yet it was the stillness within Michael that compelled her, making her want to sink inside him and give him music.

And that wasn't what she was supposed to be think-ing of, she reminded herself. *Focus!*

Strike summoned his magic from the uplink, found the travel thread linking them to the campsite, and sent them into the barrier. The world went gray-green around Sasha, and Skywatch disappeared. *Ch'ul* flowed past her, mingled songs whipping faster than thought, and then the rain forest blinked into being around her.

All around the clearing, the trees rose to impossible-seeming heights, lush and verdant and singing with life. And it wasn't just the plants and creatures that were singing, she realized after a moment; the red-gold magic had come alive at the base of her brain, singing that quiet martial theme, suggesting there was a source of power nearby. But that stood to reason; Anna had re-vealed that Ambrose's campsite was a place of power in its own right. The natural clearing, which was almost perfectly circular, had once been a cenote, one of the caved-in sinkholes that the ancients had used as both a water source and a place of sacrifice, believing the cir-cular openings to be among the earthly entrances to Xi-balba. Those sacrifices, mostly offerings of food, pottery, or small carvings called eccentrics, had remained at the bottom of the cenote even after the area ceased being inhabited by Maya or Nightkeepers. Over time, layers of leaves and debris had covered the sinkhole, eventually capping it over entirely. Now it was simply a clearing in the rain forest, with a subterranean waterway running beneath, and a cluster of offerings that gave off a background hum of magic by their very nature as sacrifices.

"Anna and Red-Boar reburied Ambrose over here," Strike said, gesturing her over to one edge of the clearing. The magi had moved him from his original spot atop the cenote to a place at the edge of the clearing. That way, if archaeologists ever found and excavated the cenote to get at the sacrificial relics within, they wouldn't find the newer corpse.

The spot Strike indicated looked like all the others, but when Sasha reached it, the air felt different—thicker, and faintly expectant. "Hello, Ambrose," she said, stumbling a little over his name, which brought the image of the demi-*nahwal*'s cruel, crazed face. "I'm keeping my promise. You'll get your funeral." Something hummed in the air, but she wasn't sure whether it was mosquitoes or magic. The thought of bugs brought her back to the last time she'd been at the cenote clearing, and cold fingers ran down her spine.

This was the first time she had been outside the bloodward surrounding Skywatch since her escape. Unsure whether Iago would be monitoring them, and whether he would try to 'port in and snatch her, the Nightkeepers were on alert. Rabbit, especially, was keeping himself attuned to any influx of dark magic.

Even on high alert, though, the magi made quick work of the exhumation, taking turns between digging and standing watch. Sasha looked away as Strike and Nate wrapped Ambrose's headless corpse in the sheets they'd brought with them for the purpose, then with a blue plastic tarp, for the sake of practicality. The tarp crinkled as they hefted the corpse out of the hole and set it off to the side of the clearing. Then they moved aside, giving Sasha a moment.

Aware that Michael stood close behind her, Sasha

stared down at the wrapped bundle. When she'd first set
out to retrieve her father's remains, she'd pictured what
she'd say or do when she found him. But none of what she
had imagined seemed appropriate now. Not when she was
hoping that she'd soon be facing his ghost, trying to get
through its madness. So in the end, she said only, "I owe
you my life. I promise I'll do my best to ease your death."

She didn't watch as Strike 'ported the body back to
Skywatch, didn't turn back until she heard the pop of air
that signaled his return. At Strike's inquiring look, she
shook her head. "No sign of him."

Strike nodded. "Then let's go ghost hunting."

Still jacked into the barrier, the magi formed a line.
Michael took the lead, hacking through the forest
growth with powerful slashes from a sharp-bladed, bone-
handled machete that he held with easy, deadly familiarity. Sasha followed close behind him, with Strike and
Leah behind her. The two other mated couples formed
the middle, with Rabbit and Sven forming the firepower-
heavy rear guard. Sasha's position in the line forced her
to watch the bunch and flow of Michael's muscles beneath his dark tank and body armor, the powerful flex of
his legs as he led them toward the temple. Heat pooled
in her belly. She told herself to look away, that she was
just making herself crazy. But at the same time, the heat
within served to intensify the buzz of magic. So instead
of pretending not to watch him, she let herself appreciate the aesthetics instead. And if that brought an ache
beneath her heart, that was her problem, her pain.

As if she'd said something aloud, Strike reached forward and gripped her shoulder, a steadying contact that
telegraphed strength and solidity, and left her with the
impression of a hug, an echo of the not-quite telepa-
thy they shared through their sibling bond. He'd asked
her once whether she wanted to talk about her and
Michael's nonrelationship, and when she'd answered

something along the lines of, "Oh, hell, no," he'd given her the space she'd needed. But it was nice that he'd asked.

Sooner than she would have expected, they emerged at the edge of the clearing, where shade-dappled orange sunlight glinted down on the entrance to Ambrose's temple. Cupping her hands around her mouth, Sasha called, "Ambrose? I need to talk to you."

The only response was a monkey's screech coming from far above. Unsurprised—she'd suspected all along that she would have to brave the temple—she started across the clearing with Michael at her side and the rest of her teammates at her back. As the magi passed through the arched doorway, the temperature dropped sharply while wan daylight gave way to shadows. Once Sasha's eyes had adjusted, though, she realized the shadows were far less than they could've been—the corridor was lit by the sun itself, with rays bouncing off highly polished sections of rock that were angled to refract the glow farther into the temple than it would've gone otherwise. "I didn't see the mirrors before."

"Lucius noticed them; they're set to show the starscript farther back," Michael said. "Still, since we don't need the script, let's give ourselves an advantage." He palmed a couple of glow sticks from his utility belt, handed her one, and cracked his own, shaking it to activate the glowing phosphorescence, which lit the scene an unearthly orange.

The small group moved along the tunnel, magic humming at a high background, there if they needed it. Sasha kept breathing, kept telling herself that every step inward they took was a good sign, a few feet closer to where she'd seen Ambrose's skull. She led them around the edge of the pit trap and consciously braced herself as they moved deeper into the temple, but it was still a sick shock when they reached the caved-in section. The skull was back at Skywatch, but the *tzomplanti* where it had rested was still there. There was no sign of Ambrose's demi-*nahwal*, though. Which meant . . . what? Was she supposed to search the ruin, hoping to find something the others had missed?

Sweat prickled at her pores, sensitizing her skin to the brush of her clothes, the heavy chill of the air as she braced her hands on her hips and called out, "I'm here, Ambrose. I'm wearing my bloodline and talent marks, and the royal *ju*. I'm a mage, a Nightkeeper. I've done what you always wanted. Now it's your turn to do what I want. Show yourself."

Nothing happened.

Anger stirred as she palmed her knife and recut her palm, deep enough that blood flowed freely, dripping to the stone floor of the temple.

Heart tripping unevenly in her chest, Sasha closed her eyes and whispered, "Where are you? I've done what you wanted; I've become what you intended. But now I need your help. Do you hear me?" She raised her voice, all but shouting, "I need you, godsdamn it. Why aren't you ever around when I need you?"

A roaring whip of wind slashed through the tunnel, all but flattening the magi. Strike and the others were driven back, shouting. They took refuge a few feet deeper down the tunnel as the gale slammed into where the space dead-ended in rubble, flinging Sasha into the wall. Panic slashed through her, and she screamed and tried to protect her face and head as the howling wind peppered her with dirt and gravel from the cave-in.

"I've got you." Michael grabbed her and turned them both toward the wall, using his body to protect her from the flying debris. She clung to him, burrowed into him. For a moment she thought it was going to be okay, that they'd gotten through the worst of it. Then thunder cracked in the tunnel, and an invisible grip picked them up and wrenched them both sideways, through a blur of gray-green barrier energy.

The world went black and they slammed down onto a hard, flat surface.

Suddenly, it got very quiet. And very dark.

Sasha lay still for a moment, pinned beneath his solidity and reassured by his steady heartbeat. "You okay?"

"I was just about to ask you the same."

"Then I guess that means we're both fine. You have another glow stick?" They'd both lost theirs.

"Yeah." He rolled off her, fumbled for a moment, and was rewarded by a wan light that started pale yellow and brightened to orange. As it did, he cursed foully under his breath, because the light showed a dense pile of rubble and the smooth walls of the tunnel they'd been in moments before . . . except the orientation was wrong, and there was no *tzomplanti*. "We're on the other fucking side of the cave-in."

"Magic," Sasha said simply. She pulled herself to her feet and dusted herself off, finding sore spots but no major injuries. "Maybe this is where we're supposed to be," she said, turning toward him. "Maybe this is the way to the—" She broke off, horrified. *"Behind you!"*

But it was too late. The demi-*nahwal* swept its arm in a wide gesture, and an unseen force yanked Michael off his feet, slammed him into the wall, and held him suspended there, several feet off the ground. Michael cursed and cast top-level shield magic, slamming his spell against that of the demi-*nahwal*. The clash of power saved Michael from being crushed against the wall, but he couldn't break free. The cords on the side of his neck stood out with the effort of holding magic against magic. "Get moving," he grated at Sasha. "What the hell are you waiting for?"

He wasn't telling her to run away, though. Snapping to action, she closed on the demi-*nahwal*. The creature

was wholly focused on Michael. Its lips were pulled
back in a feral snarl that revealed sharply pointed teeth;
its eyes gleamed with the same madness she'd seen in
her vision. Palming her knife, partly for blood sacrifice,
partly for defense, Sasha pricked her palm and called
on the magic, the music. They came quickly in a thunder
of drums, a complicated beat that folded back on itself
and then raced ahead, making her think of running feet.
"Ambrose," she said softly. "It's me. Sasha."

The creature didn't respond except to increase the
pressure on Michael, who groaned and rolled his eyes in
her direction, rasping, "Losing air here, babe."

"Don't call me babe." Steeling herself, Sasha touched
the *nahwal*'s arm, shuddering at the slippery texture of
the shiny skin that was tightly stretched over wooden
muscles and sinews. The drumbeats came faster, sounding like a monsoon hitting the roof of a canvas tent.

Magic, she thought, joy blooming as the *ch'ul* sang
through her, sweeping her up. She rode the energy flow
as it pulled her out of herself and into the man who'd
been the only father she'd ever known, for better or
worse.

Joy fled in an instant as madness surrounded her.

Anger. Rage. Insanity. The unsteady emotions spun
around her in a chaos of rimshots and timpani slams,
catching her up and sucking her into a forming vortex
of drumbeats. She screamed and fought, flailing with
insubstantial arms, trying to battle an enemy of sound.
Instinctively she grabbed onto the magic and tried to
control the drums, tried to slow their beat, to shape the
music, control the *ch'ul*. But she couldn't do it—maybe
because he was too far gone in the madness, maybe because she wasn't doing it right. She fought the noise-tide,
struggling, screaming, but made no headway. Instead, she
felt her grip on herself start to falter. Instinctively knowing she'd truly be lost if she gave up that connection, she

focused on her own body, trying to find the feeling of the demi-*nahwal*'s hand beneath her arm.

"Ambrose!" she shouted, still lost somewhere within his energy. "It's me, Sasha! Your princess." The din was incredible; she couldn't even hear herself. Still, she tried again. "Ambrose? Where are you? Help me, damn it. You're going to *kill me!*"

Her only answer was a vicious whip of mad joy, a chortle of glee that sounded all around her.

Panicking, she sought her own body, her own song, but she couldn't hear it over all the rocketing drums. "Help!" she screamed. "Help me!"

Suddenly a silver gleam cracked through the whirl and wrapped around her. She screamed and struggled, but it yanked her through the drums and madness. She was still screaming when she slammed back into her own body and found herself in Michael's arms. His eyes gleamed with silver magic and rage. Cursing, he pulled her away from the demi-*nahwal*, then backhanded the creature, driving it to its knees. Putting himself between them, he jerked the machete from its scabbard.

"Michael!" Sasha caught his arm, and held on when he tried to wrench it away. "Michael, stop!"

He didn't hear her, just bulled through her restraining grasp and lunged for the demi-*nahwal*.

"No!" Heart pounding in her throat, Sasha flung herself into the path of the sharp-edged machete. She screamed as the blade descended in a sweeping arc.

It froze less than an inch from her neck.

She hadn't realized she had closed her eyes until she was forced to open them in order to look at Michael. He was rigor-locked above her, the cords standing out on his neck and arms, muscles quivering with tension. He stared down at her, eyes dark and wild, but his own. "I almost killed you."

"You wouldn't have," she said with quiet assurance, though the fear knotted in her stomach wasn't so certain.

His expression went hard around the edges. "You're wrong about that."

He was trying to frighten her, she knew. And he was succeeding, not just because of the blade, but because of the silver magic, which was too powerful to be Night-keeper, too clean to be Xibalban. *What is it?* she wanted to ask him. *What are* you?

Not sure she was ready for the answers to those questions, she eased away and focused on Ambrose—or rather, the thing that was somehow the embodiment of Ambrose's ghost.

When she saw a familiar tic come from the otherwise motionless demi-*nahwal*, Ambrose's habitual chin twitch, she said, "I think he's coming out of it." She was slow to turn her back on Michael, and her warrior's talent chimed a warning when she did, but she ignored it to hunker down near the demi-*nahwal*. She touched Ambrose's scarred wrist, found the thunder of drums within him. "Ambrose? If you can hear me, I want you to come toward the sound of my voice. Don't think about the drums; don't listen to them. Come toward my voice." She'd seen a similar tactic work for Pim once or twice, though without the part about the drums. If that chaotic beat was his *ch'ul* . . . she shuddered at the thought of being locked inside a pattern like that. "That's it," she said when the tics intensified. "Toward my voice. You can do it."

The creature reeled and let out a keening noise as it seemed to collapse in on itself. Then it straightened and looked at her, and the madness was, if not gone, then significantly reduced. "Sasha?"

The voice wasn't Ambrose's—it was too high, gone otherworldly around the edges. But the tone was right, and the timbre. "I'm here," she said, speaking quickly because she didn't know how long he would be able to hold on to reality. "Where is the library scroll?"

"You're here," Ambrose said as though she hadn't spoken. "I'd almost given up hope." He looked past her and up, to Michael—first his face, then his forearm. A long, slow breath escaped from the demi-*nahwal*'s body. "You found them. I had hoped you'd come for my body, and see the message I left."

"Starscript," Michael explained at her sidelong look. "Lucius found it. That was what led him to Skywatch."

The knowledge that he'd tried to contact her helped somehow.

"Ambrose," she said firmly, "Where is the library scroll?"

"It's down there," he said, gesturing down the hallway. "In the tomb. The coffin will open during the solstice, and you'll find the scroll inside. It'll tell you what you need to know to summon the Prophet. He'll tell you everything you need to know." His voice dropped. "You've left it almost too late. The spell must be performed by the triad anniversary. After that, the barrier will be too unstable to form the conduit."

"Which gives us one chance and once chance only." Michael shook his head. "We should've been here earlier."

"Time happens in time," Ambrose said cryptically, then reached out toward Sasha. She nearly jerked away, but he didn't touch her, just caressed the air above her marks, pausing over the jaguar and the *ju*. "Your mother had a vision that we were all going to die. She couldn't talk Scarred-Jaguar out of attacking the intersection, couldn't go against him publicly. But you were the daughter of the sky, the daughter of the prophecy. She knew you had to live. She trusted me, her favorite brother." His voice had started to weaken, the tone fluctuating. "She told the others you were stillborn, only you weren't. You were perfect . . . but I wasn't. The scorpion spell took my magic, but the river broke something inside me. I wasn't right after that. I wasn't good for you, wasn't good *to* you. I tried. Pim tried. Neither of us was good enough. I tried to find the others, tried to find you a *winikin*, but they'd hidden too well after the massacre, and I got so confused sometimes. Then other times it all seemed like a dream. The compound was gone. Everyone I knew, everything I understood." His voice broke to a whisper. "Gone. Nothing there. Just sand. So I did my best to teach you myself. But I couldn't. You wouldn't believe."

Sasha's voice cracked. "How could I know you were telling the truth, when everything else was so screwed up?"

"Impossible, I know." His immobile face somehow reflected grief. "But then the barrier woke up. I felt it, even if I couldn't use it anymore. I went crazy—well, crazier. It scared Pim. I think it broke her. She gave up on me at long last. After she . . . did what she did, I came here to see if I could reconnect with the barrier. When I did, I hid the scroll inside the coffin, where it would be safe. But *they* found me here—the redhead and the woman. When they started asking me about the library, I knew what I had to do."

Chill fingers closed around her heart. "You killed yourself." Iago hadn't killed Pim or Ambrose, after all. Pim truly had committed suicide, out of despair for the life she'd wanted, the one she'd talked herself into believing Ambrose would give her someday. And Ambrose . . . he'd killed himself rather than reveal the library's location. He'd been loyal to the end . . . with nobody to honor him for the sacrifice.

"The gods came for me." His face lit for a second, and she heard a trill of perfectly pure melody. "They wanted to take me to the sky, but I couldn't go. I stayed here."

He reached out to her again. "I stayed for you, waiting for you to find your way, find the magic. Then you'd come. I knew you'd come." His voice had gone increasingly singsong as he lost his tenuous grip on reality.

Sasha knew the signs, knew they didn't have much time before he slipped away again. "Ambrose, listen to me," she said urgently. "We're taking your body back with us. You'll have a full funeral at Skywatch."

"Skywatch?"

"The training compound," Michael put in. At Sasha's frown, he clarified: "Leah named it. Thought it'd be good for morale."

"The canyon," Ambrose said beatifically, his voice going ragged.

"Yes," Sasha agreed. "So you can let go now. You don't have to stay here. You can let the gods bring you up to the sky. You've . . ." She trailed off, feeling something shift inside her. "You've done your job. We'll take it from here. And Ambrose . . . thank you. For everything."

His expression cleared for a moment, as though his conscious self were fighting for another moment with her. "How many of you are there?"

"Enough," she said, because what other answer was there?

"Thank the gods." He paused and reached for her, and this time she caught his hand in hers. "I'm sorry I was such a bad father."

Her heart cracked. "And I'm sorry I didn't believe. I'm sorry I stayed away so long. And I'm sorry . . ." She faltered. "I'm sorry you died alone." Lifting his dry, desiccated hand, she held it to her cheek, against the wetness of tears she hadn't entirely been aware of shedding. "Go with the gods, Ambrose."

"You, too, Princess." He exhaled and started to collapse then, losing form and shape, and drawing inward on himself. The outline of his body shimmered to vapor, then went transparent. At the last moment, his eyes locked on Michael's, and widened fractionally in a look that might've been surprise, might've been something else. "Mic—"

The word cut off as he disappeared in a flash of blinding white light that smelled of ozone and the sky.

CHAPTER SEVENTEEN

Michael growled, "Again with the 'mick' thing. What is that about?" But something in his eyes suggested that he already knew.

"Maybe it has something to do with the silver magic you're channeling." She turned on him. "Start talking. What are you doing? Why haven't you told anybody there's another type of magic Nightkeepers can tap?"

He stared at her, mouth working.

"Don't." She held up a hand. "Don't you dare lie to me."

"Sasha—" he began before breaking off, sounding desperate. Eyes wide, he said "What the hell?"

The rubble-filled tunnel shimmered, flickering in and out in a red-gold starburst ... and then the debris disappeared, leaving the tunnel clear. Startled yells greeted them from the other side, where the other Nightkeepers were uplinked for big magic. Sasha gaped at them.

Strike broke from the circle and crossed to her, caught her by the arms. "Are you okay?" He looked from her to Michael and back. "What the hell happened?" Then he looked at the tunnel beyond them. "What's down there?"

Sasha opened her mouth to explain, but then log-jammed, stopped, and looked at Michael, who said, "I think we should all probably take a look together." His eyes were his own again. There was no sign of the strange magic.

Then he turned and headed down the tunnel in the direction Ambrose had indicated, the orange glow of his light stick dipping slightly as he walked. Sasha hurried to catch up, so they were walking side by side as they came to a corner, turned it, and saw the first real carvings they'd seen in the subterranean tunnel, a row of screaming human skulls, their eye sockets seeming to follow as Sasha moved past them.

Only the first few carvings were of human skulls, though. After that, they started morphing, becoming something else entirely. The farther inward the Night-keepers went, the less the skulls looked human, the more they started to look like sharp-eared cats and dogs, and a wide-skulled bird of prey that looked familiar to Sasha, though she couldn't quite place it.

"Egyptian," Michael said under his breath, then raised his voice: "Rabbit, any of this looking familiar?"

So far, they'd been unable to identify the tomb Rabbit had seen during his impromptu vision quest, and Strike had understandably put a potential wild-goose chase to Egypt pretty low on the priority list. But Ambrose had said something about a sarcophagus. What if the tomb Rabbit had seen wasn't in Egypt after all? The ancestors of the modern Nightkeepers had fled Akhenaton's religious cleansing in 1300-something B.C. and wound up in Central America, so it wouldn't be impossible for some of the Egyptian techniques to have transferred. Only a handful of Nightkeepers had survived the First Massacre, and they had quickly assimilated into the indigenous population, eventually boostrapping the Olmec into the culture that had become the Mayan Empire. Which meant—

"If this shit is what I think it is," Strike murmured from behind Sasha, "we're walking in our first ancestors' footsteps. Literally."

She shivered as icy fingers walked down her spine as a staggering suspicion formed.

The tunnel ended at an open doorway. Lifting her glow stick, Sasha stepped through into a vaulted chamber that was roughly rectangular, its construction not nearly as regular as the architecture of the Mayan-era Nightkeepers. Which played if they assumed it'd been built by one of the first few generations of magi after the transoceanic voyage. The space seemed to have been carved out of the limestone base itself, hewn from the stone using cruder implements than the ones used to make the later pyramids at Chichén Itzá and elsewhere.

The walls were painted rather than carved, and even though Sasha had halfway expected the hieroglyphs, it took her a moment to make the transition. Her brain was used to the Mayan glyphs, the anamorphic figures and humans drawn and carved with flattened foreheads and conical skulls, heavy brow ridges and protruding noses. These painted figures didn't wear feathers and jade, weren't offering blood to the gods. No, the paintings were done in a different, though related style, one of angular figures posed stiff limbed, their catlike eyes marked at their edges with curlicues and lines, making each eye into a glyph itself: that of the sun god. Other gods were painted elsewhere around the room: the falcon-headed Horus, Bast the cat, Nekhbet the vulture, Hathor the cow, Anubis the jackal.

They were the gods of the Egyptian pharaohs prior to Akhenaton. And they were the gods of the single adult mage who'd survived Akhenaton's religious purge and had led the Nightkeeper children and their familial slaves to safety.

In the center of the room rose a huge waist-high box of carved and painted stone. The lid bore a life-size representation of a man laid out flat on his back with his arms crossed over his chest. Instead of the traditional staff and flail found on an Egyptian coffin, though, the figure held a ritual knife in one hand, an oval object in the other. A chill washed over Sasha when she recognized the latter as a highly stylized cacao seedpod, which had symbolized life and wealth in the Nightkeepers' new world.

Magic hummed in the air, latent and waiting, identifying the chamber as a place of enormous power, just as the hieroglyphs marked it as incredibly ancient, incredibly important. "Is it . . ." She trailed off, afraid to put it into words.

Strike crossed to the coffin and dropped to his knees, though she couldn't have said whether the move was shock or obeisance. Leah moved up beside him, braced one hand on his shoulder, then passed another along a line of boxed text, something that looked partway like a cartouche, partway like Mayan glyphs. "It's him, isn't it? It's the First Father's tomb."

Strike nodded raggedly. "I think so. Anna will have to translate everything and confirm, but . . . yeah. It's him. The First Father." He reached out a shaking hand, let it hover for a moment, then touched the carved stone with deeply ingrained reverence. "Gods."

Of all of them, it made sense that the king would be hit hardest by the discovery, because he'd known all along that the Nightkeepers were real, the histories were real. According to those histories, a single adult mage had survived Akhenaton's massacre to lead the Nightkeepers' children and the newly made *winikin* out of Egypt to the Mayan territories. From there, the First Father had created the original writs. He'd shaped how their civilization was to proceed along the millennia until the end-time. He'd written down the thirteen original prophecies, and then the demon prophecies that Iago had used to destroy the skyroad. The First Father had been the beginning of so many things, the wellspring of so much of the history and culture of the Mayan-era Nightkeepers, that it seemed impossible to believe he was truly a historical figure. Yet Sasha was actually standing there, staring at the sarcophagus that had been wrought by the people who had known him, lived with him, and had fashioned his last resting place after those of the god-kings they had known in another land, half a world away. And now, it seemed, that coffin also held the answer to the Nightkeepers' prayers: the library scroll.

Michael took a long look at the carvings on one side of the sarcophagus: a stylized scorpion atop a pair of wavy lines, with row upon row of hieroglyphs below it. "Hey, Rabbit. Is this your scorpion?"

The younger mage darted through the crowded chamber, glanced at the carving, and whipped out his cell phone to take a few snaps.

"I'm guessing that's a 'yes,' " Michael said dryly. But then he glanced at Strike, making sure he and the others were wrapped up in their own explorations of the chamber. Lowering his voice, he said, "Ambrose said something about using the scorpion spell to break his connection to the barrier." He paused. "What, exactly, did you ask the scrying spell right before you saw the carvings?"

Rabbit hesitated only fractionally before he said, "I started by asking how to call a new *nahwal*, and how I'm supposed to help in the war, but I didn't get shit. Last thing I asked was how to keep Myrinne."

Michael smiled grimly. Yeah, that was about what he'd figured. "So the answer was for you to get rid of the Xibalban's mark?" He supposed it made sense that the Nightkeepers' purest connection, that of the *jun tan*, would be unable to form in the presence of dark magic.

Rabbit nodded, eyeing the hieroglyphs. "If it broke Ambrose's connection to the barrier, d'ya think it'd break the hellmark connection, too?"

"Your scrying spell seems to think so." Which made Michael wonder what other connections it could break.

"What have you two got?" Strike asked from the other side of the tomb.

"Not sure," Michael answered. "Maybe nothing." But maybe everything.

He'd almost killed Sasha. When she'd put herself between his machete and her father's demi-*nahwal*, Michael had seen her, had known who she was, but he hadn't registered it or cared; he'd been too damned caught up in the raging fury. In that moment he'd hated himself, hated the world. The sluice gates had held, but somehow the Other had been inside him regardless, urging him on, bringing the blood fury it had been taught to love, to feed on.

Who the hell was he? Michael? The Other? Both? Neither?

He didn't know how he'd stopped himself from cutting her head off, and he couldn't promise he'd be able to stop himself the next time. The *muk* hovered at the edges of his soul. The dam hadn't cracked or broken; it had gone insubstantial, friable, like the barrier was becoming as the countdown to the end-time continued. And he knew, deep down inside, that if the Other broke through now, there would be no stopping it until everything—and everyone—around him was dead. Where the Other had once killed with all manner of human weapons, now his alter ego wielded the *muk* like a weapon, with deadly and precise command.

More, Sasha had flat-out asked him about the "silver

magic," which he feared meant she was already too close
to it. The Other's power had been drawn to her from the
very beginning; it wanted her goodness and life, wanted
to corrupt her, use her, destroy her balance. And that
absolutely, positively could not be allowed to happen.

He'd die first, damn it.

"Ambrose said the scroll is inside the coffin," she
said in answer to a question from Strike. "According
to him, it'll open during the solstice, and we'll find the
scroll, which will tell us how to summon something—or
some*one*—called a Prophet. It all has to happen during
the peak of the solstice."

"The solstice," Strike murmured. He looked down at
Leah, hope kindling in his eyes. "We could have the library a week from now."

"The timing will be tight," she warned, but her eyes
were alight with hope.

Rabbit was practically bouncing on the balls of his
feet, still taking pictures of the carved hieroglyphs.
"We've gotta get these pictures to Anna, ASAP, but I've
got zero signal."

Strike nodded. "You're right, we need to get Jade and
Anna on this, on all of it. We'll have to head topside,
though—there's no way I can 'port from down here, either. Too much interference."

Cell phones were pressed into service to record the
site for initial analysis, and then the magi formed a rough
line and headed out. This time, Strike and Leah led the
way, with Sasha near the end. Michael fell in behind her,
forming the rear guard. As he did so, her sex magic slid
along his skin. The darkness within him locked on the
sway of her hips, the lethal grace of her movements, and
the glitter of pure red-gold magic that sparked in the air
around her. Like matter drawn to antimatter, he reached
for her—no, the Other reached for her. Michael fought
the monster back. Barely.

When they came to the point where the spell-cast rubble had blocked the tunnel, Strike paused while the others caught up. "We need to guard the tomb entrance, or close it off or something." There had been no sign of Iago, but that didn't mean he was unaware of their success. Given the power of the tomb it seemed unlikely the Xibalban could 'port directly into the chamber itself, but he'd already proven able to zap himself into the tunnels. They had to believe he'd try it again, if he could.

"I could collapse it for real," Rabbit offered. He didn't look like he was kidding.

"Don't you dare," Leah said immediately. To Strike, she said, "I hate to split the manpower, but maybe we should post guards."

Michael prowled the area, partly to distance himself from Sasha, partly drawn by a tendril of power. He ran his hands along the tunnel walls, finally finding the point where it was strongest. "Gotcha."

"You see something?" Strike asked.

"No, but I feel it. Some sort of variant shield magic . . . there it is. Got it. I don't think this is Ambrose's spell. I think it's an older one, with an on/off switch of sorts."

He waved the others away. When they were clear of where he thought the shield would drop, he touched the magic, nudging a tendril of shield magic toward the spot he'd found. Moments later, the rubble reappeared.

Sven blinked. "Whoa. Cool."

Michael touched one of the busted chunks of debris. It felt like rock. For all intents and purposes it *was* rock, though it was an illusion, too. Kind of like him. Quickly, he showed the others how to work the spell.

Strike grinned and clapped him on the shoulder. "Good work." He turned away and headed up the tunnel, calling, "Moving out."

Michael fell into his place at the back of the line, keeping an iron grip on the Other, which—for the moment, anyway—had slipped back behind the dam, laughing softly at Michael's belief that it could be contained. *Go ahead and laugh*, Michael shot after it. *One of these days . . .*

He trailed off, because he didn't know what the hell to threaten the bastard with, given that the monster was part and parcel of himself.

When they reached the end of the tunnel, he was surprised to find that it was still daylight. It felt like they'd been underground forever, but in reality it'd been only a couple of hours . . . albeit a couple of hours during which a great many things had changed. At the thought, he fixed his eyes on Sasha, walking a few steps ahead of him.

As if aware of his gaze, Sasha glanced back as she stepped outside, into the orange-dappled sunlight. Her expression made him wonder what she saw in him in that moment, what she thought of him. "Sasha—" he began, then broke off when he saw movement beyond her, and his warrior's talent sounded the alarm.

"Get down!" He lunged for her, knocked her to the ground, and covered her body with his own.

And all hell broke loose.

The air split with gunfire and a fat fireball of silver-brown Xibalban magic, sending the Nightkeepers diving for cover. The ambush was perfectly timed and stupidly simple, with the Xibalbans dug into positions around the temple mouth, hidden in the thick underbrush, where they could—and did—fire at will. The tree line afforded them access and visibility, the slight downgrade to the temple mouth giving them the advantage of higher ground.

Michael covered Sasha as the other Nightkeepers scattered in singles and pairs, taking cover and returning fire, using basic shield magic to block the incoming fusillade. Nate snapped orders on one side, Strike on the other. That was what the magi had trained for, what they were bred to do—fight the enemy rather than retreat. But something—instinct, maybe, or his warrior's mark—told Michael that this time was different. This time they should get out while they still could.

Putting a strong shield around him and Sasha, he stood and pulled her to her feet. "We've got to get to Strike. Can you run?"

Strike and Leah were on the other side of the temple mouth, hidden behind a broken-off stela, in the shallow shelter offered by a niche in the green-covered temple wall. It was a distance of only fifty yards or so, but it looked like five times that when his shield wavered and a bullet pinged off the rock beside his head, warning that his magic wasn't strong enough. Not for this. Blood wouldn't help, he knew—her own shield magic was still too new to trust and he didn't dare touch her for a sex magic boost. *Gods*, he thought in an almost-prayer he suspected would fall on deaf ears. *Help me out here. I'm trying to do the right thing. I swear it.*

His shield settled fractionally. He figured that was as good as it was going to get. "Go!" he barked, sending her ahead of him and concentrating his shield around her, at the expense of his own protection. "Run!"

They lunged from concealment and raced across the open ground. Bullets and fire magic splattered around them, bouncing off the shield. Strike rose from concealment, shouting something Michael couldn't hear over the roar of magic and gunfire and the pounding of his own heart in his ears, his boots on the ground. Almost there. Twenty-five yards. Twenty.

Out of nowhere, a harsh rattle of dark magic rose around them and a dozen red-robes materialized, surrounding him and Sasha, weapons pointing inward.

Howling incoherent rage, Michael slammed to a stop and went for his pistols, but his hands wouldn't move;

his body wouldn't move from the neck down. Sasha, too, was frozen in place, her eyes wide and scared. One of the red-robes—average height and weight, with a bloody tear tattooed on his cheek—stepped forward, his lips drawn back in a sneer. "A nice trick, don't you think?" He flicked his eyes between them, as if checking to make sure he had the right targets, then nodded his satisfaction and hit a button on his weapons belt. "Our master has plans for the two of you."

Bullets and fireballs erupted along the perimeter of the red-robes' circle as the other Nightkeepers let rip, but the attack spent itself on the Xibalbans' shield. More teleport magic rattled, cycling up, no doubt called by whatever signal the red-robe had transmitted. *Shit*, they had a transporter who could move, not just things, but people.

Michael felt the rattle latch on and take hold of him and Sasha, and in his mind he caught a glimpse of a mountainous destination and the words "Paxil Mountain." They were about to be dragged to the Xibalbans' home base, into the hands of a man who could foul Strike's 'port lock with a thought. Once they left the temple clearing, the Nightkeepers would be unable to find them.

If Michael had been alone, and in full control of his powers, Michael would've given himself for the chance to take out Iago's army from within. But not with Sasha there. And not when he couldn't be sure of himself. Because as the dark magic twined around him, the Other reappeared from wherever it had been hiding, drawn by the Xibalbans' spell casting. A silvery fog covered Michael's vision for a second. When it was gone, he was no longer himself. Or rather, he was both of his selves, Michael and the Other. Man and weapon. The violence within him hovered on a knife point, as though waiting for the last vestige of his self-control to snap, for him to give himself to the magic.

You said you'd die for her, the temptation seemed to whisper. *What else would you do?*

In that instant, the Xibalbans' 'port magic grabbed onto them and yanked. With a roar, Michael slammed a shield around him and Sasha, cutting the 'port thread. Silver magic erupted, pouring through him, lighting him up. It was hot madness, pure temptation, and he gave in to it on a howl of mad fury and joy.

He caught Sasha against his chest, dropped the shield, and let rip with his true magic, the power the *nahwal* had warned would cost him his soul. He became the Other and the Other became him, and the resulting power was that of death.

Silver magic gushed from him, poured through him, became him. Ropy tendrils of the power spread out and curled around his enemies. Touched them. Took them.

One by one, the Xibalbans stiffened and cried out in horrible agony. The red-robe with the tattooed tear was first, his skin going gray as the silver magic latched on and seemed to *suck* the life from him. He fell, turning to dust and char, the expression of absolute terror on his face crumbling as he disintegrated. Then the men on either side of him began to crumble, their screams twisting together in horrifying agony.

With each kill, Michael felt his power increase, his soul shuddering with the terrible weight of the deaths, even as the Other exulted and grew stronger. The robed bodies fell, turned to dust. The force holding him and Sasha captive winked out of existence as the red-robes ceased to exist, and the revving 'port magic cut out as Iago aborted his plan from afar.

But Michael didn't stop. Couldn't. The killing magic spread outward away from him, into the forest where their ambushers hid. Men screamed, then stopped abruptly.

Within a minute, all Michael could hear was the howling inside his own skull. *It's done*, he told himself, not sure anymore which parts of him were Michael and which were the Other. *Pull back!* But the silver magic was within him, taking him over, more so than ever before. Mad, murderous rage rampaged through him, lighting him up and making him shudder with terrible glee.

Sasha put herself in front of him, grabbed him by his wrists. Her mouth worked, but he couldn't hear her words over the roaring in his ears, one that sounded like drumbeats and screams, and the terrible song of war, of death. The death magic rose higher within him, focusing on her even as his soul howled denial. Her eyes went wide, her skin gray.

He was killing her. Dear gods, he was killing her.

"No!" Michael roared. Taking control with a desperate effort of will, he broke his grip and flung her aside, trying to get her as far away from him as he could, trying to get some distance, some room to ... what? What could he do to stop the upward spiral, cut the feed before he unleashed death on the Nightkeepers themselves?

Sasha stumbled and fell, weakened by his magic. The Other regained the upper hand, and advanced on her. Michael was dimly aware that the others crowded around him, that he was forging through their shields. A bullet plowed into his shoulder but didn't slow him for an instant.

He was death. He was—

Death, he thought. *Yes*. He saw Tomas's face in his mind's eye, felt the *winikin*'s guilt, grief, and failure as his own, hated that he'd be breaking the promise he'd made. But what other choice did he have? Suicide was far better than this.

Lost in the thrill of slaughter, he tapped the death magic, let it spin up, spin through him. He fixed his eyes on Sasha, forced the words, his voice breaking with the effort of saying, "I'm sorry I couldn't be the man who was meant to be yours."

Then he jerked back away from her and turned the killing magic inward. At the last moment he was aware of Rabbit darting forward and grabbing onto him, getting in his face and yelling something. He caught the words "Mictlan" and "*makol*" but wasn't tracking anymore, wasn't processing. The darkness rose up to claim him. As it did, he was aware of another gripping his other arm, knew it was Sasha from the cool wash of her presence, the heat of lust.

Pure Xibalban magic came at him from one side, pure Nightkeeper from the other. They met in the middle of him, canceled each other out, and detonated to grayness. Then there was nothing. *He* was nothing. And that really sucked.

When Michael finally dropped, nobody caught him. He went down hard, unconscious, sprawled in the dirt.

A sob lodged in Sasha's throat, but she didn't go to him, didn't touch him, because she didn't want to ever again feel what she'd felt in him just now. The ugly, monstrous fury terrified her, made her want to puke. She hadn't caught any of the images she suspected Rabbit had seen, but she'd felt the silver magic and heard the screams amidst the inner music he'd hidden from her, and that had been more than enough.

Over Michael's body, she caught Rabbit's eyes and saw her own horror reflected. The young mage flexed the hand he'd touched Michael with, as if surprised it was still attached to his body.

"What. The. Fuck?" The harsh, explosive question came from Strike. He glared from Rabbit to Sasha and back. "What did you two know about this? How'd you know how to shut him down like that?"

Rabbit, looking drawn around the edges, said, "Whatever that shit was that he was channeling, it kicked on my hellmagic. I was just using the mind-bend to try to turn him off."

When Strike turned on her, Sasha shook her head and spread her hands to indicate bafflement. "I knew he was hiding something, but I didn't have any idea it was . . . whatever that was."

"You grabbed him."

"That was instinct. I had some idea of diverting enough of his *ch'ul* to knock him out, but the second I touched him, he started pulling the energy from me." Shaking inside now, she looked around at the others. "I felt like he was sucking the life out of me, and from all of you through me." And when she'd tried to cut the flow, she'd managed to stop drawing from her teammates but hadn't been able to sever the connection with Michael. He'd kept pulling her *ch'ul*, draining her, sapping her. Almost killing her. She shuddered, trying not to look at the dust piles inside the collapsed red robes. Trying not to think she could've been a dust pile of her own. "Lucky for me, Rabbit's hellmagic repelled the *ch'ul* and bounced me out of Michael's head." Which probably explained why she couldn't find Rabbit's or Michael's *ch'ul* song. They were blocked by hellmagic . . . or whatever it was that Michael had inside him. *Gods.*

"We should get out of here," Nate said urgently. "If Iago figures out that Michael's down, he might try again."

"I think we can take that as a given," Strike said, expression grim. "He'll want to get his hands on . . . whatever that was. We can't let that happen." But he didn't jump to the uplink. Just stood there, staring down at Michael as if trying to figure out what to do with him.

At that moment, Sasha was afraid of Michael. But she was also afraid *for* him. The silver magic and the thing inside him weren't the man she knew. Was there any way to separate them once again? "We're taking him with us," she said firmly.

Strike's expression went to that of the king, the man who sometimes had to make terrible decisions for the greater good. "He killed the red-robe during your rescue from the Survivor2012 compound. It wasn't Iago, after all. It was Michael."

"I didn't know." Yet she met her brother's eyes, jaguar stubbornness rising up inside her as she tipped up her chin. "Killing in battle isn't wrong."

"But he lied about it, and gods know what else. And according to his own story—if we pick through the lies—he did it *through* the guy's shield. If he can do that, he can get through the wards we've got on the storeroom." He paused, dropping his voice. "I can't have him inside Skywatch without some sort of guarantee. I can't."

"I'll stay with him," she said immediately. "He won't kill me. Not even at his worst."

Strike shook his head, but more in indecision than negation. "We don't know that we've seen him at his worst."

"We don't know *what* we're seeing," she countered, desperation increasing as the seconds slipped beneath her skin, and her warrior's mark warned that they were running out of time. "And you can't tell me you're willing to sacrifice one of your own without knowing for sure."

"Is he one of mine?" Strike asked. "That wasn't Nightkeeper magic."

"It wasn't Xibalban, either," Rabbit put in. "It was more like . . . I don't know, a mix of the two." He paused. "Strong as anything too. If we can figure out how to use it . . ." He trailed off in the face of the king's glare

"I can't risk it." Strike shook his head. "He could take us out from the inside."

"I'll vouch for him," Sasha said, feeling the moment

slipping away. "I'll blood-bind myself to him. Whatever you want." *Give him to me.*

"I won't let you endanger yourself for a guy who's treated you like he has," Strike snapped, sounding more like a big brother than a king. "He's done nothing to earn your loyalty or affection. He's a godsdamned walking dysfunction!"

"I'm not talking about him and me," she countered quickly, though it wasn't entirely accurate. "But you have to admit that this explains a whole lot of how he treated me. He was trying to keep me from getting caught up in whatever he's going through." Which sent her thoughts down a road they were probably better off not traveling, because whether or not he'd been doing what he thought was right in that regard, the fact was, he'd lied to her. He'd lied to all of them. Was her defense of him now just another brand of clinging?

"And you want to solve that by *binding* yourself to him?" Strike said. "He'd be pissed. And so would I."

"I—" Sasha broke off, caught in her own logic. "Shit."

"We need to make a decision," Nate urged. The other magi were ranged around the argument, facing out, ready to defend if—or rather *when*—Iago sent reinforcements. "We need to get Sasha back behind the ward. He wants her by the solstice, and time is running out."

"He wants Michael too," she argued desperately. "You can't leave him here. You can't."

"I wasn't going to," Strike said, his voice flat with grief.

Sasha's soul shuddered at the implication. "Don't. I'm begging you."

"I've got to do what's best for all of us," he said, back in king mode. "I've got to follow the writs."

"Except when it suits you," she threw back at him, anger kicking against what she was coming to recognize as the innate stubbornness of a jaguar. "Then you re-write. Well, then—"

"I can help him," Rabbit broke in. He'd crouched down, was touching Michael's wrist, his eyes gleaming with magic. When they both looked at him, he said, "He's got some sort of blockade in his head. It's busted, but I think . . . no, I know I can fix it."

Strike considered the offer for the longest five seconds of Sasha's life. "Can you guarantee that it'll stay in place?"

She saw the lie form in the young mage's eyes, saw it drain away as he shook his head. "No. No guarantees. But I promise I'll do my best."

Steeling herself, Sasha crouched down beside Rabbit and took Michael's hand. She didn't feel the ugly rage or the tempting silver magic now; she felt the man beneath. The one who'd rescued her, who'd made love to her. "Please, brother. Please give us a chance to figure out what this is, who he is." *And whether there's any hope for the two of us.*

As Strike wavered, a faint rattle touched the air.

"Time's up," Nate warned. He waved the others to link up, leaving a gap in the uplink, where Sasha hadn't left Michael's side, hadn't let go of him.

Logic and heartache told her to let Strike decide, that she didn't owe Michael anything. Her magic and heart, though, told her to hold on to him and never let go.

"Shit," Strike said. He reached down, grabbed her free hand, and brought up the 'port magic.

As they slid sideways into the teleport, she heard Iago's roar of rage, his shout of, "Mictlan!" Then he was gone, the temple was gone, and they were back home.

And now, she knew, things were going to get complicated.

CHAPTER EIGHTEEN

December 15
Three years, six days to the zero date
Skywatch

Michael swam back up through the fog of unconsciousness, and was vaguely surprised to find himself back at Skywatch. And alive. Given those two things, though, and what he remembered of the Xibalban ambush and his use of the *muk*, he wasn't at all surprised to find himself locked in one of the storerooms.

The hand holding his, though, was unexpected. As was his sense that Sasha was nearby. He wouldn't have expected her to want to get within a mile of him after what had happened.

He squeezed experimentally. "Hey." His voice was rough and drowsy. "I didn't think—" Realizing that it wasn't Sasha's hand he was holding, he broke off, eyes flying open to glare at the young man sitting beside his cot. "What the fuck?"

Rabbit scowled and broke the grip. "You're welcome, asshole. If I hadn't put your brain back together, you'd be a guest at Chez Xibalba right now. Or maybe Mictlan." He paused, eyes going speculative. "Did my old man put those blocks in? That's some seriously high-tech shit you've got going on in your head."

It took Michael a few seconds to figure out what he was talking about, another few to check his own brain and realize he was alone. The Other was gone. More, it was *gone* gone. There was no hint of its presence, no dark pressure anywhere. He felt like he had before he'd undergone his talent ceremony, with the critical difference that he remembered everything about his alter ego, and what it had done.

Rabbit had bent his mind, resurrecting, not the dam and sluiceways Michael had constructed on his own, but rather the conditioning Dr. Horn had used to erase his other self from his conscious mind. "Holy crap, Rabbit. You've got mad skills if you did that without the drugs and other garbage."

The younger man raised an eyebrow. "Not the old man, then?"

Michael thought of Horn's pasty, pinched face, comparing it to the hawkish ferocity of Rabbit's sire. "Not even close. Long story. It was—" Michael broke off, not because he couldn't talk about what had gone on inside him . . . but because he *could*. Rabbit's blocks hadn't just shut the Other away; they'd shut off whatever the hell had kept him from talking about it.

"Save the story," Rabbit advised, oblivious to Michael's inner *oh, holy shit* moment. He stood and headed for the door. "I'll go tell the others you're awake, get set up for an all-hands-on-deck. In the meantime, I think you've got some 'splaining to do."

Even without that warning, Michael had known Sasha was outside, waiting to talk to him. He'd felt her there, a stir of warmth and sensual awareness that was so very different from the angry lust he'd been battling for weeks now, though no less urgent for the differences.

Pulse kicking, he swung himself upright on the narrow cot. He was wearing his combat pants and muscle shirt from what he guessed was the day before, and could've used a shower. A sore spot twinged in one shoulder, and a glance showed a healed bullet wound. He thought he remembered one of the Nightkeepers—Nate, maybe?—taking a shot at him when he'd turned on Sasha. Didn't blame him. If her and Rabbit's combined magics hadn't been enough to bring him down . . .

He shuddered at the thought, and when Sasha came through the door on the backswing of Rabbit's exit, he snapped, "That was a dumb-assed move you pulled, touching me. I could've killed you."

She was wearing jeans and a button-down that followed the curves of her body, along with lace-up boots and a neutral expression. "You're welcome," she said. Which, come to think of it, had been Rabbit's first words, too.

"Don't think I'm not grateful to you both, but you damn well should've left me there," he said bluntly. "There was no guarantee Rabbit's mind-bend would work." There still wasn't, he knew; the control felt stronger than ever before, but who knew what would happen when he went for his magic?

"Iago wants you," she said, equally bluntly. "He can't have you."

"Then you should've finished me."

He expected an immediate denial. Instead, he got a long, cool look. "Is that what you would've preferred?" She held up a hand to stop him. "And no more lies, damn it. Not of commission, not of omission. I want the truth from you, even if it pisses one or both of us off."

Letting out a breath, Michael nodded. "Deal. And the first truth I'll tell you is that it was never about whether or not I wanted to tell you. I physically couldn't." He touched his temple. "They used drugs and posthypnotic suggestion to shut me down."

"They?" she asked, then shook her head. "No, don't answer that. You can tell it to everyone in a few minutes." An edged smile touched her lips. "Rabbit says you're safe to release back into the wild." The words "for now" hung between them, unspoken.

"Before we go, I need to tell you something." He reached out to her, though she still stood across the room, near the door. When she didn't move, he let his hand fall. He didn't stand and go to her, though. Didn't want to loom over her, didn't want her to fear him any more than she already must, after seeing what he was capable of, what was inside him. And it was only going to get worse when he told them the real story.

Her expression stayed guarded, but she nodded. "I'm listening."

He hesitated, trying to find the right words. He couldn't tell her everything at once, didn't even know where to start, so he went with the piece of it that belonged just between the two of them. "You've probably figured out that a big part of what's happened between us has been dictated by what's inside me, and me trying not to let it touch you."

"I'd already figured you were hiding something. I'll admit that what we saw yesterday . . . well, that was more than I'd been thinking."

She might as well have said, *beyond my worst nightmare*, because that was what he heard in her words, in her voice. He opened a hand, stared at the white scar-stripe across his palm. "I tried to stay away from you, but by the gods . . ." Giving up any pretext, he looked straight at her, let her see what she would in him. "The good parts of me want you more than anything. Unfortunately, so do the bad parts. Sometimes having you near me unsettles the balance and makes it harder for me to hold it together. Other times you bring me back to myself."

"Maybe it's not me," she suggested diffidently. "Maybe it's the three-year countdown. Big changes are coming, remember?"

"Trust me, babe. It's you." Now he did take the chance of standing and crossing to her, compelled by the better parts of himself, and the gift of honesty. He moved slowly, waiting for her to retreat. When she didn't, he stopped in front of her and lifted a hand to her cheek, cupping her jaw in his scarred palm and drawing his thumb across her smooth, pale skin. "It's always been you, even back when you were just a couple of photographs and some dreams."

"Oh." The word held a tremor, but not of fear. Eyes steady on his, she reached up to cover his hand, holding his touch against her face. But as she did so, she shook her head. "I can't. You know I can't."

"Yeah." It wasn't a surprise. But it was a lead weight in his chest. "You don't do crazies."

"I need—" She broke off, as though it were her turn to find the right words. "I'm just starting to find myself, to figure out who I'm meant to be, what role I'm meant to play in this mess. I need someone I can lean on when things go wrong, someone I know is going to be there no matter what. I don't have enough stability in me to stay strong when you start to spin off the rails. I've lived that life. I can't go back."

"I know. I don't want you to." And that was the truth too. "I wish I could undo it all."

"Jox keeps telling me that I'm exactly the way I was meant to be, that I shouldn't wish to rewind and change my relationship with Ambrose, or my decision to leave him."

"Jox is full of shit."

She looked away, snorting a laugh. "I don't think I'll tell him you said that." But when she looked back up at him, the gleam remained in her eyes. "I wish you could go undo whatever it was, too. I think I would've liked the man you would've been."

"You would've loved him," he said lightly, though he wasn't sure that was the case. Needing the contact, the woman, if only for just the next few seconds, he leaned in. And kissed her.

Sasha saw the kiss coming, could've moved away. She didn't.

He was unshowered and wearing his combat clothes; his scent was strong, though not unpleasant, as though his natural aura had been distilled to a potent, masculine jolt that fired her blood in her veins and tightened her skin, heightening sensation. His taste, too, was concentrated, his skin hot beneath the skim of her hands, his muscles bunching and flexing as he wrapped his arms around her, surrounding her with his presence.

For the first time since she'd met him, she felt that he was present in the moment, entirely *with* her. He wasn't sparring with an inner opponent, wasn't trying to blunt his responses to keep from triggering whatever lay within him. He was there, with her. Kissing *her*.

And oh, what a kiss.

He slanted his mouth across hers, touched his tongue to hers, and then slid deeper, mimicking the thrust with the drag of his hands across her ribs and hips to her ass, where they fastened, cupping her up against him as he explored her mouth, her cheeks, the curve of her neck.

Where before they had come together in a tumult, propelled by an inner drumbeat of lust and magic, now the magic was a background hum, seeming so much less important than the feel of his mouth making love to hers.

And then, finally, she heard his song, a single electric guitar with a skirr of feedback that raised the fine hairs on her arms and the back of her neck.

There you are, she thought, and gloried in the music.

She nipped her way down the strong column of his neck to his collarbone, then touched her lips to the place on his shoulder where a bullet had gone in the day before, and his healing talents had pushed it right out again. Lips stinging with the salty potency of his skin, she returned to his mouth, kissed him and twined herself around him, feeling his thick hair brush the backs of her hands, the sides of her face as they kissed long and hard, deep and wet.

An ache opened up within her, a hollowness she hadn't been aware of until that moment. She drew back and sucked in a long, shuddering breath that did nothing to fill the emptiness.

They stared at each other for a long moment, eyes questioning. *Did you feel that?* she imagined her expression said, with his answering, *Hell, yeah.*

"We should get upstairs before Rabbit comes back down looking for us," she said, though she would've rather stayed just as they were. The others needed to see him, see that he was okay. And they all needed to hear what he had to say.

"Or worse, your brother."

She grimaced. "Yeah. He's not a happy king at the moment."

"Doubt what I'm about to tell him is going to help."

"The truth is what it is," she said pragmatically, her arms still wrapped around his neck, his hands fastened to her waist, holding their lower bodies together, warm and sure, the contact enticing. After a pause, she said, "And the truth is, I was right. I like this version of you."

You would've loved him, he'd said, and she had a feeling that was the truth too. But at the same time, she knew she was in danger of falling for the man he was now, not just because of his kiss, but because of what he'd sacrificed in an effort to keep her safe, how he'd driven himself to the edge trying to do the right thing. Where Ambrose had wallowed in his own pain, rarely noticing when it caused her distress, Michael had tortured himself, nearly killed himself in an effort to protect her. Could she blame him for that?

No, of course not, her most logical self said. *But there's a difference between not blaming him and loving him, or even trusting him. Who knows what will set him off again? Ambrose had sane spells too.*

As if hearing her thoughts, or catching an echo from the bond of their magics, he eased away from her, his expression tightening to wariness. "Don't make any decisions until you've heard the whole story. It's fucking ugly."

The harshness of his voice on the last two words had her flinching back. But she nodded. "Okay. Let's go."

They left the cell hand in hand, but when they hit the stairs he released her and led the way. She followed him up, much as he'd done to her that first day. Now it was the other way around, and it was his turn to hesitate at the top step, when the assembled *winikin* and magi, who were sitting in the great room waiting for his story, all turned at once to stare.

The hesitation lasted only a moment, though. Then he squared his shoulders and kept going. Which was all anyone could do, really, she thought. Just keep going.

But as she kept herself going, heading for an empty spot on one of the long couches while Michael took a centrally located chair that had been left conspicuously empty, she couldn't help thinking that sometimes going forward wasn't enough, while other times, life took a sharp corner when she wasn't looking. And went off the road into uncharted territory.

For all that Michael had sometimes imagined being able to tell the others about the shit inside his head, he'd never come up with the right words. How could he make them understand why he'd made the choices he'd made, why he'd done the things he'd done, when he didn't even understand it himself? Or rather, he understood why he'd done it, but he didn't know what it made him, besides royally fucked-up. Was he a hero? A monster? Both?

Michael looked for Tomas, found him up at the breakfast bar with most of the other *winikin*. A thumbs-up would've been nice. He got a level stare he couldn't even begin to interpret. A glance at Sasha netted him an encouraging eyebrow lift, and he figured he'd have to make do with that. It was probably better than he deserved—*she* was definitely better than he deserved—but it helped. It was because of her that he hadn't lost it entirely back at the temple. And he suspected it was because of her that he hadn't died back there.

Taking a deep breath, he faced the big sofa, where Strike, Leah, Anna, and Sasha sat ranged together, a family unit. Figuring he'd start at the beginning, he said, "First, I owe each and every one of you an apology. I've lied to you all, both overtly and by omission. Hopefully by the end of this you'll get that I honestly couldn't tell you the truth before. It's entirely thanks to Rabbit that I can tell you now." He nodded to the young mage. "Thanks, man." Not *kid* anymore.

"My pleasure," Rabbit said, deadpan, though they both knew that messing around in his sewer of a brain would have been far from pleasant.

Then, Michael drew breath and dove in. "The truth is, I didn't exactly wash out of FBI training—a man named Maxwell Bryson recruited me into a covert arm of government ops. Washing out and taking the tech job was part of my cover." Up at the breakfast bar, Tomas jolted upright. Michael waved him down. "Don't get too excited; it wasn't nearly as sexy as it looks in the movies.

No 'shaken or stirred' for me, though I did have a gadget or two." He paused. "This was maybe a year after nine/eleven. Homeland Security was running in all different directions, and not all of those directions were purely on the up-and-up. Bryson's group wasn't new, but it got expanded to handle situations the other arms of the terror response system didn't want to—or flat-out couldn't—handle. I'm not even sure the president knew what we were up to half the time. It was like there was this reflex arc of plausible deniability built into the war on terror. Either that, or Bryson and his cronies didn't trust that there would be definitive action if it didn't come from them."

Sasha said, "You were an assassin." She didn't look all that surprised. More like things were finally starting to make some sense.

"Among other things." Michael had tried—and failed—to imagine how she would take learning that he'd been a killer even before his entrance into the Nightkeepers and their war. Granted, he'd killed in the context of another war—that on terror—but his kills hadn't come in battle, and he hadn't sacrificed his victims to a higher power. He'd killed in cold blood, and even among the Nightkeepers, that was murder. He continued, "Here's where it gets uglier still. They didn't come after me because I was top of my class—far from it. They wanted me because my psych tests showed a tendency for dissociation. I could split myself when necessary, compartmentalizing the bad stuff, shoving it to the back of my head, and more or less forgetting about it. According to Dr. Horn, who was Bryson's number two man, I was a budding sociopath, and lucky for me they found me when they did." He didn't try to stop the resentment from coloring his tone. "I bought into that because they gave me a choice—I was going to be booted from the FBI program either way, thanks to my psych evals. I could either join Bryson, or they'd cut me loose."

"An offer of therapy and some meds would've been nice," Jade said sharply.

"In retrospect, that probably would've been on the table if I'd turned down Bryson's offer. But I was young and pissed off, and I'd liked the training part of the academy. I thought I'd be a good agent, and I wanted to make a difference." He glanced at Tomas, whose expression had gone unreadable. "That's what happens when you raise a kid to save the world. Sometimes he gets there ahead of schedule."

"They trained you to kill," the *winikin* said, his voice hollow.

"According to Horn, I was most of the way there on my own. All they did was emphasize the split between the two personalities I already had going on inside my head. Using hypnosis, drugs, and some serious meditation training, Horn taught me to subsume the Other, keeping it compartmentalized until they needed it."

"The Other?" Sasha asked quietly.

He couldn't read her, wasn't sure he wanted to yet. Not until he got through the rest of it. "That was what we called my killer instinct, my alter ego. I was good at both of my jobs. Mostly I sold techware. A couple of times a month, though, I'd get a call on a second phone, with drop coordinates. There, I'd find info on the target and how they wanted it done. Sometimes it was a straight-up hit, just get it done and get out. Other times it was up to me to make it look like an accident, or frame someone else for the kill. Whatever the powers that be decided would offer maximum results." He hesitated over the one that had hit him hardest, even through the dissociation that separated him from the Other. "Once it was a kid, designed to look like a drive-by gone wrong.

The kill sparked a gang war that nearly wiped out both sides, which had been the point. But the job showed me that Bryson wasn't sticking to the war on terror anymore. And he'd started getting pretty vague on what the targets had done."

"So you got out?" Sasha ventured.

"No," he said, sticking with the honesty she'd demanded. "I stayed. Partly because by that point Horn's work was about the only thing keeping me in one piece, but also because I'd become addicted to the double life and the adrenaline high, and was using one part of myself to excuse the other, at least inside my own head. I don't know how much of it came from Horn's programming, but by the end, I was living for the hunt and the kill, existing from job to job. In the end, it was their choice to cut me loose. They said it was budget cuts and the downsizing of the terror response, but I have a feeling it was because they knew I was on the verge of going hunting on my own, without orders." He told the story as dispassionately as he could, but heard the self-disgust leaching into the words.

In the end, he'd been too dangerous even for the men who'd made him.

"I'm surprised they cut you loose," Nate said, his eyes reflecting a sort of morbid fascination. "I would've thought they'd be better off putting a burn notice on you. No offense."

"None taken, because I'm inclined to agree, though most days I'm grateful they didn't." Michael paused. "It was Horn's project, his decision. I think in the end it came down to hubris, and a certain scientific bent. He'd proven with me—and presumably others—that he could program a susceptible brain to split fully. Then he set out to prove that he could put it back together again, only better, effectively 'curing' me of my dissociative identity disorder. He reprogrammed me, cutting off my access to the Other once and for all, and convincing me I was exactly what I'd been playing for the previous three years: a decent-looking salesman who liked women and nice clothes, and had the depth of a puddle."

"And they just let you go?" Nate persisted.

"Yes and no. He implanted a compulsion: If the Other ever returned to my conscious mind, I was programmed to call in." He paused, grimacing. "The conditioning worked great, and probably would've kept me sane and ignorant for the rest of my life . . . except for the magic. The first of the memories started breaking through right around the time the barrier reactivated; I thought they were just nightmares. But then, during the talent ceremony, it all came spewing back. The Other. The jobs. Killing the kid. Everything. More, it brought this crazy power with it, though I didn't really realize it at first. My bloodline *nahwal* helped me push the Other back at first, and warned me not to let it through, and not to use the magic. The *nahwal* said that my soul balance was already tipped toward darkness, and if I used the magic, I'd tip it further. Too much, and I'd switch to channeling hellmagic."

He glanced at Jade, "It's an understatement to say that I came out of that ceremony in a really bad place, mentally. What was more, the Other's return had triggered the conditioning, and before I knew what I was doing, I was on the phone with Horn. When I realized what was happening, I shut it down, but the damage was done. Thank the gods I'd had the sense to sneak out to Albuquerque to make the call, so they didn't know to look for me here at Skywatch, but I knew they were looking for me, and they wouldn't stop until they found me and shut me up for good. So I held them off. And I started to make a plan."

"Which explains the bat phone," Sven said, with his typical inability to take much of anything seriously.

When the others just looked at him, he said, "What? You know you were thinking it. It's not like anybody had 'government agent' in the pool." It was common knowledge that the occupants of Skywatch used to speculate widely on the purpose of Michael's second cell phone, the subject of the secretive calls he got at strange hours, and what he'd really done in the outside world.

Michael found a strained grin. "What did you have, 'he owes money to the mob'?"

"Vegas, actually." Sven slid a look around the room. "Jade had 'illegitimate half-blood child he doesn't want us to know about,' Leah picked the mob, and Rabbit guessed you were some sort of gigolo."

"Shit," Michael said mildly. "I should've put in a hundred for 'borderline sociopathic assassin.' " But saying it aloud killed the brief spurt of humor that had temporarily lightened the room. He continued, "Basically, in the weeks following the talent ceremony I worked my ass off using a combination of visualization, martial arts, and the meditation tricks Horn had taught me, and managed to reassemble some mental defenses. I pictured them like a big dam, with sluice gates that opened now and then to let the Other slip through sometimes. We . . . I don't know, we reached a standoff of sorts, inside my skull. All the while, I was working on my magic and trying to hold off Bryson and Horn, and figure out how to keep them from coming after me—and finding Skywatch—without just luring them somewhere and killing them. Not because I was against killing them per se. I figured it would attract more attention than it would defuse. So I worked, and I planned, and I stalled until the spring, just after the equinox."

He looked at Sasha, still unable to see past the blank unease on her face. He said to her, "That was when Carter first got us your file. I can't necessarily say it was your photo—and what I felt when I saw it—that got me off my ass, but you were part of it. I'd also figured out the chameleon shield by then." He spread his hands, condensing weeks of sweat equity and split-second timing. "I contacted Horn and let him talk me into meeting him at a remote safe house for an 'evaluation,' knowing they would plan to take me out. Instead, I got my hands on some C-4 and detonators, ducked their attack, faked a counterattack, made it look like my detonator misfired early, and then shielded the hell out of myself when the blast went off." It had been a terrible, terrifying experience. And the Other had loved every fucking minute of it. "Horn and Bryson left, convinced I wouldn't be a danger to them anymore, and I dropped the chameleon shield and came home."

Strike nodded. "That would be when you started wearing tanks, chucked the phone, and turned into someone we could stand."

"Pretty much." Michael took a long look around, thought he saw more understanding than condemnation on his friends' faces, and let himself uncoil a fraction, thinking maybe he was going to be okay, after all. At least generally. He couldn't help thinking that Sasha was far too quiet, far too still. She looked like she'd crawled away inside herself, someplace he couldn't follow.

They would talk later, he assured himself. He didn't know which way it would go, but they sure as hell needed to talk.

"Is the Other why you don't use your offensive magic?" Sven asked.

Michael lifted a shoulder. "Depends on your definition of 'offensive.' All along, I've assumed that in blocking off the Other, I had blocked off that part of my magic. After these past few weeks, though, I've come to realize that wasn't all of it. I'd known all along that anger could bring the Other closer to the surface. When I met Sasha, though, I realized that there was more to it

than just anger." He looked at her, trying to choose his
words carefully. "Being around you, wanting you and
riding high on sex magic and frustration . . . all those
things also brought the Other forward, and weakened
the defenses I'd built up. The silver magic the *nahwal*
warned me against started breaking through more
often. It was attracted to you." He paused, then pressed
on. "The silver magic is called *muk*. It's the original form
of our power; our ancestors deemed it too dangerous to
use, because it often corrupted its user. They split the
muk into Nightkeeper magic and hellmagic, which the
Xibalbans later claimed as their own."

"I felt it," Sasha said softly. "I didn't know what it was,
but I felt it. It was . . . seductive."

Their whole relationship was tangled in the silver
muk, Michael thought. The question was whether they'd
untangle it far enough to find something that was theirs
alone.

Actually, the question was whether they'd get that
chance.

"I don't know much more about the *muk* for certain," he continued, "but I have a feeling it's attracted
to Sasha's *ch'ulel* talent, that it wants to . . . cancel her
out." He met her eyes, didn't look away. "I told you
guys that Iago was looking for one of us, back during
Sasha's initial rescue. I also told you that he dismissed
me as a lightweight, but that was when I had the Other
fully blocked. What I didn't—couldn't—tell you was
that after Sasha and I made love"—he put it out there,
staking his claim, as Strike had wanted him to do weeks
ago—"and the Other came through, bringing the *muk*
with it, Iago seemed to recognize me. He said I was the
one he was looking for, and that Sasha was going to trigger some sort of transition. He implied that after that, I
would come to him on my own. And then yesterday the
red-robe said they'd come for both of us. I think that's

confirmation that she and I are linked, not just as two people who probably should have been destined mates, but through the opposition of our magics. I don't know whether he's planning on turning me or sacrificing me outright, but either way, he's looking for some serious power."

He fell silent then. There were other details, things he could fill later. But that was the bulk of things.

After a moment, Sasha said softly, "Is the Other gone now?"

"Contained. Not gone. But I have an idea about getting rid of it, or at least the connection to the silver magic."

"The scorpion spell," Rabbit said. "The one from the tomb."

Michael zeroed in on him. "Has Anna looked at the photos you took?"

"Yeah." The young man nodded. "She even did a rough translation that makes it look as though it'll break the most recently formed magical connection." His teeth flashed. "In my case, the hellmagic connection. In yours . . . maybe the *muk* connection? Or did that come before the Nightkeeper magic?"

That was a hell of a thought. "I'm a Nightkeeper first and foremost," Michael said firmly. "How bad is the spell?"

"Nasty," Strike said. "It requires *pulque* and a particularly debilitating near-death experience to get into the in-between, which is a barren plain on our side of the entrance to Xibalba. Once you're there, you've got to find the Scorpion River, which is the first challenge the dead need to overcome to enter Xibalba. They cross over. You go for a swim."

A heavy weight pressed on Michael's gut. "Then what?"

"Another near death. If you're lucky, that purifies

your soul, breaks the magic connection and you come back." Strike didn't continue with the "if you're not lucky" corollary, but it was a given. *You don't come back at all.*

But what other choice did he have? Michael thought. He couldn't go on the way he was. "It's worth a try. When can we start?" But something changed in the air, kicking against his warrior's mark. A flash in his peripheral vision brought his attention around to the kitchen. Tomas stood, white faced, looking like he might puke at any second. "What's wrong?"

"Can we . . ." The *winikin* swallowed hard. "We need to talk. In private. *Now.*"

CHAPTER NINETEEN

There had been too many years of friction for Michael to snap to attention at Tomas's order. And he'd kept himself hidden for too long, lied to his teammates too much. He shook his head. "No more secrets."

Tomas glanced at the others, stricken. His voice broke to a whisper. "I *can't*. I made a vow."

"I didn't," Michael said. "And since I'm guessing whatever you promised to keep secret has major implications for what's been going on in *my* damn life, you didn't have the right to make the vow in the first place."

"It shouldn't have mattered," the *winikin* rasped. "No *winikin* of the stone bloodline has ever seen two in a single lifetime. There was one in our parents' generation; there shouldn't be another in this one."

"Tomas," Jox said in a forbidding voice, in full-on royal *winikin* mode. "What the hell are you talking about? And don't give me any shit about vows. Get your head out of your ass, man. The situations have changed. The *rules* have changed. If there's a secret talent passing through the stone bloodline, then fucking spill it."

Tomas glared at Michael. "You should've told me you'd been recruited to black ops."

"Why?" Michael snapped. "So you could feel like less of a failure?"

With a look at Jox, then the others, Tomas exhaled. His shoulders slumped. Then, finally, he said, "No, gods-damn it. So I could've explained what the hell was going on inside your head, and kept you from making the biggest fucking mistake of this war." The *winikin*'s voice dropped to a hiss. "You're a Mictlan; it's your talent, jerkwad. The name doesn't just mean the lowest level of hell; it's what we call a mage who wields the *muk* magic. It's a very rare, very secret talent that's sent by the gods only in times of absolute need."

"The red-robes and Ambrose both mentioned the 'mick,'" Michael rasped. "They were saying 'Mictlan.'"

"As for why I'm the only one who knows about it," Tomas continued, his voice rising a little in defensiveness, "each *winikin* of the stone bloodline knew about it, but was sworn to silence. The Mictlan himself is magically bound to maintain his silence on all matters pertaining to the talent, even to the point of lying to his king and family. There's no talent mark for the same reason. It's an avowed secret." He paused. "The king's *winikin* was the only one outside the bloodline who would've known." His voice got smaller. "I guess it didn't get passed along."

Jox shook his head. "There were things I wouldn't have learned until Strike took the scepter. Which—hello?— means you should've told me yourself, when we reunited."

"I didn't think it was necessary. Michael couldn't even summon fireballs. He was a tech salesman, for gods' sake. I didn't think there was any chance he'd become a Mictlan."

"Which is what, exactly?" Michael said between his teeth.

Tomas looked at him. Looked away. Muttered, "An assassin."

Michael's breath exploded from him. "No. Absolutely not. Been there, done that, and I want *out*."

The *winikin* ignored him and continued, "The Mictlan is a special kind of assassin who works not for his king or the other magi, but for the gods themselves." The *winikin* paused, face going drawn. "Because murder is one of the few truly damning sins, and the use of *muk* carries its own risk, the Mictlan is charged with making a single cold-blooded hit, using the *muk*. That's why it's such a secret; the target isn't necessarily one of the enemy. Sometimes it's one of us, someone the gods consider a mortal danger. The gods choose the target and show it to the Mictlan in a vision, usually in a mirror or pool of water. But it's just a single hit. I've never heard of anyone using the *muk* as fighting magic."

"Well, thanks to our complete and utter lack of communication, I now hold that dubious distinction," Michael said in a voice almost completely devoid of emotion, coming from a heart that felt like it had gone to stone. "I killed the red-robe back in Florida using the *muk*, and today I capped, what, a couple of dozen Xibalbans with it. Shit."

"Those shouldn't count against your soul," Tomas said, his words tripping one over the next as he started to babble in frantic release. "They were battle kills, not cold blood." He paused, grimacing. "I don't know how the earlier kills will affect the balance. They were part of a war, but didn't occur during a battle."

And not all of them had been part of a war, Michael thought, but didn't say because it wouldn't change the new reality of things, which was that his brief ray of hope was gone. "I can't break the *muk* bond, can I?" he said hollowly. "I've got to keep the magic and wait for my target." There was no question that he could do the job. Gods knew he'd done it too many times before. But he wanted to be done with it, wanted a *life*, damn it. He wanted to be the hero he'd thought he could be going into the FBI.

Tomas nodded. "If the gods have put a Mictlan among us, then they think there's a need for you. I can teach you how to control your talent, but I can't let you break the bond."

You don't get to make that call, Michael thought, but didn't bother because this wasn't about him and Tomas. It was about the gods needing something from him. He'd gone willingly into Bryson's employ. Could he really refuse to do the same job for the gods themselves? Maybe. But if they demanded that he kill one of the Nightkeepers . . . Yeah, he could see himself refusing that. "Have any previous Mictlan refused the charge?"

"Three of them. They all committed suicide rather than accept their targets." Tomas paused. "The first was supposed to kill Akhenaton, the second Cortés."

A chill reached up and grabbed Michael by the throat. "Fuck. Me." His breath went thin in his lungs as he said, "And the third?"

"Your uncle. He was supposed to kill King Scarred-Jaguar. He killed himself instead. If he hadn't . . ." The *winikin* trailed off, but the message was clear.

If Scarred-Jaguar had been assassinated, so many things might be different. The Solstice Massacre wouldn't have happened. The Nightkeepers would have the numbers they needed for the end-time war, and the magi would've had an extra twenty-four years of looking for answers and coming up with a solid, workable strategy for confronting the Xibalbans and *Banol Kax*. And each of the residents of Skywatch would've had that time with their families, instead of being scattered, in hiding. Waiting.

Nausea spiraled through Michael. If he knew it would prevent hundreds or thousands of other deaths, could he kill one of his own in cold blood? Maybe not. But the Other could.

What if Sasha's the target? something whispered inside him.

"What if I refuse my target but don't suicide?" Michael asked, not bothering to argue against his being a Mictlan. Hell, Iago had known it before he did. Once again, the bastard was ahead of them.

"The name Mictlan is not a misnomer. The moment your target is revealed, you have nine hours to complete the kill. At the end of the ninth hour, if you haven't completed your assignment—whether because you suicided or simply ignored the call—your soul will be yanked directly to the lowest level of hell, where you will become a powerful *ajaw-makol*."

The *ajaw-makol* were the most powerful of the demons capable of possessing a human—or Nightkeeper—host; they retained their mage powers and human knowledge, and were damnably difficult to kill. If Michael became one, the Nightkeepers were fucked.

"So let me get this straight," Strike growled at Tomas. "You knew a talent like this runs in the stone bloodline and prevents its holder from discussing it openly, and you knew that large chunks of the normal information transfer hadn't happened because of the Solstice Massacre . . . yet you never thought to mention this to me, or Jox, or, hell, *Michael*?"

The *winikin* shrank in on himself. "He'd become a salesman. And kind of a prick. How was I supposed to know it was all a front?"

Because you knew me, Michael wanted to say. *You raised me. Couldn't you see past the outside?*

Strike transferred his attention to Michael. "Going forward, it looks like you've got two options."

Michael nodded. "I can either use the scorpion spell to break my bond with the *muk* magic, and we take our chances with whatever comes from my not accepting the target . . . or I do the job I was born and trained for, and

hope the kill doesn't tip me to channeling hellmagic."
Which would be akin to having him become an *ajaw-makol*, except that he'd be allied to Iago rather than the
Banol Kax. He held his king's eyes, shaken by the thought
that, in his uncle's case, the king had *been* the target. Frustration welled up. Talk about shitty options. It's enough
to drive a guy— Michael broke off the thought, both because sanity had become a major focus the moment he'd
learned of Sasha's upbringing . . . and because he saw a
connection he didn't like one bit. A bolt of understanding hit him in the gut, and he glanced at Tomas. "That's
why the Stone males are all bachelors, suicides, or lovers,
isn't it? The bachelors and suicides are the ones with the
mind-set—i.e., borderline sociopath, dissociative personality, whatever—to accept the Mictlan talent. The lovers
don't inherit the disorder; they carry on the bloodline."

Tomas nodded slowly. "I'm sorry."

"Shit," Michael said hollowly as whatever small hope
he'd briefly had of finding a way to have Sasha for his
own died a painful death. He was a Mictlan, and a head
case. Even if his target turned out to be someone he could
see his way to killing—like Iago—and he went through
with it, he'd still be a head case, still be half a killer, if not
more. Or he could undergo the scorpion spell, break the
muk connection, and go back to a seminormal life, one
that might include Sasha. Only look what had happened
with the others. Akhenaton. Cortés. Scarred-Jaguar.
Three different powerful men. Three catastrophic massacres. Given the timing of things, he had to believe that
whatever the gods had in mind for him, it'd be big. Like
end-of-the-world big.

Could he live with that?

Damn it, Michael thought, his chest echoing hollowly.
It took him a moment to realize there was no dark anger
inside him, that Rabbit's work was holding. Thank the
gods for that much, at least.

Correctly reading Michael's overload level as reaching the critical point, Strike said, "How about we take a break. Jade and Anna can pull whatever else they can find on *muk* and the Mictlan, which probably won't be much, given the level of secrecy surrounding the talent. We'll keep working on the tomb translations, probably mount another trip out there in the next day or so. Michael . . . you can consider yourself off for the rest of the day. Take a walk. Play some vids. Blow off some steam."

"Thanks. I'll do that." Michael was acutely aware of the moment Sasha stood and slipped out of the room. He wanted to follow, but then he realized he hadn't told the others everything important, after all. Looking at Strike, he said, "During the battle, when Iago was trying to 'port me and Sasha away, I got the image of a mountain."

The king narrowed his eyes. "Can you describe it?"

"Not well enough to 'port. Sorry. But a voice said, 'Paxil Mountain.' That ring a bell?"

"Paxil Mountain," Jox said. "Yeah. That figures." At Michael's look, he elaborated, with a nod at Sasha: "It's the source of cacao and maize. Legend has it that several of the greedier gods wanted to keep the plants for themselves, so they hid them in Paxil Mountain. When the other gods discovered this, they got angry and decided to give maize and cacao to mankind. The thunder god split open the mountain and the seeds sprayed across the empire, seeding the Mayan Empire with maize and cacao."

"Is it a specific place?" Strike asked.

"I'm sure it is, or was." The *winikin* tipped his palms up. "Not one we know about, though."

"Well, that's something." Strike turned to Michael. Waved him off. "Go. You're looking too ragged for my peace of mind."

Michael nodded and left, but he didn't head for the firing range or the ball court. He headed in the direction Sasha had taken when she'd slipped from the meeting a couple of minutes earlier, toward the residential wings. He was nearly there when Tomas stepped in front of him, scowling. "You should've told me, you young idiot."

Michael felt the old, familiar tightness stiffen his neck and shoulders. "When you say it like that, I can't imagine why I didn't."

"I could have—"

"You could have done lots of things," Michael interrupted. He was suddenly sick and tired of the friction and random jabs. His priorities had shifted; he just couldn't waste his energy fighting with Tomas anymore. "And so could I. How about we agree that we both screwed up, give each other a pass on the last six years or so, and move on already?"

That brought the *winikin*'s chin down a notch. "You'd do that?"

"Consider it done."

They stood there for a moment, stuck somewhere between a standoff and reconciliation. When a hug—or even really a handshake—didn't seem to make much sense, Michael gave a stiff nod, moved around his *winikin*, and headed for the residential wing.

He hesitated at the closed door to Sasha's suite, but what could he possibly say to make things right at this point? He'd pushed her away twice, and even though the danger she brought out in him was blocked—for the time being, at least—the underlying issues remained. More, although his status as a Mictlan explained a shitload of what he'd been going through, it gave him a pretty crappy choice of actions, that between bad and worse. What right did he have to go to her now?

Thing was, he couldn't make himself give a shit. With the overt danger defused, he was through being noble, through being the better man. With the Other locked away and the anger banked, desire blazed that much higher, threatening to take him over. And this time, he intended to let it. If she didn't want him, he would go. But she was going to have to be the one to turn him away this time.

He knocked perfunctorily and, before she could answer, pushed through into her suite.

She stood in the kitchen, a mug frozen halfway to her lips. The odor of hot chocolate enriched the air, calling to something inside him, linking the scent and the woman until the two became intertwined in his sensory memory. Slowly, she lowered the mug to the counter, setting it down with a decisive click. "Michael. Did you want something?"

"We should talk."

Her eyes sparked with irritation. "Is that why you barged in here? To talk?"

"Not really, but I thought we should probably start there." He paused, steeling himself. "Or do you want me to turn around and go?"

"Why would I want that?"

"Because I'm a murderer." He put it right out there.

"You're a warrior. Warriors kill."

"It wasn't all in battle."

"It was all in war." But although she defended him staunchly, she didn't quite meet his eyes.

"Then it's not a problem for you?" he pushed, knowing they needed to get through this if they were going to go forward. Part of him said not to push, to give her more time, but what if they didn't *have* time? He couldn't believe it was a coincidence that his Mictlan powers had come online as they neared the triad threshold. Iago certainly hadn't thought so.

She sighed softly. "I'm trying to make it not be. Intellectually, I understand that killing is a part of war, whether it's a war on drugs, terror, or the *Banol Kax*. And I'm trying to accept that inwardly, as well. But I'm just not sure I'm cut out to be a warrior. The idea of killing someone—anyone, regardless of what they've done or what they might do in the future . . . in my heart of hearts, I'm not sure I can condone it." She paused. "And I don't know how I feel about what you've done . . . but whatever it is I'm feeling, it's something."

"I can accept that." He was going to have to. "I'll give you whatever time you need."

She cocked her head. Lifted her mug. Sipped. "Who said I needed time?"

His head came up, heat firing in his gut. "*Don't* you?"

"Yes and no. If we're talking about something long-term, then yeah, I would need time, and not just because of the Mictlan stuff. But that's not how this is going to work, is it?" Her eyes were a little too bright, her words a little too quick, but he didn't interrupt because he couldn't really argue the point. He was in transition, his life changing what felt like daily. Until he knew who he was, how could he offer himself up for any sort of relationship? After a short pause, she nodded. "Thought so." But she didn't look surprised, or even upset. "Then, if we're talking about something day-to-day, enjoying each other in the moment, so to speak, then I don't need time." A smile touched her lips. "Not after that kiss this morning. If that's the man you are right now, and the man you're going to be for tonight, then I don't need any time at all."

He didn't know if he understood all of what she was thinking, but he definitely did feel like the hunter she'd once accused him of being as he stalked across the sitting room, skirted the breakfast bar, and joined her in the small kitchen, which was barely big enough for one mage, never mind two. The scent of fresh herbs joined that of the rich hot chocolate. "About that kiss . . ."

"Yes?" she asked, regarding him steadily, standing her ground and not giving him an inch.

He didn't say anything more, simply closed the last small space between them, crowding her back against the counter. He slid his arms around her, caught her up against his body, and kissed her like he'd done that morning, like he'd been thinking about doing just about every second since.

She purred in the back of her throat—the sexy sound that had haunted him ever since they'd been together that first night—and returned his kiss, nipping at his lower lip and then laving the spot with her tongue. The move brought heat spearing through him, but not anger, not darkness, and the relief of that confirmation had him groaning aloud.

When he did, she planted both hands on his chest and levered herself away to hop up on the counter. The move offered him a heavenly spot to move into, between her parted legs. It also gave her leverage to block the move. "Nope. Your turn. I've told you what I've been thinking. Where is your head? It's not every day a guy has to come clean about something like your Other."

She didn't sound all that unglued about it, though. Thank the gods. And for the first time in the almost month he'd known her in person, he was able to answer with complete honesty. "I'm okay. I think I'm finally starting to accept that I'm not in control of what's going on here."

"This is news?"

"I'm slow sometimes. Sue me." He brushed a lock of dark, flyaway hair from her face, tucking it behind one of her delicately rounded ears. "The thing is, I can control my own actions, and I can do my damnedest to get ahead of Iago, and fight like a warrior. I can act with honor, or I can push the limits, depending. Sometimes, I can just say fuck the rules; I'm doing what I want. But the big stuff . . ." He paused, lining it up in his head. "There's something going on here that's bigger than you or me, or even the two of us together. We're in this . . . *structure*, I guess you could call it, that the gods conceived and our ancestors spent generations shaping. Only we've been plopped down in the middle of it without the big-ass box top that's supposed to tell us how this cosmic game is supposed to work. The massacres took away our info transfer, and Iago took away our connection to the gods. That's left us figuring out what all the pieces do, one by one. We've got a couple of the rules down. As for the rest of it, we're just winging it right now. But there I was one day, winging the shit out of things, when this folder came across my desk with a goddess inside it."

She inhaled to say something, but he touched her lips to keep her quiet. "Let me finish. I've lived part of my life an addict to blood and death, and I've lived part of it on the surface of things, and I don't like either of those lives. I'm learning to be a better man. Gods know it's not going to be an easy process. Hell, for all I know, I'll get my target tomorrow morning and I'll be forced to call the Other back, and then who the fuck knows what'll happen? But if I've figured out anything about this structure we're in, it's that while it might seem on the surface that the gods control our personal destinies, they don't. We do. Strike chose Leah despite the prophecies. Brandt and Patience found each other before the barrier reopened. Even Nate and Alexis found their way to each other on their own terms. I want that for myself. I want *you* for myself. And I'm hoping like hell you want me back. I can't promise you a future—I can't even promise you tomorrow, and I'm sorry as hell about that, because after what you've been through with Ambrose and your ex, you deserve to know there's a future, and I can't say that. What I *can* say is that I'll be here for you as long as I'm able to be. As long as you want me to be."

He paused, and when she didn't say anything, something sank inside him as his brain fed him a repeating loop of all the reasons she'd be smarter not to have anything to do with him. He'd left it too long, pushed her away too many times. He hadn't fought hard enough to find a way for them to be together despite the danger. His history and his future scared the crap out of her, and for that he couldn't blame her.

When she stayed silent, he worried he'd said too much. "Now it's your turn."

Then, finally, she smiled. "I'm thinking you had me at 'goddess.' Though the other stuff wasn't bad, either." As relief spun through him, excitement burgeoning on its heels, she eased her knees apart and linked her hands behind his neck, urging him into the space she'd created for him. "You're right that I'd ideally like to know I'm in a relationship that's going somewhere, but this isn't an outside-world situation, is it? For all we know, we're down to three years and a week left to live ... or in three years and a week, it'll all be over and we'll be able to go our separate ways. Under either circumstance, it seems silly to deny myself something special just because it doesn't fit into all of the things I wanted in the outside world."

The idea of a three-year time limit poked at Michael, irritating him. Which just went to show how much things had changed around him, within him; his longest previous relationship hadn't made it to the four-month mark. Then again, he thought with a dark kink of self-awareness, it wasn't like he was looking past the next few days, really. And that made it easier to say, "Let's give it a try and see where we can make it fit in our world."

She nodded, and her smile lost its reserve as her eyes gained a wicked gleam. Then she leaned into him, wrapped her legs around him, and sank into a kiss that promised so much more than just a kiss. It sparkled with the promise of tomorrow.

*   *   *

Heat shimmered through Sasha, taking her emotions from a poignant ache to soft acceptance, and from there to desire. She yielded to all of those things and more as she wrapped herself around Michael, anchoring herself to his solid strength. She kissed his neck, glorying in his hiss of pleasure as she found the soft spot behind his ear, and the way he shuddered at the drag of her teeth across the sensitive skin. But it wasn't just the heat that had convinced her to set aside what usually passed as her better judgment—it was the hum of rightness that had brought her to this point, and the sense that it was time for them, maybe even past time. She respected him for holding her away when he'd been certain that being with her could endanger her, could put her in the way of the darkness. There was still a kernel of fear within her, but although it disturbed her to know she was kissing a killer, one who was god-bound to kill again, at the same time, she was kissing *Michael*. He wasn't the Other; he was himself. He challenged her, yes. He excited her. He pissed her off. But she wasn't afraid of him. Maybe she should be, but she wasn't.

So she softened against him, trailing her hands down his body and up again to toy with the hair at his nape. They were aligned hard to soft; she cradled his erection between her legs, held him there by wrapping her legs around his waist as they kissed, again and again. She tugged his shirt free and ran her hands beneath, her blood firing at finally—finally—being able to touch him like this, and trust that he wasn't going to pull back this time.

Then he did pull back, but only far enough to break the kiss and say against her lips, "I applaud the idea of the kitchen, but would the chef mind transferring this to her bed?" He was smiling, but his forest green eyes were intent on hers, making the question far more serious than it seemed.

She got it, then. Twice before when they'd been together, and he'd been fighting the Other and the silver magic, they'd grappled with lust, with him standing, her pinned up against a wall. Warmth shimmered through her at the knowledge that he wanted this to be different, that *he* wanted to be different.

Smiling, she slipped off the counter, pressing fullbodied against him as she did so. Then she took his hand, feeling the ridges of their palm scars rubbing with sensual friction, and she led him to her bedroom.

There, gauzy curtains darkened the room, which was dominated by a big bed covered with a verdant green bedspread and a small army of pillows.

When they reached the bed, she turned to face him, and they stood there, staring at each other for a moment that spun out into temptation. Then, as though finally catching up with himself, he exhaled a long, slow breath that did little to release the tension gripping his powerful body. His hands came up to bracket her face; his lips softened beneath hers in a gentle, achingly tender kiss. Within moments, though, their kiss hardened to a demand and his arms came around her as his mouth fused with hers. And all she could think was, *Thank the gods*.

Heat leaped within her as he gathered her against him, then bore her down to the bed, so they were wrapped together, straining together, trying to get closer and closer still, despite the tactile barrier of their clothes. His taste exploded across her senses; his scent filled her. She caressed him, dragging her fingers through his hair, clutching at his wide shoulders.

His sleeveless shirt was slick to the touch, molding to his muscles, making her very aware of his leashed power. She sensed his desire and felt the sharp excitement of his sex magic as they boosted each other. There was no hint of the foreign silver magic, adding to her bone-deep certainty that this was right. Call it hormones or magic,

or maybe something more—she needed to feel alive,
to take something for herself after so long. More, she
needed to take him, and knew he needed her. She'd seen
the emptiness inside him as he'd looked into a future
and seen only impossible choices.

She might not be able to make those choices for him,
but she could ease him in the interim. They could ease
each other, having each spent far too long alone.

He pinned her, pressed into her. She felt the hardness
of his chest, his arms, his thighs, and the long length of
him. Hooking a leg around his hips, she opened to him
with no thought of subtlety or mystery. She wanted him;
he wanted her. They didn't need to make it any more
complicated than that. It was a freeing thought.

The mattress yielded at her back. He covered her
with his body, pressing her into the bedding, kissing
her the whole time, moving from her lips to her cheek
to the line of her jaw, then the soft, sensitive spot behind her ear. She arched against him as heat roared,
and behind it, the saber rattle of a military march that
she now knew wasn't his theme song; it was hers. The
warrior's march with the softness of strings. Awash
in sensation, in the flow of *ch'ul* and life, she slid her
hands down and tugged his shirt free of his waistband,
and ran her hands beneath, this time without the con-
straints of body armor. His skin was soft and slick in
places, roughened by masculine hair in others, and everywhere it covered the bunch and flow of muscles, the
hardness of bone.

They twined together—touching, seeking, tasting—
with a rawness she hadn't expected, a primal posses-
siveness. When he kissed her, she felt consumed. When
he ran his hands beneath her shirt, and up to touch the
sides of her breasts, then inward to cup them, tease
them, she felt branded, owned. And when he shifted to
come down atop her, then held her face in his hands and

looked deep into her eyes, she felt his hands tremble, and saw a question in his eyes.

She caught his wrists, felt his pulse thrum beneath her thumbs, and was conscious that she was touching his marks, the stone and the warrior. "What is it?" she asked.

"Nothing." He leaned in and touched his lips to hers, softly. "This is where I want to be right now."

It wasn't a vow of forever, not even a hint of something beyond tonight. But somehow it was as romantic as the most fervent promise.

Keep it simple, she told herself, and forced her lips to curve in a smile. "This is where I want to be too."

And then it *was* simple. Her body knew what it wanted, what felt good. Their magic knew pleasure, and how to seek it. The music added rather than distracting, an inner sound track that she suspected was hers alone. She eased his shirt up and off, and gloried in the feel of his masculine skin beneath her fingers, beneath her lips. They shifted together, then eased apart so she could slip out of her T-shirt and pants. Sasha moaned at the arousing contrast of the cool material of his pants against the sensitized skin of her inner thighs. They rolled across the wide expanse of mattress, feasting on each other, drawing ruthless pleasure.

Gentle turned inciting; tender turned demanding, and it became all about the heat and the flash, and the flare of magic. He moved down her body, nipping and touching, caressing and teasing. She moaned and arched against him, tried to touch him, but he shifted away. "Let me," he said, his voice a rasp of passion as he moved between her legs. "Just let me."

She would've argued, but then his tongue found her, and speech was lost to a low moan of surrender.

He gripped her thighs and spread them wide, then ran his hands up to cup her buttocks, lifting her, opening her to his mouth. He feasted, stroked, tasted, touched, all with a raw, carnal skill that brought incredible pleasure. She clutched his hair; she wasn't sure whether she meant to hold him still or draw him up her body. Then there was no more plan, no more thought, nothing but the coil of pleasure that drew tighter and tighter still within her.

He worked her ruthlessly, artfully with his hands and mouth, his clever fingers and precise knowledge of the female form, stringing the wire tighter and tighter still within her. The humming within her became a melody. Then she was crying out and shattering, pulsing against him, around his thrusting fingers and low, exultant cry.

The orgasm went on and on, gripping her, keeping her splayed out in pleasure. He moved away from her, out of her, shimmying up her body and letting her feel his hardness, his desire. He drew his lips along her breasts, the underside of her jaw, the sensitive spot behind her ear, and then her mouth.

She poured herself into the kiss, putting into it her pleasure and desire, the need to have him within her. His breath rasping in his wide chest, his flesh tight and hard all over, he rose above her and paused there, the blunt head of his shaft nudging at her opening. "Open your eyes," he ordered harshly. She did, though part of her had wanted to hide in the darkness behind her eyelids.

Their gazes caught and held, and a dangerous, treacherous warmth kindled in her chest, warning her that this wasn't just sex, couldn't be, at least not for her. And a piece of her had to believe it wasn't just sex for him, either. The look in his eyes, the open pride in his face, his total focus on her—that had to be more, had to be the same sort of connection she'd felt that first time, that she felt now.

Then he thrust within her and she arched on a cry of pleasure, of completion. The orgasm echoes that had left her flesh soft and pleased now reversed themselves and drew inward, coiling tight around the point where he invaded her, possessed her, drove her up and over another wave of orgasm, then followed her over the crest with a cry that might've been her name, might've been something else.

They came together, wrapped in each other, hearts hammering in unison, bodies shuddering. Sasha pressed her face against his hot throat, feeling his pulse against her cheek, feeling him throb within her. The humming melody became a song, familiar and lovely, but she didn't need the music or the magic to know that this was it for her, that he was what she'd been meant to find, that despite—or perhaps because of—their mismatches, they were a match. It was fate, she thought, riding high on the buzz of pleasure and the magic she was only just beginning to touch. Destiny. And if that was the case, she thought, she was in deep shit, because she had a feeling Michael didn't want to be anybody's destiny. Not even his own.

Don't, she told herself, derailing the negative thought train before it could fully form. *Don't make this more—or less—than it is. For once in your life, just enjoy the moment.*

So she did. She enjoyed the moment that he eased away and kissed her again, enjoyed the moment when those kisses became more, when casual caresses gained purpose, when postcoital bliss morphed to foreplay almost without transition. And she enjoyed the moment he came deep inside her, not just because she was locked in the throes of her own long, shuddering orgasm, but because this time she was sure he called her name.

Later, much later that night, after they'd turned to each other a third time and were wrung limp with pleasure, she said softly, "Promise me one thing?"

"What?" To her surprise, he sounded more curious than wary.

"Promise me you won't go into the scorpion spell alone. Promise you'll tell me, or if you can't tell me for some reason, you'll tell Strike. Or Jox. One of the three of us."

He nodded. "Yeah. Okay, yeah. I promise." Then he leaned in and kissed her again, and again. Then he loved her again. And in that moment, she felt that she'd come home, at least for a while.

CHAPTER TWENTY

In the week leading up to the winter solstice, the magi prepared for their singular purpose: get the library scroll from the First Father's tomb and call the Prophet.

Rabbit did his damnedest to talk Strike into letting him try the scorpion spell too, but the plan was vetoed when the royal council decided it would be far better to wait until after the Nightkeepers secured the library. Gods willing, there would be a better option contained within it.

Rabbit was pissed, but as far as Michael could tell, that had as much to do with Myrinne's deciding to stay on campus a few extra days past the beginning of the holiday break as it did with the king's decision regarding the spell. There seemed to be more trouble in paradise, but when Michael had asked after her, he'd gotten his head bitten off. He hadn't followed up, figuring Rabbit deserved his privacy if that was what he wanted. Besides, he didn't think the younger mage would appreciate his opinion of Myrinne, which started with, "She's not," and ended with, "that into you."

Michael and Sasha, on the other hand, were very into each other. It was the perfect setup, as far as he was concerned; they took each day as it came, enjoying each other without reservation, but also without expectation. Each morning, though, he awoke determined to have another day with her. And then another. He thought she was coming to trust him, reveled when she let down her guard and let herself hold onto him an extra moment, or lean on him for power or help.

When they weren't in bed together, they worked together, along with the others, working out what plans they could for the solstice. The three-year countdown was bearing down on them freight-train fast. The only thing they knew for certain was that Iago wanted him and Sasha at Paxil Mountain. The question was: Which was the better option, using them as bait to lure him into a trap, or sequestering them safely away at Skywatch? As far as Michael was concerned, the answer was obvious: she stayed at Skywatch and he went to the temple in case there was a fight. Splitting them up would make it harder for Iago to grab them both.

"Or you could stay here and I could go to the temple," Sasha had pointed out. "I know the site better than you do."

In the end, it was decided that they would both go to the temple, not the least because the *winikin* didn't want him left behind if the other magi were out in the field. A storeroom wasn't going to be able to hold him if the Other used the power of the solstice to break through. With that decision made, they turned their attention to planning for the actual solstice ceremony. In going over what Ambrose had told Sasha, Jade locked onto the word "conduit." Ambrose had said the scroll would summon the Prophet, but that the solstice was required for the formation of some kind of conduit. The original assumption was that the Prophet was a sort of guiding spirit, and the spell would open some sort of portal leading to the library, maybe because it had been hidden within the barrier, much as Skywatch had been for so many years. That, however, wasn't quite right, according to the archivist's research.

"We were correct in guessing that the library was tucked into the barrier," Jade said during one of the daily planning sessions Strike had instituted. "But this spell isn't reversible like the one that hid Skywatch, or that we believe Iago has used to hide his hellmouth. There's no way to bring the library back to earth. Instead, we need to ... deputize someone as a go-between, I guess you could say. This person, the Prophet, becomes a conduit capable of channeling the necessary information." Which sounded simple enough, but Michael heard the reservation in her voice.

"What's the catch?" he asked.

"It's a soul spell. As in, it requires the soul of a magic user to be destroyed; the magic animates the shell, using it as a golem of sorts. That golem is the Prophet." Jade paused. "It's the only Nightkeeper spell I've come across that requires an actual human sacrifice. More, the victim's soul doesn't go to Xibalba, the sky, or even Mictlan. It's destroyed. There's no afterlife, no nothing. In the case of a Nightkeeper, the person's experiences aren't even added to the bloodline *nahwal*'s collected wisdom. They quite simply *end*."

Beneath the table, Michael had felt Sasha's foot press against his in support as the others pointedly avoided looking at him.

"Does the sacrifice need to be one of us?" he asked, keeping his voice expressionless.

"Any magic user will do," she'd answered, "although that remains a small pool: one of us, or one of the Xibalbans."

"I'm in favor of door number two," he muttered. In a way he was relieved, though. It seemed logical that the gods would use the Mictlan as the executioner for a soul-spell sacrifice. Although there was no joy in the thought of killing anyone, even a red-robe, in ritual sacrifice, it seemed better than some of the alternatives he could imagine as the Mictlan's target. But in the days that followed, the Mictlan talent didn't activate; there was no hint of his victim's identity.

So the residents of Skywatch waited, and they studied, and they prepared. And each night, Michael and Sasha met in his suite or hers, or once out by the pool, where the temperature might have dipped down into the forties but the solar-heated water steamed wisps of fog into the night. Each night they loved each other, and slept in each other's arms, and pretended everything was okay, even though they both knew it wasn't. They were waiting . . . waiting for the library, for the target, for something to happen.

By the night prior to the solstice, Michael had worn himself raw inside trying to run contingencies in his head and figure out what he would do when he got his target.

He awoke near midnight, almost at the threshold of the solstice day. Even before he was fully conscious, he was aware of an aching hum of magic in the air, one that stirred his blood. He turned to Sasha, only to find her side of the bed empty and cool to the touch.

Unease stirred. He told himself to roll over and go back to sleep, that she was safe within the warded compound. But something had been off about her that night, a discord in their vibe, a wrong note or two over the course of the evening. She'd said it was nothing, that she was just keyed up for the solstice, and the planned ambush, which was still on the table, with contingency plans atop contingency plans, none of which completely satisfied any of them. And yeah, she had every right to be jacked up about that. Except he didn't think that was what she was really worried about. He was pretty sure it was something to do with him, with them.

Twenty minutes of staring at the ceiling later, he rose, pulled on dark track pants and a white tee, shoved his feet in a pair of rope sandals, and padded off in search of her. He found her, not surprisingly, in the main kitchen at the center of the mansion. The air was heavy with the scents of chocolate and dark spices, bringing a long, low tug of hunger that was more for the woman than the food.

He'd thought he'd steeled himself for the familiar kick of attraction, the lust that hadn't faded with their becoming lovers. But need hit him hard the moment he saw her stretched on her tiptoes to return a bowl to a high shelf, her midriff-cropped tee riding up, yoga pants riding down, the two exposing a strip of her taut, strong abdomen, with the soft lines of muscle on either side of her navel, where a trio of freckles drew his eye.

She turned slowly, and when she met his eyes, he saw a reflection of the burning heat that churned in his gut. "Well?" she said softly.

His body moved almost without conscious volition around the pass-through and into the kitchen, where he stopped close enough to catch her light scent over the cooking smells, close enough to distinguish the heat of her body from that of the stove. "What's cooking?"

She handed over the mug she'd been sipping from. "It's something I've been playing with."

He knew she had magic in the kitchen, knew she wielded flavors with the deftness of a trained chef and the inspiration of a mage, but still he was unprepared for what hit his taste buds the moment he took a sip. Sensations exploded across his neurons in a blaze of heat, texture, and taste that had him sucking in a breath. There was chocolate, yes, but it was more savory than sweet, taken away from the realm of dessert by a mix of peppers and salt, and things he wouldn't even begin to match with chocolate, but that somehow matched perfectly. He sucked in a breath. "Holy shit." Took another sip and rolled it around in his mouth, closing his eyes briefly as the flavors changed subtly, the peppers mellowing to something else. "Nice," he said, and this time his tone was one of reverence. "Very nice."

"That," she said with evident satisfaction, "was exactly what I was going for."

Eyes still closed, he felt her trying to take the mug back, and tightened his fingers on it. "Leave it," he said. "I'm at your mercy. Anything you want. Just ask."

He'd said it partly in play, but also because he remembered what she'd told him back in the beginning, on her first day at Skywatch. *I cook when I'm happy or sad, when I'm celebrating with friends or all alone with my thoughts*. Which of those things applied now?

He felt the air shift, felt her indrawn breath as his own, but instead of "we need to talk" or any of the female warning signs experience had taught him to expect, she surprised him by leaning in and touching her lips to his.

The kiss was as unexpected as the hint of pepper and spice he tasted amidst the chocolate on her lips, in her mouth. Setting aside his mug, he deepened the kiss, relieved to let it be easy even though a small part of him said it shouldn't be so easy, that he was skimming the surface of something he needed to be diving into. But then she shifted her hands, sliding them up his chest to link behind his neck and tug him closer, pressing her body to his, and the vibe went true, singing inside his skull with the warm sparkle of red-gold magic.

"Come back to bed," he said against her mouth. "We've got a few more hours to burn."

She let him lead her back to bed, and loved him with the passion and intensity that he needed from her, the energy that made him feel whole and alive. But even as they moved together and apart, together and apart, he was aware that she was holding a part of herself back, that she wasn't entirely *there* with him. When it was over and she lay sleeping, curled up around him, her fingers tangled in his hair, he stroked her arm, aching for what he knew was coming.

He would've asked what was wrong, but he already knew. She wasn't built for casual sex, and the sex had been far from casual with them from the very first. She'd gotten to the point where she either had to let herself fall for him or back off. And she was backing.

He couldn't blame her. More, he wouldn't try to stop her, because he couldn't say she was wrong. So he lay there through most of the remainder of the night, staring at the ceiling. And she felt empty.

When morning dawned, Sasha lay beside Michael looking into the pale orange light of the solstice day, and she kicked her own ass inwardly. *You should've told him last night. You shouldn't have come back here with him.*

She'd gone to the kitchen looking to center herself and find the words she needed to say to him. Instead, she'd let herself fall back into the heat and sex, both of which were easy with him. Too easy. It was the other stuff she was having trouble with, like trust and self-respect. And neither was his fault, really. He'd done exactly what they'd agreed to that first night they'd spent together: taking each day as it came, living in the moment, in each other.

The Other had remained at bay, so far; his music had stayed pure, his magic red-gold. He might be the Mictlan, but for now he was the man and the Nightkeeper. And her lover.

It wasn't his fault she couldn't stop wondering how long that would last, but there it was. She twitched at shadows, jumped at rattles, strung tight by the knowledge that the thing he called the Other not only could come back, but that it would at some point, when he was called on to kill. And it would be soon, she knew. She could feel the changes coming. *When in the triad years . . .*

She'd fulfilled the first piece of the prophecy by becoming a *ch'ulel*, a daughter of the gods. She didn't know about conquering death or finding the lost son, but she suspected that the time had come to defy love.

Easing away from Michael, she slid from his bed and padded to the bathroom, gathering her strewn clothes as she went. When she came back out, he was sitting on the side of the mattress with the sheet pooled at his waist, his expression schooled to careful neutrality as he looked at her. "Does it have to be today?"

She was surprised he'd guessed, but maybe she shouldn't have been. For a man who had, by his own admission, lived chunks of his life on the surface of himself, he was capable of deep insight. Deeper, sometimes, than she would've wished. So she didn't bullshit him. "I think so, yes."

"What changed?"

"Nothing. That's the problem." She held up a hand to forestall his response. "I know, it sucks and it's not fair, but there it is. I thought I could handle something day-to-day, thought I'd evolved from human to Nightkeeper, but the truth is, I can't and I haven't."

He just looked at her for a long moment, his expression bleak. "More you can't stop looking over your shoulder, waiting for me to lose the blocks and turn back into a monster."

"Tell me you're not thinking the same thing."

"Of course I am. The difference there is that I'm stuck with what's inside my own head, at least for the near future. You're not. You can walk away."

She'd expected him to be angry, had braced herself for the expected blast, telling herself not to be afraid.

But she hadn't prepared herself for this . . . this casual disinterest. "That's it?"

He spread his hands. With him naked, draped only with the sheet across his lap, the motion showcased the shift and slide of his elegant musculature and flashed the intricate black marks along his forearm. But he wasn't trying to attract or seduce her, she knew. He was inviting her to fly free. "This is a mutual thing, with both of us here because we want to be. If that's only going one way, then it's not working, is it? And it's not like I can blame you, or argue the points. I'm one mental block away from being a serial killer."

"That's not who you are," she hissed. "They took a kernel of something and turned it into a full-blown pathology. That's not you. That's programming."

"Regardless, it's part of me now, probably will be for the duration, and I don't blame you for not wanting to wait around for it to reemerge."

"You think I'm quitting on you?" Oddly, his lack of fight made her want to pick one. "If so, then say it."

"I think you're doing what you need to do."

Her anger spiked. He was saying all the right things, being mature and sensible. And it was seriously pissing her off. She'd convinced herself that he wasn't a hunter by nature, that he'd become one solely because Bryson's brainwashing had left him split from himself, unable to connect with himself, never mind someone else. But she had thought they'd gotten past that issue, that they'd forged a bond beyond the magic. But if that was the case, why didn't he fight, shout, do something to make her believe—

That was it, she realized, understanding at last what she was looking for, what she needed from him. "Why aren't you arguing with me?"

His expression flattened. For a second, she thought she saw a flash of something silver and ominous. "Maybe because I'm used to women going for the shiny exterior, then fading on me when the newness wears off."

Now he was trying to piss her off. She could see it in his eyes. But she also saw something else, something that made her wary as she said, "It'd take more than a week for me to get tired of your body, dipshit, and you damn well know it. Try again. Why aren't you fighting me?" *Why aren't you fighting* for *me?*

"Because we both know I'll lose. You've made your decision. Now do us both a favor and finish it, will you?" He sounded bored with the conversation. It was only because she knew him as well as she did that she saw the hollow anger beneath. But that wasn't enough for her anymore, not this time. She was through looking for the scraps and interpreting the hints, using her imagination to fill in the words. He'd promised not to lie to her anymore. But he wasn't telling her the whole truth, either

"I will. I am." It hurt to say, but in the way of lancing a wound. "And you know the funny thing? It's not really about the day-to-day thing, or even how the Mictlan hangs over all of it. I'm through waiting around for a man to care enough to fight. Ambrose let me go. Saul wished me luck. And you . . . I thought you were a hunter, the sort of guy who'd track his prey and fight off his competitors. But you're not. You're . . . hell, I don't know what you are, except that I can't tell if you want me because you want me, or if I'm just as convenient as Jade was."

She paused, looking for a spurt of anger to match her own, and not finding it. Waiting for the fight that didn't come.

"Well. I guess that's my answer." She turned away, willing back the tears. "I'll see you around. And don't worry: I won't stalk you. You have anything else you want to say, you know where to find me. Otherwise, I'll see you this afternoon for the final prep meeting."

He didn't say a damn thing as she exited the bedroom with her head high and her throat tight with unshed grief. And as the door closed behind her, he didn't call her back.

Heartsore, not wanting to be in her rooms, not wanting to see anyone else, Sasha headed for the greenhouse, drawn to the nonjudgmental company of growing things that demanded nothing more from her than soil and water and a soft touch.

After assuring herself the greenhouse was empty, she let herself into the space that had become hers and Jox's together, and headed along the winding cement pathway through the indoor orchard to a small raised bed. There, she'd planted her cacao seedlings a couple of weeks earlier, agonizing over their fragile roots and leaves, urging them to dig in and thrive. So far, the plants struggled onward, not thriving but not all the way giving up, either. They clung to life, but were making little headway.

I can relate to that. Settling down beside the raised bed, leaning against the sturdy masonry that made up its sides, she folded her arms atop the moist, fertile soil and dropped her forehead to her glyph-marked forearm.

She felt hollow and very alone. She was surrounded by family, by people who cared for her, who would endanger themselves to save her. Once, she would've thought that would be more than enough for her. Now, having experienced the heights that she and Michael could achieve together, and glimpsed what she thought was his true self, the man she wanted for her own, she couldn't be satisfied with mere support. She wanted more.

She wanted the magic, damn it.

A tear slid free, then another, though she didn't give in to the sobs that would have liked to come. After a while, when the few tears had dried on her face, she became aware of movement nearby—a leafy brush, a rustling breeze in the closed space. Magic prickled across her nape, and she caught a wisp of song, though the radio was off.

She lifted her head. And froze at the sight of the young, strong plants surrounding her. Where just a few minutes earlier the cacao seedlings had been thin and borderline sickly, now they were thick and dark green, and several inches taller than before.

"Magic," she whispered, realizing she'd made them grow, given them life. But if so, why did she feel so damned empty? She ached with lethargy, felt drained. Sighing, she pressed her head back down onto her forearms. Then, feeling safe and warm, and surrounded by the innocent love of growing things, though not of the man she wanted, she slept.

After Sasha left, Michael sat naked on the edge of the mattress for a long time. Not because he was aimless, but because he was fighting for fucking control of his head.

He didn't know if Rabbit's mental blocks and his own control were failing in the face of the increase in magic that came with the solstice, or if there was something else going on, but he'd barely hung on to himself as Sasha faced him down, almost didn't remember what he'd said. He'd known only that he needed to get her out of there, fast.

The old barriers had reared up, not letting him tell her what was happening, leaving her to think he didn't care. Then again, some of what she'd said was right on the mark—he hadn't fought for her, didn't intend to. He'd tried fighting with Tomas and that had never made a damn bit of difference. He'd argued with Esmee when she'd left him in the middle of his programming, trying hold on to the one familiar thing he'd had in a shifting life. He'd fought the Other and barely drew a stalemate, one that had needed to be renegotiated over and over again. Same with the women after Esmee. He'd learned the lesson often and well: He could kick ass, but if he couldn't throw a punch it wasn't worth having the fight. It just made everyone involved miserable, and didn't change the outcome one iota.

The knowledge burned within him, dark and resentful. *Get a grip*, he told himself, finally rousing from his fugue, only to realize it was later than he'd thought, nearly late morning. "Get off your lazy, fucked-up ass," he growled, but didn't move right away. He was dizzy and disoriented. And this didn't feel like the Other's work. It felt like something else entirely.

He needed to eat, that was all. He was strung up, depressed, and dumped. He needed coffee. He needed a kick in the ass.

Dragging himself to his feet, he headed for the bathroom. And froze just inside the door at the sight of the face that looked back at him from the mirror.

It wasn't him. It was Rabbit, in full-on sneer mode, his eyes hard and wild.

Rabbit, he thought, his heart clutching. *No. Oh, gods, no.*

The target will reveal itself when it's time, Tomas had said. *When that happens, the clock starts ticking. You'll have nine hours to make the kill.*

Unbidden, unwanted, the Other slipped into him, chilling his heart to stone. Under the influence of his alter ego, Michael checked the time automatically, methodically, like the executioner he was. It was just past eleven a.m. He had until eight that night to take out his target. And his right forearm bore a faint shadow: that of a hollow-eyed skull.

But even as his body went through the motions, his mind rattled inside his skull.

Rabbit. *Shit.* Sullen, pain-in-the-ass Rabbit, a loose cannon who was potentially more powerful than the rest of them put together, and who'd helped save Michael's sanity when he otherwise would've come undone for good. Sure, the kid—man, whatever—had the potential to torpedo the end-time war. But by the same token, he was just as likely to save them all in a flash of unintentional genius.

He was dangerous. He was powerful. And he was one of the last of the Nightkeepers. For the first time, Michael understood his uncle's choice, truly understood it.

"No," he grated, forcing the Other aside. "I won't do it. I fucking won't do it."

No matter what Rabbit had done in the past or what his bloodlines suggested he might do in the future, he was trying to figure his shit out. He'd started growing up at school, started taking responsibility for himself, for his magic. He and Myrinne were trying to make it work. Why, when the kid seemed to be pulling his shit together, would the gods decide he needed to die? Or was the vision even from the gods at all? The skyroad was demolished, their lines of communication cut. Where the hell was this coming from? Was it the gods or the *Banol Kax*? How the hell could he be sure?

The decision ached within him, alongside the hollowness that came from knowing that Sasha was gone, that in the end they hadn't been able to make it work after all. His head spun; his stomach hurt. He couldn't stop thinking of Rabbit's power, and his talent for inadvertently destroying almost everything he touched. Scarred-Jaguar hadn't meant to destroy the Nightkeepers; he'd meant to save them. If he'd been assassinated, there would be hundreds of magi now, an army of them. It was his uncle's sin, his bloodline's burden.

Shit, what was right and what was wrong?

At the thought, silver *muk* flared within him, buzzing death in his veins, whispering secrets and threats in the Other's voice. And, as his alter ego flowed back into him from nowhere and everywhere at once, Michael knew what he had to do. Lurching to his feet, he pulled on his combat clothes, locked and loaded his pistols, scrawled a quick note that he left propped in his bachelor-bare kitchen. Then he left his suite. And went in search of his final target.

PART V

WINTER SOLSTICE

The longest night of the year.

CHAPTER TWENTY-ONE

December 21
Winter solstice
Three years until the zero date
Skywatch

Michael knocked hard on Rabbit's door, then jiggled the handle, cursing to find the damned thing locked. He was about five seconds from kicking it in when he heard the lock click. A slow second later, the door swung open a few inches. Rabbit scowled at him through the gap. He looked like he hadn't slept in a few days; his eyes were red rimmed. "It's not time for the meeting yet."

"Come on. I need your help." Michael turned and strode off, figuring sheer bloody curiosity would get Rabbit moving. Any rational person would've asked for an explanation before taking off with the compound's resident hit man, but this was Rabbit they were talking about.

Sure enough, by the time Michael had gotten halfway around to the garage, the teen was slouching along at his heels, eventually asking, "Where are we going?"

"You still keep a stash of *pulque* up at the pueblo?"

Rabbit nodded. "It's been up there since I started school, but I don't think the shit goes bad. Doesn't go really good, either, but doesn't go bad."

"Then that's where we're going."

They snagged one of the Jeeps and they bounced their way along the track that led out past the firing range to the back of the box canyon, where a nearly vertical, cliff-clinging path led up to an intricate, multilevel group of native ruins that the ancient Puebloans had built into and out of the cliff itself. Many of the small spaces had collapsed over time, but some were still sturdy enough, and Rabbit had staked out a couple of them for his own. In the months between when Rabbit's father died and when he met Myrinne, it had been more or less common knowledge that he'd spent most of his free time alone up there, getting stoned on peyote and *pulque*, and zoning out on his iPod.

Now his stash was covered with dust and looked like it'd been worried at by a creature or two. But it didn't take him long to unearth a couple of tightly stoppered clay jugs. He held them out to Michael. "Not sure of the vintage, and it tastes like shit. But it'll get you hammered almost instantly. No doubt about that." He paused. "You and Sasha have a fight?"

Michael narrowed his eyes. "How did you know?" Mind-benders weren't supposed to be able to pick up on thoughts without physical contact, but the rules of magic didn't always apply to half-bloods.

"Saw her stomping past the cottage. Made a leap. Not sure what Strike'll think of your getting hammered right before the solstice." Rabbit lifted a shoulder, not looking particularly upset. "Might be fun to watch, though, so have at it. I'll even let you drive home."

"Fuck you. We're not here to get drunk. Or not entirely." Michael palmed his knife from his belt and held it for a moment, testing its weight as the Mictlan roared and the silver *muk* flared through him. Then he flipped the knife and offered it to Rabbit, blade-first. "Cut me."

The young man's eyes flashed with understanding, followed by reluctant respect. "Son of a bitch. You crazy bastard—you're trying the scorpion spell on the sly." He paused. "You must really love her."

"Why's that?"

"You're going against a direct order from the king just so you can wear the *jun tan* before the solstice. If you're aiming for the big gesture, that's a good one."

Michael hesitated, realizing that on one level, Rabbit was right. If he broke his connection to the *muk*, he would be able to take Sasha as his mate. *She'd like that*, he thought, knowing the symbol would matter to her. Except that she'd dumped him, hadn't she?

At the thought, the Other—or should he call it the Mictlan?—stirred, too close to the surface of his mind. Oddly, though, it wasn't trying to stop him from casting the scorpion spell, and it wasn't trying to take over and force him to kill Rabbit.

The Mictlan is just a talent, he realized. *It's up to me whether I use it.* Unlike the Other, which had been created to be partially autonomous, using his body to do the job it had been programmed to do, the Mictlan talent came with the gods' gift to mankind: that of free will.

Although the Nightkeepers' lives were largely guided by their writs and responsibilities, and the prophecies handed down by the First Father and others like him, in the end, each of their actions came down to a personal decision. Ambrose had chosen to give up his life as a Nightkeeper to carry out the wishes of his sister, the queen. Michael's parents had chosen to follow their king into battle. His uncle had chosen damnation rather than murder his king.

Now, Michael chose to try another path, one that might—just might—allow him to come out the other side whole. Because although he'd barely acknowledged the possibility, even inwardly, he couldn't stop remembering how Jade had talked about Scorpion River having the ability to purify, to take away sin.

What if it could take from him, not just the *muk*, but the Other as well?

"You going to do this?" Rabbit said, breaking into Michael's thoughts. He was trying to look cool, but jittered from one foot to the other, constantly in motion.

"Yeah," Michael said. "I'm doing it."

He sat, propping himself up against the wall and stretching his legs out in front of him. He was so mentally clamped-down that his only real thought about what he was about to do was a passing consideration that it was good there was sand underfoot, because it would soak up the majority of the blood. Hefting one of the jugs of *pulque*, he popped the top and took a swig. According to ancient Mayan law, anyone who'd had three shots of *pulque* should be considered a drunkard; four and he was criminally insane for an hour, at least. Ironic, really. The potent ceremonial beverage wouldn't just anesthetize him; it'd make him a little crazy, and help alter his consciousness so he could enter the in-between. Problem was, it would also lower his inhibitions, creating a window when the *muk* could take control. "If I try to hurt you, shut me down, okay?" he said, his words already slurring slightly under the effects of the *pulque*. "Think you can handle the spell?" he asked Rabbit as the world started to spin.

"Hell, yeah."

"Promise me you won't follow me. I'll need you to go for help if this turns to shit."

"Sure. Whatever." Rabbit reached for the knife. "You ready?"

No, Michael thought, chugging again. But he said aloud, "Yeah." He tipped the jug in a mocking salute.

"Don't fuck anything up, okay? If I make it back I'll spot you for the spell, no matter what Strike says. Deal?"

"Deal. Here we go." Rabbit began the chant they'd both memorized from Anna's translation, the spell that would send Michael to the in-between.

Closing in on unconsciousness, Michael watched fuzzily as the younger mage set the stone bloodline's ceremonial knife against his wrist, below the stone and warrior glyphs, and swiped it in a clean arc that cut through tendons, arteries, and veins in a clean sweep. Pain flashed, like bright colors behind his eyelids. Michael took his final hit of *pulque* and started seeing double. He wanted to pass out, wanted to puke. Wanted to weep like a baby. Wanted to kill. He felt a pinch on his other wrist, one that was almost lost in the spin of alcohol. The Other came right through into the forefront of his consciousness, bringing the *muk* with it. Then the world shifted hard beneath him, shuddering, then going dim as the darkness sucked him under. The last thing he heard was Sasha's voice whispering, *We're good.*

Not yet he wasn't. But maybe he would be soon.

The in-between

Lucius walked alone down a dirt path he'd walked before. The road stretched ahead and behind him, and carried the footprints of a thousand travelers before him, most barefoot or wearing rope sandals. There were no tire tracks, no hoofprints, shod or otherwise. Just footprints uncountable, silent ghosts of those who had gone before him. On either side of him, featureless gray-brown plains stretched to a limitless gray-brown horizon, a meeting between an unremarkable firmament and an unremarkable sky.

He didn't know how long he'd been there; time had no meaning in a prison that might've been a construct of his own mind, might've been someplace else. He didn't know. He'd lost contact with his body, lost contact with everything except the road that he trudged along, passing the occasional wizened, stunted tree and nothing else. Worse, his pockets were empty. Before, he'd been carrying the jade pebbles the Maya had buried with their dead, to pay their way across the dread river that wound its way throughout Xibalba. This time he hadn't given himself the damned beads. Which meant . . . what? That Cizin planned to keep him trapped there forever?

If only he had magic—

"Yeah?" he challenged himself aloud. "What would you do, seriously? What the hell would—"

A sonic boom interrupted him. The sky flashed blinding silver and the ground shuddered beneath his feet, sending his pulse jolting. Thunder? An explosion? He didn't know. All he knew was that it was the first different thing that had happened since his arrival at . . . well, wherever the hell he was. The detonation wasn't repeated, but a smudge of darkness gathered on the horizon, resolving itself into a structure of some sort. A destination.

Excitement jolted through Lucius alongside the suspicion that this was it—he was done; it was time to cross the river and enter the underworld proper. But anything was better than limbo, so he started jogging along the path, headed for the horizon shadow.

He ran past the same trees and scrub and endless gray-brown plains he'd been walking through, but the shadow drew closer, gained resolution, becoming an arched doorway made of stone and bone, guarding a ferry port that stretched out over a dark, ominous ribbon of water. It was *the* river, he knew, the entrance to Xibalba proper. The Scorpion River. And there, near the shoreline, lay a man-shaped lump. Lucius braced himself as he approached the figure, not sure what to expect. Whatever the hell he might've anticipated, though, it wasn't one of the Nightkeepers.

"Holy shit. *Michael*?"

The big mage lay as still and gray as death, but at the sound of his name he twitched and cracked open an eye. "What the fuck are you doing here?"

"That's what I was about to ask you. What—" Lucius broke off as the water beyond the stone-and-bone dock started boiling fat white froth that turned molten orange as he watched. Moments later, an unearthly, fingernails-on-blackboard screech split the air, and a huge, sinuous creature reared out of the water, raked the air with a pair of six-clawed hands, and tipped back its spiked head to scream a challenge. For a second, it flared orange and hot, like the lava from which it drew its energy. Then it went insubstantial, puffing to vapor as it turned toward the riverbank, fixing its terrible attention on the two men. "*Boluntiku!*" Lucius shouted over the boil of magma-heated water. He grabbed Michael by his shirt and started dragging him away from the river.

"No." The mage yanked away from him and lurched to his feet, staggering a moment before he found his center. "Don't touch me." Michael's eyes were wild, and held a hard darkness Lucius hadn't seen there before, along with a flash of otherworldly silver. "I don't want to hurt you."

Lucius's energy suddenly, inexplicably flagged. "What the hell is going on?"

"I've got to get in that river. It breaks the bonds of magic and purifies the soul." Michael spun, going for the autopistols he wore on his belt. Cross-drawing the weapons, he let out a roar of challenge and bolted for the ferry landing.

"You suicidal bastard," Lucius whispered. And ran after him.

Skywatch

Rabbit watched blood drip from Michael's wrists, reddening his hands and soaking into the sandy surface of the pueblo floor. It'd been maybe five minutes since he'd passed out, but it seemed like it'd been an hour. A lifetime.

"Wait it out," Rabbit told himself. "Don't shit yourself now." But it wasn't easy sitting there, watching a guy die. Especially a guy like Michael, who'd always seemed larger-than-life, larger still because he'd been able to do what Rabbit wanted and needed to do—he'd managed to live with the darkness and make it work for him. Until now. Now he lay propped up against the rock wall with his eyes rolled back in his head, bleeding the fuck out as he risked his life to break the bond with the *muk* magic.

Michael's pulse was shallow and he was barely breathing. Rabbit felt like his own systems were slowing down to match. He was cold and his energy was fading, and in the shadows inside the pueblo ruin, his skin looked gray. Hell, it *felt* gray. Then again, he'd been feeling gray overall lately.

Myrinne. He missed her, ached for her, and was trying really hard not to be pissed off at her. Their fight had been about something stupid—all their fights were pretty stupid—but this one had felt different when it ended, like it had really *ended* something. Afterward, she'd said everything was fine, but she'd stayed behind on campus, spending another week there, ostensibly to finish up an extra-credit project for one of her lab classes.

He'd tried to talk her into coming back to Skywatch for the solstice, had even offered to call in a favor with Strike and get him to 'port her there and back, just an overnight. She hadn't wanted to, though, which had bummed Rabbit out even more. She was drifting, and he didn't know how to hold on to her without turning into a creepy stalker . . . or using magic on her, which he'd promised not to do.

He reached into the pocket of his jeans and touched the little box he'd been carrying for a couple of weeks now. He'd been waiting for the right moment to give it to her, and now tried not to think the right moment might've already passed.

Michael's breathing hitched, reminding him to keep his mind on the damn job. But what exactly was he supposed to do? The spell was cast—he'd felt the magic. Michael was still bleeding out, though, and now his breathing was getting bad. How far was he supposed to let it go before he pulled the plug? And how, exactly, was he supposed to do that? Reaching out, he touched Michael's cool flesh, expecting to hear an echo of his consciousness, feel the thread that connected spirit to flesh. He got nothing. Michael wasn't home anymore; there was no sense of him, no clues where he'd gone or how Rabbit could follow, or bring him back. *Shit.* Now what? He couldn't leave Michael, hadn't brought his cell. How the hell was it that neither of them had brought a damn phone?

Maybe he could go into Michael's mind, find the connection forged by his sexual liaison with Sasha, and use that to mind-speak to Sasha. That might work. Maybe. But the longer he sat there and thought about it, the more he wondered whether he should blow the whistle. If he did, guaran-fucking-teed they wouldn't let him try the spell later. Was that selfish? Maybe. Probably. But like Myrinne said, there wasn't anyone looking out for their interests at Skywatch except the two of them.

Temptation spiraled, and something inside Rabbit whispered, *Do it. You know you want to.* It sounded almost, but not quite, like Iago's voice.

"Shut up," he said savagely. "You're not real!" Iago

couldn't get through the wards unless Rabbit initiated contact, and he sure as shit wasn't doing that. Which meant the voice was his own mind playing tricks on him. It had to be.

Cut yourself, the voice said, feeling somehow oily and dark. The world grayed out, then cut back in, and he found Michael's knife in his hand, though he was pretty sure he'd set it aside. *Cut yourself and go after him.* The voice didn't sound so much like Iago's now. In a weird-ass way, it sounded like Red-Boar, except without the insults. *He needs your help*, it said. The suggestion put a new spin on things. A rescue mission wasn't the same thing as deserting his post. The exact opposite, in fact.

Urgency gripped Rabbit, the sudden certainty that Michael was in deep shit and sinking fast. Or was that what he wanted to think, because it called for the course of action he so desperately wanted to take?

Magic hung thick in the air; the spell was still active. All he'd have to do would be to open his wrists. *Yeah.* He snorted inwardly. *That's all. No biggie.*

He'd do it, though. For Michael. For his future with Myrinne. But which thought was motivating him now? Was the voice in his head real, or a figment he was turning into an excuse?

He had to think, had to make the right call. He couldn't fuck this up; it was too big, too important. But he had to move fast, because even as he sat there, trying to figure out the right answer, Michael's chest hitched and his breathing rhythm stuttered. Hitched again. Stuttered.

This was it. He was dying.

Don't be a pussy. Do something right for once and fucking go after him! That was definitely Red-Boar's voice now. And though Rabbit could probably count on one hand the number of times he'd actually done what his father had told him in life, he was inclined to go along on this one. He took two swigs of *pulque* and got a serious buzz on. He could see and think, but the world was getting pleasantly fuzzed. Took another big swallow and quickly passed to hammered. Swaying, he lifted the knife, set the point against his wrist, and slashed. The pain was far away, but enough to make him want to puke. Instead, he gagged down another swallow of *pulque*. The world spun and yawed as he took a hack at his other wrist. Blood sprayed. Magic gathered and something went *boom* in his chest. For a second he feared it was his heart. Then it didn't matter because he was sliding, falling. Dying.

In the final instant of consciousness he heard a mocking chuckle, recognized it, and screamed inside because he knew in that moment it wasn't his father, after all. Hadn't ever been. It was Iago. Somehow he'd gotten through, grabbing onto Rabbit's soul.

Bastard! he shouted inside his own head, the rage and fear giving him a precious few seconds more contact with the world outside his failing body. Heart jolting back to a quicker rhythm, he sat halfway up, summoned the magic, and let rip with a hell of a fireball.

It exploded away from him, flew through the round-edged opening leading out of the pueblo ruin, and blasted the fuck-all out of a tree near the edge of the cliff. He felt the blaze and burn, felt the huge, awesome pleasure of destructive magic, and slipped into the darkness of Iago's hold on him. As he let himself fall, he sent a thought flying along a river of red-gold magic gone somehow gray: *Sasha, help us!*

Sasha jolted upright from her doze amidst the cacao plants, her mind a confusing jumble of dream images and the sound of her name. "Michael?" she said aloud before she was fully awake. Then she remembered where she was, and why. With a quick, startled glance at her seedlings, which were furry, thriving plants now, she shot to her feet and hurried to the mansion. It was later than she would've thought, she realized from the angle of the orange sunlight. Nearly time for the final presolstice meeting, where they would decide whether she and Michael would stay at Skywatch or hang themselves out as bait for Iago. She hoped to hell the royal council would decide on the latter; she wanted another crack at the bastard, this time with her own mage powers, and Michael at her back. They'd already proven the two of them didn't need a love bond for them to amp each other's magic. Iago wouldn't know what hit him.

Finding the great room and kitchen empty, she hurried through to the residential wing, her warrior's talent stirring to life, warning her there was something wrong. It was that warning spurring her on as she pushed through the door to Michael's suite without knocking, half-afraid of what she would find. "Michael?" she called. "You in here?" She didn't get an answer. Hadn't really expected one. The sixth sense she'd developed when it came to him—a faint hum of magic and a sense of *thereness* that had come after they'd started sleeping together again—had gone dim inside her, but she didn't know if that was because she'd given up trying to make their relationship work, or if it meant he was truly gone.

Then she saw the note on his kitchen counter, and had her answer. In square, blocky letters, he'd written: *Rabbit is with me. Either all will be well ... or it won't. If not, please remember the good stuff, and tell Tomas that he couldn't have changed this. In the end, what is meant to be will be.*

Sasha's blood chilled as she remembered the voice she'd heard in her dream, the cry for help that had awakened her. It hadn't been Michael, she realized with a sudden, sinking burst of clarity. It'd been Rabbit. He'd been the one to call for help, because Michael was already unconscious, or worse. Anger flared, but she checked it and got her ass moving.

Clutching the note, she burst out of the suite and bolted for the main room. Making a beeline for where Strike, Leah, and Jox were just emerging from the royal wing, she shoved the note in Strike's hand and blurted, "We need to find Michael and Rabbit, *now*!"

But Strike couldn't find Michael with 'port lock, and a search of the immediate mansion and cottages didn't turn them up. The magi and *winikin* gathered under the ceiba tree, trying to figure a next move. Panic gripped Sasha at the thought that the missing man had left the warded canyon and been grabbed by the Xibalbans. Michael couldn't give her the security and inner strength she needed, but she cared about him, damn it. She didn't want to lose him. Not like this. Her mind flashing to the sight of a tattered skull atop a pyramid of rubble, she said raggedly, "I saw rock walls in my dream. A ruin . . ."

A coyote howled near the back of the canyon, an almost human-timbred wail that drew her attention. She saw a smudge of smoke rising into the afternoon sky. "There!" she said, pointing. "They're in the pueblo."

After a mad scramble for first-aid kits and combat gear, Strike 'ported them all out to the pueblo, landing them on a ledge near the smoldering tree. The smell of blood hung heavy on the air, sharp and stagnant. Following the smell, or her instincts, or maybe both, she lunged for a nearby doorway—a round-cornered rectangle leading into darkness. She plunged through and skidded to a halt as her eyes took a second to adjust, another to process what she was seeing.

The small rectangular room was a charnel. Blood had saturated the sandy floor, then pooled and coagulated, bright with oxygen in places, dark with death in others. The liquid formed a single commingled pool beneath the two men who slumped shoulder-to-shoulder against the far wall, their legs stretched out before them, their heads lolled back to rest on the wall . . . and their slashed wrists turned up to the sky.

A hiss of air escaped from Sasha as her heart twisted in her chest. She was dimly aware of the others crowding into the doorway behind her, but her entire attention was focused on Michael and Rabbit. She crossed the room and dropped to her knees between the men—*the bodies*, her gut told her, because there was no way they could survive something like this. Their mingled blood soaked through her jeans to touch her skin, but she ignored the disquieting sensation as she touched Michael's face, his chest, his throat. And felt nothing. Grief backed up in her chest, making it impossible to breathe. She leaned into him, opened her magic to him, trying to find music and hearing only emptiness. On the physical level, though, she thought she felt a faint flutter. A heartbeat . . . maybe? Yes, there it was. "He's alive!"

"They both are," Strike said. He was crouched down beside Rabbit. "I've got a pulse." But his grim expression said, *They'd need a miracle to pull through.*

A miracle. "I'll heal them," she said as the others crowded into the circular room. "I made my plants grow earlier this morning; I'm getting better with *ch'ul*. If we link up, I can feed them our energy; I can do it." But even as she made the promise to herself, to the others, doubts crowded in on her. She'd never found Rabbit's *ch'ul* music, and Michael's song didn't always behave the way she expected it to. Yes, she could channel energy into them, but her gut said it would just pour right out again unless she could find their songs. Regardless, she fixed Strike with a look. "I have to try."

"I know you do." Strike hesitated. "I'll 'port us to the temple, and we'll carry them down to the tomb. You'll need extra power, and that's the strongest power sink we've found yet." He paused, expression darkening. "Besides, we'll need to be there in a couple of hours for the solstice ritual . . . and we're going to need a sacrifice."

"No!" Sasha said sharply. "Not them. One of the Xibalbans. With Michael and me both in the tomb, you can set the ambush, just like we planned. When Iago comes for us, you'll get your sacrifice."

"If Iago doesn't come, we'll still need someone," Strike reminded her.

"Maybe this was meant," Jox said quietly from behind the king, where he stood holding a first-aid kit that wouldn't even begin to address the problems confronting them. The others were ranged behind him, Nightkeepers and *winikin* alike. Anna was weeping silently, her eyes fixed on Rabbit. Tomas stood grim and stone-faced, but when Sasha met his eyes she saw real grief beneath, and thought she could almost hear him whisper, "Please," though his lips didn't move.

She nodded, resolve hardening within her. "Fine. Zap us to the tomb. But I want your word that you won't sacrifice them until I agree there's nothing more I can do." When he said nothing, she held out her bloodied hand. "Swear it."

They traded stares for several heartbeats, and in his expression she saw the war she was just beginning to understand would be a part of her life from now on, the struggle to choose between destiny and desire, between duty and emotion, friendship . . . and love. Then, finally, he nodded. "Their lives are yours."

Which wasn't what she'd asked for. But there was no way she was letting either of them die. Rabbit was too special to go out like this, and Michael . . . well, he might not have been ready to fight for her, but she was sure as hell going to fight for him, because if he died, she suspected a piece of her would die along with him, whether either of them liked it or not.

CHAPTER TWENTY-TWO

The in-between

The creature that lived in the Scorpion River was easily three times the size of a normal *boluntiku*, and had a whiplike tail that broke from the water to curl up and over its back, scorpionlike. As he ran down the ferry dock toward the creature, Michael let rip with twin salvos from his autopistols.

The jade-tipped bullets passed right through the damn thing.

"Shit!" He'd forgotten that part, how jade-tips could kill the magic-sniffing, hellborn creatures, but only when they were in their solid form—which they usually took only right before making contact with their prey.

The muddy brown water churned, boiling up from below to erupt in foul-smelling belches within the vaporish creature, which rose above him, screaming its soul-curdling battle cry as it took a swipe at him, turning solid in the last second before it made contact. Michael stood his ground, letting rip with his pistols, then dropping flat to the dock. The *boluntiku*'s long, curving claws whipped over the top of him as the creature jerked back and screamed in outraged pain. He rose up and tried for another salvo, then heard Lucius's shout of, "Down!"

Too late, he saw the wicked whip of the *'tiku*'s tail slashing through the air toward him. Then a heavy weight hit him, knocking him down and to one side as Lucius, body-slammed him to safety.

The creature's tail crashed into the place where the man had just been. The stone dock shuddered beneath the force of the blow.

"Thanks," Michael said raggedly, his ribs aching from the tackle. He dragged himself up, slapped fresh cartridges in the pistols, and snapped, "Get your ass in the water and do your best to almost drown while you're saying the spell." He rattled off a two-line prayer in badly accented Maya. "It might do something about that *makol* problem of yours. I'll hold off the *'tiku* until you're out of sight."

Michael knew that he'd been meant to find the other man, that their meeting had been far from a coincidence. He had to help the human, had to give him a chance to break the *makol*'s hold on him, and maybe even make it back to the Nightkeepers, back to Jade. Which meant distracting the giant *boluntiku* long enough for Lucius to get out into the strong current at the center of the river. When Lucius hesitated, Michael shoved him. "Go!"

The human clapped him on the shoulder. "See you on the outside." Then he ran across the dock at an angle away from the *'tiku* and jumped as far out into the center as he could. There was a huge splash when he landed, then ripples going to nothing.

The lava creature reared back and turned toward the sound, hissing.

"No, you bastard!" Michael waved to get the thing's attention. "I'm the one you want. Fight me!" Out of the corner of his eye, he caught sight of Lucius's head breaking the surface, only to sink below again. Then the river

whipped him around a corner, and the human was lost
to sight.

"Gods go with you," Michael muttered. Then, biting
his tongue hard enough to draw blood in a quick and
dirty autosacrifice, he summoned his shield magic . . .
and got nothing. Not even a flicker of red-gold power
responded to his call. Which meant he either unleashed
the *muk*, taking the risk of tipping his soul so far that the
river couldn't save him . . . or he and Lucius both died.

"*Shit*," he whispered, feeling the *muk* crowding the
edges of his brain, his soul. Then, roaring a denial, he
opened himself to the power and the Other's memories.
He smashed through the sluiceways and yanked down
the dam, then hammered at the older, stronger bastions
within him, destroying Rabbit's work, and Horn's. His
divided brain shuddered under the impact of the Other's thoughts and memories, and the oily whip of ancient
magic. The *muk* surrounded him, took him over, while
the Other howled in triumph. Michael's vision went
gray, but still he could see the *boluntiku* rearing up, tow-
ering over him.

His heart fought to reject the corrupting silver magic.
And as it did, he was helpless. Powerless.

Then the *boluntiku* screamed as it attacked, going
solid at the last possible second. Michael ducked the
creature's attack and spun aside, but could evade for
only so long; he needed to attack. Knowing he lacked
the power to fight the creature, heart breaking and soul
crying out as he did so, he yielded himself to the Mictlan and its terrible weapon. *Muk* slammed into him,
channeled through him, as, for the first time in his mage
life, he called fireball magic and his warrior's talent responded, not with a ball of fiery light, but with one of
bright, brilliant silver. The flames seethed and grew in
his hand as the *boluntiku* reoriented on him and closed
in, drawing back its terrible claws for a killing swipe.

It swung, turning solid again. Michael threw, hurling the gleaming *muk* straight into its gaping maw. Howling, the *'tiku* snapped its jaws shut on the ball of anti-*ch'ul*. It paused for a second, then let out a another unearthly howl, this one of pain rather than rage. Head whipping from side to side, it roared and cycled from vapor to solid and back. The unearthly glow of molten orange lava dimmed and died as the creature solidified a final time. Its motions slowed, grew sporadic, then stopped. The thing grayed. Then it went limp and drooped, losing form and substance as it coalesced into the river.

Water splashed, then stilled, leaving Michael alone on the stone-and-bone dock. Only he wasn't really alone. He was Michael. He was the Mictlan. He was the Other. And it was time.

Three strides carried him to the edge of the dock. A fourth sent him plunging into the water, which slapped at him with a cold shock, then swept him up and bore him into the current.

At first he paddled to stay afloat, angling his body, and started swimming for the shore. But then he stopped himself, knowing that wasn't how the spell worked. One near-death experience had been required to get to the in-between; another was necessary for absolution. Near death within near death. Double the sacrifice. *So be it*, he thought, whispering the second set of spell words and then letting himself go limp as the river churned around him.

The Other howled a warning and the *muk* rose up within him, but Michael held on to his control and forced his lungs to unlock, forced himself to inhale water rather than air. The brackish flow gushed down his throat and windpipe and he gagged, choking and spasming, spinning in the rapid current. The water slammed him into a rocky outcropping and the world went dim. Starbursts detonated behind his eyelids, and for a second he thought he heard music. Then it went away. Everything went away. As he passed from consciousness, pain ripped through his chest. Life drained from him; hope fled.

Despair welled up. He needed help, needed the gods. Needed Sasha. *Please save me*, he thought, sending the prayer into the brackish water around him. *Please help me be worthy*.

There was no answer except the darkness.

The tomb of the First Father

Sasha bent over where Rabbit and Michael lay on the floor, desperate and exhausted. She had a hand on each of their chests, her palms leaking her blood onto them, her touch giving them healing power, though not enough of it. They were still alive, but that was about all she could claim. She couldn't find their songs, couldn't follow their *ch'ul* flow to where they had gone. She was acting as little more than a magical life-support system, bleeding power into them, only to have it drain away just as quickly. She needed the miracle. She needed help. The *ch'ulel* was supposed to be able to heal. Why couldn't she find the way to that piece of her talent? What was she missing? What wasn't she doing right?

She was dimly aware of activity surrounding her in the temple room, where the others bent over the sarcophagus and spoke words of magic and reverence. She felt something deep inside her, a growing connection that brought more magic with each passing minute, though still not enough. It was the solstice, she realized. The stars and planets, the sun and moon were coming into position and the barrier was weakening.

Strike moved up beside her and dropped a hand to her shoulder. "We're down to thirty minutes."

The Prophet had to be created during the moment of true solstice, when the barrier was at its thinnest and a connection opened up, very briefly, very tenuously, to the place where the library had been sequestered. In the moments leading up to that, the Nightkeepers had to make their soul sacrifice. Iago hadn't shown up, hadn't taken the bait. The only magic users available were the ones in the tomb.

Sasha stared down at her bloodstained hands and nodded shortly, in acknowledgment rather than agreement.

Strike tightened his fingers on her shoulder—in warning, in support, she didn't know. Then he moved to rejoin the others clustered around the sarcophagus, where they labored to trip the remainder of the thirteen magically timed latches securing the lid in place.

When he was gone, she bent over Michael and Rabbit once again. She tried to summon a prayer, tried to find some hope, but in the end all she could come up with was an inner snarl: *For gods' sake, get your asses back here.*

But despite her refusal to give up on them, and her internal bravado, her eyes filmed as they locked on Michael, lying so still, his muscles lax beneath her touch. She hadn't been able to live with every aspect of his too-multifaceted personality, but there were parts of him she loved deeply—like his strong sense of honor, his honest efforts to be a better man and a worthy Nightkeeper. She couldn't even fault the need for justice that had drawn him into the FBI, and from there into the Bryson's employ. He'd never said as much, but she suspected that she'd been destined for a less battered version, one that had been raised within the traditions and canons of the Nightkeepers. And she suspected that was the man she'd glimpsed within him, the one who combined warrior, killer, lover, and friend into one honorable core that some might find frightening and violent, but she found exactly right. That man was the one she wanted.

Leaning over him, aware that two more latches had

come undone on the sarcophagus and she was running out of time, she leaned over him, touched her lips to his cool, unmoving cheek, and whispered in his ear, "Come back to me, Michael. Come back and bring me the man I could love."

The in-between

The man I could love . . . Michael awoke with the quiet, powerful words whispering around him, inside him. Humming agreement, he reached for Sasha, and touched only sand.

"What the . . . ?" Cracking his eyes he saw a flow of brown water moving sluggishly past, along a riverbank a couple of feet from where he lay facedown, feeling wrecked. *I'm still in between*, he thought, recognizing the Scorpion River. *Shit*. He'd assumed that once he'd done the near-drowning thing, he'd be zapped back to his body. Apparently not. But as he dragged himself up to a fighter's crouch, he realized something else.

The death's-head talent mark that had been on his wrist was gone. He was back down to the stone and the warrior. The Mictlan urge, as far as he could tell, was gone. The *muk* connection had disappeared, as well. The Other was still within him, though. It was contained, but it was there, waiting to emerge when his defenses were low. And perhaps it was only fitting for him to have to keep those urges and memories as punishment for the choices he'd made. But if the Other had lost its access to the *muk*, it should be his own private torture, no longer endangering his sin balance, and through that, the other Nightkeepers.

"Thank you, gods," he said softly. Yes, there would be consequences to his refusing the Mictlan's target— potentially devastating consequences—but he'd deal with whatever happened. He'd refused to sacrifice a teammate, so the Nightkeepers would deal with it as a team. And Sasha ... He thought of the whisper, thought of her. And thought that she'd been right about some things. He'd fought for Rabbit just now, and committed the Nightkeepers to future strife on the younger mage's behalf. Yet he hadn't fought nearly so hard to work things out with her, assuming it was a lost battle before it had even begun.

But not again, he decided. He was going back to her. And he was going to fight his ass off and see where it got him.

Buoyed by the thought, by the image of her that he held in his head, in his heart, he summoned his magic, not needing blood sacrifice during the solstice. The power came easily, gloriously red-gold, with no sign of *muk*. He was about to say the word that would take him back to the real world, back to his life, when he heard a low, pained moan behind him. He jerked around, then cursed viciously at the sight of another body washed up on the riverbank just beyond him.

At first he thought it was Lucius. But Lucius hadn't been wearing a hoodie. And he sure as shit didn't have a small army of marks on his inner forearm, one of which glowed bloodred among the black glyphs.

"Rabbit." Michael surged to his feet. "Godsdamn it, you were supposed to fucking wait for me to come back!" He took a couple of steps toward the kid, then stopped dead when he felt the temptation of hellmagic and saw the dark, oily shadows clinging to the young man's skin and clothes, making him look like he was lying beneath a blanket of darkness. "Aw, hell," Michael said, softer now. "What happened to you? What did you do?"

"Iago." The word was cracked, barely audible, forced through stiff lips. "He was trying to piggyback on the scorpion spell. When I blocked him, he slapped a second hellmagic connection on me. . . ." Rabbit's voice petered out, his eyes rolling back in his head.

"Damn it." Michael crouched down beside him, saw that his clothing was dry. The kid hadn't made it into the river. Iago had wrapped him in layer upon layer of hellmagic and dropped him in the in-between to die. The realization brought a glimmer of hope, and Michael reached out to shake the teen. But then he hesitated, something deep inside warning that he shouldn't touch the darkness. He'd severed his connection to the *muk* power, but the penchants of his bloodline remained. Instinct warned that if he touched the hellmagic, it would render him vulnerable to the darkness once again. And did he dare return to the river? The spell hadn't said anything about touching the powerful waters twice.

One swim breaks the bond; a second forms it anew. The whisper came in the multitonal voice of his ancestral *nahwal*. Michael didn't for a second think he'd imagined it. He wanted to rail at the *nahwal*, wanted to shout at the deaf gods, at the fates. But he knew that wouldn't do a damn bit of good, so he gritted his teeth and crouched down beside his teammate.

"Come on, Rabbit," he said, hoping he wasn't too far gone to hear. "You've got to get up. It's just a few steps to the river."

But the younger mage didn't respond. And as Michael watched, the dark haze around Rabbit thickened, and his breathing stuttered.

"Godsdamn it." Michael hesitated. He couldn't just leave Rabbit. He wouldn't. He'd made his choice already. Steeling himself against the slick, oily feel of the mucilaginous film coating the teen, he got one arm under the kid's shoulders, the other beneath his knees, and stood, lifting Rabbit with a groan of effort and heading toward the river. Everywhere he touched the teen, the darkness stuck and clung to his own skin. Every step he took toward the river put him another step back toward connecting with the *muk* power. He could feel the temptation, see the glitter of silver at the edges of his vision.

It was the curse of his bloodline.

Then he reached the edge and stepped into the Scorpion River, carrying Rabbit with him. He threw back his head and howled as the water washed part of the darkness out of Rabbit and into him, returning the Mictlan bond and his connection to the *muk*, though not the target mark. Gravity increased a thousandfold, the weight of his other self dragging him down, making his bones ache, making his soul cry out in pain.

Rabbit spasmed and jerked awake, thrashing. Michael lost his grip, regained it, and dragged the younger man to the surface. Then, realizing he still had to complete the spell, he shoved Rabbit's head under, reciting the second half of the spell as he did so.

Rabbit thrashed. Convulsed. Went still.

As life drained from the young man, Michael knew what it felt like to be a murderer. But then he pulled the young man up and out, and dragged him onto the beach. He got Rabbit on his side, got the water out. Started with artificial resps.

Rabbit came around almost immediately, and grabbed for him, latching on hard, his fingernails drawing blood.

For a second, they were linked by blood and darkness, and Rabbit's mind-bending talent. In a flash, Michael saw what Rabbit saw, knew what Rabbit knew. He felt the rage and despair of screwing up almost everything he touched, the hope that had come with finding Myrinne, the determination to turn himself around, make himself a man worthy of a mate. He felt Rabbit's insecurity, his fears when it came to protecting Myrinne, keeping her happy, and understanding what she wanted and needed from him. He felt those same emotions echo from his own soul, where Rabbit was seeing his and

Sasha's problems firsthand. More, he felt the younger mage's slashing sense of betrayal at seeing his own face in the mirror and grasping the enormity of Michael's decision, the risks he ran by refusing his target.

Then it was done. The reciprocal link blinked out of existence as though it had never been, and Michael and Rabbit sagged into each other.

"Why me?" The younger man's voice was rough and rusty, his eyes anguished. "Why did the gods want you to kill *me*?"

Michael shook his head. "No clue. Maybe they're wrong." But a shiver touched the back of his neck as he wondered whether that was what his uncle had thought: *No fucking way I'm killing the king. The gods got it wrong.*

"What if they aren't?" Rabbit said, echoing his thoughts.

"You'd godsdamned better make sure they are," Michael growled, knowing Rabbit needed to hear it, that he needed to say it. "I'll buy into the structure of the legends, but I think the details are damn well mutable. Strike was supposed to kill Leah and now she's his queen. The prophecies made it sound like the Volatile was a danger to us, but Nate's an asset, not a danger. You see where I'm going with this?"

Something kindled in the hopelessness of Rabbit's eyes. "Love helps us break the patterns."

That rocked Michael back on his heels, slammed through him with an energy that felt like magic itself. Why had it taken a punk kid to point that out? Because damned if he wasn't right. It was a small sample size, granted, but what if it held true? The Nightkeepers' magic was inextricably intertwined with the man-woman connection of sex, of love. What if—maybe because theirs was such a small group, maybe because of another, higher layer of destiny—love sometimes trumped the prophecies and the signs?

The thought was humbling. Terrifying. Exciting.

Or it's bullshit, logic said. *The kid wants to believe he and his first real girlfriend are supposed to be together forever, and you want an excuse to think you can win Sasha back, even though nothing's changed inside you.* Which was true, Michael supposed. The Mictlan's target bond had been broken, but he was still connected to the *muk*, still had the dubious talent and the Other within him. *Damn it.*

"Look," he said, fixing Rabbit with a *don't mess with me* glare, "I can't promise you that things are going to work out with you and Myrinne, and you'd damn well better not hinge your good behavior on it. Be a man and do your best. That's all any of us can ask of you."

Rabbit seemed to consider that for a moment. Then his shoulders squared and he nodded. "I'm working on it."

"Keep working." Michael clapped the teen on the shoulder. "Now, let's go find our bodies." *And hope to hell they're still alive for us to come back to.*

The tomb of the First Father

Wrung out from dividing her energies between the two injured men, Sasha felt Michael's energy flow dip alarmingly, spike, and dip again, and knew this was the moment she'd been dreading, the moment he hit the end of his reserves and her strength was no longer enough to keep his heart going, his blood flowing through his veins. Refusing to give up, to give in, she gripped his limp hand and flung the last of her fading strength toward the place where she could feel his energy draining. Calling to the others, she said, "Help me. I need more!"

Strike looked over from the nearly open coffin and

shook his head, expression drawn. "There isn't any more, Sasha." He paused. "I'm sorry. It's almost time."

She felt her fingers go numb, and thought she'd gripped Michael's hand too tight. Then she heard a thrumming, electric chord and realized it was the other way around. She froze, afraid to hope as she looked down at Michael. His eyes were open. "Oh," she breathed. "You're back."

She was peripherally aware of Strike's amazement, of the others gathering around, but she was caught up in Michael, and in his energy, which was alive and vibrant, and calling to hers, drawing it inward. Almost too late she felt the silver *muk* reach out to her, felt it begin to drain her. She cut the connection fast, but felt the ache of loss left behind. "It didn't work."

The forest of his eyes went to dusk. "It did and it didn't. Rabbit—" He broke off, glancing at the teen. "Oh, shit. He was right behind me."

Rabbit's body was still lying there, but he'd gone gray. And in Sasha's grasp, his hand was cold as death.

Somewhere in the barrier

Rabbit was halfway back into his body when he'd felt Iago grab onto his consciousness and follow, still trying to piggyback his way into the sarcophagus room, the bastard. More, through the psychic link, Rabbit could see inside the Xibalban's mind and know his plans; that knowledge chilled him to the marrow with its scope and possibilities. *No!* Rabbit's consciousness hung within the barrier's energy flow as he fought the Xibalban's hold, trying to find his way back to the in-between, to the gray-green mist of the barrier, hell, anywhere but back to the tomb of the First Father.

You can't win, Iago mocked him, giving him a shove back toward his body. *You'd be better off conserving your strength to fight me when we get there.*

And the damn thing was, he was right. Rabbit's strength was failing; his *body* was failing. Should he just let go of that connection? No, he couldn't die now. He had to get back to the others and tell them what Iago was planning, had to get back to Myrinne and tell her he was sorry for being a dick, that she could have all the time and space she needed, even if it killed him to back off. Michael had turned away from the gods by refusing to kill him. He had to be worthy of that sacrifice. And somehow, though gods only knew how, he needed to break this ungodly link he shared with Iago. It left him too vulnerable.

But how the hell was he supposed to do that? The river had washed him clean of the extra hellmagic Iago had loaded him down with, but it hadn't broken his connection to the hellmagic. What would?

Not a fucking thing, the Xibalban answered inside him, warning Rabbit that his mental shields were for shit, that the rest of his magic was falling down around his ears. His powers were crumbling, kaleidoscoping inward, along with his consciousness. Still struggling, he resisted the forces urging him back to himself, thinking that if he could stay out of his body, he could strand them both in the barrier, or the in-between.

Then he heard sudden music, a marching backbeat overlaid with electric guitar, and Sasha's voice was inside his head, impossibly strong as she called, *Get your ass back here, Rabbit. We need you!* Then she somehow grabbed onto him, latching her energy to his and pulling him home to his human shell.

Rabbit felt Iago's startled delight and roared a denial, but it was already too late. The enemy mage had grabbed onto the connection, followed it to its source. Howling despair and the knowledge that he'd fucked up again, Rabbit flung himself back into his own body, hoping to hell he got there ahead of Iago.

The tomb of the First Father

Relief and excitement flared as Sasha felt the magic connect. "He's coming back," she said, leaning into Michael's solid strength as he fed her power through their linked hands, their magic connecting despite the *muk* and the madness.

Michael continued to give her—and the rest of the room—a rundown on what had happened at the river, how Lucius had helped him, then been swept downstream, and how he'd come upon Rabbit and taken back the Mictlan talent and *muk* link in exchange for Rabbit's life.

Emotion surged through her and she tightened her grip on his hand, trying to tell him how she felt through their linked magic, even as she poured their linked energy into the healing connection she'd finally—finally—formed with Rabbit when she'd looked deep inside him, beneath the hellmagic that blocked her perceptions, and found his song—a soft tenor aria, haunting in its refrain.

"She's got him!" Michael said, triumphant. Then he said something more, and Strike answered, but Sasha suddenly couldn't follow, couldn't react, couldn't do anything as dark, oily brown magic surrounded her, latched onto her. "Michael!" she tried to scream, but all that came out was a whisper.

She was conscious of him turning, though everything was suddenly happening in slow motion. Rabbit's eyes opened, full of fear, and his mouth worked as he shouted a warning of some sort. But she couldn't follow any of it as Iago's oily magic flowed through her, into her, and he looked out through her eyes, saw the scene, and locked onto it for a 'port.

Magic rattled off-key, air exploded outward, and the big redheaded mage appeared in the center of the room, balanced atop the inner coffin that lay within the open sarcophagus. Jade, holding a scroll clutched to her chest, reeled back, eyes going wide and scared.

Strike shouted something and the others scrambled to take defensive positions, pulling their weapons as they scattered. Michael roared and lunged to his feet, shoving Sasha behind him as he cast a thick shield. Rabbit bellowed and threw fire, the shock wave practically flattening everyone in the chamber. The bright light blinded Sasha as magic sparked. Michael called something that cut off midword.

The world came back into focus around her, but it made no sense. Iago and Michael were both gone. Jade was screaming, her hands streaming blood. "Iago took the library scroll!" she cried, face etched with anguish. "And he's got Michael!"

Sasha moved toward her, throat closing in horror, but then hellmagic sparked again, harsh and discordant, and hard, hurting hands grabbed her from behind.

She screamed, drove an elbow back and tried to twist away but from her captor, but couldn't. She cried out and struggled, looked back to see Iago's emerald green eyes. Eyes out of her nightmares. The mage grinned. The oily brown magic cycled up, and Sasha's world went gray-green with 'port magic and grief. "Michael!" she screamed into the void. "Help me!"

There was no answer.

CHAPTER TWENTY-THREE

Paxil Mountain
Somewhere in the highlands of the former Mayan and
Aztec territories

The world took shape around Sasha, gray and fuzzy at first, bringing the echoes and shuffling sounds of movement within a high stone chamber. Next, she recognized the stretched, bound, hanging feeling, the strain in her shoulders and hips that had been all too familiar during her captivity. *Crucifixion.* Her soul shuddered in horror, but this was no time to pretend she was somewhere else and wait for rescue. She was one of the rescuers now.

Opening her eyes, she found herself almost back where she began—strung up on a heavy wooden cruciform, bound at the wrists and ankles. But this time, she stood on a raised dais beside a second crucifix, where Michael was tied, spread-armed and furious. She met his eyes, and a quiver ran through her at the intensity she saw in him. The shimmer might have been nerves, might've been desire—she felt both as she looked at him and the solstice magic burned within her. More, he seemed to be conveying a message, one that reached inside her and made her yearn, made her hope.

Knowing it was all too easy to confuse lust and desire when there was magic in the air, she looked away, studying the situation. The dais on which they were bound stood at the center of a conical stone cavern. The cavern's inner walls looked like they might mirror the shape of the mountain's exterior; they were carved and painted in places, though she couldn't make out the designs in the torchlight. The quasi-natural temple had probably started as a dead volcano that had been hollowed out by hand in ancient times. The interior was torchlit and spiced with unfamiliar ritual incense. Opposite the dais sat two elaborately carved thrones, one larger than the other, both of ancient design and bearing the sunburst symbol of the Aztec calendar. Tubs of soil sat on either side of the thrones, and her mind stuttered to see the familiar leaves of cacao and maize. But if this truly was Paxil Mountain, the legendary source of the vital foods, she supposed it made sense. Eight red-robed Xibalbans were ranged around the space, several clustered near what looked like a tunnel mouth leading to the outside, another couple near a prefab steel structure built up against one wall, and one each on either side of the paired thrones. One of the thrones was undoubtedly for Iago, she thought. But who was the other one for?

"Welcome to Paxil Mountain," she said hollowly, because despite the Nightkeepers' best efforts, she and Michael had wound up exactly where the Xibalban had intended all along.

"How are you set for magic?" Michael asked quietly.

A quick test run had her cursing. The solstice magic gathered within her, lit her up, made her feel powerful. But when she tried to shape the magic into a spell, it turned formless and slipped away. Keeping her voice to the same low, private murmur as his, she said, "I can feel it, but I can't do anything with it." She didn't look at him, was trying hard not to.

"Same here. Either there's a ward spell going, or it's because this is a ritual site. Most spells failed down in the tunnels beneath Chichén Itzá, too." He paused. "What's wrong?"

That startled a laugh out of her, but she stifled the knee-jerk smart-ass response and shook her head. "Later."

"Now," he countered. "Look at me."

She lifted her chin and met his eyes, knowing he would see the turmoil in hers. "You almost died back there."

"I know, and I'm sorry for putting you through that. I'll explain it all later." His tone said *much later*, but rather than an evasion, it felt like a promise. As did his direct, penetrating stare as he said, "You fought for me, kept me alive long enough to come back. I owe you for that. I hope that, going forward, you'll let me fight for you."

"I don't think we're going to have a choice on that one," she said, once again scanning the room, trying to figure contingencies. There was only one way in or out, it seemed, which could get tricky. Whoever held the tunnel controlled the situation. She continued, thinking aloud: "If we can get out of the bonds and past the ward, we still have to find the library scroll and get our asses out of here. But if we have to fight, you'd be the guy I'd choose to have my back."

"I'm not talking about fighting at your side, though I'll be there, no questions asked." Warned by something in his voice, she looked back at him and found his expression intent, his eyes heating. "What I'm saying is that I'm ready to fight with you. Against you. For you. Whatever you want to call it. You were right when you said I didn't fight hard enough to find a way for us to be together, and then to keep us together. But it wasn't because I didn't care enough or didn't want you enough. It was because I didn't think I could possibly win."

Faint warmth kindled despite the situation. "And now?"

"I still don't know if I can win, but I damn well want a chance to fight, because I don't want to do this without you. Even when we're at opposite poles and don't make a damn bit of sense together, I can't think of anyone I'd rather be with. You're stuck in my head, my heart, and my damned, beat-up soul. I'll do whatever it takes to keep you there, and to have you in my life and in my bed."

That was the starkest, most nakedly honest thing he'd ever said to her; the words cut through her wary reserve and nestled deep inside her, curling around the part of her that said he could be redeemed, that in many ways he already was. "Michael, I—"

"How touching," a mocking voice broke in, jolting her with fear and memory, closely followed by a slash of rage and hatred as Iago moved around from behind the cruciforms into her line of sight. He wore black combat clothes that closely mimicked those of the Nightkeepers; he could've passed except for the red hellmark on his forearm and the cold cruelty that shone in his emerald green eyes. "Touching . . . and borderline sickening, really. Not that it'll matter either way in a few minutes."

Sasha's breath caught when Iago casually drew the stolen library scroll out from behind his back, where he'd tucked it in his belt. He held it by one end and tapped it against his opposite palm in a hypnotic rhythm that demanded her attention as a familiar brown-haired man moved up behind him. Lucius's eyes glowed the luminous green of a *makol*'s.

Iago stepped closer to Sasha, glancing between her Michael. "To sacrifice the *ch'ulel* and Mictlan, together, during the triad threshold. Amazing. The power is going to be . . . incalculable."

"Good," Michael said, his voice a dangerous purr. "That should give me plenty to work with when I take you out."

Iago shrugged. "Big talk for a guy who's racked and tied."

"So untie me. I'll fight you fair."

Iago ignored that offer and leaned in, so his face was very near Sasha's when he breathed, "You and he are explosive together, *muk* and *ch'ul*, matter and antimatter. Your dual sacrifice will give me enough magic not only to call the Prophet, but also to raise the last true emperor of the Aztec." Anticipation lit his face with unholy glee. "Imagine it . . . Moctezuma himself as an *ajaw-makol*, at my right hand as we complete the conquest begun five hundred years ago." He turned away, gesturing for the *makol* and two of the red-robes to stay behind. "Watch them while the rest of us prepare. We've got ten minutes until the solstice enters its peak. We'll be back in five."

Sasha's breath escaped her in a hiss of dismay. *So soon.*

As Iago strode off, the red-robes and the *makol* took up guard positions on the dais. The red-robes gave the *makol* a wide berth, standing far away. The *makol*, though, took up its guard post very near Sasha; it stood looking at her with a faintly superior sneer on its otherwise expressionless face, its eyes glittering luminous green. Incongruously, though, Sasha caught a thread of music coming from it, borne on the magic of the coming solstice.

She turned her head so the *makol* couldn't see her mouth as she whispered, "Lucius is in there. And whatever sort of ward Iago's got fouling our magic, either the *makol* is standing inside it, or *ch'ul* is immune . . . because I've got his song. It's faint, but it's there."

"Son of a bitch," Michael whispered back with fierce satisfaction. "He made it out of the river." He paused. "Can you feed him *ch'ul* without the *makol* figuring out what's going on?"

"I can damn well try." Concentrating on her fledgling *ch'ulel* skills, trying to block out the knowledge that this could be one of her last acts on earth, she opened herself to the song. She found it, touched it, tried to follow it to its source, but the thread was tenuous and inconstant. Still, she channeled *ch'ul* to the point of mental contact, giving up her own because she wasn't linked to any other source.

The *makol*'s head jerked in response—apparently she wasn't so much on the stealthy side. It narrowed its eyes at her, but it seemed more amused than annoyed when it said, "Your human isn't here, Nightkeeper. He's in the in-between."

No, he's not, Sasha thought, but apparently the *makol* couldn't tell that Lucius had made it back. Maybe because the link connecting him to the *makol* had been severed in the Scorpion River? That would be a lucky break. Or the work of the gods. Hope spurted, and she sent even more *ch'ul* along Lucius's song. The moment she did, the *makol* went suddenly rigid, its eyes flickering, going from luminous to normal and back.

"Got him," Michael said on a quiet hiss of triumph. Standing some distance away, the red-robed guards were oblivious.

"Almost." Sasha concentrated as the eyes did their trick. Luminous. Hazel. Luminous. Then they finally stayed hazel. Lucius's expression animated, becoming that of a human who was wretched and disoriented, but determined to break through. He shuddered for a moment, caught in transition, unable to speak.

"Hurry," Michael ordered. "Get the guards."

Lucius nodded raggedly and lurched toward the red-robes, pulling the *makol*'s long, wickedly sharp combat knife from his belt. He was low on stealth, though; one of the red-robes turned and spotted him. Shouting a warning, the *pilli* went for his weapon. Lucius suddenly accelerated to an inhuman blur, swiping the knife across the first guard's throat, then jamming it to the hilt in the second man's chest.

Retrieving his weapon, he returned to Michael and Sasha, flowing across the space with the *makol*'s lethal grace. But his eyes remained human. He'd regained full control of his body, and apparently commanded the *makol*'s strength and coordination, as well.

He cut down Sasha first, slashing through the ties binding her ankles first, then her wrists. As he turned away, she dropped to the dais and nearly went down in a heap when her rubbery legs gave way. But she braced herself and stayed up by force of will, while Lucius cut Michael down.

"Damn glad to have you back." Michael gripped the other man's shoulder briefly, then turned and held out a hand to Sasha. "Come on. We've got to move. If we can get the scroll and get down that tunnel to open air, Strike should be able to get 'port lock on the three of us." They dropped down from the dais and headed for the prefab building, where Iago and the red-robes had gone. But Lucius warned, "N-not the tunnel." He stuttered slightly as his speech centers came back online. "It's wired to blow. Motion sensors and C-4. Iago doesn't want the Nightkeepers disturbing another of his rituals."

Sasha shuddered as claustrophobia had the walls suddenly seeming very near, but Michael said only, "We need to get that scroll first. Then we'll worry about an exit strategy."

They crept up beside the steel structure. One door was barred and padlocked on the outside; the other was cracked partway open, its padlock hanging unlatched, the bar swung off to the side. Michael took the open side, Sasha the closed side, with Lucius behind her, breathing down her neck. She felt the seconds ticking away like the throb of her pulse. The murmur of voices came from within; footsteps approached the door.

A sudden flare of Nightkeeper magic lit Sasha up, startling a gasp from her. She met Michael's eyes from his position on the other side of the door, saw his confusion. Then the stone surface beneath them gave a convulsive jerk, nearly flinging her off her feet. A deep-throated rumble sounded from the entrance tunnel, and a huge gout of dust spewed from the tunnel mouth.

Sasha's throat locked. "No," she whispered. She would have screamed, would have run to the tunnel mouth, but her warrior's talent locked her in place, and Lucius's hand fell on her shoulder, gripping tightly.

So she held her position, tears leaking down her cheeks as the door swung open. Iago's voice came clear as he boasted, "I made sure of it—put the 'port image into the kid's mind before I kicked him back to the others. He would've landed them right outside the tunnel mouth. From there, they would've walked right into the tripline."

Iago descended the three short steps, with the red-robes a few feet behind him. Michael attacked in silence, eyes lethal, tackling the Xibalban waist-high and driving him away from the door. Sasha leaped up and slammed the door on the red-robes, flipping the bar into place.

Michael and Iago struggled for possession of the library scroll. Michael landed a heavy punch with a meaty thud and Iago went limp, dazed. Roaring triumph, Michael grabbed the scroll and lunged to his feet. But before Sasha could race to join him, hard hands clamped on her and spun her around in a vicious choke hold. She gurgled and scraped at her captor's forearm, but the bloody furrows she created healed almost immediately.

Lucius! she thought. *Godsdamn* makol *just won't pick a side!* But behind the frustration, fear flared hard and hot. The emotion brought a kick of solstice magic, but the power stayed ill-defined. She couldn't call a shield or fireball, couldn't do anything useful. But she could and did feel the distant touch of Nightkeeper magic, coming from outside the mountain.

Relief was a hard, hot wash. At least some of the others were still alive—gods willing, all of them were.

The *makol* breathed against her neck. Holding her tightly, its skin and breath disconcertingly cool, the creature switched the choke hold for the sharp edge of its combat knife, digging it into her throat hard enough to bring blood.

"You're dead. You're all dead." Michael's eyes were those of the killer, but Sasha wasn't afraid. Instead, her heart leaped gladly and her blood raced with red-gold battle magic

"Take her." The *makol* handed off Sasha to two of the red-robes, one of whom dug an autopistol into her left kidney, prodding her around to face Iago. Michael was shoved around similarly, though he cursed and struggled despite the pistols.

Iago checked his watch, then the sky. "It's time. Fuck the crucifixes; get them over to the thrones."

In under a minute, Sasha found herself kneeling in front of the larger throne with a pistol to her head. Michael knelt beside her, blood running from a split lip earned in his struggles, eyes anguished when they met hers. She thought she saw a flash of silver, and whispered, "Use the *muk*."

"I can't. He's blocking it."

Damn.

Using a ceremonial knife made of cloudy gray stone, Iago cut himself deeply, digging until blood poured from his hands and tongue. The *makol* did the same with its combat knife. Eyes glowing green, all signs of Lucius banished, the demon stood opposite Michael and began an ancient chant—the transition spell that would call a *makol* from the lowest level of Xibalba. Meanwhile, Iago faced Sasha, unfurled the library scroll, and began reading from it.

When Iago paused and closed in on her, Sasha surged up, only to be slammed back down by the red-robes who held her still. She screamed as Iago sliced through her stretchy black combat shirt, then traced a line just below her ribs, where the eviscerating slash would allow her killer to pull her heart from her body in one yank. Hatred and anger wrapped around her; she leaned on them rather than letting the fear inside her.

Iago stepped back and continued to read from the library scroll as, beside him, Lucius read the *makol*-summoning spell, calling the soul of Moctezuma into Michael. Magic gathered, both dark and light, Nightkeeper and Xibalban. The magic, formerly directionless, began to take terrible shape. Images flashed across Sasha's inner eye: herself blank eyed and soulless, sitting in a featureless ten-by-ten cell, channeling information from the library into a voice-activated digital recorder; Michael, with his gorgeous bedroom eyes gone luminous green as he sat enthroned, his body under Moctezuma's control. She quailed inwardly, making a desperate grab for the magic; to her surprise, she felt a touch of *ch'ul* and caught a soft rustle. Glancing over as Iago recited the spell, she looked toward the planters only a few feet away. In them, maize and cacao plants undulated gently, though there was no breeze.

She breathed a prayer and sent them energy, having some thought of the plants bowing down to grab her red-robed captors. The maize and cacao responded, but the small amount of growth she managed to trigger wasn't going to do her any good.

Then Iago shouted the final words of the spell, raised his ceremonial knife, and advanced on Sasha, while the red-robes held her tightly.

The *makol*, too, advanced, knife raised. Only it didn't go for Michael. Still green eyed, still in *makol* form, it turned and buried its knife in Iago's chest. There was a moment of frozen shock as, grinning horribly, the *makol* said, "Compliments of the *Banol Kax*, human. My masters bid you remember who rules you in this war. They do not wish to lose Moctezuma's service in Mictlan. And they want to talk to you."

Iago went stark white, eyes rolling as he reeled back, grabbing at the knife. The *makol* closed in tighter, grabbed the haft, and started twisting and hacking. Blood sprayed a gory arc and Sasha screamed, as much in disbelief as in horror. Even as she did, though, she elbowed one of her captors in the gonads and dropped the other with a foot sweep. Bullets sprayed, but bounced harmlessly.

Michael, too, was moving. He took out his red-robes with a leg-sweep-punch combo, snagged one of the autopistols, and beckoned her. "Come on!"

Michael and Sasha broke for the thrones and took the high ground, leaping atop the stone seats and using the leverage to kick at the red-robes who tried to grab for them. Iago shouted something, his words lost to her beneath a rising buzz of magic. Sasha looked back, shocked that he was still alive.

"The spell has turned on him. He's becoming an *ajaw-makol*," Michael said. "He's already got the healing power. Soon, the only way to kill him will be to cut off his head, hack out his heart, and recite the banishing spell."

The red-robes opened fire, aiming low, trying to wound, not kill.

"Down!" Michael grabbed her and dragged her off the throne. He caught her against his strong, solid body and turned her toward the stone slab, shielding her, then fired off a quick burst with his captured autopistol, forcing the six remaining red-robes to take cover. Two were down already, not moving.

Sasha tried to feel grief, tried to find horror, and found only rage and emptiness. A need to stop the Xibalbans from doing to another what they had done to her, a drive to survive long enough to make a difference. In the end, this was the war.

Looking up at Michael, who was fierce and bloodied, she touched his cheek and said, "Can you call the *muk* now that we're not on the dais?"

His eyes flared, but he bowed his head, pressed his brow to hers. "I don't want to be the Other. Not ever again. It's a monster."

"Not a monster. A weapon. And it's your talent; it's not you." She cupped his jaw in her bloodied hands and stared into his eyes, willing him to hear her, believe her. "I was wrong about that—dead wrong. Whether or not all your kills were in battle, they were part of a larger war, on the orders of your king. That is the Nightkeeper way. It doesn't make you anything more than a mage who found his calling sooner than most of us. The magic is a tool; it's not you. Just like my magic isn't all me. I wield life but I think I've proven that doesn't make me an angel, right?"

Air escaped from him in a hiss, but she saw a spark in the depths of him—rage going to power. "Depends on your definition of 'angel,' babe." But there was such desperate need in him.

"I'm no angel," she said firmly. "And you're not a devil or a monster. Your talent is a tool from the gods, a weapon in the war. You're not any of those things. You're a man." She paused, searching inside herself for hesitation, for reservation, and finding none when she said, "You're *my* man."

He held very still for a long, breathless moment. Then he touched his lips to hers, a brief, fleeting press that promised more than a thousand words.

In a single move of deadly elegance, he flowed to his feet and moved away from their shallow concealment, stepping out into the cross fire of his enemies. His hair was slicked back close to his skull, his black combat clothes torn and tattered as they clung to his fighter's muscles. He spread his arms away from his body, indicating he was unarmed, or offering himself up as the sacrifice Iago had intended him to be. As he did, he called the *muk*. It gathered to him, clung to him, greasy and gray in her mind's eye.

The red-robes let loose, firing low, still trying to preserve their sacrificial victim. The bullets sped inward in a deadly hail, only to reverse outward when Michael let loose the Mictlan's power. It exploded from him in a thunderclap of gray death, taking the red-robes where they crouched, puffing them to dust in an instant.

It was over so quickly, there and gone in an instant, that Sasha blinked, tempted to think they had just left, or been 'ported away. But she saw the gray cast of death on Michael's skin, saw the dark grief and guilt of the man, the cold satisfaction of the killer within.

He turned back to her and offered his hand. She took it without hesitation and rose to stand next to him, leaning into him in mute reassurance. He stared down at her, eyes dark, but finally calm, as though he'd gone beyond himself, or maybe found himself. "This is who and what I am." His voice was a low rumble in his chest.

"This," she said firmly, "is war. It's justice." She took his hand, lifted his wrist, and pressed her lips to his marks. "Neither of us is perfect. Together, though, we balance each other out. And even if we didn't, I'd still want to be with you."

"Despite what I am."

"Because of *who* you are," she countered. "Now. Let's finish this."

His eyes went past her. Flattened. "Shit."

Sasha turned, her warrior's instincts firing a second too late. Not because of an attack, but because of what the lack of attack meant. Iago, badly battered by the *makol*, sagged against the larger throne, losing blood fast. But he was still alive, having survived the edges of the close-range *muk* blast by virtue of his healing powers . . . and the *makol* bond. His color was wrong, his eyes disoriented . . . but they flicked to luminous green and back again. When they went green, his face became more angular and power seemed to glow in a halo around him, as the emperor Moctezuma fought to come through to the earth.

As his eyes settled green, 'port magic rattled in the air.

"Stop him!" Sasha cried.

Roaring, Michael lunged for Iago. The Xibalban disappeared with a pop of displaced air, leaving Michael to slam into the throne, then pound it with a fist. "Gods *damn* it!"

Sasha reeled as near-prescience gripped her. Moctezuma had come to earth. And he'd possessed the strongest of the Xibalban magi, leaving the Nightkeepers with . . . what? They had nothing, and the solstice threatened to pass without their gaining the one thing they needed most: the Prophet.

At the thought, she moved around the throne, in search of their former ally . . . who might just manage to become an ally once again. "Lucius?" she called, cursing softly when she saw his feet stretched out behind one of the planters, blood splashed on the stones. Then she rounded the planter. And cursed aloud. "Michael! Come quick."

He came around the corner, his only reaction a hitch

in his stride when he saw what Iago had done to the
makol. Lucius's head had been all but severed from
his body, and his heart hung out of his chest cavity by a
thread. His eyes were closed, but his chest still moved in
a gruesome, bubbling parody of life, held by the *makol*'s
healing magic.

Sasha dropped down beside him, heedless of the
blood that soaked through her pants. "He's alive. Sort
of." She felt the *makol*'s dark magic fluctuate, heard Lucius's song cut in and out. "Iago must have said the spell.
He didn't get the head and heart all the way, though."
But the *makol* wasn't healing; he was merely existing,
his eyes flicking from hazel to green and back again.

Sasha met Michael's eyes over the laboring near-
corpse. Feeling the hard practicality of the warrior she
had become, she said, "Get the library scroll. Let's not
waste the sacrifice."

"Are you sure? He's not a magic user."

She grinned fiercely up at him. "Maybe not. But the
makol is."

Michael's expression went blank, then fired with excitement as he went for the scroll, snagging it off the
floor, where it had fallen during the melee. "*Fuck*. I can't
read it. You?"

She glanced at the glyphs, but she shook her head.
"That's beyond what Ambrose taught me. And we can't
risk my screwing it up." She looked toward the rubble-
filled tunnel. "We have to get the others in here."

Michael's eyes flashed acknowledgment, but he
turned up a hand in question. "Can you get the 'port
image to Strike through the bloodline link?"

"Not clearly enough." She shook her head. "Maybe
Rabbit . . ." He'd sent her his cry for help from the
pueblo, using the connection they'd forged when he'd
been inside her mind. But when she searched inwardly
for a hint of that connection she found nothing. "I think

it only goes one way. How about shield magic? Could you use it to clear the tunnel somehow?"

Eyes dark with frustration, he shook his head. "I don't think so. Damn it."

"Break the mountain," said a faint whisper.

For a second, she thought the words were inside her head. Then she realized they'd come from behind her. She looked down to find Lucius conscious, squinting up at her. The flesh at his throat had knitted somewhat. His abdominal cavity gaped open, but as she watched, his heart drew back into place slowly, looking sad and misshapen. Yet his eyes were fixed on her, gone hazel, though he shuddered with the effort of keeping them that way. The entire effect was macabre in the extreme.

"This is Paxil Mountain," he whispered. "Break it." His eyes stopped flickering, started to dull.

Michael's and Sasha's eyes went to the planters set on either side of the thrones. Maize and cacao. Was it possible?

"The gods split Paxil Mountain to release the seeds to mankind," she said. "But we're not gods."

"Maybe not." Michael took her hand, twining their fingers together. "But we're what's left." He lifted her hand. Pressed a kiss to her knuckles. "And I'm not through fighting. Not for you, and not for justice."

Sasha's power kicked at his words, at the quiet certainty in them. She felt the *muk* resonating from him, reaching into her. For the first time, she didn't push the sensation away, but rather welcomed it, welcomed him. Aware of the solstice magic raging around them, within them, she turned to face him. "I can't do this alone. Iago said we could create incredible power together."

"We do," Michael said softly. "We can." He paused, and his voice roughened. "You've been everything I need and want, even when I was too caught up in myself to realize it."

Her heart shuddered and went still in her chest. She saw the truth in his eyes, felt it in his touch and his energy. And for the first time, she wasn't looking at Michael, or the Other, or the Mictlan. She saw all of them in him, saw them as a single man, the united whole she'd fallen for. The real Michael didn't come from an absence of darkness, she realized with sudden paralytic comprehension. He came from balance. He was a chameleon himself, shifting among aspects of himself and his magic, but the core remained. The man remained.

"I kept telling myself you weren't real, that you were a fantasy straight out of one of Ambrose's stories. Which you are. But you're also real."

He leaned down and she reached up, in that stilled moment of time, and she heard her own music, heard his, then heard the two twine together, backbeat and chords blending to form a fully realized song. And, as the solstice slid to its peak, their magics combined, *muk to ch'ul.*

And the world around them started to shake.

Magic poured through Michael, piercing every aspect of him: light and dark, love and revenge, murder and justice. The coming of the three-year countdown fired through him, smashing his hard-won barriers to dust and opening him to all of his dissociated pieces at once. But where before that had been one of his greatest fears—the loss of control, the loss of himself—now he gave himself up to it.

He was the Other, with all the monster's trained strategy, killer instinct, and love of the hunt. He was Michael, brave enough to take any hand-to-hand challenge, yet coward enough to turn away from emotional pain. He was the Nightkeeper, with a mage's fighting drive and determination to make things right; he was the human he'd been raised as, not sure it was possible to make things right. He was the mate who'd wanted Sasha too much to heed the warnings, the lover who hadn't known what to do with her when he got her. And over it all, as the *muk* flowed through him, became him, he was the Mictlan, the wielder of an ancient magic that blended both dark and light, making a whole that was so much stronger than its parts.

Instead of fragmenting him further, the magic made him complete. His *muk* powers and Sasha's *ch'ul* magic combined in a flare of light and dark, not canceling each other out or combusting at all, but rather complementing each other, creating a balance out of the imbalance that had plagued him for so long. His human and mage aspects blended with each other, with the killer, and he became the Mictlan. The man he was supposed to have been all along, anchored by the love of the woman he'd fought for, almost too late.

Power flowed from him to her and back again, forming a feedback loop that turned the *muk* from greasy gray to pure silver, like liquid mercury running in his veins.

Aware of the trembling roar that had built around them—not volcanic, but akin to it—he changed the angle of the kiss, deepening it and sending both of them into the sex magic that had bound them from the first. He was the Mictlan and the lover. She was the *ch'ulel* and the hot warrior princess who, incredibly, loved him.

He was aware of movement curling around them as the plants grew taller and broader, seeking the walls of the chamber. The air moistened and warmed, and, incredibly, a bright light kindled above them, warming them as though the sun shone inside. He smelled green, leafy things, and felt the ground soften beneath him.

The kiss spun on, bringing heat and magic, the energies coiling together as he and Sasha embraced. Hotter and hotter it whirled, coiling into a knot of energy that gained its own momentum, started moving faster and faster, spinning up to a peak. They broke the kiss and looked at each other; he saw love in her eyes, and the forgiveness he'd sought without knowing he was seeking it.

"I love you," he said simply.

"And I you."

Triggered by the affirmation, the energy crested and broke, climaxing away from them in a tidal wave of pleasure and pressure, of life and growth and mad, pure power. The maize and cacao, grown to epic proportions, strained at the cavern, thrusting outward, seeking the sky.

A horrendous rending crack split the air, and the mountain shuddered and began to tear. Rocks rained down from above, but were caught by twining leaves and vines, a cushioning bower that protected Sasha and Michael and the dying man who would soon be their sacrificial victim. The plants shuddered with power, the volcano with protest.

The magic crested and ebbed as Michael and Sasha clung to each other, hearts pounding in unison. When the power cleared and settled, when everything settled, there was a huge, gaping crack in the side of Paxil Mountain, lined with a carpet of leafy greenery he suspected would prove to be maize and cacao, growing from the split out into the world.

The night beyond was dark, the air moist with highland vapor. Within moments, though, the night gave way to the warm glow of a rainbow fireball held by a blond Valkyrie, who sat astride a giant hawk.

Within minutes, Anna stood over her onetime friend, onetime student, onetime slave. Tears ran down her cheeks as she read from the Prophet's scroll.

Sasha sat at his head, keeping Lucius alive as best

she could. Jade sat on one side of him, holding his hand, deadly pale, her eyes intent on the rise and fall of his chest, which had closed over, but just barely. She gripped Michael's hand, not just for the power, but for support, and because part of her wasn't yet ready to believe that they'd finally found their way to each other. But even she couldn't have imagined something like what had just happened—they'd broken a *mountain* together.

More, he loved her. And she loved him. That wasn't a story or a dream; it was real. And even though his status as the Mictlan meant he could never form the *jun tan* with her, she knew they had their own form of commitment, one to the other. They were bound, even without the words or the symbols. And surprisingly, she didn't need more than that. She simply needed *him*.

Anna broke off reading the spell, looking down at Lucius with deep concern. "We're losing both of them."

Sasha couldn't argue that; she could feel it in the *ch'ul* connection, the faintness of his song. "I'm giving him all I can pull through the blood-link." But then she remembered what Jox had said once when they'd been discussing her talent over seedlings and cow manure: that the *ch'ulel* power might not work best through blood. That sometimes talents were sparked by love. "I think," she began, not sure how to say it, "I think we need to go deeper than the blood-magic in order to conquer death." It wasn't until she'd said the words that she realized she was smack in the middle of her own prophecy. She faltered, felt Michael's grip tighten, and steadied herself. "I need you all to open yourself to love, or at least respect, for Lucius. Forgiveness. He needs . . . we need to not just heal him, but give him a reason to stay."

Strike's expression clouded, but at pleading looks from Anna and Jade, he nodded reluctantly. "Whatever he needs, we'll do. He's part of this war now. One of us."

The words held the power of a vow, rippling away from the small group in a wash of magic.

The magi linked palm-to-palm, not in blood but in support. With each member added to the circle, Sasha felt an added kick of power, a notch of life pouring through her. Or not life, she realized now. Love. Acceptance.

As they linked themselves, not with blood but with the bonds of friends, lovers, and teammates, the solstice peak began to fade, the window of opportunity to close.

"Work fast," Michael added under his breath.

Anna once again began to read from the librarian's scroll.

Sasha fed the life energy toward Lucius's song, opening herself to the stranger who'd saved her before she'd even known his name, marking her palm and helping her defeat Iago's drugs so she'd be ready to run when the time came. *I owe you one.*

Still, though, it wasn't enough. The connection fluctuated. Faded. "Rabbit. I need you to go into his mind and see if you can find him."

The teen started in surprise, but then nodded, lips firming. "I'll need to cut—"

"No. No blood. Love him. Or if you can't do that, at least respect him for what he's fought against. Anchor him here, so the *makol* goes but he doesn't."

"That I can do." Pulling away from the hands on either side of him, trusting that the circle would re-form at his back, Rabbit leaned forward and pressed his palms to Lucius's chest, above the place where his heart had been ripped out and put back in, the place where a *makol*'s power began and ended.

Then, bearing down, the Nightkeepers began to pray to the gods that couldn't hear them, and to the ancestors who could.

*   *   *

Lucius was lost inside his own head. He couldn't find the sight centers, couldn't find his hiding spot as the librarian's spell echoed around him and the *makol*'s furious power sought to drive him from his own skull, sought to fling him into the magic.

On one level, he gloried in the ancient syllables, in the power he felt gathering in him, changing him. But at the same time he feared the spell, and the power, because he knew something the others didn't: that this had been the plan all along. The *Banol Kax* didn't want the Xibalbans to have the library any more than they wanted the Nightkeepers to gain the power. They wanted it for themselves, wanted it removed from the earth permanently.

He tried to scream the knowledge, tried to warn the magi who gathered around him, labored over him, trying to feed him power that he couldn't find.

But he had to find it. He couldn't let the *makol* win, couldn't let the creature reawaken wielding even more power than it had before. The Nightkeepers thought the spell would automatically take both souls, and sought to keep Lucius with them. They didn't realize the *makol* had exactly the same thought in reverse, and it had far more magic at its disposal.

Quitting? a voice said within him—not the *makol* or one of the magi, but that of his father, his brothers, everyone who had ever called him a pussy, a wimp, a loser. A geek. *Go ahead*, they said in unison, *be a loser*.

"No, godsdamn it!" Lucius shouted, raging at the darkness around him, at the *makol*'s black soul. "No!"

"Lucius!" called a voice, one he recognized, one that came from his present, not his past.

"Rabbit?"

"This way. Follow my voice."

And suddenly, Lucius's own mind took shape around him once more. The *makol* roared denial as his soul slipped from its unknowing confinement. Power wrapped around Lucius, buoyed him up, and he felt the touches of more minds all calling him back, calling him home, one stronger than all the others, not because of sexual love, but because of friendship, and a blood-debt owed.

He opened his eyes and locked his gaze on the woman who was reading the spell, the one who wore a mark that complemented his own. He reached out to her and they clasped hands. And, as if seeming to know what he needed from her, Anna said, "I call upon you to discharge your debt to me by kicking that *makol*'s ass straight to hell."

And though Lucius was nothing more than human, the slave bond he'd formed with Anna was magic; the marks were magic. In response to her invocation, they flared to life, binding him to her, and through her to the other magi. That connection, that bond of unity, roared through him in a screaming tidal wave of red and gold, heat and trust.

Cizin roared and dug claws into his brain. "Get out!" Lucius shouted, not caring about the niceties or the spell words, only that this demon got out of his head for good. He tore at the claws, pushed at the writhing thing within his own soul. The magic of the Prophet's spell peaked. A whirling vortex opened up, spearing through Lucius's skull. Or not his skull, he realized moments later when the wind slapped at him. The funnel was real, a tornado that reached through the jagged tear in the mountainside. It tugged at him, threatened to suck them all up. Arching against the wind, against the pull, he leaned on the joined magics of the magi and shouted aloud, "Gods take it!"

There was a ripping, tearing sound, and a ghostly image of his own body tore free, this one with fangs and claws and glowing green eyes. It pinwheeled its arms and legs as it was lifted away from him, hung suspended above him long enough for Lucius to look into its luminous green eyes and see the evil inside himself, the evil that had called the creature to him in the first place.

The *makol* screamed one last time, the sound growing thin as its image wavered and dissolved. Then it was gone. The tornado was gone. Lucius fell blessedly unconscious. Overloaded. But finally alone inside his own skull.

Skywatch

When strike zapped them all home, Michael sagged when his feet hit the floor, might've gone down if it hadn't been for the bodies on either side of him, Rabbit on his right, Sasha his left. The three of them propped one another up for a moment, leaning on one another. Teammates.

Rabbit was the first to peel himself away, his eyes fixed past the others to the archway leading to the pool deck, where Myrinne stood, eyes faintly uncertain. "You're here!" he said, crossing to her and stopping a couple of paces away. "How did you . . . When . . ."

The uncertainty faded a little, turning to warmth. "I hopped a plane and called Jox from the airport. I . . ." She faltered, realizing that she and Rabbit had an audience, but then seemed to realize he needed the public apology. Or maybe she needed to give it. Either way, she continued, "I didn't mean any of what I said. I was scared, I think. And maybe you were getting some backlash I should've unloaded on Mistress Truth, but couldn't because she was already dead." Her voice went soft. "I came to tell you I'm sorry. I don't want to be with anyone but you."

"I couldn't get rid of the hellmark," he said, voice cracking.

She closed the distance between them, stopping only

so he'd have to cover the last six inches or so. "Okay. We'll deal with it. Together."

At that, the fight seemed to go out of him. He let his head drop forward, let his forehead rest on hers. "You're killing me, babe."

"I'm sorry." Her voice was barely audible to the others now, and the magi and *winikin* turned away, giving the younger generation their privacy as they slipped out through the poolside doors and headed for their cottage.

For a change, not even Strike glared after them. Not that Michael was really paying much attention to his king, or to any of the others. His entire focus was on the woman whose hand remained in his, the one looking up at him with the glittering brown eyes he knew he would see in his mind's eye from now on, every time he thought of love. Of happiness.

Sasha loved him. He took the knowledge and tucked it beside his heart, where it warmed him from the inside out, chasing away the last dregs of the darkness. She had saved him. She was life; he was death. They matched, they balanced, whether the gods had intended it or not, whether they were destined mates or not. Fuck destiny; she was his, he thought, tightening his grip on her.

"Michael?" she said, turning his name into a question.

"It's okay," he said, though he wasn't really sure that it was. He'd failed to cleanse his soul, failed to discharge his duty. Which meant no *jun tan*, no mate. Was it fair to ask her to buy into that?

Too late, logic and reason said. *She already has.* And so had he. But at the same time, it was up to him to make it as right as he possibly could.

"Food," a new voice intruded. "Rest. Now." It was Tomas, dividing his glare equally between Michael and Sasha, probably because Jox had his hands full with Strike, Leah, and Rabbit.

Before, Michael would've given him shit. Now, he simply grinned and said, "Pancakes and Canadian bacon? Lots of coffee?"

The *winikin* scowled, but there was a gleam in his eye. "For one or two?"

"Two," Michael said firmly. "Definitely two." Now he had a feeling the gleam was in his own eyes, coming to life when he looked down at Sasha and found a heat in her expression to match his own. "We'll be in her suite. I like the way the herbs make the air smell."

Laughing, Sasha rolled her eyes. "Bull. You're just angling for more hot chocolate."

"Depends on whether by 'hot chocolate' you mean something else." He waggled his eyebrows suggestively, making Tomas groan.

"You're never going to change, are you?" the *winikin* demanded.

But it was Sasha who answered: "He's changed as much as he needs to. Anything more and he wouldn't be the man I love."

And that, Michael realized as the warmth unfurled beside his heart and surrounded his bruised, battered soul, was exactly what he'd needed to hear.

CHAPTER TWENTY-FOUR

December 26
Two years, three hundred and sixty days until the end

The five days after the solstice passed in a blur for Sasha, as the magi pitched in to prepare for the *wayeb* days, the five days between the end of the solar calendar of one year and the beginning of the next. Those days, which weren't even named in the calendar of the Maya, were considered supremely unlucky . . . or days of great change, depending on who was doing the proselytizing.

Because of that, and because of the jaguar bloodline's propensity to play with the rules, Strike had declared that those five days would be one big par-tay. The celebration would begin with Ambrose's funeral, which seemed fitting. Sasha and Jox had put their heads together and come up with a hell of a menu for the five-day festival. For the purpose, Jox had flown in the necessary ingredients. Since the Nightkeepers' overall desire for *pulque* was at a definite low point, the *winikin* had also brought in several other types of alcoholic ceremonial drinks. In addition, Sasha had fermented the last of her cacao seeds, and was processing the slimy mess into the hot chocolate she'd experimented on before . . . and continued to experiment on, using Michael as her eminently willing guinea pig for the various sauces and sweets.

As the sun dipped toward the horizon on the first *wayeb* day, the magi donned their ceremonial robes and knives and gathered together in the ash-shadow courtyard beneath the ceiba tree as Rabbit moved around, lighting the ceremonial torches using his pyro talent. Sasha leaned into the steady warmth of Michael, who stood at her side as the magi and *winikin* formed parallel lines through which the king and queen would formally march to begin the *wayeb* festival.

"I'm glad you made it back in time," she said in a totally nonsubtle probe.

His lips curved as he looked down at her. He squeezed her fingers where he'd tucked them in the crook of his arm, as though he'd needed the contact as much as she needed to touch him. "Wouldn't have missed it." But he didn't explain where he'd gone the night before, leaving the compound with little more than a kiss and a passable Terminator impression of "I'll be back."

She told herself the absence wouldn't have bothered her in the slightest if it hadn't been for the slightly off vibes she'd been getting from him the past couple of days. Their vibe in the bedroom wasn't in question—he was an ardent and inspired lover, and she took full advantage of his practiced skills, while polishing her own. Better yet was when she drove him beyond practice to the point of action-reaction, when he lost himself in the moment and let himself go, dragging her along with him into the abyss that was sensation and heat, and nothing of reality. And if, in those moments, some of the darkness seeped from him into her, that was as it should be. She helped him stay balanced; he kept her from becoming too settled, made things exciting. As Ada had told her so long ago, she'd found a man who challenged her, kept her guessing.

Most of the time he was loving and attentive, dark and edgy, showing her glimpses of the different men he'd been, all combining into the man she'd fallen for. Yet now and then there was something else, something that tempted her to worry. It was in his brief hesitation when she spoke of the future. He'd told her he loved her, and she had no reason to disbelieve, but she remained wary, guided by that part of her that had yearned before, been wrong before. And then he'd disappeared. He'd come back, yes, but still. It was tough not to fall right back into old patterns, hard as she tried to avoid them.

She told herself it didn't matter, that she'd decided to take him, to love him, even knowing that he wasn't able to commit to the long term. More, she lectured herself, it wasn't fair to make that decision and then blame him for being who she'd known he was.

Deliberately shoving aside the worry, she looked down the double line. The *winikin* stood together on one side, except for Jox, who was at the head of the whole pattern, with his back to the big tree. The other magi stood on the other side, along with Myrinne and a badly debilitated Lucius, who'd been heard joking that pretty soon the humans were going to outnumber the magi at Skywatch. At least, Sasha thought it was a joke.

Lucius was recovering from his ordeal, though slowly. He'd been deeply scarred by his captivity, more so than Sasha, because he had no healing magic of his own, and the Prophet's bond didn't allow Rabbit to get in there and help. More, he'd so far proven unable to form the conduit that was supposed to allow the Prophet access to the library. The theory was that there was a magical logjam going on, since the spell called for an empty body, and his was still inhabited by, well, *him*. Jade and

Anna were convinced he could learn to call the conduit himself, but first he needed to recover fully.

He mostly kept to himself, sitting atop the walls of the ball court, staring into the distance. But the few times Sasha had arranged to bump into him, she'd felt health in his *ch'ul* song, and the beginnings of acceptance.

That was all she could feel these days—her healing powers seemed to have burned out with the effort of bringing Lucius back from the brink. Similarly, Rabbit's mental powers had become seriously blunted. He could perform traditional mind-bends, but he couldn't read as deeply as he could before. Otherwise, the younger mage seemed to be doing okay; he and Myrinne were in the middle of a nauseating honeymoon period the rest were tolerating solely because it'd been generally agreed that they'd rather have Rabbit acting besotted than sulking and burning stuff down.

The magi seemed to have similarly leveled off after the chaos of the past couple of months. Brandt and Patience acted fine in public, though there was no telling what was going on behind the scenes. Nate and Alexis were solid, and Sven was . . . Sven. Jade was keeping to herself, as was Anna, who hadn't returned to Austin immediately after the solstice, which, according to Jox, was very unusual indeed. Not that the *winikin* was gossiping, he'd assured Sasha as they'd put the calendar cakes into the ovens. He was simply remarking. But she'd gotten the impression he was hoping she would talk to Anna about it. Maybe she would, too. It might take them time to decide what sort of relationship they would have— sisters? friends? something else?—but Sasha wasn't leaving Skywatch anytime soon. They had time. Some, anyway.

"Here they come," Michael said, breaking into her thoughts.

Then there was a stir of movement at the edge of the pool patio, and Strike and Leah appeared, walking together in their bloodred ceremonial robes, hands linked.

Strike was wearing his king face, but beneath that capable shell, Sasha saw love. Simply love, the beginning and ending of their magic, their lives. And the sight of it, the knowledge of it, smoothed the edges of her soul and had her leaning into Michael, the man she loved.

He brushed a kiss across her temple as the king and queen passed and took their places facing each other, while Jox presented them with the first sacrificial offering of the *wayeb* days: a bowl of maize seeds, several from each of the ears that had been passed through the blood-smoke of the magi during Sasha's bloodline ceremony. When Strike accepted the bowl, Sasha felt a small pinch beneath her heart, knowing that the seeds would be burned, symbolically returning the blood and flesh of the magi to the gods.

Instead, Strike turned and beckoned to her. "Sasha? Come here, please."

Frowning, she moved up and joined them, her heavy black robes swirling around her ankles. "Yes?"

He handed her the bowl. "Bless them, please. And then let them grow."

The pinch smoothed out and she smiled. Touching the hopeful little seeds, she felt the magic in them, the life. She sent them a song and felt them respond. Then, acting on instinct, or *ch'ul*, or maybe just a mad impulse, she swung her arm and sent the seeds flying in a glittering arc, out past the torches to the ash-shadowed courtyard. There was a ripple of laughter from the magi, a shimmer of magic from beyond the torchlight. And she knew that in the morning, there would be life in a spot that for so long had represented only death.

"Nice," Michael said when she returned to his side. "That was very nice."

Then it was time for round two of the day's ceremonies, the more somber of the two. Ambrose's funeral.

"You ready for this?" Michael asked as Jox started herding everyone toward the ball court, where they'd set up the funeral pyre so it would be downwind of the *wayeb* feast. After the fire burned itself out, the ashes would be allowed to fly on the canyon winds, as Ambrose had requested, back in another lifetime.

"As ready as I'll ever be." And, as she reached the traditional wooden structure upon which they'd placed Ambrose's wrapped body, head and all, she realized she *was* ready. She'd come to terms with Ambrose and the ways he'd failed her, the ways they'd failed each other. He had given up his own life to save hers, on his queen's orders, on her mother's orders.

The sun kissed the horizon, turning the sky to a bloody smear that warned of impending storms. The light cast strange shadows as she picked up the *pulque*-laced torch she'd prepared earlier in the day, sealing it with both chocolate and her own blood. She held it out to Rabbit, who stood with the others in a loose circle around the pyre and its wrapped bone bundle. "Will you do the honors?"

He nodded, held his hands cupped together, and whispered, "*Kaak*." Fire. A flame kindled in his palms, soft and kind, not the fireball of war. He held the spark to her torch, spoke another word, and sent the flames dancing across the alcohol-soaked brand. Then he stood beside her as she touched the torch to the pyre, and urged the flames to make it quick and do it right. She knew he'd done the same for his own father. Knew Ambrose would approve.

The others moved up around her, standing in silent support as she fulfilled a promise that had started out causing trouble and ended up showing her the way to her family, to the man she loved, whether by chance or destiny or, most likely, a combination of the two.

In losing her father she had found her family. And now Ambrose had come home. Finally. "Gods speed you to your rest," she said softly, thinking for a moment that she could see his face in the flames. "And thank you. For everything."

The bone bundle caught and flared, and the heat intensified, driving them away from a pyre that had become a bonfire. She thought Ambrose would've enjoyed that too.

"Hey." Michael touched her arm. "You good?"

"Yeah." She turned to him, smiled up at him, and felt a weight lift off her soul. "Yeah, I am." But she faltered a little when she saw the look in his eyes, the hint of reservation, of worry. "Michael, what's going on?"

He took a deep breath, tried for a smile and missed. "I know this probably isn't the right time or place to do this," he began.

Her heart took a nosedive, and all the old insecurities rose up, threatened to swamp her. "If you're dumping me, you might want to rethink. Third-degree burns on your ass won't be much fun." She tried to make it sound like a joke. Failed.

"I'm not dumping you." He sounded exasperated rather than annoyed. Then he hitched up a pant leg and dropped to one knee in front of her.

She looked down at him, at the firelight illuminating one side of his face, the darkness touching the other, and her heart stopped, simply stopped in her chest. "Michael?"

The others had gone very quiet around them; the only sound was that of Ambrose's funeral pyre. Then Michael reached into a pocket and came up with a small velvet box. Held it out to her. "I can't give you the *jun tan*, but I want—I need—you to wear something of mine; I want to know that you're mine, from this point forward.

So we'll do it the newfangled way." He paused. Took a breath. "Sasha Ledbetter, will you marry me?"

It was the moment her younger self had dreamed of. And her more mature, grounded self fumbled the shit out of it. "I don't . . . I mean, I didn't think . . . Oh, hell." She blew out a breath. Made herself stop babbling. "Yes."

His eyes glinted. "Was that a yes, you'll marry me, or are you still stuttering?"

She laughed. "A little of both?" She felt the smile start, felt warmth and heat and love expanding inside her chest, growing out beyond the bounds of her body as her eyes filled with tears. "Yes. Of course I'll marry you. I love you. Every piece of you."

"And I love you," he said. And, as the bonfire showered sparks behind them, she realized he'd been wrong about one thing: It was the perfect time and place for them, for the ceremonies of life to counter those of death.

He rose then, and flipped open the box, which held a fat, princess-cut diamond in the most exquisitely traditional of settings. Tradition for a man who was anything but traditional, she thought. It should've jarred. Instead, it fit perfectly. As did the ring.

"I love you," he said again, the words coming easily, from his heart. "I can't promise you the *jun tan* or a quiet life, but I can promise you that nobody will ever love you as much as I do. Nobody will ever need you the way I do."

The words were raw and honest. And she answered in kind, touching her lips to his before she said, "Nobody's ever challenged me the way you do, and I know I've never loved anyone the way I do you. Just love me; that's all I ask. We'll figure out the rest as we go along. Deal?"

He smiled against her lips. "Deal."

They kissed to a round of applause from the assembled group. And when they parted, something danced across Sasha's nape. A coyote howl lifted from the near distance, the wild music rising to the sky. Eyes drawn by something—maybe magic, maybe instinct, maybe just a wish—Sasha looked through the fire to the empty ball court beyond the pyre. There, in the firelight, stood a tall, lanky man with a tired face, a long gray ponytail, and a pronounced stoop to his shoulders, as though he'd spent many years trying to look smaller than he was, trying to blend into a life he hadn't chosen.

"Ambrose," Sasha said, tears welling up to spill over and track down her cheeks. She lifted her hand in a wave, saw her new diamond glint in the firelight. "Thank you."

The spirit—ghost?—lifted a hand, returning the wave. The fire distorted the air between them, but she could swear she saw a smile on the spirit's face, and no hint of madness in its eyes. For a moment, she imagined he looked like the man she'd glimpsed on his good days, in the gaps between obsessions. And in that moment, she imagined that all was forgiven between them both.

It is, she heard in the crackle of the fire, in a multitonal voice that shouldn't have existed outside of the barrier. Michael stiffened at her side, letting her know he'd heard it, too. Then the spirit's form wavered. And disappeared.

"What did he mean by that?" he asked quietly.

"It means all is forgiven." She lifted their joined hands to her cheek, rested her face on his strength. "It means we go on from here and do the best we can do."

"That I can manage." He gathered her close, pressing her against his broad chest and rocking her gently as the others ringed the bonfire once again.

Strike and Leah, Nate and Alexis, and Rabbit and

Myrinne paired off, the mated couples wrapping together while the other magi and the *winikin* stood apart and alone. They watched the fire burn down, even knowing that Ambrose's spirit had passed onward. Sasha suspected each of them saw something slightly different in the flames—scenes of the past, of futures near and far.

She had fulfilled three-quarters of the prophecy: She'd become a daughter of the sky, a *ch'ulel*; She'd conquered death, bringing Rabbit, Michael, and Lucius back from the brink; and she'd defied love—or at least what she'd thought she'd known about what she wanted when it came to falling in love—by claiming Michael for her own despite all the reasons they made no sense together. As for the lost son . . . well, time would tell.

The next six months would be critical. They needed to call the Triad, deal with Moctezuma, and figure out where the *Banol Kax* would strike next. Each of those things seemed an insurmountable obstacle in isolation. In sum, they could be seen only as impossible. Yet rationality said that a dozen magi wouldn't be enough to save the world when the prophecies spoke of hundreds. So far they might not be kicking ass, but they were holding their own. Over the next few months, the next three years, they would continue to do the same.

"It's not going to be easy," Sasha whispered, pushing slightly away from Michael's chest so she could see the firelight play on his face. "The next few years, I mean."

"No, it's not. But whatever happens, we're in it together." He tapped the ring, the symbol he'd known she needed, and had come to need himself. "That's a promise."

She smiled up at him, touched her lips to his. "I like the sound of that."

The next three years—and the future beyond—were wreathed in shadows and darkness. But she had a family now, and a lover. A fiancé. There was strength in that, and power. And, in the beginning and the end, there was love. And it was in that love she wrapped herself as stars prickled in the sky and the fire burned low, leaving the Nightkeepers in gathering darkness, standing together as a team, as a family.

Her family.

Read on for a sneak peek at the next book
in the Final Prophecy series
by Jessica Andersen,

DEMONKEEPERS

Coming from Signet Eclipse in April 2010.

Skywatch

It was almost full dark when Strike materialized himself and Jade beneath the ceiba tree. The mansion was only dimly lit, making it seem far away, while the stygian silhouette of the training hall loomed very near. But despite the darkness, Jade appreciated the king's tact; the absolute last thing she wanted to do was see the others. She wasn't sure she could handle doing the *Hi, how have you been* routine right now, as she'd been gone nearly ten weeks, taking a crash course in ancient Mayan glyphs and language . . . and getting some distance.

Yeah, she'd needed the miles. At that, she'd still be far from Skywatch if it hadn't been for Strike's message. She wasn't sure which was worse: the secondhand booty call, or the fact that she'd volunteered for it. *It's the right thing to do*, she reminded herself. *Lucius needs to trigger the Prophet's powers, and he's not getting it done on his own. This isn't about us; it's about the magic.* More, it was her chance to be on the front lines for a change.

"Okay," she said under her breath. "Here goes everything."

But when she headed for the mansion, thinking to sneak in through a side door, Strike shot out a long arm and aimed her in the other direction. "He moved into one of the cottages a couple of months ago. Said the mansion made him feel claustrophobic after being trapped inside his own head for so long."

"Oh." She tried not to let that rattle her, even though when she'd pictured what was going to happen, she'd always envisioned being in the safely familiar three-room suite a few doors down from her own. *Not a big deal*, she told herself. *It's just a change of scenery.* Experience, both as a woman and as a therapist, had taught her that people didn't fundamentally change; only peripherals did. Human, Nightkeeper—it didn't matter. Some people were good, some bad, most a mixture of the two. She knew Lucius, trusted him. Wasn't scared of him. She could do this.

"Problem?" Strike asked, the darkness making his voice seem to come from the air around them rather than from the man himself.

Shaking off the thought—and the quiver of nerves it brought—she said, "Of course not. Which cottage?" There were thirteen of them in two rows of six, with lucky thirteen on the far end, off by itself.

"The very last one; you'll see the lights. Nate and Alexis are spending the night in the mansion. With Rabbit and Myrinne at school, you'll have privacy." He pressed something into her hand. "Take this."

Feeling the outlines of one of the earpiece–throat mike combos the warriors used during ops, she didn't ask why. "Who's going to be on the other end?" Even knowing that the mike would only transmit if she keyed it on, she couldn't help picturing a voyeuristic tableau in the great room.

"Either me or Jox. Unless you'd prefer Leah."

The king was doing his best, she realized, to maintain the illusion of privacy while keeping her safe, letting her know the warriors stood ready to come to her defense if the sex magic went awry and Lucius's dark tendencies once again drew the attention of the *Banol Kax*, or even opened him up once again to *makol* possession. Which had been just one of the numerous daunting possibilities that had been thrown around, only to be set aside because the Nightkeepers were running out of options.

"Whatever you think is best," Jade said, just barely managing not to tack on "sire" at the end. *I'm not following orders this time. This was my idea. My choice.* Raising her chin, she said, "Don't worry about me. I know Lucius."

The king's answer was slow in coming. "You know, becoming the Prophet has . . . changed him."

Anna had said something along those same lines earlier, when Jade let her know the booty call had come through on schedule. Now, as then, Jade waved off the concern. "He's not the Prophet yet. If he were, you wouldn't need me. Would you?"

Strike didn't have an answer for that one, and that fact pinched somewhere in the region of her heart. With the information in the archive virtually exhausted, her value as a librarian was almost nil. Given her inability to tap her scribe's talent, she didn't bring much in the way of a unique skill set to the Nightkeepers . . . except in the matter at hand. She and Lucius had a history, and she was the only female mage who remained yet unmated. More, in the wake of her and Michael's failed affair, she'd proven that she could be sexually involved with a man and not lose her heart. She and Lucius ought to be able to return to the friends-with-benefits arrangement they'd had previously, and use the generated sex magic to trigger the Prophet's powers.

That was the theory, anyway.

Realizing that Strike was waiting for her to make her move, she inhaled to settle a sudden flutter of nerves, and said, "Okay. Wish me luck."

She halfway expected him to come back with something about getting lucky. Instead, he said, "Remember, you can bail at any point. I wouldn't have called you today if you hadn't volunteered, and if I didn't think this might be our answer. Still, I want you to promise me that you'll stop if it doesn't feel right."

Pulling back in surprise, she glanced at his dark silhouette. "But the writs say—"

"Fuck the writs," he interrupted. "They might be a good rule of thumb, but they're not perfect by a long shot, and over the past couple of years we've certainly proved that they're not immutable. So now I'm telling you—hell, I'm *ordering* you—to make your own decision on this one. Take me and the others out of it. This is between you and Lucius."

Jade drew breath to *Whatever you say, sire* him, but then stopped herself, thought a moment, and said, "With all due respect, that's bullshit. There's no way I can possibly take out all the other variables. I'm here right now because we're out of other options. If we don't get our hands on the library soon, we might not even make it to 2012, and we sure as shit won't have enough firepower to defend the barrier. So you don't get to tell me to take all that out of the equation, just so you can feel better about what I'm about to do. If it doesn't bother me, then it shouldn't bother you. And if it does, that's not my problem."

There was a moment of startled silence; then Strike said, "Huh."

Jade didn't know if that meant he was offended, taken

aback, or what, but told herself she didn't care. "What? You didn't know I have a spine?"

"I knew. I wasn't sure you did." He made a move like he was going to touch her, but then stopped himself. Letting his hand fall, he said only, "Good luck, then. And remember the radio in case . . . well, just in case."

Without another word, he spun the red-gold magic and disappeared in a *pop* of collapsing air, leaving her standing there thinking that the 'port talent was a hell of a way to get the last word in an argument. Not that they had been arguing, really, because they were both right: She couldn't separate the act from the situation, but it *was* her choice. Strike had called only to tell her that the other magi and their *winikin* were out of ideas, and that a midday blood sacrifice channeling nearly the power of the full equinox had failed to trigger the Prophet's power. Her response to the information was her responsibility. "So why are you still standing here?" she asked herself aloud.

"Perhaps because you're wondering whether Strike and Anna were right to try to talk you out of this," a familiar voice said from the doorway of the training hall, which was a pitch-black square against the building's dark silhouette.

Jade's pulse skittered at the sound, then started pounding hard and heavy as she heard the rasp of clothing, the pad of approaching footsteps. Swallowing to wet her suddenly dry mouth, she said, "Eavesdropping, Lucius?"

"Considering that you've been discussing my sex life, or lack thereof, with the royal council, I'm not feeling very guilt-ridden." The timbre of his voice was deeper and richer than she remembered, as though experience had lent new layers to the tone. The difference sent a fine shiver racing along the back of her neck.

It's just Lucius, she told herself, as she'd been doing

since she'd initially broached the sex magic idea to the royal council. For the first time, though, she wondered whether she'd sold herself on a lie. Granted, human beings didn't fundamentally change, not at their core. But what if the human being wasn't entirely human anymore? Did the same rules apply? And what if he truly wasn't interested in her any longer? Some of the things he'd said to her the night before she left for the university had dug in and taken root, continuing to sting long after the fact. She'd told herself he'd been lashing out, confused from the Prophet's spell and stressed over the new pressures . . . but what if he'd meant every word?

Reminding herself that she could do this, that she *had* to do this, she said, "Part of me is glad you overheard. It saves me from explaining why I'm back. Although I can't imagine the idea comes as a surprise."

"I'd certainly prefer trying sex before ritual sacrifice," he said, his tone carrying a very un-Luciuslike bite. "And I understand the math. So, what does that make you . . . the Nightkeepers' sacrificial victim?"

"Don't be a dick. I'm a volunteer, not a victim." But heat rushed to her face, and she was grateful that he couldn't see her blush in the darkness. "I'm trying to help here, Lucius. If you want to turn me down, do it. But don't make me into the bad guy because I'm offering."

There was a long beat of silence before he exhaled, long and low. "I don't think badly of you. And . . . I don't want to turn you down."

Heat curled in her chest, then moved lower as her body awakened, seeming to suddenly realize what she'd been talking about all along. Sex. With Lucius. Although subsequent events hadn't allowed her to dwell on the memories, their one spontaneous, somewhat rushed coupling in the archive had lit her up like nothing had done before, not even being with the far more polished Michael when the two of them had both been running hot with transitional hormones and their first taste of sex magic. Where Michael had been skilled and considerate, Lucius had been raw, teetering on the borderline of control. Where Michael had held a portion of himself apart out of necessity, Lucius had been entirely *there* with her, making her feel as if there hadn't ever been anybody else for him, never would be; that he didn't see her as support staff, a backup, or a fill-in for what he'd really wanted.

Would it feel that way again? *Only one way to find out*, she told herself, blood humming suddenly in her veins. "Well ... if I'm offering, and you're not turning me down, why are we still standing here?"

Clothing rustled again as he closed the distance between them. His body heat caressed her lightly, bringing an answering stir of warmth within her. *Touch me like you did that day in the archive*, she wanted to say, but was afraid to because he'd told her flat out that his feelings for her had changed. Tonight wasn't about them; it was about the Prophet.

"Light a fox fire," he said. "Just a small one."

It was one of the few small magics she commanded, and one that had fascinated him, especially when she had sent it dancing from her hand to his and back again. Thinking that was what he wanted, that this was foreplay of a sort, she cupped one hand and used the power of the equinox to call the magic. A tiny light kindled, starting pinpoint-small and then expanding outward to a ball of cool blue flame that lit just her and Lucius. She looked up at him, smiling, expecting to see his remembered joy in the minor spell.

Instead, serious eyes looked at her out of a stranger's face.

"*Gods!*" Jade jerked back, shock hammering through her. "Who ... ? What the—" She broke off, realizing that he wasn't a stranger, not really.

The man standing opposite her resembled Lucius, but he wasn't for an instant the man she'd known. He was perhaps what Lucius would have been if he'd gotten the big-and-burly genes of his brothers and father along with the tall-and-borderline-willowy set he'd inherited from his mother's side. Combined, they had yielded a frame that was only maybe an inch taller than that of the man she'd known, but carried twice the mass in muscle, all of it layered onto bone and sinew as though sculpted there. He was wearing new-looking jeans; she doubted his newly powerful thighs would've fit into the old ones. The T-shirt with the bar logo was familiar, but there was nothing familiar about the way the shirt stretched across his chest and arms, and hinted at a ripple of muscle along his flat abs.

And his face . . . gods, his face. Features that had been pleasantly regular before were sharper and broader now; his jaw was aggressively square, his formerly borderline-too-large nose had come into perfect proportion, and high cheekbones and broad eyebrows framed hazel eyes that she knew, yet didn't. He watched her with an unfamiliar level of intensity as he held out his right hand, palm up, so the fox fire lit the dual marks on his right forearm: the black Nightkeeper slave mark and the red quatrefoil hell-mark of the Xibalbans. She'd seen them before, of course, but back then the marks had seemed out of place, magic unwittingly imposed on a mere human. Now, though, they looked . . . right. As though they belonged.

Jade didn't know why the sight made her want to break and run.

"Well?" he asked her softly.

"You look . . ." She trailed off, not sure he'd be flattered by her first few responses, which involved steroids and testosterone poisoning, clear evidence that her scientific, analytical side was trying to buffer the shock. So she went with, "different."

In fact, he looked amazing, reminding her of the long lunches she'd spent at the Met on her student pass, wandering through the Greek and Roman art galleries and imagining the carved marble and cast bronze coming to life in a raucous stampede down Fifth Avenue. He was that perfectly imperfect—human, yet something more now. And that *more* had her nerves skimming beneath her suddenly too-sensitive skin.

It's just Lucius, she told herself. Only it wasn't. He'd broken the rule that said people didn't fundamentally change. And—oh, gods—she'd offered herself to him. More, she'd fought the whole damn royal council long distance for the opportunity, and she'd brushed aside Strike's and Anna's concerns when they had tried to tell her that he wasn't himself. In her rush to finally escape from her backup role, she'd thrown herself headlong at . . . what? What was he now? He didn't command the Prophet's ability to reach the library, yet there was clearly magic at work, changing him into something more than himself.

"Not exactly what you were expecting when you volunteered for sex-magic duty, was it?" he asked, his eyes dark and inscrutable.

"I . . ." What was wrong with her? Where had her words gone? She was the one with the answers, the cool-blooded scribe who didn't get rattled. But right now her body was saying one thing, her spinning brain another, and her verbal skills had gotten lost in the cross fire.

His not-quite-familiar mouth curved in a humorless smile. "That's about what I figured. I wish they had warned you."

That, at least, she could respond to. "They tried. I wasn't listening. But . . . you could've called me, or e-mailed." She'd posted her contact info in the mansion's kitchen, just in case. "I hate thinking of you going through all this alone."

"I haven't been in the mood for company."

Feeling her magic—or maybe her nerve—fading, she let the fox fire go out, plunging them back into darkness that shouldn't have been as much of a relief as it was. But it was easier not to look at him as she said, "What *are* you in the mood for?"

"That, dear Jade, is entirely up to you."